Praise for N

"*Newport* has it all: intrigue, scandal, and séances to summon a spirit that will not rest. The slow unraveling of tangled secrets will keep you turning pages long into the night."
—Deanna Raybourn, *New York Times* bestselling author

"Jill Morrow's *Newport* is a portrait of a long-lost era, a sophisticated drama, and a gripping mystery all in one. Full of delicious prose and surprising twists, this book is a delight, an engrossing read that goes down like a glass of the finest champagne."
—Simone St. James, author of *The Other Side of Midnight*

"Past and present collide in 1920s Rhode Island as long-buried secrets begin to come to light in this mesmerizing novel of love, loss, and redemption. Beautifully written and vividly detailed, *Newport* is an elegant and mysterious tale that will keep you entranced from beginning to end."
—Ashley Weaver, Edgar Award–nominated author of
Murder at the Brightwell

"A delicious plunge into the gilded lives and mansions of another era, *Newport* sends you swimming through an intricate mystery involving money, tragedy, bittersweet love affairs, and voices from the beyond, until you arrive at the whirlwind ending. It's everything you need for literary escape: a ripping good read."
—Beatriz Williams, *New York Times* bestselling author

NEWPORT

Also by Jill Morrow

The Open Channel
Angel Café

NEWPORT

A Novel

JILL MORROW

wm

WILLIAM MORROW
An Imprint of HarperCollins*Publishers*

P.S.™ is a trademark of HarperCollins Publishers.

HarperCollins books may be purchased for educational, business, or sales promotional use. For information please e-mail the Special Markets Department at SPsales@harpercollins.com.

FIRST EDITION

Designed by Diahann Sturge

Library of Congress Cataloging-in-Publication Data has been applied for.

ISBN 978-0-06-237585-8

15 16 17 18 19   ov/rrd   10 9 8 7 6 5 4 3 2 1

To Elise and Sofia, my own personal angels

Acknowledgments

Newport could not have been written without the support and talents of many people. I am grateful for each of them:

To Nora Frenkiel, Emily Levitt, Gwen Mahoney, Shawn Nocher, and Sherry Audette Morrow. *Newport* was born in your critique group, and thanks to your expertise and gift for clear-eyed reading, the story found its voice. To Sherry—who happens to be my sister-in-law—thank you for sharing your writing and editing skills above and beyond critique group. Why, who *wouldn't* want to spend family holidays and events hashing out plot points and character issues? I appreciate your letting me borrow your credibility.

To Eva Kapitan, Gary Garth McCann, and Carolyn Sienkiewicz. *Newport* came to your critique group fully formed. Thank you for thoughtful comments and insights that allowed it to mature into a more cohesive work.

To Eliza Graham and Kristina Riggle, beta readers extraordinaire. Thank you for your willingness to fit complete reads of my manuscript into your own tight writing schedules. Kris, additional thanks for figuratively holding my hand whenever necessary, which occasionally meant several times a day.

To my agent, Ann Collette, whose love for this story allowed me to fall in love with it all over again. Thank you for believing in both *Newport* and me.

To my editor, Amanda Bergeron. Your enthusiasm for *Newport* was delightfully contagious, and your vision helped my dream become reality. What an absolute privilege to work with you and your team at HarperCollins!

To my parents, Roz and Stan Morrow. How I wish you were here to share this with me! I will always be grateful for your love and support, and for my memories of Mom with her nose in a book and Dad with the constant curiosity of a lifetime explorer.

To my daughters, Elise and Sofia, who have always believed in me more than I believe in myself and who make me happy and proud. You are among my greatest joys and the reason I do what I do.

And, finally, to Tom. We are very different from each other, yet somehow it works. Thank you for being my partner, my friend, and the love of my life. This book is all the more special to me because I can share it with you.

NEWPORT

CHAPTER
1

The lighthouse on the shore flashed its beacon in time with each rolling heave of Jim Reid's stomach. His knuckles whitened around the metal railing of the boat as he leaned forward, willing the wicked water to swallow him up whole and end his misery now. "Holy Mother of God," he groaned.

"Good grief, Mr. Reid. We're crossing Narragansett Bay, not the high seas." Adrian de la Noye's words cut through the nighttime dimness of the ferry deck. Disembodied in the shadows, his silken tone carried the same authority it did when summing up a complicated case before a Boston jury.

For at least the tenth time since they'd boarded Adrian's Pierce-Arrow town car earlier that day, Jim swore beneath his breath at his own weakness—soft Irish words that he remembered from childhood but could no longer translate.

"Sorry to be such a wet blanket," he said. "I'm doing the best I can."

There was a pause as Adrian considered. "Of course you are," he said. "You always do, my boy. You always do."

The smell of phosphorus hung on the air as a match arced through the darkness toward the cigarette in Adrian's mouth. Illuminated briefly by the flame, his chiseled features appeared almost otherworldly, his dark hair and eyes conjuring images more akin to pirates and gypsies than to prosperous middle age. Jim would have traded even his fresh new Harvard Law School sheepskin for some of that smooth coolness. It wasn't likely he'd ever attain it without some sort of miracle. He was tall and lanky, with fair skin that blushed at the slightest provocation and a sandy-colored cowlick that doomed him to be viewed as more boyish than manly by nearly every female who crossed his path.

"Here." Adrian handed him the cigarette. "It will settle your stomach."

Grateful, Jim pulled in a deep drag. Even he could manage some degree of cleverness with a cigarette resting lightly between his fingers. Sometimes smoking felt like the most valuable lesson he'd learned in school. The god-awful queasiness began to subside.

Adrian lit a cigarette for himself and leaned his elbows casually against the ferry's railing. The lighthouse receded off to the left, leaving the gentle glow of the stars to wash across the deck. Jim pushed his wire-rimmed glasses farther up his nose and let out a long, relieved sigh.

The smoldering tip of Adrian's cigarette picked up glints in his gold tie pin, making the fine amethyst stone at its center glitter. Jim winced as he remembered one more thing he had to do: search the floor of the town car for his own tie pin, which he'd flung there in annoyance after stabbing himself one time too many that day.

"We've almost reached Aquidneck Island," Adrian said. "Newport is a short drive from the quay. I'll need only a moment to send Constance a telegram. She'll want to know we've arrived safely."

"Do you think we'll find any place open?"

Adrian shrugged. "We'll manage something."

For as long as Jim had known Adrian de la Noye—and that was practically all of Jim's twenty-five years—the man had never seemed ruffled or out of place. Such ease was to be expected in the sanctified halls of Andover and Harvard, which Jim had attended on Adrian's dime. Adrian had been born to fit into places like that, and he called both institutions alma mater. As far as Jim was concerned, each school could consider itself darn lucky. What surprised him more was that Adrian was equally at home in the Reid family's noisy South Boston row house, where a seemingly endless number of Jim's siblings, nieces, and nephews had tumbled across Mr. de la Noye's well-dressed knees throughout the years. For all his accomplishments, Adrian seemed to require little more than the comfortable life he shared with his wife, Constance, and their two children back in Brookline.

Jim glumly flicked his ashes into the bay. He himself never quite fit anywhere. Overeducated in his boyhood neighborhood, but not of the usual social class found at Harvard, he was a perennial fish out of water, getting by through the sheer power of his mind.

"Ah." A husky female voice behind Jim's shoulder startled him. "Real men smoking real ciggies. Please, darlings, tell me those are Fatimas."

Adrian reached into his coat pocket as both men turned to face the woman behind them. "They are. May I offer you one?"

"I thought you'd never ask."

The woman was of average height, dressed in a light frock well suited to a sweet young thing. She needn't have bothered. The way she stroked Adrian's hand as he lit her cigarette marked her as anything but sweet, and it was obvious that she hadn't been young in years. The stylish dropped waist of her dress could not conceal a matronly thickening about her middle, and beneath her gay cloche and bobbed fair hair, her jawline had begun to sag.

She plucked the match from Adrian's fingers and tossed it into the water. Then, insinuating herself snugly between the two men, she leaned back against the ferry's rail and dragged nicotine deep into her lungs. The exhaled smoke wafted into the air, borne on vapors of alcohol. The woman swayed, evidence more of her own intoxication than of the ferry's movement. Adrian steadied her before she could tumble into his arms and then took a discreet step to his left. Jim didn't bother to move at all. It didn't matter that the woman's arm had just brushed his wrist. He could drop his trousers and jump up and down on the deck were he so inclined; he was sure she'd never notice.

"I can't resist Fatimas . . . or the men who smoke them," the woman said. "Virginia tobacco can't hold a candle to the . . . virility . . . of a true Turkish blend."

Adrian flashed a polite smile. "Indeed," he said.

It was the same everywhere they went. Whether the female was a doll or a chunk of lead, she always chose Adrian. Jim sighed, wondering what it would be like to leave every woman in your wake weak-kneed with desire. Granted, this one wasn't worth it. But how was it that Adrian was never even tempted to slip? Given the opportunity, Jim would have been delighted to slip nearly every time.

"The name is Chloe," the woman said. "Lady Chloe Chapman

Dinwoodie to the rest of the world, but you may now consider yourself my friends. Excuse me." She bent down, lifted the hem of her dress, and withdrew a contraband flask from the garter tied around her pudgy leg. "Drinkie?"

"No, thank you," Adrian said.

Recognition hit Jim like a smack to the side of the head. "Say, you're . . ."

Adrian corked his flowing words with one veiled glance. "Mr. Reid has perhaps heard of your father," he said. "Bennett Chapman's contributions to the textiles industry are very well known."

Chloe's expression soured. "Damn the old coot. I'm missing a weekend of parties in New York to ossify in Newport because of him." She threw her head back and took a long swig from the flask. Adrian met Jim's gaze over the swallowing motion of her throat.

"Yes, sir," Chloe Dinwoodie said, coming up for air. "Let's drink to good old Pop and his contributions to the textiles industry."

"His success is admirable," Adrian said mildly.

"Then let's drink to good old Pop and his contributions to Chloe's lifestyle." She again extended the flask in a silent invitation. Adrian shook his head. "Let's drink to the family manses in Boston, New York, London, and Newport," she continued. "And let's not forget how that money bought me a titled husband, too. A shame the fool's a fairy, but he does come with benefits."

She tossed her half-smoked Fatima over the ferry railing. Adrian wordlessly extended another.

"You're a dear man." Chloe waited as he lit a match, then pulled his hand closer to guide the flame toward the cigarette now clamped between her bright red lips.

Adrian did not move away this time. Instead he bathed her in one of those intimate gazes Jim recognized from his mentor's arsenal of cross-examination techniques.

"Of course you'd rather be elsewhere," Adrian said. "Newport certainly isn't the jewel she used to be. What coaxed you away from the glitter of New York?"

Chloe's fingers tightened around his wrist. "Oh, only dire circumstances could do that, I assure you. My father wants to change his will."

Jim's face burned with the flood of a hot red flush. Words bubbled to his lips.

Adrian intercepted them with the graceful stealth of a panther. "I assume the change is not to your advantage," he murmured.

Chloe's round-eyed stare resembled a mesmerized trance. "Advantage? It's a disaster! Nicholas and I—Nicky's my brother—will be flat out of luck if he goes through with it. Right now we stand to get everything when my father kicks the bucket . . . meets his maker . . . you know. But now Pop wants to marry this . . . this gold digger."

"Ah. There's a woman involved."

"Isn't there always? Anyway, that's why Pop wants to change his will. And if he goes through with it, Nicky and I get a yearly stipend apiece, and that's it."

"I see your difficulty," Adrian said. "But how can you stop him?"

Chloe dropped her voice to a confidential whisper. "Pop's got his Boston prig of a lawyer coming up to draft the new will tomorrow. Nicky says that if we can prove our father is nuts, the will must legally stand as is. Nicky's a dull stick, but he's smart about things like this."

Adrian's voice dropped as well. "Can you prove that your father is incompetent?"

"Oh, yes." Chloe stepped forward until only an inch separated the lace of her collar from Adrian de la Noye's well-tailored vest. "With what's been going on around his place lately? Oh, absolutely yes. You know, I don't believe you've told me your name."

Jim could almost see the noxious alcohol fumes snaking their way up Adrian's nostrils. Adrian abhorred inebriation, deemed it sloppy and unnecessary. It probably required a supreme act of will for him to stand still, smiling blandly as Lady Chloe Chapman Dinwoodie walked her fingernails up his chest.

A snicker worked its way through Jim's nose. He quickly turned away, disguising his laughter with an unconvincing sneeze. This tendency to lose his composure at the mere thought of the absurd was yet another bad habit he needed to conquer.

A sudden movement on the deck stopped his sniggering flat. Farther down the rail, a figure crouched, half hidden by a weathered box of life preservers. Startled, Jim leaned forward. The figure jumped under his scrutiny and flattened itself against the box as if trying to disappear. It was too late; Jim had seen plenty. He identified the cap and knickers of a young boy, noted that the figure was small and slight. But, most important, he knew without a doubt that for some reason, this boy had been listening intently to every word.

"Hey!" Jim lunged toward the life preservers, but the boy was faster. The small figure skittered across the deck and out of sight.

"May I offer assistance, Mr. Reid?" Adrian appeared instantly at his side.

Jim's shoulders sagged as he blinked at the empty space before him. "I'll tell you later, when there's no fear of ears. It's probably nothing; I'm just a little jumpy."

"Any particular reason?" Adrian threw a glance toward Lady Dinwoodie, who now slumped against the ferry rail like a deflated balloon, lost in an inebriated haze.

Jim shook his head, hard. "This whole trip reeks, that's all."

"In what way?"

"I don't know. It just feels . . . off. Taking this trip to the old man's summer cottage in the first place—"

"Mr. Chapman has been a valued client of our firm for many years."

"—then running across his daughter like this . . ."

"An admittedly awkward coincidence, although I found her comments most enlightening."

"You had no idea that Bennett Chapman's will might be contested?"

"Not an inkling. Naturally, we'll readjust our plans accordingly. We'll stay in town tonight and visit Liriodendron tomorrow. That will give Lady Dinwoodie an opportunity to compose herself."

Jim removed his spectacles to massage the crease in his brow. "You don't think she'll remember us the second we knock on Liriodendron's door?"

They turned as one toward Chloe Chapman Dinwoodie, but she had tottered away, presumably in search of new prey.

A corner of Adrian's mouth turned up. "Given the amount of bootleg she's consumed, Chloe Dinwoodie will be fortunate if she remembers how she arrived at Liriodendron in the first place. I suspect we'll register as nothing more than a bad dream. Suppose we wait in the car. That will save us from meeting the charming lady again."

With a resigned sigh, Jim followed his mentor to the auto. He was no longer particularly connected to his Irish past, no more so than any other first-generation American born and raised in South Boston. Why was it, then, that he could now hear the lilting voice of his departed Granny Cullen, who'd always claimed that the blood of ancient Celtic soothsayers warmed her veins? He'd grown up with her predictions and warnings, and this one trumpeted as loudly as any of them: "Little good ever comes of mixing where you aren't wanted." Despite Bennett Chapman's invitation, it was clear that most of Liriodendron's occupants would be more than happy to slam the front door in Adrian de la Noye's face.

"Adrian . . ." Jim stopped still on the deck.

Adrian turned toward him, one eyebrow raised in inquiry.

Jim hesitated. He was indebted to Adrian's kindness, could never have come this far without his patronage. But it was more than that: dashing, sure-footed Adrian de la Noye was everything he wanted to be. Summoning superstitions from the old country would only further emphasize the differences between them.

"Never mind," Jim said slowly. "I'm tired, that's all."

"All the more reason for a good night's sleep before we visit Liriodendron. I'll need that sharp mind of yours, Mr. Reid. I've grown to depend upon it."

Jim followed along in silence, trying to forget that his granny's predictions had seldom been wrong.

CHAPTER
2

Adrian de la Noye navigated the Pierce-Arrow down Bellevue Avenue as if he'd done so only yesterday, a fact that irritated him no end. His last visit to Newport had been some twenty-three years ago. He'd been around Jim's age then, recently graduated from law school and just back from a Grand Tour of Europe. It would have pleased him now to find that memories from that time had faded into oblivion.

Newport had changed, and unwelcome memories or not, Adrian approved of the shift he'd noted while driving from the ferry last night. The patina of pretension he remembered from years ago had dulled somewhat, lessened as society wealth siphoned away either to other resorts or to former President Wilson's reviled income tax. Still, one needed only to look at the lavish mansions lining either side of Bellevue to realize that, despite the more pronounced presence of the navy, despite the increased influx of immigrants and the workingman, Newport would always keep a soft spot for the glittering doyennes of the social order—the ornaments who'd made the town sparkle in its heyday.

Adrian tamped down his distaste and, for the fourth or fifth time since they'd docked the night before, reminded himself that he'd been rescued long ago from that mindset.

In fact, he'd spoken to his favorite personal angel just last night.

"You sound worried." Constance's lilting tones had soothed like honey. He'd have paid the hotel clerk twice over for the privilege of using the telephone. "What's wrong?"

He knew his wife well, knew he had interrupted her evening cup of tea and the *New York World* crossword puzzle she enjoyed working after Grace and Ted kissed her good night and disappeared into their bedrooms. She'd most likely taken a cookie or two up the stairs to enjoy with her tea, probably the rich, buttery shortbread she baked to perfection. The thought had made him smile: wise men did not interfere with Constance and her sweet tooth. In truth, wise men rarely interfered with Mrs. de la Noye at all. Her ethereal prettiness hid a steel trap of a mind, and those who underestimated her once never did so again.

He'd pictured her so very clearly: telephone receiver grasped loosely in one graceful hand, candlestick body of the phone raised close to her soft lips. He'd longed for home so badly then that it had nearly robbed him of breath. He'd ached to envelop his wife in his arms, to brush away the blond tendrils that always escaped the casual twist of her hair, to gently kiss her cheek.

"Adrian?" Constance's voice had crackled through the wire.

He'd quickly submerged his yearning. "It's . . . unpleasant . . . here without you. It feels wrong."

"You've been away on business before."

"This is different."

"Is it Newport, then?"

He'd licked dry lips. "It might be."

"I see." There'd been silence as she absorbed his words, but it had been a comfortable silence. Constance never required excessive explanation. "Adrian, listen to me. I don't know the source of your unease, but I'll swear to this: you're a good man with a good heart. Nothing can change that unless you allow it. Just finish the task at hand and hurry back. I miss you."

He'd lost the line then, listened as Constance receded into a field of sputtering noise. But it had been enough to remind him of the man he meant to be.

Jim's drawl brought him back to Bellevue Avenue and the mid-morning sun. "Can you imagine walking through that front door at the end of a hard day?"

The chateauesque lines of Belcourt filled the passenger-side windowpane. Adrian remembered seeing that mansion go up back in the 1890s, listening to tongues wag over the eccentricity of its owner.

"Actually, Mr. Reid, that's the back of the place. The entrance is on Ledge Road, around the other side."

Jim let out a low whistle as his gaze took in the massive house. "It's obscene. Is Liriodendron like this?"

"I've never been. But I wouldn't be surprised. Summer cottages built in Newport were meant to impress."

"Summer cottages." Jim's snort was understandable. One of these "summer cottages" could have housed his entire family—parents, siblings, nieces, and nephews included.

"It's a different world, is it not?"

Jim slid him a sideways glance. "But one with which you're familiar."

Jim Reid had yet to recognize his own many gifts, one of which was an innate sense of observation. Adrian took great pleasure not only in this but in the young man's ability to effortlessly gather clues and weave them into a fine tapestry of reason. Watching Jim's mind work was almost worth his own slip into momentary transparency.

"Yes," Adrian said simply. "I spent some time in Newport in my youth. I had friends here."

Jim left a wide-open pause just perfect for filling. Adrian declined the invitation, guiding the town car into a smooth right turn instead. To their left, the ocean opened out in sparkling ripples of deep blue and white.

Jim turned to study the sea. "I noticed you booked the hotel room for another night," he said. "How long do you expect we'll be in Newport, given the unforeseen complications?"

Another gift: the young man knew when to change the subject.

"I don't know yet," Adrian replied. "It's hard to tell exactly how much of a complication Lady Dinwoodie will be once sober. And we've yet to meet brother, Nicky . . . also known as the 'dull stick,' I believe."

"Do you think the old man is afflicted, as they claim? What's he like?"

"The 'old man,' as you so succinctly put it, can be difficult. Still, he's made more money for our law firm than half our other clients combined. Do you know much about him?"

"Some."

"Bennett Chapman made a fortune in cotton textiles after the Civil War."

"Gainfully?"

"Now that's a question I've never asked. Breathe deeply, Mr. Reid. There are few sensations as cleansing as a lungful of fresh salt air."

Jim obliged, dissolving into a fit of coughing as his chest expanded beyond its usual habit. Adrian gave him a moment to fumble for his missing handkerchief, then passed over his own without a word.

"Thanks." Jim made use of the neat silk square, crumpled it up, and shoved it into his pocket. "Mr. Chapman must be rather up in years."

"Eighty next month."

"Hmm." Jim's fingers tapped out an impromptu jazz rhythm on the dashboard of the automobile as he considered. "Well, then, there's a chance that Lady Dinwoodie is correct. What if the man's truly not right in the head?"

"Then I suppose we won't be drafting a new will after all."

"Bennett Chapman might take his business elsewhere."

"I know."

"Could the firm absorb the loss?"

Adrian hesitated. "That would remain to be seen."

The younger man nodded, apparently satisfied with the answer.

Jim Reid had been slightly more than a toddler when they'd first met, but Adrian had recognized the boy's sharp intelligence even then. He'd have funded the child's education no matter what his ability, but it had taken no more than a few minutes of watching the boy scrutinize him from the safety of his father's lap to realize that any money spent on the lad would be money well spent. Indeed, what had begun as a favor—compensation for a debt that Adrian had known he could never fully repay—had reaped so much more than expected. Years of shepherding Jim Reid through the halls of academia had provided Adrian with not only a law associate, but a friend.

Jim tugged at his too-short jacket sleeve in a futile attempt to cover his knobby wrist. It was well past time for a trip to a tailor. No man—especially one of Jim's imposing height—could expect to find well-fitted perfection hanging ready-made on a rack at Filene's. Adrian filed away a mental note to make arrangements with his own tailor once they returned to Boston.

"This is the place," Jim said, staring through his spectacles at a circular driveway to their left.

A large white mansion sat planted at the apex of the drive, a northern paean to southern antebellum architecture. Adrian took in the graceful white columns that guided the eye from porch floorboards to ceiling, the well-manicured lawn with its early summer flowers in riotous bloom, and the expanse of ocean rolling behind the house in an endless carpet of motion. He'd never set foot in this house before, couldn't even recall what had once occupied this prime ocean-view site. But that didn't matter. The indulgent opulence of Liriodendron transported him back more than twenty years in time, back to a place where he'd never wanted to find himself again.

"You've stopped in the middle of the road," Jim said.

Adrian thought of Constance, of the solid dining room table where he, Grace, and Ted enjoyed their breakfasts before departing each morning for the office and school. He thought of the soft quilts on their beds, the worn leather chair just waiting for him by the

fireplace in his study. He had a place there, a family eagerly awaiting his return.

"Just getting my bearings, Mr. Reid." Eyes steady on the horizon, Adrian gave the Pierce-Arrow's steering wheel a firm spin to
the left.

Newport hadn't changed nearly enough.

Fortunately, he had.

CHAPTER
3

Catharine Walsh reached for her hairbrush, whacking her hand against a heavy glass bowl of rose petal potpourri on the way. Swallowing back a mild expletive, she flexed her fingers then grasped the handle. The rough tug of the bristles through her dark, bobbed curls felt good. At least it reflected action. The pervasive air of lethargy in the guest room left her cranky and on edge, and she knew from experience that neither state of mind allowed for clarity of thought.

She was staying in Liriodendron's Flower Room, a bucolic guest bedroom so festooned with floral imagery that staring at the walls too long made her eyes water and her nose itch. She was not given to sentimentality, so the delicate blossoms everywhere oozed more romanticism than she cared to handle at one time. The room faced the sea, which should have offered nothing more than soft breezes and the gentle whisper of surf. Instead, voices floated through the open window—the same quarrelsome voices that had encouraged Catharine to feign a headache that morning instead of joining Bennett Chapman at the dining room table for breakfast. The Chapman heirs had arrived in a flurry of self-importance last night, the plastered Lady Dinwoodie relying upon her chauffeur to keep her upright, her older brother, Nicholas, striding stiffly through the front door nearly an hour later. Catharine had fled to her room before coming face-to-face with either. The meeting she dreaded was unavoidable, but she still had the right to put it off for as long as she could.

She drifted toward the bedroom window to take a peek. Just as she'd suspected, these two neither looked nor sounded better in the morning sun.

"I can't help it if I've a delicate constitution!" Chloe Chapman Dinwoodie's high-pitched voice made one ponder the relative benefits of deafness. Her white chiffon frock danced in the breeze as if searching for the adolescent girl it was meant to adorn. Catharine stifled a groan. Chloe was a few years older than her own forty-three. Why had no one told Lady Dinwoodie that clothing and affectations charming on a young woman of eighteen merely made her a frump at forty-five?

But meeting the indisposed Chloe was nowhere near as unnerving as the thought of dealing with her brother. Catharine hung back, determined to ignore the low rumble of Nicholas Chapman's voice. Yet despite her will, she found herself edging closer to the window, drawn to him like Faustus to Mephistopheles.

"You're a drunk, Chloe," Nicholas was saying. "There's nothing delicate about that. I'd appreciate it if you could reform just long enough to assist me. Employ the same wits you use to circumvent Prohibition, and we can't help but succeed."

Chloe sank down into a lawn chair, limp hand draped across her forehead. "Oh, all right, Nicky. Tell me what you have in mind."

Catharine ducked behind the curtains as Nicholas spun toward the window, his narrowed eyes scanning the façade of the house. But his check was apparently habit, a perfunctory move provoked by a suspicious mind. As brusquely as he'd turned toward the house, he bent toward his sister, his black suit and beaky nose conjuring images of a crow. Strands of his thick blond hair rose and fell like pieces of straw in the brisk wind.

"It's just as I expected," Catharine murmured, resting a hand atop the dresser to steady herself. "There are no surprises here." It took a few more deep breaths than she'd anticipated, but eventually the thumping of her heart slowed to a more reasonable rate. She brushed a nonexistent speck of dust from the front of her dress and straightened up, jaw set.

The Chapmans' voices were no longer audible, but that didn't matter. Catharine knew very well why Bennett's children had made the inconvenient trip to Liriodendron, and it certainly wasn't to bestow warm nuptial blessings and wish her well.

A soft knock on the door drew her away from the tableau unfolding outside.

"Excuse me, ma'am, but I've a note for you." One of the housemaids stood in the hallway, a folded piece of paper extended before her. Her Irish brogue was as thick as if she'd just disembarked from the boat that morning. Catharine veiled her irritation: Bennett still adhered to the last-century affectation of importing domestic help from the British Isles, as if guests might actually believe they'd somehow stumbled into one of the great family manor houses of Europe.

She took the paper from the maid's waiting hand. "There's no need to 'ma'am' me, Nellie. 'Miss Walsh' will do just fine."

Nellie burned pink. "Mr. Chapman hopes that your headache is much improved. He wants you to accompany him out to the terrace to meet his son and daughter."

"Will Miss Amy be joining us?"

Nellie glanced toward the note. "I'm not sure."

A real headache started pounding above Catharine's left eye. Amy apparently had taken off again, galloping who knew where, leaving Catharine alone to face the lions.

But it wasn't fair to drop her foul mood onto Nellie. The poor young thing was merely the messenger, after all. "Oh, very well. You may tell Mr. Chapman that I'll be along in fifteen minutes."

"Shall I wait until you've read the note, ma'am? In the event you wish to reply?"

"Yes, of course. Thank you for thinking of it, Nellie." Catharine unfolded the paper in her hand. As expected, her eyes met Amy's hasty scrawl.

Dear Aunt Catharine, Amy had written in large, loopy letters. Catharine could already tell that this note would be yet another that raised more questions than answers. *I'm not in the mood to meet them yet. I've gone for a walk. I hope you understand.*

It took everything she had not to crumple up the page. *I hope you understand.* As if it would have mattered whether she understood or not. Amy would have done precisely as she pleased anyway. And, since she was twenty-two years old, that was probably her right.

Nellie remained in the doorway, a picture of practiced serenity. As Catharine met her gaze, she realized that the maid was not as young as she'd originally thought and that her knowledge of Liriodendron ran far beyond the linens and silver.

"Please send somebody out to find my niece," Catharine said evenly. "And inform her that her presence is requested on the terrace. Immediately."

Nellie nodded, then retreated down the hall.

Catharine waited until she could no longer hear the maid's footsteps before stepping back into her bedroom and closing the door firmly behind her.

She'd never expected this wedding business to take so long. When she and Amy had arrived in Newport six weeks ago, she'd expected to be Mrs. Bennett Chapman by mid-May. Now it was June. This had dragged on long enough for Bennett's progeny to come swooping down like vultures.

An exclamation from Chloe brought her back to the window. There were no discernible words, but Lady Dinwoodie's discontent was evidenced by her piercing whine and fluttering hands. Nicholas whipped about to face the ocean, his shoulders so squared that pebbles could bounce off the hard plane of his back. His comment to his sister was carried away by the wind, but his anger remained clearly etched in each line of his rigid stance.

Catharine sank to the floor and rested her head against the wall. Neither Chloe nor Nicholas had a right to be angry about anything. They'd been spoon-fed every advantage right along with their childhood farina. Even now, decades out from beneath Daddy's roof, neither had any apparent cause for complaint. The Chapman heirs were well-off even without their father's will. Chloe's foppish

British husband had enough personal wealth to keep her in more than crumpets for the rest of her life, and Nicholas owned a lucrative percentage of the family's textiles empire. There were no grounds for griping—or for bad behavior.

Yet they behaved badly quite frequently. Lady Dinwoodie's outlandish New York antics had reached even Catharine's local newspaper back in Sacramento, where people usually didn't give a fig about East Coast snobs. And as for Nicholas Chapman, even the society pages had long ago stopped calling him an "eligible bachelor." Everybody knew by now that he was too much of a selfish tightwad to ever share his wealth with a wife. Of course, as far as Catharine was concerned, no amount of money could ever make that hateful man marriageable in the first place.

She sighed. There was nothing for it but to go out to the patio and meet the loathsome two. She smoothed her dress—low-waisted and simply cut, its deep vermilion hue flattered her dark coloring and hugged her body. Current fashion may have favored boyish figures, but Catharine knew that men preferred curves. Mother Nature had made her far more alluring than Chloe Chapman could ever hope to be, even without the girlish flounces on her frocks and a personal fortune to call her own.

In the scheme of things, she decided, she had no other choice but to look upon the arrival of the wretched offspring as an unfortunate intrusion, a bump in a road that should have gone more smoothly. But it wasn't yet a disaster.

Catharine took one last steadying breath, raised her chin, and sailed from the room.

CHAPTER
4

Jim nearly tripped over a small marble statue of the Three Graces as he and Adrian followed the black-and-white-uniformed maid through Liriodendron's foyer.

"Steady, Mr. Reid." Adrian caught him with a firm hand beneath the elbow.

"What's it doing at knee level where no one can see it?" Jim glared down at the offending sculpture. Arms entwined about each other's naked bodies, the Graces paid him no heed.

"It's art," Adrian said. "It's not accountable to you."

Art or not, Jim thought there was too much of it. He was as big a fan of conspicuous wealth as the next man, but how could a body ever rest at ease in a place that felt more like a museum than a home? He craned his neck to peer into a side parlor as they passed by. Just as he'd suspected, one couldn't hope to settle comfortably on the plush sofa there. A fierce gray Zeus posed in a nearby alcove, threatening to hurl thunderbolts at the slightest provocation.

This was not to deny that Liriodendron was beautiful. It was, in an old-fashioned, lavender-and-crepe sort of way. It reminded Jim of afternoon teas in downtown Boston hotels, where powdered matrons sipped sweet weak oolong from paper-thin porcelain cups and stubbornly denied the existence of a chaotic world outside.

He let out a low whistle as they passed through the French doors leading to the ballroom. Although acquiring an escape like Liriodendron was a privilege few could afford, at least the breathtaking ocean vista sparkling beyond the wall-to-wall windows was still available to all, free of charge.

The outside of the house was every bit as grand as the inside. Fragrance from a thousand flowers hypnotized, and colors bloomed pure and clean against a vibrant green carpet of grass.

Jim stopped for a moment to take it all in, quite sure that he could happily adjust to living this close to heaven. The click of footsteps against flagstone terrace jarred him from his reverie. Adrian now walked well ahead, led by the little housemaid, who every now and then shyly grinned up at him.

Jim turned his back on paradise and jogged to catch up.

The terrace wrapped around to the right of the ballroom, bordered on its edge by a waist-high stone retaining wall. An elegant wrought-iron table sat beside the wall, a silver coffee service on it hinting that, at the very least, one might expect to get a good cup of java before leaving.

Not as cheering was the sight of Chloe Chapman Dinwoodie,

draped across a chair like a discarded fur throw. A man with a head of graying blond hair stood behind her, one hand tapping a regular rhythm against her shoulder.

The stiff arm the man extended toward Adrian might have been attached to a wooden soldier. "Nicholas Chapman." His voice hit the ground before Jim and Adrian had even stopped walking. "My sister, Lady Dinwoodie. You, I believe, are my father's attorneys. We know why you're here. It's vital that we speak with you before my father joins us."

Adrian returned the handshake as if such abrupt greetings were the height of propriety. "Adrian de la Noye. Allow me to introduce my associate, James Reid."

A cloud crossed Lady Dinwoodie's face. "Have we met?" she asked, confusion lacing her words.

Adrian accepted her limply proffered hand with an apologetic smile. "I'm sure I'd remember the honor, madam."

"Oh." She withdrew her hand and settled back in the chair, brow still furrowed.

"We have little time, so I must be blunt," Nicholas said, although it was obvious that he was seldom otherwise. "I'm sorry you've wasted a trip, but it will be quite impossible to change our father's will."

Adrian raised an eyebrow. "Mr. Chapman has been my client for many years. I am at his service."

"No, you don't understand. Our father is not in his right mind."

"He's nuts," Lady Dinwoodie added helpfully.

"Ah." Adrian rocked back on his heels. "And why do you think this?"

Nicholas jerked his head to the left as wheels on gravel sounded from the side of the house. "My sources say you're a smart man, Mr. de la Noye. I'm sure you'll see for yourself."

A man in a wheelchair rolled into view, accompanied by a striking dark-haired woman in a red dress. It didn't require a formal introduction to know that this was Bennett Chapman, millionaire many times over.

Although seated in a wheelchair, Bennett Chapman looked as fit as could be expected for a man of nearly eighty years. His white hair was plentiful, his beard trimmed close to his face. He looked as if he'd spent a lifetime working near the sea, for his complexion was ruddy and his chest and shoulders still broad. In fact, he wore the uniform of a commodore, although it wasn't clear why: Bennett Chapman had never served on any vessel more official than his personal yacht.

But even if his body had aged, Chapman's eyes still demanded attention. Blue and penetrating, they seemed capable of peeling away the layers surrounding any story until a kernel of truth was exposed. Nicholas and Chloe had each inherited the color but not the intensity of that gaze. Nicholas's eyes darted from side to side as he inspected each person in the group; Chloe's looked likely to fill with tears at the merest perceived slight.

"Mr. de la Noye!" Bennett Chapman's voice gusted across the terrace like a strong north wind. "And this would be the praiseworthy Mr. Reid I've already heard too much about. Damn, Adrian, did you take the slowest route possible to get here? I see that my children have insinuated themselves into your good graces. Meet my intended, Miss Catharine Walsh."

Jim squinted toward Miss Walsh. She was no coed, but he

thought her a looker all the same. If he had to guess, he'd say she was younger than both Nicholas and Lady Dinwoodie. And if first impressions of her determined mouth and spectacular figure held true, the Katzenjammer Kids had met their match. Here was a lady who wouldn't be easily steamrolled.

But suddenly Miss Walsh's Cupid's bow lips dropped open. Her dark eyes widened. Jim followed her gaze straight to Adrian, who pulled back as if pricked by a thorn. Miss Walsh regained her composure quickly, covering her slip by offering a graceful hand in greeting.

"So pleased to meet you, Mr. de la Noye," she said, and the even pitch of her voice made it clear that she intended to remain fully in charge of the matters at hand.

The smile she turned toward Jim packed maximum wattage. "And you, Mr. Reid. How kind of you to make this trip out to Newport on Mr. Chapman's behalf." Her hand rested in his and, for a minute, it was hard for him to think about anything else as he met her liquid gaze.

"Catharine, meet the children," Bennett Chapman ordered, and Miss Walsh was gone, leaving behind only a trace of perfume.

Adrian's stare remained fastened on Catharine Walsh as she strolled across the terrace. Jim was not surprised to see the look of dismay on his face. Adrian had little patience for melodrama, and what had begun as a cut-and-dried task was rapidly sinking into a tangled family saga more commonly found in a dime novel. A flush had deepened his coloring. Then, with a slight shake of his head, Adrian returned his full attention to the scene unfolding before them.

"Catharine, I present Nicholas and Chloe." Bennett rolled himself to Miss Walsh's side. "Not much to look at, but I'm obliged to claim them. Children, my bride-to-be."

A grimace splashed across Chloe's face. Nicholas's glare flicked over and past Miss Walsh as he turned abruptly to address his father. Miss Walsh paled and clasped her hands behind her back, making it clear that no friendly hand would have been presented to him even had he wanted it.

"You're in no state to marry," Nicholas told his father. "You're lucky we haven't carted you away, put you someplace where people can prevent you from making stupid decisions like this."

"And you're lucky I don't beat the stuffing out of you," Bennett Chapman said. "God, you're an obnoxious prick, Nicky. Always have been."

"Do you see what I mean, Mr. de la Noye?" Nicholas Chapman demanded. Chloe slumped in her chair, the perfect picture of despair, but her reaction might have been due more to a hangover than to any deep emotional pain. Miss Walsh remained still, as regal and proud as a figurehead on a ship.

Adrian walked toward the coffeepot on the table. "May I?" he asked, lifting it.

"Oh, by all means," Bennett Chapman said. "And pour me one while you're at it."

"My God!" Nicholas exploded. "This isn't a damn garden party!"

"Well, it's meant to be, you newt," Bennett Chapman said. "It's not my fault you and your sister decided to intrude. I didn't invite you."

Nicholas took a step toward Adrian. "Mr. de la Noye, I implore you."

Adrian concentrated on the steady stream of coffee flowing from pot to cup. "Although there are many who would insist otherwise, willingly entering into the state of matrimony is not de facto proof of insanity. Your father's decision to marry is not necessarily the product of a deranged mind."

"Damn." Bennett Chapman stared up at the sky. "So they've decided I'm cuckoo, have they?"

Nicholas ignored him. "Oh, it is in this case, I assure you. If I could speak with you and Mr. Reid privately . . ."

Adrian passed the coffee cup to Bennett Chapman. "I'm afraid I can't do that. Your father is my client, not you. Coffee, Miss Walsh?" Their eyes locked. Adrian quirked an eyebrow, a silent question that Jim suspected had absolutely nothing to do with coffee.

Miss Walsh turned away to study the sea. "No, thank you," she said.

"Oh, Nicky, who cares about privacy?" Chloe's hand flopped over the side of her chair. "Do you think this little gold digger deserves it? Go ahead and ask Pop the question. Just do it."

A muscle twitched at one side of Nicholas's mouth. "All right, although it doesn't sit well to expose the family's warts in public. Father, suppose you tell these gentlemen exactly why you've asked Miss Walsh to marry you."

Jim fumbled the cup and saucer Adrian had just handed him. The elder Mr. Chapman was a little too comfortable spewing the unvarnished truth. One could only hope he would apply some tact to his answer.

But Bennett Chapman seemed to change before their eyes. Instead of the fiercely outspoken man who'd rolled himself out onto the terrace, a dreamy man settled back in the wheelchair, eyes glistening with tears.

"Why, Nicky," he said in a soft voice. "I explained all this to both you and Chloe when I telephoned to announce our engagement. I thought you understood."

"Explain it once again."

Bennett Chapman cradled his cup in both hands. His expression, so fearsome only a second before, took on the defenseless cast of a child. "Your mother wishes it," he mumbled into his drink.

Chloe's pale skin flamed pink. Nicholas's fingertips whitened against her shoulder.

Jim took a quick swig of coffee as the missing puzzle piece of information clicked into place. No wonder the younger Chapmans were so prickly. Nobody in society wanted to admit to the stain of divorce in the family. Even Adrian had stiffened, although Jim couldn't imagine that this was information he didn't already know.

"I'm sorry." Adrian's tone was gentle. "But, Mr. Chapman, could you repeat that for me?"

Bennett Chapman raised brimming eyes to meet Adrian's question.

"Of course I'll repeat it, Mr. de la Noye. I'm not ashamed. Elizabeth—my first wife—told me to marry Miss Walsh. She not only endorses this union, but blesses it. And, as I am to marry Miss Walsh, it is only fitting that I amend my will to reflect her importance in my life. Elizabeth feels very strongly about that as well."

Adrian set his coffee cup down onto the table. His stare landed hard on Catharine Walsh, as insistent and unavoidable as a guiding hand to the chin. Lesser men had faltered under this wordless inquisition, but Miss Walsh met it full on, locking her gaze in his until the two seemed intertwined. A breath of wind gusted between them, raising the hair on their heads and sending Miss Walsh's skirt swirling against her legs.

"You needn't waste your time in confrontation, Mr. de la Noye." Nicholas Chapman's voice broke the standoff. "She'll admit to nothing. But I'm sure she knows as well as you do that Mother died over thirty-five years ago."

CHAPTER
5

Adrian pulled away from Catharine Walsh's magnetic stare, forcing himself back to the business at hand. His mind rapidly sifted through facts. He'd spoken to Bennett Chapman via telephone only last week. The man had seemed perfectly sane then, had even relayed his corporation's stellar quarterly financial figures.

"Crossed over, perhaps, but certainly not gone," Bennett said now. "Is it so difficult to believe that my Elizabeth would stay in touch with the husband she adored?"

"It's difficult to believe she'd stay in touch with anyone at all." Chloe fumbled for the flask in her garter, apparently thought better of it, and reached for a cigarette instead.

As his client looked dreamily out at the horizon, Adrian recalled that there had indeed been something unusual about that last telephone conversation: Bennett Chapman had been very nearly pleasant. In fact, he'd sounded so different from his usual dour self that Adrian had mentioned it to Constance just before dinner that evening.

He suddenly remembered her response. "He's in love," she had said, carefully lighting the dining room candles as she did every night.

"Ah, women." He'd smiled as soft candlelight enveloped them. "Always ready to assume romance in any situation. What makes you so certain that our Mr. Chapman has a paramour?"

"Oh, nothing so tawdry as a paramour, Adrian. A sweetheart, perhaps." Her brow had puckered in concentration over the last stubborn wick. A wisp of pale hair escaped a hairpin to rest against her cheek. Adrian reached out to tenderly tuck it behind her ear, breath catching as she caught his hand and pressed it firmly against her heart. Caught off guard, he'd pulled her closer, the insistent echo of his own heart more than pleased to give away the depth of his longing.

"Why, darling!" Constance had curled against him. "Shall I hold dinner?"

He'd pulled in a deep breath, regaining his composure before dropping a soft kiss onto her lips. "Constance, my dear—the children," he'd whispered, raising her gaze with a gentle finger beneath her chin. "They'll be down at any moment."

Constance had squeezed his hand before releasing it. "My dearest Adrian," she'd said with a sigh. "You keep so much bundled up inside. You needn't, you know; you're perfectly safe with me. Anyway, Mr. Chapman's romantic state is obvious. Do men honestly believe they achieve contentment on their own? Without good women behind you, you're a troubled lot, always searching for peace. Mr. Chapman has been an unpleasant blowhard for years. You say that today he was jocular, eager to make conversation—he's in love."

As usual, Constance would not be surprised to learn she was right. But as Adrian watched Bennett absently pat his fiancée's hand, he was willing to bet that Catharine Walsh was not the cause of the anxious longing etched into the old man's face.

"Need we continue this conversation?" Nicholas asked in a low voice. "My father's state of mind should be obvious to you both."

"Sir." Jim Reid set his coffee cup on the table and crouched before the wheelchair until he and Bennett Chapman were nearly eye to eye. "When was the last time you . . . spoke . . . to Mrs. Chapman?"

"When was that, Catharine? Two nights ago?"

"Where did this conversation take place?" Coming from Jim, the question verged on innocent. With his long limbs and open Irish face, he was as unthreatening as a puppy.

Bennett Chapman inched himself forward in his wheelchair, eager to share. "In the parlor. How Elizabeth would have loved that room had she lived to see it! I don't know how they bring her to me, Mr. Reid, but it's a miracle . . . amazing."

"'They'?"

"Catharine's got something to do with it, but it's her niece, Amy, who really accomplishes the feat. She just has a way about her that calls Elizabeth back to speak."

Both Chloe and Nicholas had turned a chalky shade of white. This time Chloe did draw out her flask, and nobody made a move to stop her.

Jim set a reassuring hand on the old man's knee. "Are we talking spiritualism here, sir?" he asked.

"I don't know what you'd call it. I don't even care. It brings Elizabeth back, and that's all that matters."

"It's . . . it's a séance, then." Chloe gulped.

Adrian drew back, stunned. This was an old trick. False spiritualists had delivered messages from "the beyond" for decades, feeding eager patrons exactly what they wished to hear in exchange for profit.

He turned slowly toward Catharine, pinning her with a cold stare. "Miss Walsh, I'd like to pursue this matter further with you. Privately, if you'd be so kind."

Her face remained an exquisitely controlled mask. "I've no doubt that you would, Mr. de la Noye." She pronounced each syllable of his name with studied precision. "But I'm sure you'll understand when I refuse your request."

For a moment her features wavered in his vision, contorted by a slow, simmering anger that started somewhere behind his eyes and threatened to boil over. He pulled in a deep breath and, through sheer force of will, harnessed his tongue.

A small whirlwind of yellow and pink flew between them, coming to a stop at Catharine's side. "So sorry I'm late," it trilled.

"Father, who is this?" Nicholas demanded sharply.

"Why"—Bennett Chapman broke from his daze—"it's Amy. Amy Walsh. She's Catharine's niece. Weren't you listening, you dolt? I just mentioned her name."

Amy Walsh looked as if she'd fallen from a doll maker's shelf. She was a tiny fairy of a young woman with wide blue eyes and delicate skin. Despite the current rage for bobbed coiffure, her blond hair cascaded over her shoulders in whimsical curls. She wore a smart pink frock and white T-bar shoes, which showed off her neat figure and pretty legs to perfection.

"I'm a houseguest," she explained guilelessly, rounding Bennett's wheelchair.

Jim rose to his feet, accepting her hand before it could become obvious that Chloe and Nicholas were snubbing her. "Charmed, Miss Walsh," he said. "James Reid—Jim—at your service."

"Any other houseguests, Father?" Nicholas asked. "Any chance we could buy some snake oil or swampland in Florida? Have you filled all of Liriodendron's guest rooms with charlatans and frauds?"

"Nicky!" Bennett Chapman frowned. "Curb your tongue or I'll thrash you."

Nicholas turned from his father, apparently well used to the barbed words thrown his way. "Mr. de la Noye, need we say more? You may return to Boston at any time."

Adrian reached for his pocket watch. "We'll leave either late this afternoon or tomorrow morning. It depends on how long it takes to complete your father's will."

"But you can't change the will." Chloe's words floated doubtfully out to sea on the wind. "Nicky says our father is crazy." She crumpled against her brother as Bennett Chapman half stood, eyebrows lowered. Catharine placed a calming hand on his shoulder. He took the cue and settled back in his chair.

"Handle the matter, Adrian," he commanded.

Adrian acknowledged the order with a curt nod. "I'm not convinced of that, Lady Dinwoodie," he said.

"How can you say that?" Nicholas asked. "I'm aware that your firm gains a great deal of profit through my father—I can see why you'd want to remain in his good graces. But the man actually believes everything these charlatans tell him. If that's not insanity, I don't know what is!"

"This is America, Mr. Chapman. We're allowed to believe as we choose."

"Have you ever attended a séance, Mr. de la Noye?"

"No."

"I have. Knocks and whistles, disembodied voices . . . only the most gullible and unhinged could possibly believe that such communication is real. The very fact that my father trusts these quacks is proof of his incompetence."

"Your father is not a danger to himself or to others. He successfully manages both his business and his household. I see no signs of incompetence in that."

Nicholas took a slow, deliberate step away from his sister's chair. "Perhaps you choose to misunderstand me, sir. I'll speak plainly. You draft that will and I'll contest it. Believe me, Mr. de la Noye, I have the connections to make you look as unbalanced as my father really is. By the time I'm through, you'll be lucky if you can get a clerking position, let alone maintain a profitable law practice."

Adrian calmly returned his watch to his vest pocket. "Are you threatening me, Mr. Chapman?"

"You may interpret my words however you wish."

"But what if it's all true?" Jim's comment sliced through the uncomfortable silence. "What if Elizabeth Chapman really has come to call?"

Even the seagulls' screeches overhead sounded incredulous.

"I suggest you rein in your associate, Mr. de la Noye," Nicholas Chapman said.

Adrian dismissed his words with a raised hand. "Please, Mr. Reid, continue."

Jim shrugged. "My granny believed such things. Not a day went by that she didn't pass on some pearl of wisdom she'd 'heard' from my departed grandad. And there was nobody more solid and down to earth than my granny, I can tell you that."

"I am not a quack," Amy said in a clear little voice. "I am not something to belittle. I merely help Mrs. Chapman say what she can no longer say on her own."

"And how do you—" Adrian turned toward her, accidentally catching Catharine Walsh's gaze along the way. That vulnerable curve of the neck . . . the way one of her eyeteeth slightly over-lapped the tooth beside it . . . Somewhere in the distance he heard Jim Reid clear his throat, an obvious prompt for him to continue. But Catharine Walsh looked away, taking all his words with her.

Jim filled the breach. "I've a proposition," he said. "Mr. Chapman, am I correct in assuming that you and Lady Dinwoodie allege your father's incompetence based on his willingness to believe the inconceivable?"

"Of course. That shouldn't require any further explanation."

"I am not a charlatan." Amy's pink cheeks made her appear even more doll-like than before.

Jim studied her for one long moment before folding his arms across his chest. "I believe you have a right to prove that to us, Miss Walsh. I suggest a séance."

"Oh, dear God," Nicholas Chapman started, reaching for the flask in Chloe's hand.

"A séance?" A broad smile lit Bennett Chapman's face. "You mean . . . we would all be present for a conversation with Elizabeth? Splendid! How I'd like for you to meet her, Adrian!"

Adrian forced himself back into the moment, quickly catching Jim's intent. "An excellent plan, Mr. Reid, and, Mr. Chapman, one that I believe you and your sister may find more suitable than you think."

"Why would we acquiesce to this stupidity?" Nicholas demanded. Catharine winced as his hand slammed down onto the table.

"Because it may prove the easiest way to get what you want," Adrian said. "Here are the terms: if Miss Amy Walsh presents reasonable evidence that one could believe she communicates—"

"Preposterous," Nicholas snapped.

"—with your mother—"

"We could give it a whirl, Nicky," Chloe said. "Séances are all the rage in New York."

"—then you must accept that your father is in his right mind."

Nicholas grunted.

Adrian's voice grew hard as steel. "If that is the case, you will allow me to draft his will in peace. There will be no public complaint on your part, no repercussions whatsoever against either myself or Mr. Reid."

"And? Do continue, Mr. de la Noye. Tell me the part I most wish to hear."

"If we deduce that Miss Walsh offers your father no reason at all to believe, then the will stands as is. Mr. Reid and I will pack our bags and return to Boston immediately." He turned to the man in the wheelchair. "Mr. Chapman, you are my client. It's your decision. Are you agreeable?"

Bennett Chapman rubbed his hands together in anticipation. "Oh, absolutely. I look forward to it."

"And you, sir?" Adrian faced Nicholas.

Nicholas slowly withdrew a gold cigarette case from his pocket. He flipped it open with studied calm, examining the contents carefully before choosing a brown-papered cigarette. "The risk is more yours than mine. The agreement will be written and signed, of course."

"Of course."

The cigarette case slapped shut. "And, in the event fraud is uncovered, Miss Walsh shall be prosecuted to the fullest extent of the law."

Amy gasped. "I—"

"Not you." Nicholas pointed a long finger at Catharine Walsh. "Her."

Catharine drew herself up to her full height. A slight tremor ran down her left arm. She clenched her fist to stop it, but the gesture was not enough to curb her fury. Adrian watched her lips compress into a tight line and recognized the feverish glint in her eyes.

His words tumbled out as if released from years of captivity. "I hardly think that necessary, Mr. Chapman."

"Oh, I think it very necessary indeed, Mr. de la Noye." Nicholas delivered a smile stolen directly from the serpent in the Garden of Eden. "Those are the only terms I'll accept. Otherwise, you go right ahead and draft that new will. And I'll go right ahead and employ every contact I have to contest it. Win or lose, I'll see to it that both you and Miss Walsh are dragged through the mud."

"Accept his terms, Adrian," Catharine said quickly. An inadvertent hand flew to her mouth, partially concealing her bright red blush. Jim's eyebrows rose above the wire frames of his spectacles.

When she spoke again, her tone was cool. "I've nothing to hide, Mr. de la Noye. Accept his terms."

Adrian veiled his own surprise at her slip before turning toward Nicholas Chapman. "Very well, then. Mr. Reid will draft the paperwork. When do we meet?"

Amy blinked. "Mrs. Chapman comes in her own time, not at my bidding. I can't just command her to appear."

Nicholas reached for his cigarette lighter, flicking up the flame with one sharp motion. "Then I suggest you put in your request for her appearance now. Send her an invitation. A telegram. Do whatever it is you do to summon her, for we shall all be waiting with bated breath to see her after dinner tonight."

"Tonight?" Amy squeaked. "But—"

"Splendid!" Bennett Chapman beamed. "Of course, Mr. de la Noye, you and Mr. Reid will remain at Liriodendron as our guests."

Chloe heaved herself up from the chair, catching her brother's arm even though he'd failed to offer it. "I'm exhausted. Should you need to interrogate me more closely about any of this, Mr. de la Noye, you'll find me in my room. Alone. Any time."

"Stop talking, Chloe," Nicholas ordered, half dragging his sister across the flagstone patio to the French doors.

Bennett Chapman waited until his children had gone. "Greedy little tyrants," he said. "Have some coffee, Catharine, and maybe a scone. You missed breakfast this morning."

"No, thank you." Catharine's shoulders sagged. "If you'll excuse me, my headache has returned. I need to lie down."

"If you say so. I'm feeling rather peaked myself. Damn those children of mine. They can make you old before your time. Roll me back to my room, Catharine, will you? Oh, I'm so looking forward to the séance! It brings me great comfort to see Elizabeth's fondness for you."

Catharine Walsh didn't answer. She merely gripped the wheelchair handles and pivoted Bennett Chapman to face the house.

Jim turned toward Adrian, eyebrows raised in question, but Adrian was watching as Catharine pushed the chair toward the ballroom doors, her eyes straight ahead and her color high.

"Come along, Mr. Reid," Adrian finally said, snapping his attention back to Jim. "We've work to do."

CHAPTER
6

The séance would be held in the parlor, the Zeus statue presiding. Jim shoved his hands deep into his pockets and longed for the after-dinner brandy he'd just abandoned on Bennett Chapman's library desk. He'd have preferred to stay in the plush library longer, enjoying both the contraband alcohol and the Gauloise cigarettes his host had provided the men after dinner. It didn't matter that the air between Adrian and Nicholas Chapman crackled with mutual contempt; Jim had seen worse just strolling around the block in his neighborhood. Besides, the raised hackles in the library were far preferable to the tension they'd all endured at the dining room table earlier that evening, where men and women alike had sat at awkward attention beneath the salty language of Bennett Chapman's incessant commentary.

But all leisurely enjoyment of Liriodendron's luxuries had vanished with Amy Walsh's knock on the library door.

"I'm ready," she'd said, as cheerfully as if announcing a madcap game of charades.

Bennett Chapman's face had lit from within like a Chinese lantern. "Gentlemen, you've all finished your drinks, haven't you?"

And, as he'd watched Adrian drain the last of his brandy and set down the glass, Jim had known that, half-full glass or not, he had no choice but to follow their host out of the library and down the hall.

Now Amy Walsh led the men from the library to the parlor, Bennett Chapman at her side. He'd eschewed the wheelchair this evening, choosing instead a fine wooden walking stick topped with an intricately carved ivory elephant. His step seemed sure as he crossed the parlor threshold.

Seven chairs had been arranged in a loose circle about a round table. A candelabra with four lit tapers was set in the middle, placed atop a maroon cloth that covered the table from top to floor on all sides. Nicholas lifted the edge of the cloth and examined the space beneath the table before retreating to stand like a sullen sentinel beside the parlor door.

Amy seated herself in the chair directly opposite the doorway, with Bennett on her right. Cool and composed, Catharine sank gracefully into the chair beside him.

"Are we to sit in any special order?" Chloe's brittle voice floated from her spot by the fireplace.

"It doesn't matter," Amy started to say, then caught herself. "No, wait." She closed her eyes and tilted her head. Jim exchanged a questioning glance with Adrian, who gave a slight shrug.

"I guess it does matter tonight," Amy said, eyes still closed. "Mr. Reid is to sit at my left. The younger Mr. Chapman is beside him, then Lady Dinwoodie and Mr. de la Noye. Aunt Catharine, you and Bennett may stay where you are."

Bennett leaned forward. "Is that Elizabeth who says so? Oh, she always did love arranging a good dinner party!"

"I suspect it's Mrs. Chapman." Amy opened her eyes. "But it's mostly just a feeling for now. No words."

"Perhaps the message is from your spirit guide." Chloe drifted toward her assigned seat. She seemed particularly tired this evening, as if even lifting her fork at dinner had required too much effort. She hadn't touched a drop of wine during the meal and had refused even the offer of an after-dinner cordial.

"Spirit guide." Nicholas almost spat the words.

"I'm unfamiliar with that term." Adrian slid Lady Dinwoodie's chair out from beneath the table.

She dropped into the offered seat. "To contact loved ones on the other side, most mediums rely on the aid of one who has already crossed over. Have you never heard of Florence Cook and her Katie King? Of Mrs. Piper and the Imperator?"

"When did you become an expert on otherworldly communication?" Nicholas's words frosted the air.

Chloe's chin quivered. "I've . . . had an interest in séances for quite some time now," she said faintly.

She brought to mind a cornered doe searching for an escape from the barrel of a hunter's gun. Jim opened his mouth to save her, but Adrian spoke first.

"I'm not at all surprised that Lady Dinwoodie has an interest in such things," he said. "She is a sophisticated society woman, after all. It's her responsibility to stay well informed about the current fads and fashions in entertainment."

He seated himself in the glow of Lady Dinwoodie's grateful smile.

"Please extinguish all lamps except for the small one on the bookcase by the door," Amy said.

"Allow me." Nicholas Chapman strode through the parlor, turning off every lamp in his path. The room grew dimmer with each click. Amy's wide eyes gleamed in the candlelight. Catharine flinched as Nicholas swept past her. She sat still as a stone, her face an unreadable blank. Lady Dinwoodie bit her lower lip as her brother extinguished the last light and took his place in the chair beside her.

"Remember," Amy said, "I've no guarantee that Mrs. Chapman will come."

"She'll come." The anxious note in Bennett Chapman's voice made Jim turn his way. Understanding dawned as he took in the older man's crisply creased black suit, expertly knotted tie, and freshly barbered hair. Bennett was seeking the approval of the woman he'd married decades before.

"We must all hold hands," Amy said.

Jim reached for Nicholas's hand on his left and Amy's on his right. Her fingers fluttered so lightly in his grasp that he felt they might float away if he didn't enclose them completely. Across the table, Catharine hesitated briefly before allowing her hand to rest against Adrian's open palm. He acknowledged her touch with an expressionless nod but did not close his hand around hers.

"Should we shut our eyes?" Chloe asked.

"I have no intention of doing that," Nicholas said. "I don't plan to miss a thing."

An uncomfortable silence descended upon them as all attention turned toward Amy. She had already closed her eyes, her face in repose reminiscent of a Renaissance Madonna.

"We have visitors tonight, Mrs. Chapman," Amy said politely. "Won't you join us?"

Chloe squirmed in her chair. "Oh, dear. I do hope we needn't worry about anything as odious as ectoplasm."

"Shhh!" Catharine frowned.

Amy's cheeks grew exceedingly rosy. Her small hand curled into a fist against Jim's palm. He resisted the urge to slide his chair a little closer to hers.

Seconds dragged into minutes. The grandfather clock in the entrance hall chimed the quarter hour, each toll an indictment. Outside, the sky darkened a shade.

Nicholas's chair creaked as he shifted position. "I'll endure five more minutes of this nonsense. If nothing has happened by then, the matter is settled in my favor."

"There is no prescribed waiting time written in our agreement," Adrian said.

"Perhaps you have more hours than I to waste in the pursuit of folly, Mr. de la Noye. Five more minutes."

"Oh, I'm quite certain they won't mind at all," Amy said suddenly to no one in particular.

Bennett Chapman leaned forward. "Is she here?"

"She says that you should be able to sense that by now . . . that if you think about her, you'll know exactly where she's standing."

The candle flames wavered as Bennett obediently closed his eyes. A small smile pulled at one corner of his mouth. "Why, of course. She's near the fireplace."

"Very good indeed," Amy said.

"She's wearing that blue gown I liked so well, the one she first wore to a ball at the White House. Rud Hayes and his wife, Lucy, were such splendid hosts, even if one had to resort to trickery to get a drop of liquor in their house; excellent practice for this wretched Prohibition, if I do say so myself. Good evening, my sweet Elizabeth."

"Oh, for the love of God." Nicholas yanked his hand from Jim's, slamming it hard on the table. "Are we to believe—"

One candle blew out as a chill laced the room.

"We must clasp hands," Bennett said sharply.

"This is stupidity!"

"Do as he says, Nicky." Illuminated by the remaining candles, Chloe's anxious face resembled a pale, floating moon.

"Mrs. Chapman is approaching the table," Amy said calmly. "She is very pleased to see you all here tonight."

Jim's mind raced in an effort to organize this new influx of information. Granny Cullen had certainly never relied on eerie effects or rituals to dole out the comments she claimed came straight from his grandfather. He remembered her standing in the bright light of the kitchen, paring knife pointed in his direction: "Your Gran'da says you're to cut your hair and straighten your spine. Stand proud, young man!" He'd grown used to receiving pithy commands from the beyond delivered in the midst of whatever mundane chore Granny happened to be doing at the moment. He'd believed them, too: why doubt when Granny's pronouncements were nearly always right?

But he'd expected more here—instruments for the spirits to play, perhaps, or the adoption of strange voices and mannerisms as "Mrs. Chapman" spoke. Instead there was simply Amy, looking lovely but ordinary as she sat in her chair with her eyes closed, speaking in her usual tone of voice while delivering words she claimed belonged to someone else.

"Is this all that happens?" Nicholas demanded.

"Of course not," his father said. "We talk about old times. And your mother offers the advice she's been robbed of giving in physical form. You may ask her anything you wish."

"Ask *who* anything I wish? There's nobody here. Mr. de la Noye, I implore you to halt this travesty now."

Adrian sighed. "I'd like to hear more, Mr. Chapman."

"Your mother regrets that she wasn't present to temper your rash disposition while you were growing up, sir," Amy said, and a murmur of agreement from Catharine underscored her words. "She would have remained on this earth longer had she been given the choice."

"Don't fret, Elizabeth," Bennett whispered. "We all understand."

Amy's voice softened. "Lady Dinwoodie, your mother brings words meant for you tonight. She recognizes your sorrow and longs to share the burden. She has a message from someone you miss very much."

Chloe wrenched her hand from Adrian's, but not in time to cover the gasp that escaped her mouth.

Nicholas half rose in his chair. "Mr. de la Noye. You must stop this at once."

"No, Nicky. Wait." His sister struggled to her feet, each tendon in her neck taut. "Please, continue."

Adrian placed a gentle hand on her shoulder and guided her back into her chair. "Lady Dinwoodie, there is much resting on this session tonight, and it's necessary to ensure that justice is served. Will you allow me to ask the questions?"

She slumped against the back of her chair, too distracted to return her hand to his. "Please do. I'm not sure I can."

He turned toward Bennett Chapman. "And you, sir—may I respectfully ask that you remain silent as well?"

"Indeed." The old man's eyes shone. "I am content simply to bask in Elizabeth's presence."

Adrian faced Amy, who sat quite still with her eyes closed and a sweet smile on her face. "Am I speaking to Mrs. Chapman?"

"You are speaking to Amy Walsh," Amy said. "But I hear Mrs. Chapman and deliver her words."

"I've heard that some . . . spirits . . . speak through their mediums. You don't do this?"

Amy gave a slight shudder. "How ghastly. No, Mr. de la Noye. I don't choose to give myself over to something I can neither see nor control."

"So, if I ask a question of Mrs. Chapman, you will give me her response."

"If she so directs, yes."

"Very well. Mrs. Chapman says she has a message for Lady Dinwoodie. Who is it from?"

Once again, Amy tilted her head as if listening. "Lady Dinwoodie lost a loved one in the Great War."

"Is this true, Lady Dinwoodie?" Adrian asked gently.

"Don't offer any additional information, Chloe," Nicholas interjected. "A skilled swindler will use every piece of information you provide to strengthen her own conjectures."

Chloe bit her lip. "It's true, though, Nicky. You know it is."

"Of course it's true. *Everyone* lost a loved one in the Great War. If ever a quack wanted to hit a bull's-eye with a guess, this was the one to make. Very well then, Miss Walsh. So the generalization fits: the Chapman family endured a loss in the Great War."

"Mrs. Chapman tells me that it was a beloved child." Amy continued as if nobody had spoken at all.

This time, both hands flew to Chloe's mouth. "Please, Nicky, I must hear . . ."

"But your mother tells me that she must speak to you about certain matters before we go any further," Amy said. "There are . . . habits . . . that must cease. It is imperative that you stop your abuse of alcohol, Lady Dinwoodie."

"The obvious conclusion of anyone who has observed you for more than five minutes," Nicholas muttered.

"You cannot continue to live as if your life doesn't matter to anyone." Amy's voice had receded into a mildly hypnotic singsong. "Your mother says that each day compromises your health and well-being a little more. The surest way to honor and remember someone you loved is to live well on their behalf."

A single tear made its way down Chloe's cheek, leaving a light trail in her heavy makeup foundation. "I know," she whispered. "It's just so hard to go on."

"The vast amount of money you spend on bootleg and other means of dissolute behavior could be spent in better ways."

"It was only a matter of time before money entered this conversation," Nicholas said. "Mr. de la Noye, if you won't ask the crucial questions, then you must allow me to do so."

Adrian handed Chloe his handkerchief and turned back to Amy. "Would Mrs. Chapman be so kind as to give us more information about the departed? Where was the place of death?"

The room grew even quieter as Amy paused. Bennett Chapman's

eyes widened slightly, then tracked a short path along the table to settle on a spot between his children's seats. Catharine leaned forward, gripping the table as if she feared the room might sway.

"A German artillery shell . . ." Amy began.

Chloe started to tremble.

"Another easy guess." Nicholas shot a quelling glance at his sister.

" . . . hit an Evacuation Hospital on the Western Front," Amy continued. "But all is well, Lady Dinwoodie. You're not to grieve. Your child is happy and at peace."

Chloe's fingernails scrabbled against the table as she again struggled to her feet. "I must hear . . ."

Nicholas rose as well, clamping his fingers around his sister's wrist in a grasp so tight it would surely leave a mark. "Not a word, Chloe." His head snapped toward Amy. "Tell us, then, Miss Walsh," he said. "What words of wisdom does Chloe's deceased son have for her today?"

"Nicholas!" Bennett Chapman's voice cut through the challenge. "For the love of God!"

Chloe's face contorted.

Amy's eyes opened wide beneath Nicholas's penetrating stare. She raised her gaze to meet his. "Why, Mr. Chapman," she said, surprised. "I should think you'd know that your sister did not lose a son in the Great War."

The lines around Nicholas Chapman's mouth grew deeper. His jaw clicked as he clenched his teeth.

"She lost a daughter," Amy finished.

Nicholas remained rigid as Chloe's shoulders shook with sobs.

CHAPTER
7

Adrian quickly rearranged his features into bland neutrality. Nicholas Chapman was correct: fatalities conjured from the Great War were safe bets. But it was harder to explain Amy's knowledge that Chloe's loss had been a daughter rather than a son. Of course, it was nothing that a little research couldn't uncover. Catharine Walsh had certainly ingratiated herself into Bennett Chapman's confidence and could have easily received such information. But Catharine looked just as startled as everyone else at the table. Her cheeks had flushed scarlet, and the fingers of her left hand now fanned across her swanlike neck. Bennett, too, looked slightly ill, as if he'd stashed away this family tragedy with no intention of ever revisiting it again.

"My poor Margaret," Chloe whimpered. "My poor, poor baby. She felt such a strong calling to nurse the wounded. She was a

British citizen through her father, you know, and when Britain went to war . . ."

"No more, Chloe." Nicholas placed both palms firmly on the table and leaned in, an inquisitor in search of a victim. "This is information anyone could discover. Don't let it deceive you." His chin jerked in Catharine's direction. "How much more family knowledge have you coaxed from our father, Miss Walsh?"

Burgundy glints shone in Catharine's hair as she straightened in the dim glow of the candlelight. Her mouth curled into a sneer. "I'm sorry to deflate your insufferable ego, Mr. Chapman, but the subject of you and your sister rarely comes up."

"Catharine!" Bennett sounded as if he might send his fiancée to bed without dessert. "They're boorish brats, but they are still my children. There's no need to insult them."

Nicholas folded his arms across his chest. "Very well, then, Miss Walsh. Have your little acolyte tell me something you couldn't know."

Adrian started as Catharine's fingers intertwined with his. He felt anger quiver through her like an electric current. He doubted she was even aware that they still held hands. The proud set of her shoulders . . . that flare of delicate nostrils . . . Somewhere deep inside him, a long-closed door finally burst its safety locks, creaking open with an invitation as teasing as a siren's song.

He carefully extricated his hand. "I believe that Amy—rather, Mrs. Chapman—has more to say."

Amy's eyes flickered beneath her closed lids. "She does indeed, Mr. de la Noye."

"Please, are the words for me?" Chloe asked anxiously.

"Your Margaret wishes you peace," Amy said. "She wants you to know that she was able to bring great comfort to many brave boys, and that she would do it all again if given the opportunity. She felt no pain in her death and sends great love to you."

Chloe laid her head in her arms as deep sobs wracked her body. Neither her father nor her brother made a move to comfort her. Bennett merely stared into space as if awaiting celestial orders, while Nicholas glanced impatiently at the clock on the fireplace mantel.

Jim rose from his place and circled the table.

"Stay seated!" Bennett cried. "You'll break our chain and Elizabeth will leave us!"

"No." Amy's eyes flew open. "No, she's still here."

Jim placed an awkward hand on Chloe's shoulder and bent toward her. "I'm sorry for your loss," he said. "The sacrifice was too great to ask of either of you, but I am grateful for your daughter's selflessness. She was a true hero, Lady Dinwoodie."

Chloe gazed at him through wet eyes. Slowly, she reached up to squeeze his hand. Jim waited until her breathing sounded less ragged before turning back toward his chair.

Amy did not speak until he'd returned to her side. "Mrs. Chapman thanks you for your kindness," she said, reclaiming his hand. "You have a stout heart, boyo."

Jim blinked. "And who says that?" he asked, his voice light.

"I don't know." Amy frowned. "But Mrs. Chapman says that you will."

"It's what my granny always called me."

Nicholas Chapman groaned. "You've the map of Ireland splashed across your face, Mr. Reid. Here's another lucky guess that has hit its target."

Jim sank into his chair as if underwater, his brow furrowed in thought.

"I believe we're finished here," Adrian said quietly.

"We are in agreement at last, Mr. de la Noye," Nicholas said. "I'm afraid you've most likely missed the last ferry off the island tonight. You can catch one early tomorrow. As for you, Miss Walsh . . . I'll give you one last evening with your niece before I make good my promise to call the authorities."

"There's no need to call anybody." Adrian rose to his feet, frowning slightly as he brushed a speck of lint from the sleeve of his dinner jacket. "This matter has been settled in your father's favor, not yours. Mr. Reid and I will draft his will according to his wishes."

A vein pulsed in Nicholas's temple. "You must be joking. You can't possibly believe that 'Mrs. Chapman' is real."

"That was never the question. We don't sit here tonight to prove the existence of life after death. We need only agree that your father has reason to believe such existence might be possible."

"Anybody of right mind can see through the fakery here!"

"I don't think it's fake, Nicky," Chloe said in a tiny voice.

"And why should your opinion matter, Chloe? You're a lush."

She did not look up from the tablecloth. "I haven't had a drop this evening. And I must confess that this isn't my first séance. I've been to several since Margaret died, dreadful spectacles filled with parlor tricks and silly spirit voices. But this . . . this feels different. I believe that my Margaret's words have come through Miss Walsh."

"My dear girl." Bennett Chapman's eyes brimmed with tears. "I always knew there was a good egg beneath that foolish shell."

Adrian did not retreat from Nicholas's cutting stare. "You considered your father incompetent because, in your mind, no sane person could believe that the words Amy Walsh delivers might come from any source other than herself. Yet here's another who believes that very thing. Is she incompetent as well?"

Nicholas rounded Chloe's chair until he stood face-to-face with Adrian. He was the taller of the two, but Adrian didn't even blink as the other man's angular figure bent toward him.

"What about you, Mr. de la Noye?" Nicholas asked. "Do you believe?"

"What I believe, Mr. Chapman, is irrelevant."

"A lawyer through and through, aren't you?"

"I'll take that as a compliment, sir."

Nicholas whirled toward Amy, long finger pointed at her nose. "Very well, then. No more vague pronouncements. No more information inveigled by your aunt from my father. Tell us something you could not possibly have known before."

Amy shrank against the back of the chair, her wide eyes and tousled blond hair making her resemble a grade-school girl instead of an adult. Her breathing came in short little gasps.

"Behave yourself, Nicky," Bennett Chapman commanded. "I won't have my guests harassed. You're frightening the girl with your loutishness."

"Oh, her type doesn't frighten easily, I guarantee. Let me guess: 'Mrs. Chapman' is no longer with us . . . there are no more messages to be had for this evening, and it's all my fault."

Amy bit her lower lip. "No," she whispered. "She is indeed still with us. I don't understand at all. I thought she required a solid chain, that she needed things to be done just so . . ."

"Has she more to say?" Bennett Chapman and Chloe spoke at the same time.

"You needn't speak further if you're tired, Amy," Catharine interjected.

"I am tired. But Mrs. Chapman is so eager tonight. I can't deny her the voice. Lady Dinwoodie—for Margaret's sake, she begs you to love your husband. He is a good man at heart and suffers his own grief over the loss of his beloved daughter. You should grieve together rather than alone. He will take care of you if you let him, and you will not feel so lonely."

"Again, tell us something we don't know," Nicholas muttered beneath his breath.

"And you, sir . . ." Amy's eyes fluttered shut. "Your selfish, loutish nature has denied you the company of your child . . ."

"I have no children."

"You do indeed, your mother says. One."

Catharine, Chloe, and Bennett sat in shocked silence as, for the first time that evening, Nicholas fumbled for words.

"I am not aware . . ." he began, genuinely surprised.

Amy's voice dropped in both tone and volume. "Your mother says that you should be."

Catharine recovered first. "There you have it," she said, breathing hard. "You asked for information you did not know before."

"Obviously, I meant information that could be proven. This is insanity. What am I to do, travel the world in an attempt to prove that I've no offspring?"

"That shouldn't take much, boy," Bennett Chapman said. "You've never been much of a lothario, after all."

"Stop." Jim leaned toward Amy, who was swaying unsteadily in her chair. "Miss Walsh—Amy—are you all right?"

"There's a bit more, I think." Her voice was barely audible. Her cheeks, so pink only moments ago, now looked unnaturally pale in the candlelight. "I have to say it; she'll be most displeased if I don't."

"I disagree." Jim kicked his chair from beneath him and dropped to one knee beside her. "It's time for you to stop."

Amy's head lolled to one side as she struggled to find the words. Catharine half rose from her chair.

A warning jab gnawed in the pit of Adrian's stomach. He covered Catharine's hand with his own and gave it an urgent squeeze. The expression she turned his way was just as startled and helpless as he himself suddenly felt.

"You must stop her," he said softly, fighting back an unexpected sense of unease.

"Dear God, don't I know it."

The intimate tone of her voice nearly robbed him of breath. Decades fell away as he stared from those chocolate-colored eyes to her full lips, noted the rise and fall of her breasts beneath the deep-rose dinner dress she wore.

Their eyes met. Catharine's breath caught.

She tugged her hand from his to hurry to Amy's side. "Amy," she said, giving her niece a gentle shake. "Enough. You must stop."

Amy opened glassy eyes and stared unseeing into her aunt's face. "The message is about a girl named Cassie and . . . and someone in this room. Mrs. Chapman is most insistent that it be delivered."

Then her eyes rolled back as she crumpled into Jim's waiting arms.

CHAPTER
8

The contours of the parlor floated before Catharine's eyes. She watched Jim carry Amy to the sofa, but the action was something from a dream, disjointed and barely rooted in reality. Chairs rattled as Bennett, Chloe, and Nicholas rushed across the room. Jim's voice rose above their babble, a touch of calm in the midst of a verbal storm.

"Back away," he ordered. "Give her space to breathe."

"Does your niece faint often?" Adrian's breath felt soft against Catharine's ear.

She gave an inadvertent shiver as his shoulder brushed hers. "No," she said. "This is the first time."

She felt him study her for a moment and turned toward the insistent gaze. She could read his face so easily. The combination of concern and distrust in his eyes embarrassed her, gave her the impetus she needed to turn away and rebuild her defenses.

Her heels clicked against the hard oak floor as she hurried toward the sofa. "Amy!" Everyone cleared a path as she approached except for Jim, who remained crouched beside Amy, her small hand wrapped in his.

Catharine gently cupped Amy's chin. "Amy. Wake up!"

"Should we ring for a doctor?" Chloe twisted the handkerchief she still held in her hands.

Catharine ignored her. "Amy!"

The young woman moaned and turned her head to one side, nestling her cheek against Jim's chest.

"Are you all right?" Jim asked.

Amy slowly opened her eyes. Color returned to each cheek as she struggled to sit. "What happened?"

"You fainted," Jim said.

"Goodness! How embarrassing." She winced as she swung her legs over the side of the sofa. "That's never happened before."

"I find that hard to believe," Nicholas said. "Really, it was a most effective addition to your act. I must applaud your sense of drama."

Catharine forced her words through clenched teeth. "My niece is not a liar, Mr. Chapman."

"You lack the credibility to make that assessment, Miss Walsh."

She advanced toward him, right hand raised to strike his smug face. Suddenly Adrian was between them, the familiar spice of his cologne making her head reel.

"We recognize a legal presumption of innocence in this country, Mr. Chapman," Adrian said, calmly lowering Catharine's arm. "So, unless you've evidence to the contrary, I must believe that Amy Walsh is telling the truth."

Chloe pushed between her brother and her father, coming to

a halt at Jim's side. "Miss Walsh . . . may I call you Amy? Were there further messages? Did you hear anything else before you swooned?"

"Yes, do tell us." Bennett sank onto the sofa. "Is Elizabeth still with us?"

"No." Amy pressed her palm against her forehead. "No, there's nobody here now. But there were other messages . . . I remember . . ."

Catharine's words tumbled out, halting Amy's hesitant flow of words. "You needn't worry about this now, Amy. You've done enough tonight."

"I agree," Adrian said. "I think it best that you retire for the evening."

Amy frowned. "No, it's all right. It's coming back to me now. The first message is for you, Bennett. It's from Mrs. Chapman. She urges you to marry Aunt Catharine as quickly as possible."

"What a surprise," Nicholas said. "And does 'Mrs. Chapman' offer any reason why this marriage must take place?"

Amy either did not catch his sarcasm or chose to ignore it. "She hasn't told me why," she said. "But she is most insistent. She says it's extremely important."

"How very like Elizabeth." Bennett smiled. "Still looking out for my welfare despite our distance from each other. We should set a date, Catharine."

If hatred alone could ignite fires, Nicholas's stare would have sent Catharine through the ceiling in a ball of flame. A torrent of blistering words fought to leave her lips. It took all her will to bite them back. "Yes, Bennett," she said evenly. "I'm willing. Why, we could do it now, if you'd like. Call the clergyman of your choice; I'm ready."

Chloe's insistent whine chopped through the tension. "Amy, had Margaret anything more to tell me?"

Everyone turned toward her, startled by her myopia. Her desperation almost inspired pity.

"No," Amy said. "Not this time."

"But you said there were other messages."

"There's one other. But it's not for you. It's . . . it's for a man, I think. Someone a bit profligate who should have known better and . . . geez, I've an awful headache."

Adrian's hand froze midway to his cigarette case. His expression remained serene, but a vein pulsed in his forehead.

Catharine hooked a determined hand beneath Amy's elbow and guided her to her feet in one smooth, even motion. "That's enough for tonight," she said, avoiding Adrian's eyes. "Everyone, please excuse us."

"Wait a minute." Nicholas's fingers curled around her upper arm as she passed by. Catharine gasped and wrenched her arm away, leaving his hand poised in the air like a set of claws in search of a victim.

"Don't touch me," she snapped. "Ever."

"Oh, Nicky, stop behaving like a Neanderthal," Bennett chided from his spot on the sofa, but it was Adrian who once again appeared at Catharine's side.

"Mr. Chapman," Adrian said, "suppose you tell us what's on your mind from several steps back on the carpet?"

Nicholas speared Catharine with one last glare before allowing his hand to drop to his side. Her eyes narrowed in response.

"I apologize," Nicholas said smoothly, reaching for his cigarettes. "But let me point·out that we still disagree about my father's state of mind."

"You are the only one in disagreement." Adrian did not offer a light. "The rest of us—including your sister—understand that reason enough exists for your father to believe this communication might be real."

"Our written agreement says nothing about a majority decision." Nicholas cupped one hand around the end of his cigarette as he lifted a flaming match to its tip.

"But, Nicky," Chloe started, "Amy knew so much about Margaret. You can't possibly believe that she could create all that from thin air."

"I do not deny that Miss Walsh is a very convincing young lady. And her aunt"—he exhaled the cigarette smoke in Catharine's direction—"is too clever by half. However, since ambiguity does indeed exist regarding unanimous agreement, I propose another séance, to take place tomorrow night."

"I hardly think that necessary," Adrian said.

"I didn't expect you would, Mr. de la Noye."

Catharine drew herself up. "I don't understand, Mr. Chapman. What do you hope to gain by this? You've made it quite clear that we'll never change your mind."

Nicholas took another long drag of his cigarette, then crossed the room to the Tiffany lamp on the sideboard. "That you won't," he said, flicking its switch with a resounding click. Light pooled across the dark wood of the sideboard as he continued toward the next lamp.

"Then what's your point?" Jim asked, planting himself a little closer to Amy.

Nicholas turned on another lamp. "I may not understand how anyone could be drawn into such stupidity, but I do understand that most people are motivated by material gain. Miss Walsh would not have initiated this spiritualist scheme unless there was something she wanted. It's quite clear what she wants from my father. I even understand what she wants from my sister and me. The upper class has ever been a target for hoi polloi. But why draw Mr. Reid into it? And, if my suspicions are correct, why Mr. de la Noye?"

"Mr. Reid and I have arrived merely to fulfill a request from our client," Adrian said. "Nobody has drawn either of us into anything."

"Really?" Nicholas lit the final lamp and turned toward him. "Let's consider, Mr. de la Noye. Each one of us here tonight got a . . . message, shall we say . . . from the great beyond. Pure claptrap, of course, but messages all the same. Husband heard from wife, mother from daughter. I received information regarding a child who most assuredly doesn't even exist. Why, even Mr. Reid here was given words purported to come from his grandmother, who I can only assume is now part of the heavenly choir."

Amy shrugged. "The spirits are always grateful for the opportunity to speak to those they love."

Nicholas ignored her. "And now it seems that there was one message left—one message that could not be delivered due to Amy Walsh's human frailty. I'm betting, Mr. de la Noye, that the message is for you."

A deep red flush flooded Catharine's face. "And what would that prove?" she demanded. "I'm quite sure that Mr. de la Noye is willing to forgo confirmation of your theory. You don't care about the message at all, do you, Mr. de la Noye?"

Adrian's mouth twitched. "No," he said. "Of course not. There's no need to revisit the spirit world on my behalf."

"Then do it on mine," Nicholas said. "Allow me the chance to enlighten you, Mr. de la Noye. You may not be able to sway me to your way of thinking, but perhaps I can sway you to mine. If I am correct, perhaps *you* will be the one to call the authorities and end this charade once and for all."

"Why would we do this?" Jim demanded. "It has nothing to do with our original agreement."

"I disagree. If these women are perpetrating a blatant fraud, then only the most incompetent—my father, perhaps—would allow themselves to be swept into it. Perhaps if you'd drafted our agreement a bit differently . . ."

"This is ridiculous," Catharine said. "I've Amy's health to think of. She's not a trained monkey, able to perform on demand. She—"

"No, it's all right." Amy shook Catharine's hand from her shoulder. Her blue eyes glittered in a too-pale face. "Mrs. Chapman would very much like an opportunity to speak with you all again. Tomorrow night is fine."

"Elizabeth has returned?" Years fell away as Bennett struggled hopefully to his feet.

Amy listened for a moment. "She's gone again," she said finally.

"How convenient," Nicholas murmured. "I don't remember Mother being quite this peripatetic when she walked the earth."

"Then we shall meet again tomorrow night." Chloe flushed pink. "Father, let me help you to your room. I want to hear everything—everything!—Mother has told you."

Bennett enclosed his daughter's hands in his own, his face glowing with delight. "Catharine, you don't mind if I spend some time with Chloe, do you?"

"No, Bennett, of course not." Catharine's smile looked as if it might shatter.

"Chloe." Nicholas extended a warning hand toward his sister, obviously no more comfortable than Catharine with the upcoming father-daughter tête-à-tête.

"Oh, leave me be, Nicky." His sister offered their father a steadying arm. "I'm not your puppet; I can have a conversation with my own father if I please."

Catharine stood quite still as Bennett's papery lips scratched against her cheek. "Good night, my dear," he said. "I shall see you at breakfast."

"I need air," Amy said as Bennett and Chloe left the room. "I'm going for a walk."

Catharine automatically took her hand. "Give me a moment to fetch my wrap."

"No." Amy's little hand slid from Catharine's and into the crook of Jim's elbow. "Mr. Reid, may I prevail upon your protection for half an hour or so?"

A crimson blush painted Jim's face as he straightened from his slouch. "You bet. Of course. Delighted."

Catharine opened her mouth to speak. Adrian stiffened. But neither Amy nor Jim spared the slightest glance behind them as they left the room.

Nicholas stubbed out his cigarette in the ashtray by the door. "Tomorrow, then," he said.

Adrian pulled his attention back to the tall man before him. "I will not be held hostage here indefinitely, Mr. Chapman," he said. "If we are unable to conclude this matter tomorrow night, I shall refer you to Clause Eight of our agreement, which allows a neutral third party to decide the outcome of our dispute."

Nicholas nodded. "Very well, Mr. de la Noye. But I very much doubt it will come to that. You are ultimately a man of reason. I trust your level head will prevail. Good night."

Catharine closed her eyes in an attempt to make sense of the situation. Why on earth had Amy agreed to another séance? The atmosphere at Liriodendron was too explosive. A hornet's nest of questions floated about these posh rooms, and the mix of sitters was decidedly volatile.

"We must talk."

Adrian's low voice cut through her reverie. Her eyes opened wide as she faced him. She'd expected anger from him, indignation at the very least. But his stare seemed more mournful than malevolent. He made no effort to move toward her, did not so much as extend a hand in her direction. It was as if he'd placed her under quarantine.

An anxious flutter ricocheted through her stomach.

"Please, Cassie," he said, and the ache in his voice cut a swift incision through her heart.

She turned and bolted from the room.

CHAPTER
9

February 1898

"You're a drunken sot," a female voice proclaimed, and a bucket's worth of water splashed across Adrian Delano's face.

"Hey!" he protested, sputtering from his horizontal position on the ground. Remaining flat on his back, he wiped his face with one hand as he tried to recall exactly where he was. Outside. Definitely outside. That was terra firma beneath him, frozen and hard, dusted with snow. The air was so cold that each breath drawn into his lungs hurt. Stray facts hammered at his foggy brain. He remembered disembarking from the S.S. *New York* in New York City hours earlier, just returned from the European tour he'd begun after last year's graduation from Harvard Law School. That meant it must be February (although he wouldn't even try to fathom the date).

The information was dull, but at least it made sense. He still needed to determine where he was and why he was wet.

He propped himself up on his elbows and struggled to open his eyes. An angel's face floated across his blurred vision, its eyebrows lowered, lips pursed.

"I couldn't sleep," the angel said. "I saw you fall and thought that someone ought to bring you into the house before you froze to death. Now that I'm here, though, it appears you've swallowed enough alcohol to prevent that. Can you stand?"

Everything came together with a sobering thud. He was back at his family's estate outside Poughkeepsie—sprawled in the front yard, to be precise. The angel dropped her bucket with an exaggerated clang and Adrian winced, finally understanding exactly what had happened.

The young woman—she was too unforgiving to be an angel—extended a hand. He grasped it and allowed her to help him to his feet. He was too cold to even entertain the notion that he should be mortified by his condition.

"A fine mess you are, Adrian Delano," the woman said and, shocked into cognizance by the frigid early morning wind, his whirling mind placed her as well.

"Cassie? Cassie Walsh?"

"Very good. And now you'll want a medal, I suppose."

"You've grown up." His voice grumbled through his shivers.

Cassie gave a weary sigh. "Between university and Europe, you've been away for a very long time."

Cassie was the cook's daughter, an amusing little spitfire who'd spent her childhood turning up for games of chess or backgammon in the Delano family quarters when she was supposed to be peeling potatoes in the kitchen. She was five years younger than Adrian, and he'd actually enjoyed shielding her from her mother's wrath, claiming he had no idea where she might be as she pressed her small self against the back of the parlor door in hiding. She'd written him once at school, an oddly solemn letter about how dull the place was without him. He'd responded with a brotherly letter or two, but nothing since November of freshman year.

He caught a glimmer of his disorderly self through her eyes and wished he were still drunk enough that it didn't matter. "So," he started weakly, hoping to remind her of the friends they'd once been, "who's been saving you from scrapes since I've been gone?"

Her dark eyes were relentless. "Nobody," she said. "And it doesn't look like you're up to the task anymore, either."

He gave up. "Not at the moment, anyway," he said. "Might I have a cup of tea? And would your mother have a slice of her splendid Madeira cake laid away?"

Cassie Walsh studied him for a moment. Then she turned on her heel and led him toward the servants' entrance. He remained upright by concentrating on the swing of her thick, dark braid as she walked. A hem of vanilla-colored lace peeked from beneath her pink chenille bathrobe. Her bedroom slippers left shallow footprints in the light snow as they rounded the side of the house. The poor thing would probably catch her death of cold, and it would be his fault—one more casualty of his reckless, stupid decisions.

A dull headache started at his temple. "Damn it, Cassie. I've botched everything up, haven't I."

Her hand hovered above the doorknob. "Yes," she said. "You have."

He'd left the S.S. *New York* with every intention of quickly traveling home to Poughkeepsie. A chance meeting with friends, a comradely supper in the city—even the women who'd joined them during the course of the lengthening evening—had all seemed logical at the time. His parents had expected him home for dinner, but now, in the warm kitchen of his family's estate, the clock above the pantry showed that it was half past two in the morning. There was no point in trying to justify his actions to Cassie in the face of such damning evidence.

Instead he accepted the tea towel she presented and wiped the remaining rivulets of water from his face and hair. Then he sank into a chair at the kitchen table and propped his chin in one hand. "Very well, Cassie Walsh. There are some years between us now, but we've always been straight with each other. Should I cower at the thought of meeting with my father this morning?"

Cassie lit the flame beneath the kettle before standing on tiptoe to lift a teapot down from a shelf. "You've returned from Europe only because he ordered you home at once. What do you think?"

Adrian's cheeks burned. Even the help knew of his disgrace. But of course they would: gossip crossed the ocean faster than any bird could fly. His biggest mistake had been believing that his stellar academic record would shield him against wagging tongues. Even he had to admit that his European achievements had had more to do with drinking and carousing than with intellect and potential. He'd suspected that fact as he'd escorted the Comptesse de-What's-Her-Name through the theaters of Paris, ignored it while drinking his way through Rome, and embraced it thoroughly as he'd gambled away a ridiculous sum of money in London.

"I see," he managed to say. "Well. Perhaps I'll be off after I've had some tea, then. Father and I can talk later, once I've had the chance to redeem myself a bit. I'll leave a note to let my parents know I've returned safely to the country."

"Off? You've just arrived."

"I'm invited to a wedding in Newport this weekend, a friend of mine from Harvard. I'd planned to leave this afternoon, but perhaps it would be wise to postpone my reunion with my parents just a little longer. I'll have my things sent."

Cassie lifted the cover from a cake plate and there it was, the fragrant Madeira cake Adrian had craved for so long. The thought of it warmed him even more than did the steaming radiator in the corner.

He jumped as Cassie sank a knife into the cake with more vigor than necessary. She slapped a piece onto a plate and thrust a fork in his direction, tines pointed straight at his chest.

"You infuriate me," she said.

He fell against the back of his chair, startled. "I've only just come home. What could I possibly have done to you?"

Her cheeks flamed red. The cake plate trembled in her hands. "You've got everything—wealth, education, a sure position with your father's firm—and you don't care. You're willing to fritter it all away in scandals. And such scandals! Good grief. They were third-rate at best."

The skin beneath Adrian's collar burned hot. "I'd remember your place," he began in a low voice.

"And I'd remember yours." The plate clattered onto the table before him, the noise slicing through his head. Cassie spun around to the kettle, lifting it from the stove to the teapot in one smooth, easy arc. "To think I once looked up to you," she murmured beneath her breath. "To think I once believed you might help me."

Adrian sat frozen in his seat, longing to humble her with a few harsh words. She was insolent beyond belief.

But she was also right.

"You don't want what I have, Cassie," he answered quietly. "The benefits of my station come with too many expectations."

Her back remained rigid as she poured boiling water into the teapot. "Poor Adrian Delano," she said, although the tone of her voice did not match the words at all.

ADRIAN SLUMPED AGAINST the leather chair behind Bennett Chapman's library desk, allowing its cushioned back to relieve some of the tension from his shoulders. That night's séance had shaken him well beyond its worth.

He prided himself on planning for all possible contingencies, but nothing in the world could have prepared him for this. Cassie Walsh did not belong here. She belonged securely wedged in memory, anchored to a time passed through long ago.

He reached for his cigarette case, examining the cigarettes nestled there as if each one were a work of art. He chose precisely, lifting a lighter from the desk.

The twentieth century had been kind to her. She was older, of course, but he had long ago come to see increasing years as a gift rather than a burden. Her chin-length curls were a departure from the luxurious mane he remembered, but her eyes—those eyes!—were as deep and beautiful as the ones that still occasionally haunted his dreams. He exhaled a long stream of cigarette smoke into the still air of the library, lost in the undercurrents of a life he'd once known.

Cassie Walsh—Catharine—was not his concern. He'd already

allowed the distraction of her presence to affect him adversely: he should have dictated a more thorough agreement about the séance to Jim. He would slam the door on the past and jam the deadbolt securely into place.

But Bennett Chapman was his client. He couldn't ignore Cassie's presence at the older man's expense. He knew all too well that while Cassie had missed being born with a silver spoon in her mouth, she more than made up for it with a silver tongue.

His wedding ring glinted in the dim light as he stubbed out the cigarette in an ashtray. Straightening, Adrian reached toward the telephone and his wife.

CHAPTER
10

I t's cooler out here than I thought," Amy said, skimming down Liriodendron's front steps and onto the circular driveway.

Jim followed more slowly, waiting for his eyes to distinguish the flat of each step from its edge before stepping forward. He reached the bottom of the short flight and slid his spectacles up his nose. "I'll wait if you want to fetch a shawl or something."

"No. I'd rather freeze than go back into that place."

He took her in from head to toe. She was indeed clad in something pale blue and flimsy. Still, he doubted that her shiver had anything to do with the temperature of the night air.

He shrugged off his dinner jacket and draped it across her bare shoulders. "Here. It looks better on you, anyway."

Her sunny smile was thanks enough, but the Sir Galahad moment still ended all too soon as she turned and darted down the driveway.

He hurried to keep up. "Where are we going?"

"Cliff Walk. The Forty Steps at the end of Narragansett Avenue. You wouldn't have an auto at your fingertips, would you?"

He hesitated. "It belongs to Mr. de la Noye."

"Oh, never mind. Calling for it would take an eternity anyway. We'll walk. It's not quite two miles."

He quickly computed the sum: two miles there, two miles back . . . alone in the moonlight with a girl who had the potential to make his pulse unreliable. This was luck, pure and simple.

A soft breeze lifted the blond tendrils around Amy's face as she walked briskly toward Bellevue Avenue. Jim's jacket, too big in all directions, threatened to swallow her whole. She tugged it more closely around her, an unconscious action that nearly sidelined his vigilance by melting his heart.

"Have you been to Newport before?" she asked as they turned onto Bellevue.

"No."

"Cliff Walk skirts the ocean. You'll like it. It's one of my favorite places in this town."

"You've been here before?"

Her shrug was nearly indiscernible in the fuzzy darkness. "Nope. But I get antsy if I sit around in one place for too long, and we've been at Liriodendron since May."

"An invitation from Mr. Chapman, I assume."

"Of course. It was nice of him to ask, considering we'd only met in April. I suppose the rich are more accustomed to entertaining than we mortal folk are."

Jim mulled over this new nugget of information. Bennett Chapman hadn't known the Walshes before April? It was now mid-June.

Even the most sentimental sap would have to question the swiftness of Cupid's arrow.

"I can show you around Newport in the daylight, if you'd like," Amy was saying. "I can't believe you've never been here before. Boston isn't that far away."

"Yeah, well, my family doesn't run in these circles." He nodded toward the massive outline of Belcourt to his left. "Do you travel with your aunt often?"

"I live with her." Amy picked up her pace. "I've always lived with her. She took me in after my parents died. My father was her brother."

Apparently Catharine Walsh had either a soft heart or a strong sense of duty. Somehow, Jim hadn't expected either. "Where do you two live?"

"Sacramento." Amy stopped suddenly, posed in the middle of the sidewalk like an escaped Liriodendron statue. "You're just chock-full of questions, Counselor. Am I on trial?"

"Not at all," Jim said, grateful that the darkness hid his sudden blush. "Just getting to know you better, that's all."

A smile broke full across her face as her small hand crept into his. "Well, that's just ducky," she said, pulling him into a brisk walk. "I think that getting to know each other better is an awfully good idea."

Jim shoved his free hand into his pocket, breezing past architectural splendors with scarcely a glance. Sacramento was quite a long journey to undertake just to visit someone you really didn't know. Surely there was a life left behind, obligations dangling back in California. At least one of the Miss Walshes had to have a job that put food on the table. As for Bennett and Catharine's engagement, no matter how many ways he tried to calculate the days of its inception, he came up with the same answer: whirlwind.

It took a minute to realize that a woman—a pretty one at that—had just flirted with him and currently held his hand. The tips of his ears burned. Was this what practicing law did to a man? For years he'd dreamed of being the object of flirtation. Now that it seemed he actually might be, all he could do was interrogate the cuddly young lady in question.

He took a deep breath as they turned onto Ruggles Avenue. A whiff of Amy's perfume went straight to his head, inspiring pleasant ideas that had no business being there. The press of her fingers against his was enough to make his legs unsteady. And when she turned those big eyes up toward him, it didn't take much to imagine an invitation beckoning behind the flutter of her lashes.

Instead, more questions fell from his mouth. "Tell me about the late Mrs. Chapman. Did she just join you at the dinner table one night? Do you regularly conduct séances back in Sacramento?"

Amy dropped his hand and sped ahead. Her words floated back over her shoulder. "No, I do not regularly conduct séances back in Sacramento," she said, and he thought she sounded more puzzled than perturbed. "Do you think I'm a quack too, Mr. Jim Reid?"

"Of course not." She moved faster than any human he knew. The pale edge of her frock peeked out from beneath the jacket. He used it as a beacon, picking his way across the cracks of the unfamiliar sidewalk as carefully as he could.

Amy had almost reached the corner before turning to see where he was. "Are you all right, slowpoke?"

"Yes. I don't see very well in the dark, that's all."

She doubled back. "You don't?"

Jim pointed to his spectacles. "I've worn these for as long as I can remember. I do just fine in the daylight, but my night vision is atrocious. It's the reason I couldn't go to war. To be honest, I couldn't have driven us anywhere tonight even if the car had been smack-dab in front of us."

There. It was out. He hated mentioning his eyesight. It was one more reminder that he was less than a strapping specimen. His grandmother had always told him to thank God for his superior intellect, but women had never cared much about the workings of his fine mind. They'd always smiled indulgently at him, calling him a real pal while clinging to the muscled arms of his handsome, brickhead friends.

Amy Walsh seemed to take the information in stride. "Why didn't you say so? I wouldn't have left you back here on your own."

Jim flinched. "I don't like talking about it. In fact, I'd be much obliged if you didn't mention my eyesight to anyone."

"Of course." Amy hooked her arm through his. "Why would anyone need to know?"

She brushed against him as they turned onto Ochre Point Avenue. Jim cleared his throat and tried not to think about how warm she felt against his side. Questions tickled the roof of his mouth. This time, he managed to hold his tongue.

"Okay, Mr. Lawyer," Amy said after several minutes of silence. "You've had your turn. May I ask some questions now?"

He couldn't stifle his indulgent grin. "Only if I have the right to cross-examine afterward."

"You may examine to your heart's content," she said demurely, and he resisted the urge to stop in his tracks to take his own pulse.

"Are you friendly with Mr. de la Noye outside the office?" Amy asked.

He deflated a bit. Maybe this interlude was about Adrian after all.

"He's charming," Amy continued, squeezing the crook of Jim's arm. "Do you know him well?"

Whether or not Amy was yet another woman intrigued by Adrian de la Noye, Jim could never be anything less than loyal to the man who'd taken such good care of him over the years. "I've known him practically my whole life. He's not only a mentor, he's part of the family."

Her eyebrows rose. "How did that happen?"

"He and my father served together in the Second Massachusetts Infantry during the Spanish-American War. They'd already become friends when the regiment shipped out to Cuba, but then my father saved Adrian's life at El Caney and, well, helping to look after me was Adrian's way to repay him. I'm the youngest of our brood, you see, and Da's health was never quite the same after the war. He died when I was twelve. Thanks to Adrian, though, I've always had everything I need."

"He's got some money, then. I thought so. Does he come from a wealthy family?"

"I couldn't say."

She didn't miss a step. "Really? You don't know his background?"

Jim shrugged. "I know his wife and children; I've met some of his friends and colleagues. Sure, he's obviously well-off. But he's always been just Adrian to me."

"And it never occurred to you to ask questions." The statement verged on accusatory.

Jim lengthened his stride, forcing Amy to skip to keep up with him. "No," he said, challenging her to refute his statement. "It never did."

"I see," she said, deliberately dragging their pace back to its original speed. "Well, you've explained that relationship as best you can, I guess. I don't suppose you can tell me how he knows my aunt?"

Up to this moment, he'd assumed he'd been the only one to notice a connection between Adrian and Catharine Walsh. He passed Amy a sideways glance. Her expression was as guileless as ever, those big blue eyes belying any concept of deviousness. She was adorable, easily the cutest little thing he'd seen in quite a while. But so were kittens, and they made him break out in hives.

"What makes you think he knows your aunt?" he asked casually.

"Don't you think he does?"

Jim stroked her fingers, hardly aware that he was doing so. "Oh, you're good, Amy Walsh. A natural-born lawyer."

"Turn right at the corner," she replied. "We're nearly there." She entwined her fingers through his and held on tight.

Jim reminded himself that he was here in Newport solely for business purposes.

"We're on Narragansett Avenue," Amy said. "The street ends at Cliff Walk. The Forty Steps are wonderful—I hope you'll like them as much as I do."

The breeze lifted her hair, teasing it around her graceful neck. Jim allowed his gaze to wander there. He was close enough to see that vulnerable spot near the collar of her borrowed jacket, right below her ear, a place just begging for a nuzzle.

Too many questions still dangled. How had Amy and her aunt met Bennett Chapman? Did Amy make a habit of speaking for the dead, or did Elizabeth Chapman have an exclusive agreement? And just how did Adrian know Catharine Walsh?

The answers to those questions could affect the wishes of his client in detrimental ways. Jim regretfully disengaged his hand from Amy's.

The street ended; the ocean spread before them in a dark vista of motion. A staircase appeared as they drew closer to the sea, dropping down the side of the cliff to a stone balcony just above the water.

"Come." Amy reclaimed Jim's hand, giving it a squeeze. "We'll take the steps as slowly as you want."

But there was no need to go slowly at all. The sea air filled Jim's lungs as they started down the steep incline, cleansing his crowded mind with salty vigor. With this entrancing young lady on his arm, his footing felt sure.

"Back around the turn of the century, servants from the summer cottages used to come here at night to play music and dance," Amy said. "Can you imagine how lovely that must have been?"

He gazed across the star-dappled sea, straight out to the point where water met sky in a velvet union of darkness. He could see those servants. His Irish ancestors, mostly, smothered by starched uniforms and stuffy protocol during the day, free to let loose at night and dance by the ocean to the swirling pipes of home. This may not have been their native country, but it was certainly their sea. It cradled Mother Ireland, had carried their boats safely to this land of opportunity.

He could almost feel the pressure of Granny Cullen's hand on his shoulder as her familiar words echoed through his mind: *You've a good mind, boyo, but never fear to follow your heart.*

Yes, there were still questions, but maybe they didn't all need answers at the moment.

"All right, Miss Amy Walsh," Jim said. "Let's talk about these supernatural powers of yours. Can you read my mind?"

Her eyes met his. "Yes. But that's just because you're a man."

Jim hesitated, then slid an arm around Amy's waist. Together they studied the bright moon.

CHAPTER
11

They scattered after dinner the next night like billiard balls following a good break. Nicholas left first, his quiet "Until later" more ominous than any loud, dramatic exit could ever be. Catharine was relieved to see him go. She preferred to partition her battles, handling each in its proper turn. The time to deal with Nicholas Chapman would come. For now she had a more immediate concern: Bennett's interest in her company seemed to be waning.

He wore his age badly tonight, turning toward Lady Dinwoodie for assistance as he struggled to his feet from his seat at the head of the table.

"Let me help you, Bennett." Catharine quickly rose from her chair. "Will you be retiring to the library with the gentlemen?"

He waved her away. "No, no, not tonight. I'm sure our guests will understand if I leave them to their own devices for a bit. I'd like to sit in the parlor for a while before we begin. Perhaps Elizabeth will arrive early and we can spend some time together."

"But the séance isn't scheduled to start for over an hour."

"I'll come with you, Father," Chloe said as if Catharine hadn't spoken at all. "I wouldn't mind sitting there myself." She crooked her arm. Bennett took it, and they left the room chattering about Elizabeth as if she awaited them in the parlor with coffee and cordials.

Chloe had been an unpleasant drunk, but at least she'd been fairly predictable while in her cups. It was hard to tell what to expect from this newfound filial devotion.

Adrian rose next, and Catharine forced herself to study the fleur-de-lis pattern on the wallpaper behind his head. She hadn't realized how much she'd relied on the laughable illusion that he didn't recognize her. Now, with no doubt that he did, she felt utterly exposed, as if every move she made were subject to intense scrutiny. And what to do about the persistent emptiness that threatened to invade her every time their eyes met?

"Mr. Reid?" Adrian directed a sharp stare across the table at his associate.

Jim and Amy sat beside each other, chairs closer than Liriodendron's housekeeping staff could possibly have placed them. A rosy blush dusted Amy's cheeks as she laid a proprietary hand on Jim Reid's sleeve, leaning close to murmur into his ear. Catharine could have pinched her. Things were complicated enough without mixing in an infatuation.

"Mr. Reid?" Adrian repeated, and Jim pulled away from the spell of Amy's feathery whisper. "May I speak with you?"

"Yes." Jim clambered from his chair like a student caught cheating. "Of course."

Catharine watched them go, her mood sinking with each passing second. Adrian appeared so polished, the well-heeled image of a successful man. But she could see behind his poised façade. He was no more pleased about this newfound alliance between Jim and Amy than she was.

Amy lifted her water goblet to her lips, dreamy gaze set on some faraway landscape that only she could see. "I think I'll take a walk."

"I'd rather you didn't," Catharine said, voice low.

"Don't worry. I'll be back in time." Amy set the goblet onto the ivory tablecloth and pushed her chair back.

Catharine rounded the table, halting at Amy's side. "What are your intentions toward Mr. Reid?"

"Oh, I don't know. What are yours toward Mr. de la Noye?"

"I have no intentions toward Mr. de la Noye. In case you've forgotten, I am an engaged woman. I might even be a married woman someday. Isn't there some way you could just prod Mrs. Chapman along a bit, one way or the other?"

Amy's cool blue gaze pinned her in challenge. Catharine narrowed her eyes and glared back. They could sit here all night as far as she was concerned. At least she would know where Amy was.

Amy broke first, leaning back in her chair with a sigh. "You know I can't make Mrs. Chapman do anything. She's been unpredictable from the start."

That was true. In all the years Amy had read palms and told fortunes back in Sacramento, nothing had prepared them for Mrs. Chapman. That shouldn't have been the case: they had dabbled in the spiritualist game for so many years that it had become routine, an easy and relatively harmless way to make a little extra money. Yet no matter how often Catharine ran the past months' events through her mind, she couldn't unravel the mystery of Mrs. Chapman.

SACRAMENTO HAD PROVED a fine place to lay down roots, temperate and teeming with possibilities. Catharine had found a job managing a cigar stand in the lobby of the city's finest hotel, a position that offered not only a modest salary but the chance to establish influential contacts as well. Wealthy men behaved in basically the same way wherever she came across them. A flirtatious smile here, a flattering comment there, and gentlemen passing through the hotel on business naturally assumed that every word leaving their lips was a pearl of great worth. Financial and social tidbits flowed freely, delivered by entrepreneurs keen to impress the striking lady behind the counter. Catharine had reaped a steady harvest of professional secrets from men who coaxed her from behind the cigar stand to dinner and a night on the town.

It hadn't taken much analysis to convert these clandestine tips into wise personal investments. It was easy to confide during dinner dates that Amy had a gift that increased the capital of all who paid for her spiritual readings. The gentlemen always chuckled indulgently—until Catharine tossed out a stock tip or financial morsel that only a professional could know. Suddenly, the fish was hooked. And once back at the Walsh home, Amy reeled him in by listening earnestly to the "great beyond," then passing along information that other magnates had indiscreetly whispered into Catharine's listening ear.

It seemed a benign way to build a little nest egg. The captivated men often returned with their ladies, who pined for readings filled more with romance than finance. Catharine made it a habit to read every article she could about the nation's prominent families. That, combined with a survivor's instinct for mining details, meant that Amy always had something of plausible interest to say. The two of them had lived more comfortably over the years simply by transferring information from one party to the next.

But Bennett Chapman had been different right from the start. Because the Chapman family business was so strongly centered on the East Coast and in Europe, Catharine had never expected to come face-to-face with anyone connected to it. The day Bennett approached the hotel humidors had sent her head spinning at the unexpected twist of kismet.

It was hard to make conversation at first. Bennett was more snappish than most, seemingly immune to pleasantries or banter of any sort. But then his fingers had brushed hers over a Hoyo de Monterrey. For one brief, unguarded moment, their eyes locked. Bennett grumbled and turned away, but not before Catharine realized that, despite his bad-tempered exterior, he had the same needs and vulnerabilities as every other powerful man she'd met. An afternoon's worth of companionship at their home might even do him good.

"A tarot reading," she'd suggested lightly. "Just as a diversion from your busy schedule. Who knows? Perhaps you'll get a decent stock tip from the other world."

"Waste of time," he'd growled, but he'd come to the house anyway, unable to resist the chance to bolster his fortune.

Amy had reached for her tarot deck, serene smile in place. "Let's choose a significator for you, shall we, Mr. Chapman? That's the card that will represent you in this reading." She withdrew the King of Cups from the deck and placed him faceup on the Queen Anne coffee table between them. "He'll suit you fine."

Catharine settled onto the sofa beside Bennett as Amy shuffled the cards. His hand trembled a bit. She straightened her spine against a jab of remorse. There was no reason to feel guilty. She and Amy were only giving this man information he'd pay three times as much for elsewhere.

Amy spread the cards in a neat Celtic Cross on the coffee table. She did this spiritualist thing particularly well, for she possessed not only an aura of innocence but a true knack for reading people. When those natural abilities combined with the information Catharine provided, Amy's readings were both engaging and effective.

"Do you see this card atop the significator?" Amy asked, pointing. "This card represents your situation as it stands now."

Catharine glanced at the card, idly studying its depiction of Adam, Eve, apple tree, and serpent. It didn't much matter which card Amy turned up. Her readings always had less to do with the cards themselves than with whatever words would satisfy their listener. Still, it was ironic that she'd presented The Lovers turned upside down to a man who obviously had no use for other people.

"Love reversed," Amy said, almost to herself.

Bennett Chapman paled. "How do the cards know anything about me?" he asked, and Catharine looked up from the cards, startled by the quaver in his voice.

"It's a mystery," Amy intoned. "Shall I continue?"

He placed both hands on the head of his walking stick and pulled himself to the edge of the sofa. "Yes, yes. By all means!"

"The next card represents what crosses the situation, good or bad. You are lonely, sir, aren't you?"

This was a definite deviation from the usual script. Typically this was the point where Amy introduced a financial tidbit, some hint of promised wealth.

But Bennett Chapman's response came quickly enough that it was clear she was onto something. "Yes," he said, and the word was so hollow that it was all Catharine could do not to stare at him. Here in her tiny parlor, this powerful millionaire, this captain of industry feared by many, suddenly seemed nothing more than a forlorn old man. She turned toward Amy, willing her to proceed at a quicker pace. Where was the clever stock tip that would pique Bennett's curiosity? What had happened to the sage advice meant to encourage his return for several more readings?

Instead Amy doubled over in her chair and clutched her stomach.

"What's wrong?" Catharine jumped from her seat. "Are you ill?"

All color drained from Amy's face as she turned toward Bennett Chapman. "Who is Elizabeth?" she asked.

He started as if a jolt of electricity raced through his body. "Elizabeth?"

"Yes. There's someone here named Elizabeth who wishes to speak with you."

Startled, Catharine instinctively cased the parlor. Only the three of them sat there, shrouded in the afternoon shadows. Was Amy speaking of spirits? This sort of thing had never been in the repertoire before.

Bennett began to shake. "Elizabeth? Here? My God. She is . . . was . . . my wife. She passed away long ago."

"She sends her love," Amy said. She looked almost as surprised delivering the words as Catharine felt hearing them. "She knows you have been thinking about her lately."

Bennett's shaking became so pronounced that Catharine could not help but place a firm arm around his shoulders. Tears slipped from his eyes, but he did not seem to notice as they trickled down his cheeks. "Of course I've been thinking about her," he whispered. "She was my wife, after all, and as I approach the end of my days, I am overcome with . . . she was quite a woman. No one will ever measure up to her."

Amy's voice softened. "She says that she cannot bear your aching. She wants only for you to be happy. If you care about her memory, she says, you will take another wife to make your last days on earth comfortable and sweet."

"Another wife?" The words flew out of his mouth on a puff of forced air. "But—"

"She says that the opportunity is nearer than you think." Amy spoke faster now, as if she were reading aloud. "She says you should marry my aunt, Catharine."

"What?" Catharine barely recognized her own shocked voice as it echoed through the room. It did not surprise her that Amy knew some biographical facts about Bennett Chapman. Heavens, there was plenty of information about this man—and others—stashed away in the metal strong box they kept in their safe. But what on earth could have prompted the unexpected marriage message? And why hadn't Amy said anything to her before blurting it out in the midst of a reading?

Bennett's grasp tightened around the head of his walking stick.

No longer frail and malleable, he shot to his feet in a rage. "Fraud!" he shouted. "This is a despicable scheme to get your hands on my fortune, isn't it? You ought to be horsewhipped! As it is, I'll be paying a visit to the authorities on my way back to the hotel!"

"Sir, please." Catharine stood as well, resting a hand on his sleeve. He shook it off. "Please, Mr. Chapman, we mean you no harm."

He whirled toward her, brow lowered and walking stick raised to strike. She recoiled. Then, suddenly, his anger seemed to subside a bit. His gaze stayed hooked to hers, mellowing as he studied her face. Catharine blinked. What could he possibly have seen in her desperation?

"I'm sorry," Amy whispered, "but Elizabeth has more to say."

"Enough!" Catharine said, stare still linked to Bennett's. "Amy, no more!"

"I've no choice." The misery in Amy's voice made them both turn her way. "I . . . I don't know what's happening any more than you do. I just started hearing words that needed to be said. I know it's bold of me but, please, could you just listen a little longer?"

Bennett sank to the sofa as if his legs could no longer support his weight. Perplexed, Catharine followed suit.

Amy continued. "Elizabeth understands your disbelief and implores you to give her a chance to prove that it is she who comes to you now. She asks you to remember your wedding day, how the skies cleared of rain just before the ceremony and how the cherry blossoms bloomed outside the church."

Bennett gasped.

"She gave you a gift that day. Do you remember?"

"Of course!"

"Yes, your pocket watch. You still carry it. The inscription on the back—do you recall what it says?"

"Yes," he said. "How could I ever forget?" He fumbled with his watch chain for a moment, then drew out a gold watch. Flipping it over in his hand, he fixed Amy with a challenging eye.

She didn't hesitate. "It says 'Elizabeth Jane and Bennett William, May 15, 1869.'"

Silently, Bennett Chapman turned the back of the watch toward Catharine so that she could read it. Her eyes absorbed the words.

"Yes," Bennett said slowly. "How did you . . ."

"Elizabeth says that if you remember the essence of your life together, you will listen to her advice and marry Catharine. She bids you farewell, now. Until next time."

Bennett Chapman visited frequently after that, mostly to talk to Elizabeth but, after a little more than a week, to begin courting the woman his late wife had directed him to wed. Bewildered, Catharine allowed the courtship to unfold. It was, after all, a brilliant idea. But how had Amy come to it? How did she know the personal details Elizabeth shared visit after visit? And did she even realize how neat a package she was wrapping? But her questions yielded no answers. Either Amy kept her secrets well, or she honestly didn't know why the thoughts—why Elizabeth Chapman—had suddenly arrived in her head.

CATHARINE PULLED HER attention back to the dining room and stared at the young woman before her. "Amy. Notwithstanding Mrs. Chapman, the marriage idea is still incredibly good. But the door is rapidly closing here, and I don't wish to get caught in its slam."

Amy stood, her smile serene. "I understand," she said. "I'll meet you in the parlor shortly before nine."

Catharine watched her go, thoughts buzzing through her head like bees set free from a hive.

CHAPTER
12

Adrian glanced at the library clock as he waited for the telephone operator to connect his call. 8:20. Jim would join him in ten minutes, and together they'd make their way to the parlor for the evening's séance. His fingers drummed against Bennett Chapman's desk blotter: ten minutes left to steel himself for yet another potential disaster.

"Adrian!" Constance's voice through the telephone wire was like velvet wrapped around his heart. "I've been looking forward to your call all day."

He sank into the leather chair behind Bennett's desk. "And you, Constance, are my lifeline. Sometimes it feels as though I'll never be allowed to leave Newport and come home to you."

"Oh, but you must." He caught the teasing note in her voice. "The egg man happened to bring me the most wonderful gift today."

Adrian raised an eyebrow. "Gift?"

"A thank-you for the almond croissants I gave him last week. I'm afraid he's quite addicted to them, and between you and me, they do nothing for his figure. Anyway, he's brought me a bottle of wine—purely for medicinal purposes, of course; I wouldn't dream of breaking the law—and I won't open it without you. Work hard and come home, my darling, so that we can enjoy the pink of health together."

He couldn't help but smile. "Believe me, there's nothing I want more. I have so much to tell you when I get home."

"More than I've heard so far?"

"Much more. If I believed in such things, I'd say this whole house is bewitched. And Mr. Reid! Even our sensible Mr. Reid has fallen under the spell. Traipsing through the evening with a young woman who could prove our client's undoing . . . he has lost his head entirely."

He pictured her reaching for her teacup, tucking her feet up beneath her as she settled more comfortably against the plush chair pillows. "Would this young lady be Miss Amy Walsh?"

"The same. I can't imagine what he's thinking."

Her low laugh made his blood run warm. "Oh, yes, you can, Adrian. I've spent enough time alone with you to know you can. But let's politely assume that he's thinking he's finally met a pretty woman who sees his worth. Have they kissed?"

"Now, how would I know that?" he asked lightly.

"You'd know," Constance said, and it occurred to him that she was right. For better or worse, a change came over a man once he fancied himself desired by a pretty woman. He walked with squarer shoulders, his head held higher than before. Although Jim and Amy had returned to Liriodendron quite late last night, Jim's general demeanor remained more cub than lion.

"No," he said, "I don't believe they have. There's still hope. If we can finish our business here quickly enough, perhaps they'll never get the chance."

"Oh, but perhaps they should. He's a good man, our Jim. It may take a little romance to help him realize that."

"My sweet Constance. You are ever the romantic."

"As are you, my darling. Heaven only knows why you try so hard to hide it."

"Perhaps. How are the children?"

She sighed. "They miss you, Adrian. And so do I. Hurry up and come home."

It was time to finish the call, but he picked up the hesitation on the other end of the line. Constance seemed to expect something more. He waited, knowing that she would ask her question soon enough. There had never been anything reticent about Constance de la Noye.

"Adrian—tell me about Mr. Chapman's fiancée. Will Catharine Walsh be good to him, do you think, or is she nothing more than a callous gold digger?"

There was no logical reason for his jaw to tense the way it did. "Why do you ask, my dear? Is your finger itching?" His wife swore by her pinkie, which she claimed itched whenever her intuition sensed something amiss.

"Yes," she said. "It itches like mad, although I don't think that has anything to do with Mr. Chapman. It's just that he's an old man. Rapscallion or not, he deserves to live his last years in peace. I hope you'll see to it that nobody takes advantage of him."

Anyone who tried to take advantage of disagreeable Bennett Chapman would return carrying his own head. "Of course, Constance. He's my client."

"Do it because he's your fellow man. Look after him, Adrian."

It was not a reminder he cared to hear. He could brush away his own doubts about Catharine Walsh, chalk them up to suspicions born of a mistake long past. But Constance's concerns were not so easily dismissed. She had a way of making him feel accountable for his actions. He had no desire to tarnish the shining vision of him she held so close to her heart.

"Yes, sweetheart," he said quietly. "I will look after Mr. Chapman as if he were my own father."

"Better than that," she said, and he was pleased to hear some tartness return to her voice. "You and your father are barely civil to each other. Well. As it appears you'll be delayed another few days, I'll have fresh clothing for you and Jim sent first thing in the morning."

"You are an angel."

"More like a goddess. Good night, my love. Sweet dreams."

He cradled the telephone receiver in his hand for several minutes after the line went dead. Constance knew him so well, often understood his thoughts before he could even articulate them. Did she sense that there were still parts of his life he'd never shared?

A sudden breeze fluttered the library curtains. Outside, a branch snapped. The telephone receiver clattered atop the desk as Adrian realized he was not alone.

He was on his feet in a flash, leaning out the window in a matter of seconds.

But all he could see was the small figure of a boy, sprinting across Liriodendron's manicured lawn as if there were a race to be won.

CHAPTER
13

February 1898

Adrian Delano," Cassie purred, gliding into the train compartment as if she belonged there. She tossed two new carpetbags onto the seat across from his, eyes glittering. "I thought I'd surprise you, dear, keep you company on this inconvenient trip. Surely you didn't expect me to stay away!"

Adrian looked up from his prone position across the plush seat, arm draped against his still-pounding head. He'd stayed in Poughkeepsie just long enough to bathe and make arrangements to have his baggage sent to Newport. He had, in fact, escaped the house only minutes before the time his parents usually awoke. Since avoiding confrontation had been of paramount importance, there'd been no time for what he needed most: sleep.

But here was Cassie Walsh, bathing him in a gaze so adoring

it seemed as if he must have dozed off and entered dreamland after all.

The conductor followed her into the compartment. "Your wife is most persuasive, sir," he said, chuckling.

"Wife?" Adrian struggled to sit upright.

"I've told him everything, Adrian." Cassie cast a demure glance toward the floor. Her cheeks, rosy from the cold, gave the perfect imitation of a blush. "I simply couldn't help it. I told him all about our secret wedding, how we mean to announce it properly once you return from this trip, how you'd let only a journey of the utmost importance separate us . . ."

"Wife?" The word trailed into the air.

"You're a fortunate man, sir." The conductor smiled. "She adores you. You can take it from an old veteran of marriage: such devotion is hard to find. Congratulations on your wedding."

Cassie reached for Adrian's hand as she slid into the seat beside him. "Please don't be angry with me, darling. I know we didn't plan it this way, but I just couldn't bear to be away from you."

"But . . ."

She squeezed his hand, hard. Surprised, he stared her full in the face. Her pink lips parted slightly; her eyes widened. Beneath the veil of bravado, he recognized the same pleading expression that had led him to rescue her from jams so many years ago. He drew back, startled.

"A fortunate man," the conductor repeated. "Now, if you'll just pay her fare, sir, I'll leave you to each other's company."

Unable to extricate his gaze from Cassie's, Adrian slowly reached for his billfold.

Cassie's hand slipped from his arm as the train conductor closed the compartment door and left them alone. She moved to the opposite end of the seat, the lingering warmth of her body the only evidence that she'd ever sat beside him at all.

Adrian cleared his throat. "I believe you owe me an explanation."

She closed her eyes and leaned her head back against the seat cushion. "My family has served yours for decades. This is simply a small favor in return."

It was baffling. Had he not felt so incapacitated from his revels the night before, he'd have gotten to the root of this situation before it could spiral so out of hand. "Your mother—like her father before her—is not an indentured servant. She's paid fair wages for her services, as you will be should you choose to remain a part of our household staff."

"Choose?" She grimaced but did not open her eyes. "A fine lot you know about my choices. Go to sleep. You're in no condition to speak of this now."

He'd been dismissed, and on his own nickel. There was little he could do about it now. All the privilege he'd been born into, all the Harvard law degrees in the world couldn't help him until the alcohol-induced fog cleared from his brain.

Cassie's eyes remained closed. A small furrow creased her brow, and pale lilac crescents shadowed the delicate skin beneath her lowered lashes.

She was obviously running away. Did he really need to know the reason why? She was old enough, after all, and despite earlier years of escapades and games, she was none of his concern. It was a compliment that she trusted him enough to include him in what was surely the biggest adventure of her life.

He glanced at her again, this time catching the vulnerable curve of her cheek as it rested against the fur collar of her too-big winter coat. The image of the spirited girl he'd known merged with the wilted waif before him until he could not quite tell where one left off and the other began.

He cleared his throat. The world was a far more ruthless place than Cassie Walsh could possibly imagine. At the very least, he had a moral obligation to see her safely onto the next train.

"We'll continue this conversation later," he said firmly, if only to be the one to officially end the exchange.

But the only response was the deep, even breathing of sleep.

CHAPTER
14

W̲e're here as before, Mrs. Chapman." Amy's clear voice broke through the stagnant parlor air. "We do hope you'll join us."

"Yes, please do, Elizabeth."

Jim opened his eyes at the desperate tinge in Bennett Chapman's voice. From across the table, Adrian met his inquiring stare with a small nod. They were in agreement: even if Bennett was sane, his nearly tangible yearning for his late wife's presence made him appear more foolish than was wise in this situation.

Adrian's eyes closed again. Jim suspected that he should follow suit, but the parlor felt claustrophobic tonight, and he was loath to return to the cloying darkness that waited behind closed lids. Instead, he allowed his gaze to travel around the table, studying each séance participant in turn.

Nicholas Chapman shifted in his chair. Jim narrowed his eyes, wondering how anyone could direct such ill will toward his own kin. Nicholas, who'd been given every advantage, had a chip on his shoulder so big he should have been walking with one set of knuckles grazing the ground.

"Is Mother coming?" Chloe's hopeful voice drew Jim's attention her way. For the second evening in a row, she had refused all alcohol at dinner. She reminded him of a cave animal emerging into sunlight after a long period of hibernation.

"She's probably powdering her nose in anticipation of her grand entrance," Nicholas said.

"Stop it, Nicky. She won't come if we're disrespectful."

"Oh, she'll come. The Misses Walsh wouldn't have it any other way."

"Please." Amy frowned. "I can't concentrate."

Adrian and Catharine Walsh sat beside each other, as cool as two strangers on a streetcar. Jim glanced at their loosely held hands. Amy's echo of his own hunch had been a relief, proof that his intuition wasn't off after all. Somewhere, somehow, those two had met before. He'd need to stay sharp if he wanted to catch the details of their story, though: Adrian sure wasn't talking.

He didn't need to look at Amy. Where she was concerned, it was better to finally close his eyes and let images from last night flood his mind. She'd been beautiful with the moonlight dancing through her hair, and she'd fit perfectly in the crook of his arm. They'd stood at the base of the Forty Steps for quite some time, gazing out at the sea, exchanging the occasional word but mostly just savoring the sensation of having each other so near. For the first time since he could remember, Jim had felt practically debonair. Amy had laughed at his jokes. She'd listened intently when he spoke, sharing her own thoughts with an endearing confidence that no other woman had ever entrusted to him before. It had been she who'd initiated their first embrace, tucking herself against him as if she'd belonged there all along.

He'd resisted the urge to kiss her at least three or four times, leaning toward her only to draw back before she could catch the drift of his intentions. What if she pulled away, utterly appalled by his misinterpretation of sisterly affection? His minutes with her were too wonderful to muck up with eager stupidity; it was better to wait until he had a clear read on the situation. Besides, there was something delicious about the anticipation.

"Elizabeth!" A smile wreathed Bennett Chapman's tired face. "You've come!"

"Has she, Amy?" Chloe asked eagerly.

"She has indeed." Amy remained serene, although Jim felt her hand tense in his. "Do you see her, Bennett?"

Jim winced at the question. He'd have to find a tactful way to advise Amy that the fewer details she coaxed from Bennett Chapman, the stronger their case would be.

But Mr. Chapman's answer surprised him. "No," he said. He sounded like a child whose long-awaited Christmas gift had failed to appear beneath the tree. "I don't. I just feel her presence, that's all."

"Sometimes," Catharine suggested, "that can be enough."

"Has she something to tell us?" Chloe's pitch edged up half an octave. "Did she bring Margaret with her tonight?"

Amy paused, a stenographer taking dictation. "She greets you on Margaret's behalf, Lady Dinwoodie, but no, your daughter is not with her. Mrs. Chapman says that this was her decision, not Margaret's. There is much of importance to say tonight, and she fears for my stamina."

The hair at the back of Jim's neck prickled. Someone's stare had raked past him, and he was willing to bet a week's pay that the scrutiny wasn't ethereal. He opened his eyes a slit. Sure enough, Nicholas Chapman's eyes were wide open. Although he still held hands with Chloe to his right and Adrian to his left, he leaned forward in his chair, his glare now boring a hole through Amy's forehead.

"I have a question," Nicholas said. "Surely my mother will deign to answer it."

Amy hesitated. "You must understand that Mrs. Chapman no longer focuses her attention on the physical plane. She has moved on. While certain earthly recollections remain strong in her consciousness, others have been pushed aside for thoughts of more cosmic consequence."

Nicholas snorted. "Oh, of course. Nevertheless, I will ask my question. When I was a small boy, I had a favorite toy. What was it?"

"Oh, for heaven's sake, Nicky." Chloe rolled her eyes. "You're enough to make me need a drink. It's hardly important."

Nicholas continued as if his sister hadn't spoken at all. "It's important to me. Our mother would know this."

Amy chewed her bottom lip for a moment, listening. Catharine's mouth twitched. Bennett Chapman relaxed in his chair, a look of such dreamy contentment upon his face that it appeared he'd happened upon a glorious symphony nobody else could hear.

The silence stretched for what seemed an excruciating length of time, although no more than a minute or two passed. Finally Amy shrugged. "Your mother doesn't say."

Nicholas wrenched his hands away from both Chloe and Adrian. "I have proved my point. This young lady delivers only information she's been fed by her aunt. If Catharine Walsh has not supplied a particular fact, then 'Mrs. Chapman' is incapable of responding."

Catharine's eyes flew open. "That's a lie!"

Nicholas raised his voice. "Mr. de la Noye, only the most gullible fool would allow these women to manipulate him like this. Admit that my father is incapable of managing his affairs, and we can bring this unpleasant matter to a close."

Amy wandered into the fray, undaunted. "Mrs. Chapman has a message."

"Of course," Catharine said quickly. "Amy, Mrs. Chapman's message must surely be for Bennett. Right?" She squeezed Bennett's hand, but the old man remained in a state of blissful reverie, eyes closed, small smile hovering about his mouth. He seemed not to have heard her at all.

If Catharine's words were meant as a hint, Amy chose to ignore them. "No," she said. "Mrs. Chapman sends her deepest regards to her husband, but these words don't concern him."

"Then whom do they concern?" Adrian's words were calm, but his knuckles were white.

"I'm not sure. Mrs. Chapman says that the recipient of the message will know. I can only hope she's right, because I don't understand it at all."

"Then why say it?" Catharine yanked her hand from Bennett's tepid hold, knocking her forearm against the table. "Really, Amy, what purpose could this possibly serve?"

Amy's eyes remained closed. "Mrs. Chapman says that there was more to Cassie's story than met the eye, and that honor must be restored. Does that make sense to anybody here?"

Nicholas swiveled in his chair, steely gaze resting on Adrian's face. "Does it, Mr. de la Noye? I have little doubt that the so-called message is for you."

"So you remarked last night, sir," Adrian said, face immobile as he met the stare.

"Everyone else here has received a little drop of otherworldly wisdom. It's your turn."

"Mrs. Chapman has more to say." Amy continued like a small steamroller, oblivious to anything that might stand in her way.

"Go on," Nicholas ordered.

"Something happened here, in Newport," Amy said slowly. "But it wasn't recent, and I don't understand what Mrs. Chapman is trying to tell me. I see the image of a train . . . an alliance, perhaps . . . 'reputations are nothing more than masks we're forced to wear,' Mrs. Chapman says."

Across from Jim, Catharine's palm slapped against the top of the table. "Amy, this doesn't seem to concern anybody here. Perhaps you aren't hearing correctly."

But Amy's eyes remained closed, her low voice merciless in its recitation. "This Cassie Mrs. Chapman mentioned before was . . . expecting a child when she left Newport."

Catharine's hand flew to her mouth, but not in time to prevent her gasp.

"Oh, dear God," Nicholas groaned. "Is that the only thing 'Mrs. Chapman' can think of to say to people? That they've somehow involved themselves in procreation?"

Jim squinted in the dim light of the room; every ounce of color had drained from Adrian's face.

"Mr. de la Noye," Nicholas continued, "do you have the slightest idea what she's rambling about? Because if nobody here understands these words, then you must admit that your client is a raving loon."

Adrian sat so still that he might have been carved from ice. Jim leaned forward, anticipating a logical explanation, but his mentor was clearly incapable of finding words, much less saying them.

"Well?" Nicholas prodded, a grim smile of satisfaction shadowing his face.

Jim stumbled to his feet. "I understand Miss Walsh's words," he said, clearing his throat. "The message is for me."

Adrian's head snapped toward him. "Jim . . ."

Jim stared him down. "The words make perfect sense," he said.

"They do?" Nicholas sounded genuinely surprised.

"Absolutely."

"Mr. Reid," Nicholas continued, "would you care to explain?"

Jim glanced from Nicholas to the rest of the table. Even Amy gaped at him, her mouth wide open. "Um . . . no," he said. "It's . . . a personal matter." He sank back into his chair.

"Mr. de la Noye." Amy's eyes didn't leave Jim's face. "Mrs. Chapman says that you should draft the new will as quickly as possible."

"There's still no proof!" Nicholas shouted. "None!"

"And Mr. Chapman . . ." Amy dragged her gaze from Jim to Nicholas. "Your mother says that your favorite toy was a dapple gray rocking horse that once belonged to your father. You called it Clover and rode it until the bow rocker cracked."

Chloe sprang like a coil from her chair. "She's gotten it, Nicky."

"Clever deceit, that's all it is!" Nicholas too shot to his feet, rigid finger pointed at his sister. "You will lose a fortune if you believe her, Chloe! How can you let that happen?"

"Because the words are true. You know they are!" She pushed his hand away, breathing as hard as if she'd just run a race.

Catharine tugged at Bennett Chapman's sleeve, guiding him back into the present. "Bennett, is it still your intention to change your will?" she asked.

Her fiancé roused himself from his dream, caught in a cloud of irritation as he rejoined his guests in the parlor. "Of course, Catharine. Whatever Elizabeth wishes is my wish as well."

"Not yet," Adrian said.

"Mr. de la Noye, I'm not quite sure I follow." Catharine drew each word from the icebox. "Bennett Chapman is your client. You have a responsibility where he is concerned."

"Precisely." Their gazes locked. Jim averted his eyes, suddenly embarrassed to observe so closely.

"Tell me of your hesitation, Mr. de la Noye," Bennett Chapman said, and his lucid tone brought a welcome touch of reason to the proceedings.

Adrian nodded. "Certainly. I assure you, Mr. Chapman, that there is nothing I would rather do than follow your directive and draft your will to your satisfaction. I still have every intention of doing so. But I would like to attend just one more séance first."

Bennett smiled. "I can't blame you for that, Adrian. They're rather addictive, aren't they?"

"And, with your kind permission, sir, I would like to speak privately with your fiancée. Since I assume my firm will handle her legal affairs as well as yours once you're married, I would appreciate the opportunity to become properly acquainted."

"That won't be necessary," Catharine snapped.

"Catharine!" Bennett looked puzzled.

Catharine burned red. "I'm sorry, Bennett. It's just that I already have an attorney back in Sacramento."

Bennett placed a solid hand on her shoulder. "Mr. de la Noye has taken care of my legal concerns for a very long time now. I consider him more than simply my attorney. He is a friend; I trust him implicitly."

Nicholas cut through their exchange like a runner suddenly back in the race. "May I ask why you've suddenly changed your tune, Mr. de la Noye?"

"No." Adrian rose from his chair. "You may not. Miss Walsh, shall we walk?"

Catharine stared from his drawn face to the rigid arm he offered her. Then she lifted her chin and sailed past him from the room.

CHAPTER
15

Catharine's pace remained smooth and dignified until she reached the top of the stairs. There she took a sharp right and raced down the hallway, her breath coming so hard that she had to lean against the doorjamb outside her bedroom for a moment to keep from fainting.

She gave the doorknob a firm twist and slipped into her room, locking the door behind her. Hardly thinking, she dragged a suitcase from beneath the bed, tossed it atop the mattress, and began to sweep the contents of her bureau drawers into it.

How on earth had Adrian found her here? No, that was stupid. He couldn't have been searching for her. Adrian was sharp, had always been sharp. If he'd really wanted to locate her, he'd have done so years ago. As for her own inability to uncover any information about him these past twenty-some years . . . well, now she understood why. Adrian Delano had become Adrian de la Noye.

Only four drawers emptied and the suitcase wouldn't close. There were still dresses in the closet to pack, as well as shoes and toiletries.

She threw herself back against the soft pillows of the bed, flinging an arm across her face to stop angry tears from falling. She was usually so good at keeping images from the past locked firmly away, separated from day-to-day consciousness like snakes trapped in a wooden crate. Now she was so rattled that she couldn't even pack properly.

Of course, she hadn't run away from anything in a very long time.

Even steps sounded in the hallway, coming to a stop outside the guest-room door.

"Miss Walsh."

Catharine hoisted herself upright on the bed at the sound of Adrian's voice. She heard the click of his cigarette case, followed by the scrape of match head against striking surface.

"I will wait here all night if need be," he said.

She knew that he would. For all his flaws, Adrian had always kept his word. She'd recognized a man of honor lurking beneath his disreputable façade twenty-three years ago when he hadn't immediately tossed her from his train compartment in a fit of righteous rage. There was no need to doubt that the Adrian here at Liriodendron, fully grown and respectable, was any less reliable.

She rose wearily from the bed, scooping up the ashtray from her nightstand on her way to open the door.

He stood just across the threshold. The tip of his cigarette burned bright above one cupped hand. Wordlessly, Catharine extended the ashtray. Adrian took one last drag of his cigarette before stubbing it out. Years fell away as she stared into his dark eyes. As if of their own accord, her fingers reached out to stroke his cheek. He flinched at her touch.

"Oh, Adrian," she murmured, pulling her hand away. "Do you really hate me so much?"

"No," he said, and his pain caught her off guard. "Not anymore."

She swung the door open all the way and motioned him into the room. His gaze fell on the bed, and she knew that he hardly noticed the suitcase atop it. He shook his head and offered his arm instead.

Catharine hesitated for a moment. Then she set the ashtray down on the bureau and slipped her hand through the crook of his elbow. Closing the bedroom door behind her, she allowed him to lead her toward the stairs.

CHAPTER
16

February 1898

Cassie shivered as she followed Adrian Delano from Newport's train depot out to Marlborough Street. The air was cold, damp with moisture from the nearby harbor. The chill cut straight through her wool coat, raising prickles on her skin. Worse, Adrian's stiff posture pointed more toward irritation than she'd anticipated. He hadn't made a move to carry even one of her carpetbags when they'd changed trains earlier, and he did not offer to carry them now. This was not a good sign. Adrian may have slipped into disgrace, but he was still a gentleman at heart.

She measured her steps to his, following close enough behind him to be his shadow. Sooner or later he'd have to acknowledge her presence.

A minute or two passed before he stopped at Thames Street. "I can pretend I never saw you, if you'd like," he said, not bothering to turn around. "I'll even give you train fare home if you need it."

"Home?"

"You're running away, aren't you? I assume nobody knows about this little trip."

"Of course not."

"I won't tell anyone, either. You can give your family whatever excuse you choose to explain your absence. Hopefully they'll be kind."

Apparently she'd been deluded by the quick wit she remembered from her childhood, by his willingness to listen and help her through precarious situations as she grew up. This version of Adrian was dimmer than she'd expected.

"Don't be silly," she said. "Why would I go home?"

He turned to face her, confused. "Do you have friends here then?" he asked.

"Who would I know in Newport, Adrian Delano?"

A combination of comprehension and disbelief splashed across his face. "Oh, no, Cassie, I can't help you. My family summers on the Cape, remember? I've only visited Newport on occasion. I don't know anybody here well enough to recommend your services."

She could not prevent the harsh tone that crept into her voice. "Of course you'd assume I want to tie myself down to a lifetime of menial labor."

His brow creased. He'd slept off his drunkenness only to awaken to an entirely different problem, and she almost felt sorry for him. Almost—but not quite.

"How long will you stay in Newport?" she asked.

"I don't know yet." He lifted a tired hand to massage the back of his neck. "Cassie. What do you want from me?"

"I want to stay here with you. I want you to introduce me to your friends."

He stared as if a cat had spoken.

She let both carpetbags drop with a thud to the hard ground. "Don't you understand? I'm leaving Poughkeepsie."

"Why would you want to do that? You've got a home in Pough-keepsie, a position . . ."

"I'm trapped in Poughkeepsie. I'll work myself into the ground for other people there, and my mother will make me marry the housekeeper's horrid son. If I'm to be scuttled about like chattel, I may as well tie myself to a wealthy man. Introduce me. I'll do the rest."

It took a moment for her words to sink in. Then Adrian turned and started up Thames Street as if walking quickly enough could expunge the thought from the air. "As I said, Cassie, if you need train fare home, I'll give it to you. But I want no part of this lunacy."

She grabbed both carpetbags and hurried to catch up with him. "You needn't act shocked. It's not like you're untarnished, you know. Your reputation is in shreds after all your tomfoolery in Europe. Who knows? I might even be able to help restore your honor. I can be very charming."

"You can't seriously believe that introducing our cook's daughter as a marriage prospect will enhance my status."

"No. But introducing your delightful cousin might."

He stopped. "You're in over your head. If there's one thing

this circle knows, it's pedigree. You wouldn't last a day with that ruse."

"Oh?" Her voice was acid. "I'm a better actress than you think. I've plenty of fodder. Observing the Delanos is the only way to break the monotony of tidying up after them. I'm your second cousin Kate. On your mother's side."

"I don't have a second cousin Kate."

"You do now, and I know enough family background to make it sound real."

"That's daft," Adrian said. "Even if your scheme actually worked, what would happen after the wedding when the truth came out?"

"It wouldn't matter then."

"Of course it would. There's my reputation to think about, your honor . . ."

To her own chagrin, she actually stamped her foot. "We've already discussed the state of your reputation, and my honor is my own concern. I'll handle it. I've already thought all that through."

His sigh contained more weariness than anger. She was startled by his sadness. The Adrian she remembered was lively and intelligent, so full of potential that an occasional fall from grace could be considered merely mischievous. The man before her was still handsome, but his dark good looks had taken on a sallow cast, and new lines had formed about his mouth.

"What's gotten into you, Adrian?" she whispered. "You used to have so much promise."

"And look where it's gotten me," he said beneath his breath. "Wedged securely under my parents' thumbs. They've got my life all planned, right down to the sort of woman I'll marry and the Supreme Court seat they're sure I can add to the family's list of achievements."

"Well then." She set down her carpetbags and laid a gentle hand on his coat sleeve. "Your situation is not so different from mine. Unlike you, however, I have no intention of escaping by drinking myself to death."

He stood still before her, his coat flapping in the wind as he studied her face. She stared back, raising her chin to meet his gaze.

"You may stay with me until tomorrow," he said quietly. "Then I'll give you train fare to any destination you choose. Do you understand?"

"Where are we staying?" she asked, careful to keep any touch of eagerness from her voice. "Which grand house has offered hospitality?"

"It's off-season. One of my friends has a small cottage on his family's summer property. The gardener usually lives there, but he's visiting his daughter for the duration of the winter. I've arranged to stay there."

"Small cottage?" Cassie's voice squeaked. That meant no constant whirl of society, no chance meetings in the hallway with wealthy gentlemen in celebratory moods.

"Rustic." Adrian's lips curled around the word with a little too much pleasure. "I've come here to think, Cassie. I need some peace."

She frowned. "Fine time for you to locate your conscience, Adrian Delano."

She thought she detected the start of a genuine smile on his face. "Why should it matter to you?" he asked, and there was a glimmer of the boy she remembered from long ago. "You won't be here beyond tomorrow morning."

Her hand brushed against his as she bent toward her carpetbags. "Of course," she said.

He plucked the heavy bags from her grip and continued up Thames. She pushed through the silence and fell into step beside him.

CHAPTER
17

Amy flounced from the parlor, leaving Jim to stagger after her like a kite tail caught in a wicked crosswind.

"Amy! Wait!" One didn't need prior experience with women to recognize that this one was steaming mad. Jim's long legs made short work of the space between them, but it was harder to penetrate the nonphysical distance. He'd never imagined that pink satin evening slippers could click so loudly against a marble floor.

"Amy." He spoke to her profile as she yanked open Liriodendron's front door and sailed down the porch steps. This time she didn't wait for him to maneuver the stairs. Instead she barely touched ground before turning right and heading toward the back of the house.

Jim picked up his pace, praying that his feet would instinctively make solid contact with each individual stair. Using Amy's pale curls as a guide, he quickly closed the gap between them.

"What's wrong?" he demanded, sliding his arm around her waist.

Amy jerked away. "You are," she said, not breaking stride. "I don't ever want to talk to you again, Jim Reid. You're a bounder, nothing but a cad."

He stopped short, wondering how someone who'd had so few chances at romance could possibly be in such hot water with a woman. Then the analytical portion of his brain took charge.

"Wait a minute. Amy! You've got it all wrong."

She headed toward the rocks of the coast, a part of Cliff Walk that came with no promise of safety. Jim raced across the grassy lawn, stopping when the soles of his Oxfords pounded stone.

"Okay." He raised his voice above the crash of the waves. "I'm relying on your decency here, Amy. I can't see."

She wasn't that far ahead of him. He watched as she stopped short, poised on the rocks like a bird about to take flight. Her dress rippled about her like gossamer, exposing her slender legs as it undulated in the chilly night air.

"Don't think I don't know that you did that on purpose," she said, but she turned toward him, skimming back across the rocks as if the craggy surface were the smoothest dance floor. "Why did you follow me out here, anyway?"

Jim waited until she'd alighted in front of him before reaching out to grasp her shoulders. "That message at the séance tonight . . ."

Her brows lowered, and he saw that he was on the right track. "Yes, that message was most illuminating," she said. "Who is Cassie, Mr. Reid? Mrs. Chapman was clearly most anxious that someone know of her delicate condition, and you're the only one to whom the message made sense."

If ever there was a time to lie, this was it. Telling the truth would be the ultimate act of disloyalty against Adrian. But as he looked at Amy's pouting mouth, at the hurt in her eyes, a stab of annoyance flashed through him. He'd signed on as Adrian's associate, not as his sacrificial lamb.

Always tell the truth, his Granny Cullen had said. But would she have said that even if telling the truth left his friend vulnerable?

He cleared his throat. "About that message, Amy."

She folded her arms across her chest. "Yes, Mr. Reid. About that message."

"I've never been to Newport before, kiddo, remember? I didn't understand that message any more than you did."

Amy blinked, eyes widening as she absorbed the meaning of his words. "Then why did you say that you did?"

"I don't know. It seemed the right thing to do at the time. Where'd that message come from in the first place? Where do you get this stuff? I thought you were supposed to be clairvoyant. Why couldn't you—or Mrs. Chapman—figure out that I was lying through my teeth?"

His hands slipped from her shoulders as she turned away. "I'm not in the business of detecting lies," she said. "And I don't understand Mrs. Chapman any more than you do. She comes when she pleases and says whatever she wants."

"You don't even choose the topic of conversation?"

"Of course not. What do I know about the workings of Elizabeth Chapman and her family?"

He stepped cautiously across the rock, coming to a stop by her side. "That's something I'd like to know myself," he said.

She swung toward him. "What are you implying?"

"What really brings you and your aunt to Liriodendron, Amy?"

"You already know that. Mr. Chapman invited us."

"After an acquaintance of only several weeks? That trek from Sacramento to the East Coast isn't exactly a Sunday jaunt to the park. Nobody travels that distance without some solid assurances. It sounds like you and your aunt have followed the Chapman family for quite some time now."

"Why on earth would we do that?"

"That's what I'm dying to know."

He had to admit that she looked stricken, her pretty mouth a shocked little O and the hint of tears shimmering in her blue eyes.

With a sigh, he reached out and tugged her toward him, stroking her silky hair as she sobbed against his chest. "Tell me, Amy," he said.

Her muffled voice floated up from the depths of his white shirt-front. "There's nothing much to tell. I owe everything to Aunt Catharine. She's taken care of both of us for such a long time, seen to it that I've had all I need even when times were tough. Yes, sometimes that's involved telling a fortune here and there, but what's the harm in that? It makes people happy."

"Did you conduct many séances back in Sacramento?"

She raised her eyes to his. He looked away, not ready to lose himself in the sweet abyss of her gaze. "Mrs. Chapman is the only . . . person . . . I've ever spoken for," she said. "And I don't like it very much, I can tell you that."

"You don't?"

"Of course not. There's something creepy about it, don't you think?"

She lowered her head back to his chest, leaving him to stare out at the sea as her words flowed through his mind. If Amy didn't like feigning Mrs. Chapman's words, then why did she do it?

The answer smacked his brain before he could even ask the question out loud.

"Amy," he said warily, "are you telling me that Mrs. Chapman is real?"

There was nothing sweet and needy in her gaze this time. She backed away from him, scowl replacing the quiver of her lip. "Of course. Did you think I'd made her up?"

Jim's arms dropped to his sides.

"I told you," Amy said. "I am not a fraud."

He swallowed hard. The thought of an ectoplasmic Elizabeth Chapman floating through the parlor seemed insane. But, then, Granny Cullen's pronouncements had always felt real enough, so much so that he'd always accepted them without question. After all he'd experienced growing up, he owed it to Amy to at least let her try to prove that she wasn't off her rocker.

"All right," he said, trying to organize his thoughts. "All right. So Bennett Chapman invited you and your aunt out here from Sacramento, and you came along with Mrs. Chapman in tow."

She shrugged. "If it makes you feel any better, Aunt Catharine and I are used to traveling. Aunt Catharine lived in New York City when I first came to stay with her, you know. We moved to Chicago when I was three, then on to Denver, and finally out to Sacramento just before I turned thirteen."

Jim stroked his chin, trying to arrange the random snippets of information into some recognizable pattern. Adrian had obviously understood Mrs. Chapman's message—nothing outside of extreme shock would have caused his mentor's uncharacteristic loss for words and subsequent need of rescue. Nor was it an absurd leap to presume that Catharine Walsh might have gone by the diminutive "Cassie" at one point in her life. But the rest of the story . . . how was he supposed to fill in the details when Adrian closed up as tight as a speakeasy every time the subject arose?

"Don't blame me," Amy said primly.

"Huh? For what?"

"For the fact that you never thought to ask Mr. de la Noye any questions."

She looked awfully smug. Jim made a face at her before turning his attention back to his thoughts.

Adrian had been a fixture at the Reid home for decades, included by Jim's father and later his mother in both family celebrations and heartaches, willing to lend a hand during dark days. Jim had never questioned why. Like everyone else in his family, he could recite by heart the story of how his father had risked his own life in Cuba during the Spanish-American War, dragging a wounded Adrian to safety under a barrage of enemy fire. He understood implicitly that repaying that debt was one of Adrian's greatest joys. Yet with all that, he had to admit that Amy was right: he knew very little about the life Adrian had led prior to his adoption by the Reid family. Why had he never considered that strange?

Of course, it was no odder than the idea that the late Elizabeth Chapman would interrupt her eternal rest to deliver messages about two people she'd never even met.

Amy's small palms rested against his chest. "Jim."

He glanced down to meet her gaze.

"Will it always be this way?" she asked. "Will we constantly waste beautiful moonlit evenings with dry interrogations?"

His stomach flip-flopped as she nestled closer. "Aren't you curious about Mrs. Chapman's message?" he asked, cradling her in a loose hug. "Don't you want to know what it means?"

"Yes." Her voice was velvet. "But not all the time."

Jim jumped as her soft fingers stroked his cheek. She felt small and delicate in his arms, a Dresden doll come to life. One inch closer and he'd vow to slay the Minotaur for her.

"Jim. You're still thinking, aren't you?"

The reproach stabbed his heart.

Amy sighed. "Silly," she murmured. "For a smart boy, you sure can be thickheaded."

She wrapped her fingers around his lapels and pulled him down toward her. He thought briefly that the whirling of the rocks might make him lose his balance and plunge them both into the sea. Then he realized that the rocks weren't moving at all.

Amy stood on tiptoe, so near that he could feel her soft breath against his cheek. He bent instinctively toward her, lips tingling as they drew closer to hers. "Amy," he whispered in her enticing little ear.

"Yes, Jim?"

"Do you think your aunt could be Cassie?"

Amy groaned. Then her mouth landed on his, and anything else he'd meant to say floated out to sea on the ocean breeze.

CHAPTER
18

You're looking well." Adrian opened Liriodendron's back French doors, ushering Catharine Walsh onto the terrace with the formality of a trained escort.

"Thank you." Her fingers slipped from the crook of his arm. "The years have been kind to you, too."

He appreciated the cool distance between them. With so much time gone by, they were little more than strangers now. There was no reason to resurrect anything as messy as emotion. On the other hand, this was still Cassie Walsh beneath the fine clothes and stylishly bobbed curls. He recognized her reserve for what it really was: a diversionary tactic.

He leaned back against the stone retaining wall. "Cassie, surely you realize that I have questions for you."

"Catharine." Her voice was sharp. "You may call me Catharine or Miss Walsh."

Her claws were still intact. "I understand," he said.

"I thought you might, Mr. de la Noye." The syllables of his last name tripped off her tongue.

He did not reply.

"Good." Catharine gave a curt nod. "I'm glad to see that we're in agreement."

He saw that she had already determined which information she would share, regardless of the questions asked. Still, her wide eyes and set jaw could not divert attention from the trembling of her left hand. Despite all efforts, she'd been unable to fully submerge her apprehension. She was vulnerable—perhaps every bit as vulnerable as he himself felt.

He chose his words carefully. "Miss Walsh, it's to your advantage that we find Mr. Chapman competent to amend his will."

"Of course he's competent."

"That's hard to defend when he says his marriage proposal to you is based on advice received from his deceased wife."

The gauzy sleeves of her dinner dress fluttered in the breeze as she clasped her hands before her. "I can't help that. It's not my fault Elizabeth Chapman decided to surface."

"Are you sure about that, Catharine?"

"Yes!"

"You're asking me to believe that Mrs. Chapman is not a product of your imagination, something you've created for your own benefit."

"She most certainly is not!"

Adrian paused, surprised by the flash of fear that crossed Catharine's face.

"All right," he finally said. "Suppose I take you at your word.

Surely you can see how convenient it seems that the ghost of this magnate's first wife should so enthusiastically choose you to be his second."

"Of course I see it." Her eyes rested on the inky horizon. "I'm not a fool."

"Yet you have no idea whatsoever why Elizabeth Chapman thinks Bennett should marry you."

She whipped around. "No, Adrian, I do not!"

He raised an eyebrow. He could understand her determination to see this marriage through. Bennett Chapman was worth more money than most people dreamed about. But even the smack of the waves against the rocks could not disguise that jagged catch in her breathing. Perhaps Catharine had nothing to do with Mrs. Chapman's arrival, but he'd wager that she knew a little more about the ghost's edict than she was willing to share.

Once upon a time, he'd been privy to this woman's hopes and dreams. He'd assumed then that he could interpret every turn of that pretty mouth, each veiled glance.

He'd been wrong.

He turned to scan Liriodendron's serene façade. It rose high above the terrace, pale and gracious, glowing like a pearl in the soft moonlight. There were no signs of hastily withdrawn figures, no swaying curtains. As far as he could tell, they were quite alone.

He stepped closer to the woman before him and lowered his voice. "Catharine, I must ask you . . . the message Amy delivered at the séance . . ."

She glanced up to meet his gaze, her expression blank. "Which message? Mrs. Chapman seems to have quite a bit to say."

"You know which one."

She turned away, fingers trailing through the air in a dismissive wave. "That question goes beyond your professional purview, Counselor," she said.

"Yet I have every right to ask it." Without thinking, he caught her hand in both of his. It fit as if he'd last cradled it only minutes ago. Years peeled away, whipping about them in a whirlwind of unbridled memory. Surprised, Catharine leaned toward him, lips parted.

He should never have come here.

Catharine yanked her hand from his as if burned. "Have you any further questions?" she asked, struggling to catch her breath.

"Yes," he said, voice hard. "So many. But I'd be much obliged if you'd just answer the one I'm asking. Was there a child?"

She raised her chin like a queen receiving subjects. "You needn't worry, Adrian Delano. There is no child. Good night."

He watched her leave the terrace on heels too low to cause the lack of balance in her walk. The response was classic Cassie. Of course there was no "child." Any child that might have been had grown up long ago. Not exactly a lie, but perhaps not exactly the truth either.

She was as beautiful as she'd remained in his memories. Worse, she still possessed the magnetism that had drawn him to her in the first place, that spark he'd never been able to rationalize away.

He gripped the edge of the retaining wall. One more séance. That was all it should take to find the answer Cassie herself would not provide. Then he and Jim would draft the will and leave Newport forever.

CHAPTER
19

February 1898

It was still afternoon when Adrian followed the housekeeper into the gardener's cottage off Ruggles Avenue, but it might as well have been two in the morning. His fatigue ran far deeper than body alone. He tried to concentrate on the woman's words, managing to catch the ones he thought might be most important: "I've had them place your trunks in your room . . . I'll be in with meals . . . you'll find me up at the house should you need anything else, Mr. Delano."

"Thank you so much for your kindness, Mrs. Vickery."

He jumped at the sound of Cassie's clear voice behind him. Despite their shared streetcar ride across Newport, he'd nearly forgotten that she was still with him. How had he managed to ignore the housekeeper's raised eyebrows when they'd first entered the cottage together?

"Oh, dear," Cassie sighed, mouth pursed in a fetching pout. "I'm afraid my little whim has proven inconvenient to everyone. Even Cousin Adrian had no idea I planned to travel with him today. It was a surprise, but perhaps an ill-conceived one. I apologize for my rashness."

Adrian straightened. "No, I'm the one who should apologize. I should have offered both proper introductions and an explanation when we first arrived. Forgive me, Mrs. Vickery. I returned from Europe just yesterday, and exhaustion has played havoc with my manners. This is my cousin . . . Miss Kate Weld."

His eyes met Cassie's. Her glittering smile could have saved Alfred Dreyfus from Devil's Island.

Oh, why the hell not. He'd told worse fibs in Europe. She'd be leaving in the morning, anyway.

He set Cassie's carpetbags onto the tiled floor. "My cousin will be staying here tonight, leaving for Boston tomorrow."

"I wish I'd known," Mrs. Vickery began. "I'd have made up the second bedroom. If you'll give me but a moment, I can—"

"Oh, no need to trouble yourself." Cassie's dimples flashed as she laid a confiding hand on the housekeeper's arm. "If you send over the linens, we can certainly manage. It strengthens the character to fend for one's self now and then. It will be fun, like family summers on the Cape. Isn't that right, Adrian?"

"Quite." He watched as she guided Mrs. Vickery to the door. He'd have to remind "Cousin Kate" that "summers on the Cape" included a small flotilla of household help.

Cassie waited until the garden gate clicked shut before turning back to face him. "There," she said with a shrug. "That wasn't so hard, was it?"

Adrian rested his aching forehead against the cool wall of the parlor. "I can't even say that you're ruining me, can I? I arrived in a compromised state."

He jumped at the touch of her soft hand in his hair. Her fingers slipped down the nape of his neck to gently knead his tight shoulders.

"Perhaps you should rest," she said. "I imagine we have plans tonight."

In for a penny, in for a pound. He was too tired to resist, even when she insisted on injecting that awkward "we" into the conversation. "I'm invited to a late dinner at the Phillips's home tonight. Peter Phillips is best man in the wedding, and his sister Marjorie will be hostess tonight."

"Hmm. Who else will be there?"

"I have no idea. I haven't been paying attention." He closed his eyes. The soothing rhythm of those fingers against his shoulders was pure magic.

"Surely there will be a bachelor or two on hand. You've been invited, after all."

"I suppose it's possible."

She stepped away, brow puckered in thought. "You must, of course, let our hostess know that I will be joining you tonight. It's maddening to have unexpected guests intrude. Can you think of an acceptable reason to bring me along? Oh, I know! My visit is a surprise, but I'm just out of mourning for my dear papa and . . ."

He remembered that her inventiveness had always made him smile. "I haven't invited you to join me."

"Oh, Adrian, you must. Please. It's my only hope. I won't embarrass you, I promise."

He turned toward her, surprised by the tinge of desperation in her voice. Her back remained as ramrod straight as ever, but he noted the slight slump of her shoulders, the faint circles shadowing her eyes. Her fragility took him by surprise. Somehow, he'd supposed her invincible, as utterly impenetrable as an ironclad warship.

"You're as tired as I am," he said.

The fact that she was too weary to argue spoke volumes.

He rested a hand on her shoulder. The bones beneath his palm were more delicate than he'd expected. "You can rest inside," he said. "I'll make the necessary arrangements for tonight's dinner, then nap out here on the sofa. We can make up the other room later."

"You'll take me with you tonight then?"

He hesitated briefly, considering. It was only one night. What difference would it really make? "Yes," he said.

"Thank you, Adrian," she said softly. "For everything. I'll never forget this kindness."

Something in her eyes threw him off balance, made him feel as if he had no control over either the situation or his actions within it. He lifted his hand from her shoulder. "You'd best make your mark tonight, Cousin Kate, because I'm packing you off tomorrow."

Undeterred, she stood on tiptoe to kiss his flaming cheek. "I understand," she said, then turned toward the bedroom, closing the door softly behind her.

CHAPTER
20

Sunlight streamed across Jim's bed, bathing him in brilliance impossible to ignore. He flung an arm across his eyes in a useless attempt to ward off the brightness. Only a sap would forget to pull down the shades before falling into bed the night before. With a groan, he rolled over and burrowed his face more deeply into the soft down of his pillow.

Intoxicating images flickered against his closed eyelids. Amy cuddled in his arms, her pliable curves tucked up against him as if there were no place she'd rather be. He could still feel her satin strands of hair brush his chin as the ocean breeze wrapped itself around the two of them standing on the rocks. Her smooth skin . . . those incredible lips . . . the inscrutable look in her blue eyes as he'd bent closer and closer . . . Most amazing of all, it hadn't been a dream.

He flopped onto his back, grin tugging at the corners of his mouth. Lord, he'd been such a jackass. His mind, always too active, had wasted so much time analyzing how to make that first kiss perfect. Yet even without a well-constructed plan in place, kissing Amy had been as easy as eating ice cream. That first kiss had melted into another, the next one into even more, until he and Amy had ended up breathless, her small hand stroking his chest as he drew her close.

And, incredibly enough, it would probably happen again.

A loud knock on the bedroom door pulled him back into the daylight. He squinted at the clock on his nightstand. Seven forty-five. Later than he usually slept, but certainly not beyond the bounds of decorum.

"Who is it?" he called, hoping that Amy stood beyond the door.

"Adrian."

"Um . . . just a minute." He fumbled for his spectacles, not even bothering to hide his disappointment. Had he promised to meet Adrian this morning? His mentor rarely initiated meetings prior to breakfast.

He hopped from the bed, snatching his robe from a corner chair on his way to the door. The trousers he'd worn yesterday tangled in his feet and nearly sent him sprawling headfirst across the floor. He shoved them away with his foot, yanking his bathrobe over his union suit as he reached for the doorknob.

"Come in," he said, cracking the door just enough to peer through.

Adrian tapped the door open and entered the room. His gaze flickered across the mound of clothing on the floor, traveling upward to rest on Jim's face. Jim unconsciously raised a hand to smooth his ruffled hair.

"Late night, Mr. Reid?"

"Somewhat. You know how it is."

Adrian closed the door behind him. "Possibly," he said. "But perhaps you'd best tell me all the same."

Jim shifted his weight from one foot to the other.

"Well?" Adrian waited.

"Sorry. There are some things a gentleman just doesn't divulge."

Adrian winced. "Oh, Jim."

"What?" It was hard to appear cool while clad in an old blue bathrobe, but Jim did the best he could. "There's nothing to worry about. We're still welcome here. It was only a walk."

"With Amy Walsh, I presume?"

No matter how casual his nod, Jim couldn't prevent the hot flush that burned his fair Irish skin. He squared his shoulders. "Yes."

Adrian left a long pause. Jim kept his mouth shut.

Adrian finally turned toward the window. "Would you be so kind as to draft Mr. Chapman's will this morning? I want to leave for Boston immediately following tonight's séance."

"No matter what its outcome?"

"No matter what."

"What of Nicholas Chapman?"

"Damn Nicholas Chapman."

The tightness in Adrian's voice was new. Jim unconsciously stroked his chin, considering. "He could ruin you."

"I'll take my chances." Adrian's gaze remained fixed on the distant horizon. "It's time we left this place."

Jim studied the other man for a moment. Adrian looked as well turned out as usual, dressed casually in cuffed white flannel trousers and a pale-green argyle sweater. But the lines bracketing his mouth were more pronounced this morning, and a slight puffiness around his eyes made it clear that he'd gotten even less sleep than Jim had himself.

Unbidden, one of Granny Cullen's favorite sayings sprang to his mind: *Even a small thorn causes festering.*

With a sigh, Jim knotted the bathrobe cord more firmly about his middle. "Adrian. Do you remember that infamous night just before my first-year law school exams?"

A dry smile flickered across Adrian's mouth. "The night I opened my front door to find you in a drunken heap on the doorstep?"

"That's the one."

"That would be a hard night to forget."

They hadn't talked about that incident in years, but it still had the power to make Jim cringe at his own stupidity. He'd studied until he was cross-eyed, yet emerged from the library with a sickening premonition of failure. Drinking the night away had seemed a perfectly logical solution at the time. He'd then compounded the error in judgment by giving the cabbie Adrian's address instead of his own.

"I was mortified," he said, shaking his head. "I still can't believe I showed up in that state after you'd done so much for me. You probably wondered why you'd even bothered."

"Nonsense. You were overwhelmed, that's all. You needed no more than several cups of strong coffee and a soft bed."

Jim crossed the room to stand by Adrian's side. "The sympathetic ear and dose of reassurance you provided didn't hurt, either. The point is, you listened without judging. Your faith in my character got me through a rocky time. I've never forgotten your kindness in the face of my idiocy."

"It wasn't idiocy, Jim." Adrian buried his hands in his trouser pockets and turned to face him. "It was a youthful mistake, that's all."

"Which we all make on occasion." Jim rested a tentative hand on his mentor's shoulder. "Adrian, please. I can never repay the kindness and trust you've invested in me all these years, but let me try. I could never judge you harshly."

Adrian held his gaze. "I'm not sure I know what you mean," he said evenly.

"Oh, I think you do." Jim plucked his spectacles from his nose, suddenly absorbed in cleaning them with the cord of his terry cloth robe. "You're not in fighting form, and that's unusual. I'm guessing the K.O. has something to do with Catharine Walsh."

"Are you now?" Adrian's face remained an immobile mask.

"Perhaps I can help. You should at least let me try."

Adrian returned his attention to the window, staring so hard that it took everything Jim had not to peer outside as well. Instead, he lifted his spectacles up to the light for inspection, aiming for nonchalance.

"And what if the situation requires information from Miss Amy Walsh?" Adrian asked quietly. "You're a good man, Jim. I'd hate to compromise your loyalties."

Jim returned the spectacles to their proper perch on his nose, blinking until Adrian's profile wavered into focus. "It's a little late to think about that, isn't it? I already compromised my virtue on your behalf at last night's séance."

For the first time since they'd arrived at Liriodendron, Adrian's smile was warm and genuine. "So you did. Very well, then. I'll have the auto brought around after breakfast. Some conversations are best had off premises. Which reminds me: our little eavesdropper from the ferry is here."

"The kid?"

"The same. I've made a few discreet inquiries but have no information."

A clatter of footsteps in the hallway made them both jump. Chloe Chapman Dinwoodie flung open the bedroom door, not even bothering to knock. "Come!" she cried.

"What's wrong?" Adrian hurried to her side.

"It's Miss Amy. We were chatting in the dining room—she, Father, and I—and all of a sudden, Mother broke through."

"I don't understand," Jim said. "Do you mean that . . . out of the blue . . . the late Mrs. Chapman has arrived? Without the trappings of a séance?"

Chloe's nod was almost lost in a flurry of hair and fabric as she turned on her heel and raced back down the hallway. "Mother sent me to fetch you both, along with Catharine. But I can't stay—I don't want to miss a thing!"

The frenzied pounding of her feet faded as she ran toward Catharine's room.

"Well," Adrian said in a low voice. "Either Elizabeth Chapman is a very real entity with a mind of her own, or the Walsh ladies are every bit as calculating as Nicholas claims they are. What's your opinion?"

Amy? Calculating? Someone so soft and sweet—someone who kissed the way Amy did—could never be calculating . . . could she? Arguments jumped and reeled through Jim's mind, twisting themselves until he could not determine where one ended and another began.

"I thought we believed in the Walshes' veracity," he said. "That Bennett Chapman isn't nuts . . ."

"Oh, I believe our client is perfectly sane. But greater men than he have been taken in by well-woven schemes. Bennett has been given every reason to believe that the spirit of his wife is real. That doesn't make him incompetent; it merely proves he's a human being with an Achilles' heel. It's time we got to the bottom of this, don't you think? Dress quickly; I'll meet you in the dining room."

Another of Granny Cullen's sayings cut through the din in Jim's mind as he turned from the door: *Put silk on a goat, and it's still a goat.*

Deep in thought, he shut the door with a solid thump.

CHAPTER
21

Catharine burst through the dining room door, hoping to stem the chaos before it could careen into disaster. "What is the meaning of this?"

Her words faded as she absorbed the scene before her. Seated at the foot of the table, Nicholas wore his customary sneer, but a curious twitch plagued his mouth. Chloe sat to his left, the rapturous expression on her face a throwback to the Romantic portraiture of saints. Beside her, Adrian managed neutrality worthy of Switzerland.

But it was Bennett who caught her attention, causing her to stop halfway to the dining room table.

"Catharine!" Bennett's voice, strong and hearty, belonged to a man at least thirty years younger. His cheeks glowed with more than good health. He seemed lit from within by an inexplicable glow, infused with vim that hadn't before been there. He stood, walking stick clattering to the ground as he left his place at the head of the table to stride to Catharine's side. "Take your place. Elizabeth has come to call."

Puzzled, Catharine allowed him to hook a firm hand beneath her elbow and guide her toward her usual seat at his right. She hazarded a brief glance at Adrian as she settled into her chair. He gave a nearly imperceptible nod across the table toward Amy.

Catharine's gasp echoed in the quiet room. Amy's skin, usually so creamy and smooth, had the sallow, dry look of paper. Dark circles rimmed her blue eyes, and she slumped in her chair as if the weight of the world had become too great to carry. "Amy, what's happened?"

"I don't know," Amy said in a monotone.

"Mother has come." Chloe's words tumbled over themselves. "She has much to say, but doesn't want to begin until we've all gathered. Where is Mr. Reid?"

"He's on his way." Adrian's gaze traveled from Catharine to Amy, then back to Catharine again.

"Congratulations," Nicholas drawled. "An impromptu conversation with Mother—it's a clever move, however unbelievable. You ladies are more ingenious than I thought. Unfortunately, I'm hungry. Surely we can either eat breakfast first or begin our spectral conversation without Mr. Reid?"

Amy tilted her head, listening. "Mrs. Chapman would prefer that we all be present."

"And we are." Jim hurried across the threshold, peering into Amy's face as he slid into the chair beside her. "Good grief, Amy. Are you all right?"

She turned glazed eyes his way. "I'm not sure," she said.

He searched her face for another moment, then laid a gentle hand atop hers. "I'm no expert, but it seems to me you shouldn't do this right now. It's not agreeing with you."

"No, she must!" Chloe leapt from her chair. "Mother is here waiting . . . perhaps she's brought my Margaret as well."

Amy swayed in her chair, glassy gaze now riveted on Chloe's trembling form.

"Fine lot any of that will matter if Amy keels over." Jim raised his eyebrows in Catharine's direction, his open stare more commanding than expected. "Miss Walsh. Surely you share my concerns about your niece's well-being."

His words jolted Catharine from her shock. "Of course I do, Mr. Reid."

"Then perhaps you could escort her up to bed."

"No!" Chloe's desperate cry pierced the air. "Don't listen to him! He just doesn't want to hear from Mother again, that's all. After last night, he's afraid she'll reveal even more about his sordid personal life!"

"That's uncalled for," Adrian said firmly. "I've known Mr. Reid since he was a child. I can vouch for his sterling character."

Chloe snorted. "Nevertheless, Mr. de la Noye, since you want to hear from Mother just as much as I do, I suggest you silence your associate. You're the one who wanted another séance in the first place."

"That's correct, Lady Dinwoodie. I did. But I don't need to compromise Miss Walsh's health in order to obtain the information I seek."

Jim placed a firm hand on Amy's shoulder. "Go with your aunt, Amy. This can wait until you're feeling up to it."

"Coward," Chloe spat as Catharine half rose from her chair. "You'd deprive us all of Mother's company just to prevent more of your grimy past from surfacing. But I'm not surprised. You didn't even have the guts to fight in the Great War, did you? Unlike my Margaret, you stayed home and let others die on your behalf!"

Jim's jaw tightened as protests from Adrian and Catharine erupted around him.

"Enough." Catharine stood so suddenly that her chair nearly tipped over. "Amy, come with me. We're finished here."

"Blossom, you are behaving badly." Amy's flat tone cut through the hubbub.

Nicholas froze. "What did you say?"

"Blossom," Bennett repeated. "Chloe. Only your mother ever called you that."

Chloe dropped into her chair. "My God," she breathed.

Amy's voice grew stronger, its force contrasting with her stony face. "Lady Dinwoodie, your mother says that Mr. Reid does not deserve to be maligned in this way. He had good cause not to fight. His vision is so poor that the military wouldn't let him enlist. Why, he can hardly see at night."

Jim grabbed the edge of the table, cheeks scarlet. "Amy! You promised—"

"Mrs. Chapman has called you all here for a reason," Amy continued. "She says that she's waited long enough for you to accept responsibility for your past actions. She'd hoped that an intimate weekend gathering such as this would inspire you all to set things right, but since that does not appear to be the case, she will say what needs to be said. Time grows short."

"Elizabeth, my dear." Bennett looked crestfallen. "I'm trying my best to do all you ask."

"She says she understands this and recognizes your efforts. The fact remains, however, that you have yet to marry Catharine Walsh and that your will remains unchanged. These matters must be amended as soon as possible."

"Yes, Mother seems to have a rather one-track mind where marriage to Miss Walsh is concerned." Nicholas shifted in his chair. "Why? Ask her why."

"You may ask her yourself," Amy said. "She's passed over, not deaf."

"Where is she?" Chloe swiveled her neck to scour the room.

"By the sideboard," Bennett said, eyes misting in awe.

"Good," Nicholas said. "Ask her to fetch some toast while she's standing. I'm famished."

"Nicky!" Chloe rapped her brother's hand.

"I have a few questions for Mrs. Chapman, if she'll allow the imposition," Adrian said.

Catharine stiffened at the steel wire that ran through his words. "I don't think that wise under the circumstances, Mr. de la Noye. I have my niece's welfare to consider."

"I certainly understand, Miss Walsh. But since it seems Mrs. Chapman plans to stay until she's had her say, perhaps it would speed the process if I—"

"Mrs. Chapman would be delighted to answer your questions, Mr. de la Noye," Amy interrupted. "She wonders what has taken you so long to ask."

"Don't, Adrian." Catharine swung around to face him, gripping the back of the chair to keep her balance. It was no use. Her legs turned to rubber as she sank into her seat.

"Ah." It was Amy's voice, but the expression on her face was one Catharine had never seen before. The pinched look about the nose . . . that slight narrowing of the eyes . . . for a brief moment, it was as if someone else had borrowed Amy's facial features for their own use. "You'd prefer I set matters straight in your own house, Miss Walsh? That's certainly part of what must be done. I can start there if you'd like."

"'I'?" The rest of the room fell away in a hush as Catharine stared across the table at the young woman she knew so well. "Amy . . . please. You can't possibly understand what you're saying."

Amy's eyes widened with confusion as she stared back, but at least she was thoroughly Amy again. One hand fluttered to her stomach. "Aunt Catharine, Mrs. Chapman says . . . Mrs. Chapman says . . ."

Catharine threw a quick, panicked glance in Nicholas Chapman's direction. To her left, Bennett's chair creaked as he leaned forward, eagerly awaiting his late wife's words. To her right, Adrian's gaze pierced her straight through, searching for answers. She dared to meet it. The detachment in his dark eyes made her stomach roil. She'd once kindled a most wonderful fire in that gaze. It seemed a blasphemy that it held nothing but emptiness for her now. Suddenly, her fingers itched to trace the line of his chiseled jaw, to pull him so close that nothing could separate them ever again.

Letting him go had been the biggest mistake of her life. And in another moment, the reasons she'd done so probably wouldn't even matter anymore.

She lifted her chin like a prisoner facing a firing squad. "Very well, Amy," she said. "Out with it. I'm ready."

Amy obliged, her words a relentless wave. "Mrs. Chapman says . . . that despite what you've told everyone for years, you're not my aunt at all."

"Catharine!" Bennett twisted toward her, startled. "Is this true?"

The shock on Amy's face tore at Catharine's heart. "You're my mother."

CHAPTER
22

Voices converged in utter pandemonium as Adrian stared at the young woman across the table. A vein in his neck throbbed; he raised a hand to shield it from curious eyes. At least no one could hear the booming thoughts racing through his mind. With difficulty, he made himself concentrate through the din. Bennett Chapman was still a client with interests to protect, no matter how topsy-turvy his own world had just become.

"You're my mother," Amy repeated, her small voice fading away like a vapor.

"Catharine. What does this mean?" Bennett bent toward his fiancée, brows lowered over eyes so piercing that any other woman would have cowered in her seat.

"Oh, I think that's obvious," Nicholas said. "It means that one way or another, your intended has led you astray. Either she's a proud mama who has neglected to mention the fact, or the dearly departed 'Elizabeth' isn't as accurate as an all-knowing spirit should be. Which is it, Miss . . . Mrs. . . . Walsh?"

"'Miss' will do," Catharine said, skewering him with a look so full of hatred that it seemed blood should be pooling at his feet. Her voice softened as she turned toward her fiancé. "Bennett, you deserve an explanation, and I will answer your questions in private, away from the inquisition."

"I'm sure I have even more questions than he does." Amy sat so still that it seemed a statue had spoken. Jim moved as if to take her hand but stopped mid-motion. Instead he folded his arms across his chest and averted his gaze to a spot somewhere above Adrian's head.

The explosion of laughter from Nicholas's end of the table ricocheted through the room. "Which will it be, Miss Walsh? Do you still vouch for Mother's otherworldly existence? You can choose to be a whore or a fraud. Take your pick."

Catharine's chair clattered to the ground as she leapt to her feet. Adrian shot up as well. "That's enough," he snapped, glaring at Nicholas. Jim sent him a quelling glance from across the table. Nicholas raised an eyebrow.

A dull thud started in Adrian's left temple as he settled back in his seat. "I won't tolerate vulgarity," he said.

Catharine's deadly stare nearly bore a hole through Nicholas Chapman's forehead. "In answer to your question, Mr. Chapman, you may call me whatever you wish. You can't hurt me. Rest assured that I would never have chosen to reveal this information—especially to you. At my own expense, it appears I have proved that the spirit of your mother is indeed real."

"This could still be a cleverly staged fraud," Nicholas said, but for the first time, his words faltered. Only the most accomplished actress could counterfeit the look of shock on Amy's face, could fake the way she trembled in her chair. Furthermore, it was hard to refute the damage done to Catharine's reputation through this most recent revelation.

Catharine slowly righted her chair. "Bennett, I will speak with you whenever you wish. And I will certainly release you from our engagement should you so choose."

Bennett hesitated. "I will hear you, of course. But I am obliged to follow Elizabeth's directives. It seems to me that she has known your story all along yet still encourages our union. I will go forward with this marriage."

"Are you truly this foolish?" Nicholas asked, dazed.

"Stow it, boy," Bennett growled through gritted teeth. "Can't you see I need to keep your mother happy?"

Catharine swayed slightly in the wake of Nicholas's sputtered oath. "Then make the arrangements today," she said. "Let us be done with it, or I'll pack my bags and return to Sacramento. One way or another, I will leave Liriodendron with my pride intact."

Bennett straightened in his chair at the ultimatum, more business tycoon than besotted lover. "I'll do so this morning, after breakfast."

Catharine nodded her acquiescence, color high. Adrian's pulse quickened as she turned his way, but her gaze merely grazed him, coming to rest on Amy instead. Her tone softened. "Amy, I ask your forgiveness. You must understand that I had good reason to alter the truth. I owe you an explanation, but I will not provide it here. You may come to me whenever you're ready."

"You may be waiting for quite some time," Amy said flatly.

Catharine held her gaze. "And perhaps I would deserve that. But you'll never know unless you speak with me, will you?"

Head high, she walked toward the dining room door. For a fleeting moment, Adrian entertained an image of greedy subjects pawing at their queen, demanding that she deliver yet one more act of largesse before mounting the platform to the guillotine.

"I don't care." Amy struggled to stand, as winded as if she'd just run a mile. Catharine paused at the sound of her voice. "I'm tired of it all," Amy continued. "I'm tired of those here who think I'm a fraud, of you others who humor me simply because you believe I'm a conduit to *her* . . ."

"Her?" Chloe looked up. "Is Mother still with us?"

"Yes, she's still here." Amy gave an exhausted shudder. Jim's arms tightened across his chest as if tethered there. "And yes, she has more to say. But do you know what? I don't think I feel like being her puppet anymore. I've had enough."

"But surely she's come for a reason!" Chloe cried. "You must tell us what she wants."

"Must I?" Amy sank back into her chair as if her legs could no longer support her. "Must I really?"

"Of course not." Catharine stared Chloe down from the doorway. "You are beholden to no one, Amy. You needn't do anything against your will."

Amy melted against the back of her chair. "Tell that to Mrs. Chapman. She won't leave me alone if I don't speak for her. Actually, she won't leave at all. Her message is for you, Bennett. You're to make arrangements for the wedding now, not after breakfast. This marriage must take place within the next few days."

Bennett's eyes remained fixed just to the right of the fireplace mantel. "Dear Elizabeth," he said, but his voice was strong. "I am happy to do your will."

Nicholas's fist pounded the table. "Father, I won't allow it. You can't possibly—"

"I can do whatever I wish." Bennett rose to his feet with the agility of a man half his age. He strode toward the door, stopping at the threshold to deliver a sharp peck to Catharine's cheek. "I'll place the telephone calls now. Mr. de la Noye, I believe I've clearly stated my intentions regarding my new will. Go ahead and draft it. No need to fret, Nicky; you and your sister will be invited to the wedding."

His brisk footsteps retreated down the hall, leaving them all to stare at the walking stick he'd left behind.

"Mrs. Chapman will be waiting here," Amy said to no one in particular.

"She needn't," Catharine said. "I've certainly heard enough."

"And I've said enough," Amy shot back. "But since she apparently won't leave until she's satisfied she's gotten all her ducks in a row, you'll come back later to hear what she has to say . . . for my sake. You owe me at least that."

Chloe brightened. "Are you saying that Mother will remain in this room all day?"

Nicholas stared at his sister in disgust. "Oh, absolutely, Chloe. She'll be levitating near the fireplace, just waiting for a plummy moment to deliver her next dramatic revelation."

"Bravo," Amy said. "That's exactly where she is. Do you see her, too?"

Nicholas blanched.

"I feel faint." Amy closed her eyes.

"Well." Chloe squirmed in her seat. "Perhaps if we all just sit here and have a lovely chat with Mother, you'll feel better."

"No." Amy's eyelids fluttered open as she slumped down farther in her chair. Catharine started toward her, arm outstretched, but Amy stopped her with a well-aimed glare.

Adrian cleared his throat. "Mr. Reid, suppose you escort Amy to the gardens." He ignored the pleading refusal that flickered across his associate's face. "The salt air will do her good."

"Yes, please." Amy turned doe-like eyes toward Jim, who shrugged helplessly. "Perhaps I'll feel better after a little walk. You and I could have breakfast on the terrace, Mr. Reid. This room is starting to give me the creeps."

"So there's to be no more conversation with Mother now?" Chloe asked as Jim rose and offered Amy a rigid arm.

"Oh, don't worry. She'll be here. She's waiting for your father." Amy slipped her fingers through the crook of Jim's elbow and pulled herself from her chair. His eyebrows rose slightly in surprise as she slumped against him. "Please, Mr. Reid. Take me outside."

"Perhaps I could join you two on the terrace," Chloe began, but she might as well have spoken to the wall. Jim and Amy left the room as if they hadn't heard a word she'd said.

"Well." Chloe's disappointed gaze darted from Nicholas to Adrian to Catharine. "Here's a jolly crew. You all look as if you might draw weapons. I'll take breakfast in my room, where it's safer. Fetch me when Mother is ready to speak. Lord knows there's nothing to do here when she isn't around."

Adrian barely noticed her exit. His stare enveloped Catharine, but her figure refused to remain constant in his vision. Instead, a young woman with a mesmerizing smile and a mane of thick hair danced through his mind. His fingers twitched as he remembered how sweetly her waist had once yielded beneath the span of his hand. Her skin, tinged with rose, had incited tremors each time she'd brushed against him. Set free after so many years, a Pandora's box worth of memories swirled through his consciousness, stabbing at his solar plexus until it seemed the front of his argyle sweater should be bloodstained.

Catharine's haunted eyes met his and, for the first time, he saw that she was drowning alongside him.

He looked away. "Miss Walsh. I'd be much obliged if we could talk."

"Yes," she said, staring at the floor.

"You'll have to wait your turn," Nicholas said. Adrian turned toward the foot of the table, cursing himself for forgetting that the other man had stayed behind.

Nicholas's smile was anything but genuine. "Forgive the intrusion, but I'd like to have a few words with you as well . . . Mr. Delano."

Adrian stiffened.

"Oh, I'm sorry, Mr. de la Noye. My mistake," Nicholas said. "But it's an easy one to make, isn't it? Have a seat. You and I can chat over breakfast."

Adrian didn't need to look in Catharine's direction. Quick footsteps in the hall made it clear that as long as Nicholas stayed sniffing around the past, she planned to stay as far away as possible.

CHAPTER
23

February 1898

I'm hoping to catch a Vanderbilt at one of these hoity-toity dinner parties," Cassie Walsh said as Adrian handed her down from the brougham in front of the Phillips residence. "Newport teems with them, doesn't it?"

Adrian smiled. A few hours of rest had worked wonders; he'd awakened feeling nearly human again. "In season it does. Your timing isn't quite right, Miss Walsh. Had you chosen to run away in June, your society marriage prospects would have tripled."

She lifted her hand from his and buried it deep in her fur muff. "I'll make do," she said, studying the Phillips residence. It was more a well-appointed home than a lavish mansion, but its sprawling architecture, Bellevue Avenue address, and landscaped grounds made it clear that Peter and Marjorie Phillips had grown up wanting for very little.

Cassie eyed the gingerbread trim. "I'll settle for a well-to-do professional man, a lawyer or doctor, perhaps. It's not as if I'll ever be allowed to break into the Four Hundred, after all."

Adrian's smile flattened. "That's correct."

"Of course, I'd hoped that since one of your relatives—*our* relatives—married an Astor some fifty years ago . . ."

"Very good. You've studied well. Then you already know that I'm not on that esteemed list either, and that Mrs. Astor would require even more credentials from a distant cousin on my mother's side."

Cassie's gloved fingers smoothed his sleeve. "Even though the Delanos are connected to the Roosevelts by marriage? The Roosevelts are on the list, aren't they?"

He didn't even try to hide the sarcasm that trickled into his voice. "Goodness, Miss Walsh, you ask too much of America's royalty. How dare you even think of sullying the precious bloodlines?"

"God, Adrian. You wealthy are an affected lot."

"And yet you wish to join the ranks."

"*Your* ranks." She stopped dead in the middle of the front walk. "Why shouldn't I want the best? You'll stay near me tonight, won't you? Come to my aid if I do anything wrong?"

"I'll do what I can," he said, wondering even as the words left his mouth what it was about Cassie Walsh that could make him agree to such folly.

He caught sight of a tiny dimple in her cheek as they reached the front door. "Good," Cassie said. "I'm tired tonight. That may put me a bit off my game."

Game. Adrian forced a pleasant expression to his face as the Phillips's door swung open. That was as good a term as any for the evening that lay ahead.

He didn't wonder that Cassie was tired. Despite her original intention to rest that afternoon, she'd instead set about unpacking his trunks with the zeal of a Salvationist. It hadn't taken long to discover why she'd developed a sudden interest in sifting through his luggage. Leaning against the bedroom door jamb, he'd watched in amazement as she withdrew several frocks from his largest trunk.

"You were sending the trunks anyway," she'd said, rummaging past his packed clothing. "It seemed a waste of space. You can rest in this room if you'd like. I'll be very quiet."

He'd dropped gratefully on top of the counterpane, too exhausted to argue. Slipping in and out of sleep, he'd been distantly aware of her puttering about the cottage. She'd gone from pressing her clothes to hanging them and had eventually disappeared down the hall to run a bath. Even as he'd dozed, the scent of patchouli had tickled his nostrils. He'd smiled through his dreams, unsurprised that Cassie's choice of fragrance would contain spicy notes rather than floral ones.

Cousin Kate. What madness. What long-ago spell had this cook's daughter cast that allowed her to weave him so thoroughly into her plans? This masquerade would never work anyway. His colleagues weren't fools: they'd know at once that she wasn't of their class.

He winced at his own elitism. How exactly would they know? Years of tending to his younger sister, Edith, had made Cassie as much an expert in manners and fashion as any daughter of society. And, as Marjorie Phillips introduced her to each of the other ten guests gathered in the parlor, he had to admit that no one seemed to suspect their new acquaintance was anyone other than Kate Weld, Adrian Delano's distant cousin come to call. James Heyward raised an interested eyebrow as Cassie praised Newport's beauty. David Houghton, ignoring the presence of his own wife, leaned toward her in that solicitous way Adrian recognized from their university days on the prowl. And Peter Phillips, their host—Peter, lush and letch extraordinaire—smiled broadly at the young woman before him. He looked like the wolf come across Red Riding Hood in the wood. Adrian glumly noted that Cassie was the prettiest woman in the room.

"She's quite lovely." Marjorie Phillips interrupted his train of thought. "Why haven't we met this little jewel before?"

"My apologies." Adrian stepped to one side to peer around his hostess's blond head. "I've been remiss." Cassie dimpled at something Peter said. Adrian sighed. He'd have to warn her later about his friend's rakish ways.

Marjorie moved closer. "We're about to enter the dining room. You'll escort me, won't you?"

"Of course," Adrian said reflexively, watching as Peter offered Cassie an arm. He wondered which lady his friend had just dropped in order to escort "Cousin Kate" to the table. That meant she'd sit at Peter's right for the evening, that he'd have her full attention . . .

"Mr. Delano . . ." Marjorie smiled coquettishly. "Your arm?"

"Arm? Yes, of course." It was too early to offer it—a good hostess repaired to the dining room behind her guests—but Adrian was too preoccupied to remember that Peter's older sister had set her cap for him quite some time ago and so allowed the proprietary grip on his sleeve without protest.

He'd already admitted to himself that Cassie Walsh was beautiful. He'd had no choice: she'd swept into the cottage parlor earlier that evening, a pre-Raphaelite vision in white organdy. Startled, his gaze had traveled from the flow of gauzy fabric about her rounded hips, past her tiny cinched waist and daring décolletage, straight up to her huge brown eyes and loose chignon of wavy dark hair. The realization that this angel was his cook's daughter, a girl who'd grown up in his own household, had captured his breath.

The pearls dripping through her gloved hand had reminded him at once that it was perfectly acceptable to breathe.

"Those belong to my sister," he'd said, surprised.

"Yes." She'd extended the triple-strand choker toward him. "I know. Your great-aunt Rose had them sent to Edith as a sixteenth-birthday gift. Could you help me put them on? The clasp is difficult."

"But . . . they're not yours." That bewitching undercurrent of patchouli had again become a distraction. Without thinking, he'd accepted the proffered pearls.

"Of course they're not, Adrian. How could I ever afford anything from Cartier? Edith let me borrow them for my grandfather's wake while you were away at school, so I think she would have lent them again had I been able to ask her. I couldn't very well wake her up in the middle of the night to check, now could I? You can bring them back home when you go."

She'd turned her back to him, waiting. Adrian had slipped the necklace around her graceful neck and fastened it, and the transformation had been complete. Every debutante he knew proudly displayed pearls such as these. Illuminated by their luster, Cassie Walsh disappeared and Kate Weld emerged, aglow with excitement for the evening about to begin.

"Thank you." She'd reached out to adjust his white bow tie, and he couldn't help but notice that Edith's pearls would be shown off to perfection.

She was a puzzle, this Cassie Walsh.

Marjorie gently tugged him toward the dining room. "Your cousin is quite an addition to the party," she said. "I admit, I could have throttled you when you changed my guest list at the very last minute, but perhaps this was providence. Peter seems quite taken with her."

Indeed. Adrian escorted Marjorie to her chair and seated himself beside her, gaze riveted to the head of the table. Peter rose to propose a toast. Cassie's eyes shone as she smiled at him, champagne glass raised. The words of the toast blurred in Adrian's ears as he followed the delicate arc of her arm. He only knew when the toast ended because everyone else raised glasses to lips in response. Pasting yet another stale smile onto his face, he followed suit.

Was Peter Phillips really Cassie's choice? He was prosperous enough. His credentials weren't all that different from Adrian's own: solid position in a respected family law firm, enough inherited wealth and family reputation to receive reasonable social invitations . . .

A discreet "ahem" signaled that a footman stood beside him, waiting. Adrian absently selected several oysters from the offered platter.

Peter was a cad, an out-and-out womanizer. Cassie was naïve if she thought she could mold him into the faithful sort. Adrian frowned as he lifted his oyster fork to his mouth and chewed.

"Is everything all right?" Marjorie leaned toward him, concerned.

"All right? Of course. The entire evening is perfect, and you were very kind to allow my cousin to be a part of it."

Marjorie looked doubtful. "If it's all so perfect, perhaps you'll come down from the clouds and talk to me. I feel as if I'm having a conversation with myself! Tell me of Europe—did you enjoy Paris? It's quite my favorite city in the world."

"I can understand why." It was easy enough to launch into a safe conversation about Paris in the autumn. It required very little thought.

Surely Cassie would blunder, say something that revealed her as nothing more than a charlatan. Adrian froze as Peter's voice floated down the table, asking where Miss Weld had hidden herself for so many years.

Tears pooled in Cassie's eyes. "I debuted rather late, I'm afraid, due to the untimely death of my father." Her sadness apparently brought out the gallant in Peter, who bent toward her with concern, handkerchief at the ready. Cassie brushed away a tear, lifted a brave chin, and rallied. "Forgive me, Mr. Phillips. This is a party, and we are to be gay. I'd much rather hear about you."

A skillful return. Cassie could take care of herself.

"Mr. Delano," Marjorie prodded. "You are miles away."

"I'm sorry." He leaned back to allow the footman to remove his oyster plate. "I'm afraid I feel a responsibility toward Miss Weld. This is her first trip since her father's death. She took the loss rather hard."

Marjorie relaxed. "That's admirable, and I understand perfectly. I just wondered if there might be something . . . more. Exactly how distant a cousin is she?"

Adrian silently swore to become a more attentive guest.

He managed through the vermicelli soup and turbot in lobster sauce, through the spring chicken with peas. Cassie's melodic voice grazed his ears as he savored the palate-cleansing punch served after the fourth course, but he could not distinguish her words. He didn't have to: the enthralled look on Peter's face said more than words could have. The situation was so clear that Adrian had little appetite for the several courses that followed the punch. Only by glancing at the menu card placed between him and Marjorie could he determine what exactly had been served.

"Adrian." Peter Phillips glanced toward the dining room door as the ladies swept from earshot after dinner. "Miss Weld will accompany you to the wedding Saturday morning, won't she?"

For the first time he could remember, Adrian had no thirst for the tawny port just poured. "She hasn't been invited. She leaves tomorrow."

Peter's eyes glittered. "I'll see to it that she's welcome," he said. "Bring her."

CHAPTER
24

A re you hungry, Mr. de la Noye?" Nicholas Chapman settled back in his chair at the end of the dining room table.

"No." Adrian remained planted by the dining room door.

"Well, I'm ravenous. Would you mind if I rang for breakfast?"

"Yes, I would. I'd prefer to hear what you have to say as quickly and briefly as possible. I have a great deal to accomplish today."

"Drafting my father's new will, perhaps?"

"It's on my list."

"Maybe not," Nicholas said. "I did get the name right before, didn't I? You're Adrian Delano. Your family hails from upstate New York."

"I don't deny that."

"Yet you go by the surname de la Noye."

Adrian shrugged. "Our original family name was de la Noye. I reverted back to it a long time ago."

"So I've been told. You fought in the Spanish-American War, were wounded and received a Medal of Honor under that name. I believe it was in Cuba that you began your friendship with young Mr. Reid's father, was it not?" Nicholas rose and walked toward the coffee service on the buffet. "You must admit that on the face of it, changing your name was an odd decision. After all, you come from a family of some prominence. Giving up the Delano name surely meant sacrificing some of the privileges that came along with it."

Adrian paused before answering. The man had obviously made inquiries. "I found it preferable to rely on ability rather than pedigree."

"Ah." Nicholas poured himself a cup of coffee from the silver pot, added two lumps of sugar, and stirred well before turning back to face his adversary. "I hadn't pegged you as a man of the people."

Adrian reached for his pocket watch. "Despite your extensive research, it appears you don't know me very well after all."

"No. But I do know human nature, and men just don't change their last names for purely selfless reasons."

Adrian flipped open the cover of his watch and pointedly checked the time. He had faced opposing counsel like this before, lawyers who flung half-baked suppositions through the courtroom in the hopes that something would stick due to the mere momentum of the throw. Nicholas clearly had some facts at his fingertips, but it was hard to tell exactly which ones. Key components were missing. Did the man honestly believe that Adrian himself would eagerly step forward to fill in the gaps?

He closed the watch with a loud click and returned it to his pocket. "You seem to have invested a great deal of effort into exploring my past, Mr. Chapman."

Nicholas smiled. He shouldn't have. He had the insincere grin of a patent elixir salesman. "A considerable amount of money as well, Mr. Delano."

"It is legally de la Noye, sir."

"De la Noye, then. Forgive me. It's hard for me to remember that, since I had some association with your family in the past."

Adrian's eyebrows rose. "Excuse me, but have we met before?"

"No, sir, not at all. Your sister, Edith, was one of the young ladies I considered courting many years ago, but you were away in Europe at the time . . . sowing your own wild oats, as I recall. But, yes, I attended a few soirees hosted by your family. It's ancient history now, brought back only because you've come to call at Liriodendron."

Adrian nodded politely. "Are we quite finished here, Mr. Chapman? My last name is unimportant to the proceedings at hand."

Nicholas raised the porcelain cup to his lips and carefully blew steam from the top. "You're right. It doesn't matter what you choose to call yourself. But the reason you reverted to de la Noye in the first place might have some significance." The coffee reached its destination, and Nicholas took a deep swig.

"I've told you the reason."

Nicholas eyed him from across the rim of his cup. "The real reason, Mr. de la Noye. The one you'd prefer I keep to myself."

Years of practice and training had taught Adrian to temper his reactions. He was an expert when it came to controlling both his expressions and his gestures. He could not, however, prevent the heat that rushed through his veins. Was this a bluff? There was no way to know.

"Mr. Chapman, let me make sure I understand. Are you saying

that you'll reveal some unknown nugget from my past should I move forward with the execution of your father's new will?"

Nicholas cradled the coffee cup in both hands. "You are as smart as my sources say. Yes, Mr. de la Noye. That's exactly what I'm saying. But the reverse is true as well: if my father's current will remains intact, your secrets are safe with me."

"What of your father's marriage to Miss Walsh? I've nothing to do with that decision."

The delicate cup landed on the buffet with such force that Adrian expected it to crack in two. "You leave Miss Walsh to me," Nicholas said.

Adrian fixed the other man with a steady gaze. "Miss Walsh is not my concern," he said. "She is not my client; your father is. That's as far as my interest in this matter runs."

"Is it now?" Nicholas met the stare. "Ethics are of no use to a lawyer, Mr. de la Noye. Surely you've learned that."

Both men started as determined footsteps sounded in the hall. Adrian spoke beneath his breath. "I will take your words into consideration."

"Consider quickly. Time is short. Oh, by the way—regards to your wife and children. Dear Constance was your stenographer before your marriage, wasn't she? Lovely lady, but hardly of your class."

Adrian bit back his response as Bennett Chapman strode through the dining room door. The older man seemed to have gained even more vitality during his trip to and from the telephone.

"It's done," Bennett said, squaring his shoulders beneath his navy blue blazer. "I've spoken to an old friend of mine, Judge Thomas

Bourne. He'll arrive from Boston by four o'clock tomorrow afternoon to marry us in the parlor."

Adrian nodded. "Judge Bourne? A good choice. He'll see to it that tomorrow proceeds smoothly indeed."

Nicholas looked as if the floorboards had cracked beneath his feet. "You can't be serious."

"No need to fuss, Nicky. As I've told you before, you are certainly welcome to attend the ceremony. Where is Catharine? She might want to order flowers for the parlor, plan a wedding dinner—I suppose we should arrange some sort of honeymoon . . ."

"Bennett." Adrian clapped a firm hand on his client's shoulder, angling him away from his son's furious glare. "I've only one question for you: have you reached this decision through your own volition? Is this marriage what you really want?"

Bennett's shoulders slumped slightly beneath his palm, but his gaze remained fixed and true. "Yes. I am fully cognizant of my actions."

Adrian's hand dropped back to his side. "Then congratulations to you, sir. Please accept my every wish for your continued happiness."

"You'll stay through tomorrow night, Adrian, won't you? It would mean a great deal to me to have you and Mr. Reid attend the marriage ceremony. And you, Nicky—I would never consider asking you to be my best man, but will you stay to see me wed?"

"You can't be serious," Nicholas repeated, but his father's attention had shifted toward the fireplace. His businesslike demeanor melted away as he studied the spot to the right of the mantel, eyes misted by the pleading gaze of a supplicant.

His voice, when it came, seemed far away. "I understand that neither of us cares for the other very much, Nicky, but your presence during this ceremony would please your mother greatly."

"Oh, for the love of—"

"Look closely. She's still with us, standing by the mantel. Wait, she has more to say . . ."

"You can hear her?" Adrian asked.

Bennett blinked, momentarily nonplussed. "I suppose I can. What a wonderful turn of events! Perhaps I won't need to bother Amy anymore if I can speak with Elizabeth on my own—oh?" He squinted. A faint whiff of lavender wafted through the room; both Adrian and Nicholas froze.

Bennett nodded his head as a dreamlike smile wreathed his face. "Very well, then. Of course it's all right. Anything you wish, my dear."

"What's happening?" Nicholas demanded.

His father shot his cuffs as he turned toward him, once again the consummate businessman. "No need to concern yourself. Your mother simply prefers that we continue to speak through Miss Walsh for the time being, and only when we are all present together. She agrees, however, that Mr. de la Noye would be a delightful addition to the wedding guest list, and says that your presence, Nicky, is obligatory. Plan to stay, Adrian."

"Perhaps Mother herself would like to be a guest at the wedding," Nicholas said sourly. "It would give her a chance to meet Judge Bourne."

"She already knows Judge Bourne," Bennett said.

Adrian glanced up, a germ of an idea racing through his head. "Mr. Reid and I would be honored to attend your wedding," he said slowly. "I'll draft a will that you and the new Mrs. Chapman can sign immediately following the ceremony. Judge Bourne can witness it."

"An excellent idea, Mr. de la Noye. No wonder I retained you so many years ago."

Nicholas faced his father, but his words were for Adrian. "You're imposing, Father," he said. "Surely Mr. de la Noye's family longs for his return to Brookline as quickly as possible."

"Oh, they'll see me soon enough." Adrian finally reached for a coffee cup. "You've never met my wife, sir. A wise, resilient woman, if you'll indulge my bragging. Constance always reminds me that any task worth doing is worth doing well. She'd be disappointed if I were to leave this one in the middle."

"Then I take it I'll be sharing some very interesting information with Judge Bourne tomorrow night," Nicholas said evenly.

"I'm sure we will be at no loss for conversation." Adrian extended his cup. "Would you be so kind as to pour me some coffee? Bennett, Nicholas had a splendid idea a moment ago. Perhaps Elizabeth could attend the ceremony."

Bennett clapped his hands together with delight. "Are you suggesting a séance, Mr. de la Noye?"

"Why not? The late Mrs. Chapman obviously approves of the marriage."

Nicholas nearly dropped the coffeepot he'd just lifted from the buffet. "You would . . . let Judge Bourne know Father believes Mother is here?"

Adrian held his cup steady as Nicholas poured. "Why not?" he repeated.

"You're as mad as my father is. Because the minute you inform the judge that Father thinks a ghost is attending the wedding, you prove my case."

"We'll see," Adrian said, meeting the other man's gaze squarely. "Perhaps it's time to invoke Clause Eight of our agreement, the one that allows a neutral third party to decide the outcome of our dispute. Judge Bourne should do nicely. Maybe you should ring for breakfast after all. I'm suddenly hungry."

"I'll inform the housekeeper on my way out." Nicholas deposited the coffeepot onto the buffet with a loud thump. "You'll excuse me. I've a telephone call to make."

"Don't mind him, Adrian," Bennett said as his son left the room. "I'm sure my recent decisions have rattled him, but Nicholas is usually more bark than bite."

"No trouble at all. Would you join me for breakfast? I'd like to hear more about Elizabeth."

"She'll be so pleased." Bennett turned toward his chair at the head of the table. "So pleased."

CHAPTER
25

Jim half carried Amy out of the house, listening as her ragged breathing grew calmer the farther they got from the dining room. It was as if a stranglehold had been pried from her throat, and not a moment too soon. By the time they reached the back terrace, a hint of pink had returned to each of her cheeks. Even her grip on his arm felt steadier—sure enough, in fact, that he felt no compunction about plucking her fingers from the sleeve of his flannel jacket and stepping abruptly away from her side.

Amy looked up, startled. "Are you all right? I know it was creepy back there, but that's my problem, not yours."

"You really take the cake, don't you?" Jim jammed both hands into his pockets and turned away.

"I don't understand."

An angry buzz started in his ears. "Don't bother to look confused, Miss Walsh. I've got your number now. You're a calculating flirt. Worse, you're a fraud."

He heard her indignant gasp. "How dare you!"

He whirled around to face her, finger pointed at her nose. "I was brought up to believe in the spirits, but after your performance today, it's clear that 'Mrs. Chapman' is composed of nothing more than scraps of information nicked from clueless dupes like me."

Amy's mouth dropped open. "How can you say that after what I just went through back there? It was like some horrible wave was trying to suck me under and drag me out to sea! It took everything I had to break free—I couldn't wait to get out of that room. And to think I was about to thank you for helping me!"

His own naïveté made him wince. "Save your breath. I'm finished with it—*all* of it."

"You can't just walk away, Jim Reid. I need you!"

He batted away the thought that she might actually mean it. "For what? There are plenty of other men out there for you to make fools of, and you do it so awfully well. Can't say I didn't bring it on myself, though—I should have realized that anything I told you in confidence could and would be used against me."

Her lower lip trembled. "I don't understand. I would never hurt you on purpose."

He shook his head hard, trying to shield his sense of reason from her plaintive tone. "Darn it, Amy, why did you have to tell everyone that I can't see in the dark? You promised me you wouldn't."

"I told you before," Amy said in a small voice. "I have no control over anything Mrs. Chapman says."

"Forgive me if I don't believe that anymore."

"Jim." Her hands scrabbled across his chest, gathering his jacket into two large hunks. "Jim, please. I'm scared to death. I think . . . I think I could have died in there."

He looked down at her and breathed a silent curse. Were those real tears welling up in the corners of those clear blue eyes? How did she manage to look so utterly helpless, like a bird that had just fallen from its nest?

"You handled yourself just fine," he mumbled, staring down at his scuffed buckskins.

"No, Jim, listen." The crack in her voice made his eyes lock with hers. "I'm afraid to go back in there. I don't want to speak for Mrs. Chapman anymore."

"Then don't."

"I don't think I have a choice," she whispered.

His brows lowered in concern. Carefully, he disengaged her fingers from his lapels and led her over to one of the wrought-iron chairs by the table. "What do you mean? Who's forcing you? Is it your aunt?"

"Don't you mean my mother?" she demanded flatly.

He dragged a chair to her side and sat. "Of course. Your mother. Amy, level with me—after all these years, did you honestly have no idea that Catharine Walsh was your mother? Not even an inkling?"

She glowered at him. "No, of course not. She told me that my parents died when I was a baby. I was just a kid, Jim. Why would I question information like that?"

He cleared his throat. "Well, you're not a kid anymore. It's time to take responsibility for your life, and that includes your actions here. You and Catharine made money in California by hoaxing folks with fake psychic phenomena, didn't you."

She at least had the grace to blush. "Not exactly. Besides, this isn't anything like that."

"Oh, I understand that part. This is a bigger fish, a bigger scam. If you've seen the error of your ways and don't want to do it anymore, then tell Catharine you've had enough. She can't force you to do something you don't want to do."

"She's not forcing me. She wants to see it end, too."

He looked puzzled. "Then I don't get it. Who's forcing you to continue the charade?"

"Her." The word dropped to the flagstone like a two-ton weight. "Elizabeth Chapman. It's like she's on a mission or something. Each time she comes, her presence gets stronger and stronger. When we started, she was content to tell me what she wanted to say and then hover in the background while I repeated it. This last time it took every ounce of strength I had to keep her from rushing through me to deliver the words herself. I don't know if I can keep pushing her back. Don't you see, Jim? One day very soon, she's going to totally take over my mind, and I don't know if I'll ever get it back."

She was either truly scared or she'd missed her calling to go on the stage. A fine sweat misted her forehead as her hands began to shake. Jim felt his own fingers grow cold.

"Okay, Amy," he said. "Say I decide to believe you when you tell me that Mrs. Chapman is real. Say she isn't some cleverly crafted fiction of yours, set up for the sole purpose of parting the rich from their money. Why has she come? What does she want?"

Amy looked so miserable that he couldn't stop himself from wrapping a protective arm around her shoulders. "I'm not sure," she said, leaning her head against his chest. "She always seems happy to see Bennett. That's what struck me most in the beginning—her eagerness to reunite with the man who I suppose was the love of her life."

Jim mulled over her words. He'd excelled at case analysis in law school. Even now, his ability to extract a cogent argument from a pile of facts was among the strongest of his legal skills. But this situation offered no solid, tangible details. Assuming Mrs. Chapman really did exist, she certainly didn't adhere to the laws of physics. Even the law of cause and effect would prove worthless here. Clearly, this was something entirely different—this was a matter of the heart, and no rational deduction could help him where that was concerned.

"What else do you feel when you deliver Mrs. Chapman's words?" he asked.

Amy nestled more comfortably into his arms. He instinctively tightened his hold. "She's very eager to see Bennett and Aunt . . . and Catharine . . . married. She pushes hardest when she delivers that message, as if she wants to fly through me and set the matter to rights herself."

"Yes, it's clear she wants that wedding to happen as quickly as possible. Does it stem from concern about her widower's happiness?"

"I don't think so. I feel there's something else she wants to say, something of great importance that she hasn't been able to voice yet."

"Why? You don't block any of her words, do you?"

"No, of course not. Good grief, I'd be happy if she'd just spit it all out and leave me alone. Apparently the right moment hasn't come yet. She's waiting for something to happen, but I don't know what."

Jim fell silent. Why had Elizabeth Chapman chosen this particular young woman as a conduit for her messages? Surely there were other "psychics" available, and they lived a heck of a lot closer to Liriodendron than Sacramento, California.

"Amy, do you remember why Bennett Chapman was out in California when he met you?"

"He was on his way home from a business meeting in San Francisco. He visited Sacramento on a whim. Now he believes that Elizabeth may have guided him there." She stopped. "Why so many questions?"

"It's just the way I'm made," Jim said slowly. "Whenever there are a lot of puzzle pieces scattered about, I feel obliged to fit them all together."

"I understand perfectly," Amy said with a sigh. "I'm usually that way, too. Problem is that in this case, I'm one of the biggest puzzle pieces of all. Before this morning, I assumed I was Amy Carolyn Walsh, daughter of Charles and Susannah Walsh. Now I have no idea who I am."

"Why don't you ask your mother?"

"Why should I believe anything she tells me?"

Jim nodded. The response, though harsh, was understandable.

"Will you help me?" Amy reached up to pull him close.

His guard was slipping, and fast. Her lips were so close, and there was nothing he wanted more than to kiss them. What a dandy distraction that would be, the perfect way to give his busy mind a rest.

Too bad he couldn't escape the feeling that that was exactly why Amy had placed herself in his path.

With a sigh, he reached up and disengaged her arms from around his neck. "What would you like me to do?" he asked.

A shadow crossed her face, but she continued as if nothing unusual had passed between them. "I'm sure there will be more séances," she said quietly. "I don't think they can be avoided—Mrs. Chapman is determined to deliver her final messages, and even if I don't want to be her mouthpiece anymore, I have no doubt she'll find a way to speak through me. That's what happened this morning."

"And?"

"You've got to make sure I come back."

The skin on the back of his neck prickled. "Back?"

"Don't let her take over forever, all right?".

He searched her frightened face, longing to find a hint of deceit shadowing her lips, a guilty blink or two, anything that would let him believe that she was nothing but a clever con artist. One false note and he could righteously walk away. But no matter how hard he looked, all he could detect was fear. Amy wasn't lying.

He knew the right thing to do.

He grasped her trembling hand in his. "You have my word," he said.

CHAPTER
26

February 1898

Cassie Walsh observed Peter Phillips from beneath lowered lashes as she bid good night to their host and hostess in the parlor. Tiny red spider veins snaked beneath his fair skin, and the voracious expression he sported had probably become so habitual that he had no idea it was even there.

"A pleasure, Miss Weld," he said, holding her hand in his for a second too long before release. He tried to capture her eyes as well, but the amount of liquor he'd consumed eliminated any possibility of a straight gaze. "You'll come to the wedding with your cousin Saturday morning, of course."

Cassie opened her mouth to respond, but Adrian, appearing just behind her right shoulder, spoke first. "We'll see. Family obligations may require my cousin to depart tomorrow morning as planned."

"Ah." Peter straightened. "Then you must plead my case, Adrian. You're a far better litigator than I. Tell your family that good company has done wonders to ease your sweet cousin's sorrow."

Cassie did not need to look to know that Adrian wore a bitter smile. She'd caught that same expression on his face throughout the evening as Marjorie Phillips prattled gamely in his ear, hoping for a positive reaction of any sort.

"Your wrap, cousin," he said now, dropping her evening cloak across her shoulders as if it weighed a hundred pounds. She found herself with no choice but to let final pleasantries float on the air behind them as he tucked an insistent hand beneath her elbow and propelled her out into the frigid night.

"I'd prefer to walk back to the cottage," he said, starting down the front walkway. "It isn't far. Or are you wearing ridiculous shoes more suited to fashion than practicality?"

It was cold, but the challenge in his voice sent hot blood coursing through her veins. Besides, a bracing slap of frosty air would probably do him good. She'd noticed him drain several glasses of wine throughout the evening, each with less enjoyment than the one before.

"Of course we can walk," she said haughtily. "I'm hardly the fragile flower you usually escort; women in service can't afford to be. Tonight was a refreshing change for me."

"Change?" His mouth twitched. "Oh, you served tonight. Make no mistake about that."

The dark undertone in his voice raised her hackles. She swallowed back a sharp retort as he left her to dismiss the waiting carriage. Adrian wasn't the only one who'd had a bit too much wine that evening. There was little to be gained through a tipsy spat, though, especially one in which she might not be in top form.

He returned to her side, grip firm as he plucked one gloved hand from her fur muff and slipped it securely through the crook of his elbow. "Let's go," he said.

Cassie glanced at him as they walked down Bellevue Avenue. In her younger days, Adrian Delano had reminded her of a medieval knight. With his keen gaze and sharply cut jaw, there seemed little reason to alter that perception now. His gait was sure, his muscles tight where her fingers rested on his arm. All he lacked was a sword.

"So," Adrian said, and she remembered a little too late that not all sword slashes were physical. "Is it your intention to trade yourself from one sort of service into another?"

"I don't understand," she said primly.

"Oh, I think you do." His voice was silky, inescapable in the darkness.

She sighed, too tired to keep up a pretense. "Why are you so shocked? For better or worse, you knew why I wanted to come here. Are you simply surprised that I've captured someone's eye so quickly?"

"Peter? All you had to do to catch Peter was bait your hook with décolletage . . . which you did. Now, reeling him in will require actual work."

"How insulting you are!" She stopped short and tried to yank her hand away from his arm. He held on tightly with his free hand.

"Cassie, listen to me. Do you know anything at all about Peter Phillips?"

"Yes." She studied the tips of her shoes peeking from beneath the hem of her dinner gown. "I can tell quite a bit about him. He drinks too much and is a horrible flirt. He will never be faithful to the woman he marries and will grow corpulent and childish as he ages. But since his money comes from family wealth as well as a professional salary, he can be counted on to provide a steady income. Am I correct?"

Adrian's shoulders sagged. "And that's better for you than what's back in Poughkeepsie?"

"You don't know the half."

"Then tell me."

"No!"

He studied her for a moment, and she knew exactly what he saw. She'd allowed a little too much emotion to creep into her response; the concern on his face could only be a reaction to fear reflected on her own. She pulled her hand from his grasp and continued briskly down Bellevue, snapping the spell that had fallen between them.

Adrian reached her in three long strides. "You're too clever and beautiful for the likes of Peter," he said. "If you only knew how my friends and I pity whatever poor lady the man ends up marrying."

"I don't need to know that. I already know how you and your friends regard women of my station, and it certainly isn't as ladies."

This time, he was the one who stopped, so suddenly that she stumbled into him. He caught her in his arms, righting her beneath the glow of a nearby streetlamp. "That isn't fair," he said, resting his hands on her shoulders. "I've never treated you with anything less than respect, even when you were a pigtailed little nuisance hiding from your mother."

She stared at him. She saw nothing of the drunk she'd lifted off the lawn in Poughkeepsie the night before, nor of the sallow wreck she'd accompanied to Newport earlier that day. Beneath the brim of his top hat, Adrian's eyes were clear, and she recognized that firm set of his mouth from the days she'd watched him ponder his next backgammon move in the clandestine games they'd shared.

"I'm sorry," she said. "You're right. You've never been anything but kind to me. But, honestly, what do you expect me to do? I don't have your abundance of choice."

A carriage rumbled down Bellevue, its illuminated lamps a reminder that they stood on a very public street. Adrian's arms dropped from her shoulders to his sides, leaving behind a warm tingle where his palms had rested.

She slid her hands into her muff and fell into step beside him. He smelled pleasantly of cologne, tobacco, and wine. She drew in a deep whiff, startled by how familiar he seemed.

Adrian cursed himself for not anticipating that Cassie would be even more beautiful in the moonlight than she'd been in the diffused candlelight of the Phillips's dining room. He hadn't expected the unfortunate wave of longing that threatened to engulf him each time he glanced her way.

Her vulnerability stabbed at his heart. It had been easy enough to protect her years ago when she'd risked little more than a tongue-lashing. It was harder now that the stakes were so much higher.

"Cassie . . . you were frank with me last night, and I hope you'll allow me the same liberty now."

"Say what you want." Her gaze remained fixed straight ahead. "You won't offend me."

He cleared his throat. "Men like Peter Phillips do not always harbor honorable intentions."

Her laugh sliced through the air like broken glass. "Was that meant to be a profound revelation?"

"I know you see him as a gentleman, but . . ."

"Don't worry. I am well aware of the shortcomings of your class."

Her bitterness broke the steady rhythm of his gait but did not prevent him from continuing. "You're young, Cassie, and you grew up in our household, where such . . . shortcomings . . . do not exist in great excess."

"The men in your family are no different from any others of your class." Her voice was hollow. "You all believe you've got the right to take whatever you want, whenever you please."

"That's not true!"

"Oh? Can you honestly tell me that your exploits in Europe have been greatly exaggerated?"

"I regret Europe with all my heart." His retort was sharper than intended.

She turned toward him, surprised. "No need to pillory yourself, Adrian," she said gently. "We each do what we must to stay afloat in a given situation. At least you have the capacity for contrition, which is more than I can say for many." Her hand latched on to his elbow again, sliding down his arm until their gloved fingers intertwined. Adrian accepted the offer of absolution with a grateful squeeze.

The outline of the cottage came into view, stark against the winter sky. Inside, Mrs. Vickery had lit the lamps, and the windows glowed with soft light. Surrounded by barren branches, the place seemed lonely, eager to welcome any signs of life across its waiting threshold.

Cassie shivered as Adrian unlatched the garden gate.

"Are you cold?" he asked.

"A little." She hesitated, then allowed herself to rest against him. He understood at once how hard it was for her to admit weakness of any sort.

"So am I," he told her, wrapping a steady arm around her waist to help ward off the chill.

"I've missed you more than I thought," she murmured into his coat. "I'd forgotten how easy it is to talk to you. You've always seemed to know me so well."

He fumbled for the key as they walked up the cottage steps. "I'm honored that you think so," he said, opening the door and ushering her inside.

Cassie stopped in the middle of the room, eyes closed. "So cold," she said.

He could see that she was. Her cheeks were rosy, her lips a little chapped. A visible shudder raced through her.

"Poor Cassie," he said, suddenly remorseful. "I'm sorry. I shouldn't have insisted on the walk. I was feeling peevish."

"No, I liked the walk. I just need a few minutes to thaw."

He peeled off his gloves. "Give me your hands."

She held out her hands as obediently as a child. He worked her gloves over icy fingers, then enclosed her hands in his. They felt like little blocks of ice.

"You *are* cold," he said, stroking her fingers.

"Insubstantial evening wear." She managed a smile through chattering teeth. "And perhaps you were right after all about the impracticality of my shoes."

"You should have told me." He eased her closer, arms tight around her in an effort to calm her shivers.

She nestled against him, one errant strand of hair brushing his cheek. "Your mood was wicked enough when we left the Phillips's house. I was too tired to dodge your barbs."

It didn't take long for her shaking to subside.

"Better?" Adrian peered down at her.

She nodded. Then, without a word, she coiled an arm around his neck, tugged him toward her, and kissed him.

The kiss was sweet, nothing at all like the frenzied encounters he'd experienced in Europe. And yet, he sensed insistence beneath it, an invitation to so much more. Her hand slipped inside his overcoat to rest against his shirt; as if of its own accord, his finger traced the outline of her small ear, coming to rest beneath her chin. Her lips tasted of champagne, and it seemed that he could never drink enough.

Then, with a surprised gasp, she stepped out of his embrace. "Thank you, Adrian," she said, her cheeks pink. "I'm much warmer now."

He struggled for air as she backed away down the short hallway, ducking into the first bedroom as if it offered respite from a storm.

"Oh, look!" Her voice, steadier now, floated through his ears as he slowly removed his coat. "Mrs. Vickery has made up the other room after all. Shall I take that one?"

He watched her retreat, trying to find his voice. He wanted to tell her that he'd be happy to share his bed with her, that he'd be happy to share any space at all with her. Instead he simply nodded. "Take whichever room suits you," he said finally, tossing his coat onto the nearby sofa in an attempt at nonchalance.

She appeared in the hallway again. She'd discarded her cloak and her shoes, and pulled combs and pins from her hair as she walked. "Forgive me, Adrian, but I need to sleep. I'm exhausted. Must I really leave tomorrow?"

He stared, mesmerized, as thick locks of hair dropped about her shoulders in an uneven rhythm. "Stay," he said, and his tongue felt thick in his mouth.

She was in his arms again, and this time he was well aware of the press of her full breasts against his chest. "Thank you," she whispered into his ear, and was gone before propriety demanded that he ease her away. "Good night," she called over her shoulder. "I'll see you in the morning. Don't stay up too late."

He sank down onto the sofa as the bedroom door closed behind her, unable to face the visions of Cassie that would surely invade his dreams.

CHAPTER
27

Adrian propped himself on the edge of Bennett's library desk, one hand wrapped around the telephone receiver, the other holding a small tintype in a silver frame. A stern-faced woman stared back from the portrait, her piercing eyes an indictment of every decision he'd ever made in his life. He grimaced as he once again took in her stiffly boned bodice and the prissy little ruffles sewn at the shoulders of her dress. With her light hair plastered flat from a center part and that accusing glare, Elizabeth Chapman had clearly added a touch of disapproval to every occasion she graced.

Constance came on the telephone line so quickly that it was almost as if she'd anticipated his call. "I'd hoped to hear from you," she said, and the breathless lilt in her voice told him that she'd been working outside in her garden.

"You sound pleased with the world," he said. "Digging in the dirt, my dear?"

"The roses are growing wild, finally in full bloom. All of my flowers are splendid—there will be vaseloads to greet you when you come home. And the sun—simply glorious today! I dragged myself inside only because I had a feeling you might phone."

He could picture her, and it was far more pleasant than studying Elizabeth Chapman. Constance's blue eyes would be bright from a morning spent in the fresh air, her blond hair swept into a haphazard twist beneath the wide-brimmed straw hat she wore to shield her fair complexion from the sun's hot rays. Even with the hat, he knew his wife would go to bed that night with a mild sunburn across her nose and cheeks. Her skin would be warm to the touch, as yielding and fresh as ripe fruit.

Adrian allowed himself to savor the thought for a moment before continuing. "So you expected my call."

"I did. And you know that my intuition is seldom wrong." Her tone was prim, but he caught the playfulness behind the words.

"Very well, then, Mrs. de la Noye," he teased. "Your intuition led you into the house just as the telephone rang. Has it anything to say about the call itself?"

He heard a rustle and assumed she'd lifted the hat from her head. Much of her hair would escape its knot now: Constance never had enough hair pins. "Well," she said, "I'm afraid it says you aren't coming home today."

"Your intuition is correct. I'm so sorry, my dear. You know I'd like nothing better."

"Fortunately for you, I know that only a good reason would keep you away."

"Bennett Chapman has asked me to stay for his wedding. He and Catharine Walsh are to be married by Judge Thomas Bourne in Liriodendron's parlor early tomorrow evening."

"How lovely! Do send my regards, and tell the judge that he must come to dinner soon. Mr. Chapman must be delighted after spending so many years alone. I'll send a gift from the family tomorrow."

"Thank you."

"You sound less than thrilled, Adrian. Is there more?"

He glanced again at the picture in his hand. Elizabeth Chapman looked as if she might begin barking orders at any moment. "You'll remember that the late Mrs. Chapman brokered this marriage. I never met her. She passed away years before I'd even entered law school. But as you can imagine, I've developed a keen interest in her over these past few days."

"Of course," Constance said. "She keeps popping up in the oddest of places."

"I just came from an interesting breakfast alone with my client. He told me everything about his Elizabeth, spoke in great detail for over an hour about their years together."

"You've told me how overjoyed he is to be in contact with her again. They must have shared a wonderful marriage."

Adrian turned the tintype facedown on the desk. Since he hadn't married Elizabeth Chapman, he was under no obligation to endure her censure. "Now, that's where I'm baffled, Constance. They didn't. The union was an utter failure."

Even his usually loquacious wife was momentarily stunned into silence. "Goodness!" she finally said. "Are you sure?"

"Bennett's morning coffee might as well have been wine for as much as it loosened his tongue. I felt like a priest hearing confession. The marriage was arranged. He and Elizabeth were ill suited from the start. It seems he spent most of their years together . . . how to say this delicately . . ."

"Adrian, kindly dispense with decorum."

" . . . catting about."

"Frequently?"

Adrian thought of the satisfied curl of Bennett Chapman's lip as the old man recounted each extramarital conquest. "Incessantly," he said.

"Oh." He'd always appreciated his wife's ability to strip emotion from fact. She did not disappoint him now. "How interesting. Then why do you suppose Elizabeth Chapman has gone to such trouble to come back and suggest this second marriage?"

"That's what I'm hoping you can tell me. I'd originally thought she might want to see Bennett happy, but now I'm not so sure. I could use a woman's point of view in this."

"Hmm." He imagined his wife sinking into the chair beside the telephone table, brow furrowed in thought. "You're quite right, Adrian. After what he put her through during their years together, I doubt she cares a fig about his happiness now. The disenchantment probably made her rather dour."

"You can't imagine," he said, not even bothering to turn the tin-type faceup.

"Oh, but I can. You may forget any idea that she's returned through love. There's something else at work here."

"My thoughts exactly. Revenge, perhaps?"

"Is Catharine Walsh so odious?"

An image of young Cassie Walsh flooded his thoughts. It took a moment to remember that Constance had never heard of Catharine before this association with Bennett Chapman. "No," he said. "She's not."

If Constance wondered about his brief hesitation, she kept it to herself. "Perhaps I am a romantic, Adrian, but I prefer to think that once we pass to the other side, we become our better selves. I would hope that Mrs. Chapman has moved away from anger and pettiness. In addition, I can quite understand Mr. Chapman's affection for the wife he treated poorly during her lifetime. He's probably relieved to find that she's forgiven him. But something else prevents Elizabeth Chapman from enjoying her eternal rest. This is a lady with intent. What does Jim think?"

"We've yet to speak of it."

"You must remedy that. Jim Reid is a smart young man with a heart of gold. I'm sure he'll be able to help you."

"It's that heart of gold that concerns me most these days."

"Oh dear. Amy Walsh?"

"The same."

"Then guide him, Adrian. Don't leave him floundering. Our Jim deserves some happiness."

Adrian reached for the tintype. The frame was heavy and intricately carved; he was sure it was pure silver. Bennett Chapman had surrounded himself with the best his fortune could buy, from the fine food and bootleg liquor that graced his table to expensive objects of art that pleased the eye. Yet captured forever within the confines of this ornamental frame was the image of a wife who had grown to despise him. Even now, tucked away each night between luxurious sheets of Egyptian cotton, Bennett's grown children sent evil thoughts his way as they drifted off to sleep. No, Adrian didn't envy his client's substantial wealth. He had only to think of Constance and the children to know that he was the richer man.

"Adrian." There was a hint of weariness in his wife's voice now, but she quickly masked it. "Do what you must, but hurry home when you can. I miss you so very much."

"I miss you, too," he said, swallowing hard. "Constance . . . perhaps we should talk when I get home. There are parts of my life I've never shared with you . . . incidents that happened years before we met . . ."

There was a pause. "Do these incidents affect our present?"

He thought briefly of Amy. She was twenty-two years old. Would it even matter?

Constance continued. "Are you happy? Do you still love me and the children?"

"With all my heart."

"Then let your demons go, Adrian. We can certainly talk about them, but it's not necessary on my account. I knew you had a past when I met you, remember? You were jaded by war, had separated yourself from the Delanos . . . you were clearly damaged. But you were also intent on helping the Reids and earning your way in this world through your own merits. I knew a good man when I saw one, and I still do. You've no need to explain to anyone chapters of your life that were closed long ago."

He couldn't argue the point just yet. In some situations, it was best to gather facts before plunging in. "You're a remarkable woman, Constance de la Noye. Have I told you lately how fortunate I am to have you?"

"Not nearly enough," Constance said calmly. "But that can be easily remedied."

He fumbled for his cigarette case with one hand. "I'm afraid you may hear some unpleasant stories in these next few days. Nicholas Chapman is on a rampage."

"Oh, he's employed investigators? Then you may hear stories as well."

"Excuse me?"

"Have you ever considered that *everyone* has a past, Adrian de la Noye? When you employed me as your stenographer, you only asked if I could take and transcribe shorthand."

He slowly lowered the cigarette case to the library desk. "Darling. Is there something I should know?"

There was a long pause. Then Constance sighed. "No, darn it all. Aside from leaving the occasional broken heart here and there, I am perfectly spotless. But every once in a while I think it might be nice to be a woman of mystery. Hurry home, dearest."

Adrian smiled as the line went dead.

CHAPTER
28

Jim sat on the terrace for quite some time after Amy left, long legs stretched before him, feet resting atop the stone retaining wall. Amy's perfume, enmeshed in the threads of his tweed jacket from the hasty hug she'd delivered before leaving, mingled with the fresh salt air. Damn that hug. He thought he'd safely stowed away every romantic notion he'd ever had concerning the younger Miss Walsh, but that was before she'd flung herself into his arms, eyes shining with soft tears as she gazed up at him.

"Thank you, Jim," she'd said, a penitent picture of humility. "I don't deserve your kindness."

She'd drifted away before he could utter a protest, weaving her way back to the house like a weary little fairy in search of a leaf upon which to rest.

Had she wanted him to follow her? Should he have? In the end he'd jammed his hands into his pockets and turned toward the sea, tired of being every girl's buddy.

A jingle of keys stirred him from his reverie. Adrian crossed the flagstones from the house, the determined cadence of his steps indicating that there was a task at hand. Jim straightened. Adrian's jaw was set, his eyes clear. Finally—the composed man he'd admired for years had returned.

"Welcome back," Jim said. "So good to see you again."

"I've come from the house, not Outer Mongolia." Adrian did not break stride.

"I'm welcoming you back to rationality." Jim scrambled to his feet and fell into step beside him.

Adrian quirked an eyebrow as they rounded Liriodendron's massive corner. "I hadn't realized I'd ever left that state."

"You're joking, right? I thought I'd lost you for good. I was ready to telephone the good Mrs. de la Noye in the hopes that she knew of some antidote I could slip you."

"Come now, Mr. Reid. Surely it wasn't that bad."

Jim shortened his stride as he checked to see that no one was in earshot. "Oh, no? Let's just say that the sharp lawyer I know would have figured out days ago that Catharine Walsh wasn't Amy's aunt."

Adrian stopped. "I beg your pardon?"

Jim stopped too, nailing his mentor with a guileless stare. "Catharine Walsh grew up in your childhood home, didn't she? Surely you should have known whether or not she had any brothers or sisters, and you would have inquired as to which one had been lost."

He waited as Adrian brushed a nonexistent speck from the front of his sweater and looked up.

"That seems a bit of a stretch, Mr. Reid. Wherever did you get the idea that Miss Walsh grew up in my childhood home? I've certainly never told you that."

"Didn't have to." Jim folded his arms across his chest. "Do you remember what you used to tell my Granny Cullen every time she cut you a slice of her Madeira cake?"

"I've always had a weakness for Madeira cake. And your Granny Cullen had a wonderful way with it."

"So you often said. You'd tell her it must be a gift of the Irish, since the only other person in the world who could produce such a splendid Madeira cake was your family cook while growing up—a Mrs. Mary Walsh, another fine lady of Irish extraction whom you admired very much."

Adrian remained planted in the grass, a study in neutrality. Jim plunged on.

"It's no secret that you know Catharine Walsh. Maybe the Chapmans are too self-centered to figure it out, but Amy and I noticed at once. In fact, I'm willing to go out on a limb here and say that Catharine is the Cassie the late Mrs. Chapman spoke of last night."

"Oh, you think so, do you?"

"It's a mere deduction, but it makes sense to me. I'd never even heard of Miss Walsh before this trip, despite the fact that you've introduced me to various friends over the years. Yet you obviously know her fairly well. She shares a last name with a beloved servant from your past, and 'Cassie' is a common diminutive of 'Catharine' . . ."

Adrian began walking again, no more hurried than before. "I've called for the car. It should be around front by now. Suppose you come for a ride with me? I've an errand or two to run before we draft Mr. Chapman's will."

Jim quickened his pace to catch up to him. That was it? There'd be neither confirmation nor denial? In a way, it was a good sign. It meant that Adrian had regained enough possession of his faculties to give nothing away.

They slid into the Pierce-Arrow in silence. Liriodendron slipped away behind them as Adrian navigated the circular driveway and drove out the front gate. Jim leaned his head against the back of the seat and closed his eyes. Leaving the mansion was like leaving a well-appointed prison. If only he didn't feel a nagging pull back again, as if he'd left something important behind.

"Not bad, Jim," Adrian said. "I always knew you had it in you."

"What?"

"Yes, Cassie Walsh grew up in my boyhood home."

Jim blinked up at the automobile ceiling. "You're kidding. I'm right?"

"Why are you so surprised? You've a fine mind. Very well, then. What else have you deduced about me?"

"Not much. You're a man of many secrets. You'd have me believe you sprang fully grown from a battlefield during the Spanish-American War, and that only because of the actions of my father."

"There's some truth to that. Your father saved me in more ways than one."

"But you had to have a life for him to save in the first place."

"And?"

Adrian's pause was so expectant that it seemed a shame not to fill it. "Okay. You obviously come from a privileged background. There's nothing nouveau riche about your manners or your tastes; you've an eye for the finer things in life, and you know how to use them. You've also the means to acquire them. Now, I know your law firm provides a comfortable income, but you must have an alternative source of funds somewhere. Your kindness toward me and my family is a blessing, but certainly not an inexpensive one."

Adrian's eyes stayed glued to the road as he turned the steering wheel to make a smooth left turn. "True on all counts. My compliments."

"You seldom mention your parents. Are you still in touch with them?"

"Yes. When necessary."

"I bet your marriage didn't sit well." Jim slid his mentor a sideways glance.

"Now you're guessing," Adrian said.

"You agreed earlier to give me more information about your past."

"Not so. I agreed to give you enough information to aid our current situation. Be patient, Jim. I intend to keep my promise, and more, but allow me to choose the time. By the way, I've suggested to Bennett Chapman that we invite his late wife to join us for the wedding ceremony tomorrow night."

Jim twisted in his seat to face him. "You mean . . . as in a séance?"

"Any other way would be positively gruesome, don't you think?"

"Hmm. Are you sure this is wise? Having Bennett Chapman talk to his late wife in Judge Bourne's presence might only prove Nicholas's contention that his father is not of right mind."

"Again, you'll have to trust me."

Amy's tearful plea for safety played through Jim's mind like a stuck gramophone record. "I'm surprised Amy has agreed to do this."

"I haven't asked yet. After her explosion in the dining room this morning, I wasn't sure she'd be open to the request."

"Oh. Well, she won't be." Jim settled back in his seat. "She's scared to death."

"Scared?" Adrian frowned as he shifted gears.

"Apparently Mrs. Chapman gets more insistent each time she comes to call. Amy wants to keep her away. She's afraid that the late Mrs. C will show up one day and take up permanent residence inside her head."

Adrian paled, but it didn't stop him from continuing. "We're still missing crucial information. We need another opportunity to speak with Mrs. Chapman."

"You can suggest it, but . . ."

"I was hoping *you* would suggest it."

Jim smacked his palm onto the seat between them. "Ask me to do something else."

"I can't. It's clear that Amy Walsh wants nothing more to do with this, but it's crucial that we meet at least one more time. If anyone can persuade her to do so, it's you."

"Why me?"

"Need I really elaborate?"

"There's nothing between us anymore. I'm finished with it."

Adrian guided the automobile toward the curb, slowing to park. Down the cobblestone street a ways, several navy recruits escorted a group of giggling town girls toward a movie theater. Jim sighed as their laughter floated back to the town car. What would it be like to ask Amy out on a bona fide date, to casually slip an arm around her waist as he plunked down change for a ripping Douglas Fairbanks adventure? Or Valentino. Maybe Valentino would be a better choice. Amy might go all swoony over Valentino, and all those romantic feelings would have to transfer themselves *somewhere* . . . Without the trappings of Spookyville, was there a chance he and Amy might actually have a grand time together?

"Constance believes that a good woman might very well be the making of you," Adrian said, following Jim's gaze to the boisterous crowd down the street.

"Don't tell me that," Jim said glumly. "I thought your wife liked me."

"She does. Quite a lot. And not only is she an excellent judge of character, but I've learned over the years that her instincts are usually correct." Adrian turned off the auto. "I need to send a telegram, and then we'll go back to Liriodendron. That will give you plenty of time to speak with Amy before we begin drafting the will."

Jim opened his mouth to protest, then thought the better of it. His words wouldn't really matter anyway. Adrian had made up his mind.

Another thought struck him. "Adrian."

Adrian paused halfway through the auto door.

Jim cleared his throat. "Do you believe it's really Mrs. Chapman coming through?"

Adrian slid back behind the steering wheel, gaze focused straight out the windshield. "I didn't at first. But Mrs. Chapman delivers messages that undermine her messengers. She tells secrets nobody wants revealed. With that in mind, it's only logical to believe that neither Miss Walsh would choose to invent her."

"Logical?"

"Yes." He turned toward Jim, a hint of a smile crossing his face. "And don't forget: I knew your Granny Cullen too."

Jim followed him out into the sun. So Adrian believed. Knowing that made him feel more confident about his own instincts.

Talking to Amy would be about as much fun as bouncing a ball against his head. There wasn't much he wouldn't rather do. But perhaps the only way out of this situation was to help it finish in the same way it had begun.

CHAPTER
29

February 1898

Cassie slept deeply after the Phillips's dinner party, lost in the eiderdown and silence of the cottage guest room. Her dreams, born of fatigue and too much rich food and wine, churned through her mind in restless swirls. Most of them vanished before she could even begin to decipher them. But as dawn stretched into midmorning, they seemed to acquire a reality of their own, dragging her through landscapes and emotions she had no desire to visit. The down pillows, so soft and inviting throughout the night, transformed themselves into hellish clouds intent on smothering her. She clawed at her throat as strong fingers entwined around it. Spectral hands pushed against her shoulders, pinning her to a mattress that suddenly felt as unyielding as a hardwood floor. She knew what came next. Time was short. Struggling against drugged tides of sleep, she opened her mouth to shriek before an expected hand could clamp it shut.

"Cassie."

She heard her name but could not respond. Tears streamed down her face, and her shoulders shook with gulping sobs that seemed to come from her very core.

"Cassie!"

The spell of the nightmare shattered, releasing its ghosts into the air. Cassie's eyes opened. Adrian Delano leaned above her, one hand on her shoulder, the other grasped around the bedpost. His was the only familiar shape in the room. It took a moment to re-member that she was in a cottage in Newport, Rhode Island, as far away from Poughkeepsie as she had ever been in her life.

"Here." Adrian fumbled in his pocket for a handkerchief. Her senses still shrouded by the dream, Cassie could do nothing more than open her hand. He pressed the handkerchief into her palm and closed her fingers around it. "Are you all right?"

"I . . . I'm sorry. It was a dream, that's all. Did I wake you?"

She realized the moment the words left her lips that he'd been awake for some time. He was dressed in tweed knickerbockers, boots, and a collarless white shirt. He hadn't shaved, but his cheeks beneath the shadow of beard looked more olive than sallow this morning. He seemed full of light, as if a sunbeam shone down upon him. In fact, the whole room seemed brighter.

She pulled herself up to sit. "There's so much light! It's quite late, isn't it?"

"Yes, but it's more than that." He glanced around and found her robe hanging on a bedpost. "Here, put this on and come look."

He discreetly turned away as she slid from beneath the quilts and slipped the robe over her flannel nightgown. She padded across the chilly floor to join him at the window. Outside, the garden was blanketed with snow.

"It's beautiful!" she cried. "But what about the wedding tomorrow?"

Adrian looked like a cat about to purr. "There may be fewer guests, but I'm sure it will go forward as planned."

"Why do you look so pleased? It's not as if you've never seen snow before."

"This means we don't have to call on anyone today, and no one will call on us. No need to be sociable. I couldn't be happier."

"No!" She tugged her bathrobe more tightly around her. "I need those calls! I can't afford to lose a single opportunity if I'm to convince Peter Phillips—"

His gaze skewered her. "Oh, I don't know that it matters all that much, Miss Walsh," he said, and the sudden detachment in his voice made her shiver. "Between Peter's drinking and your determination, a day or two shouldn't make a whit of difference."

She tried to ignore the shame that washed through her. It was one thing to battle fate on her own, pushing bullishly through to achieve a necessary end. It was quite another to see the callousness of her plan reflected in Adrian's eyes.

"I can be very persuasive indeed," she said, but the words sounded as hollow as she felt and fell far short of bravado. Unexpected tears welled up in her eyes. She turned abruptly from the window, swiping them away with the handkerchief still crumpled in her hand.

"Cassie . . ." Adrian laid a tentative hand on her shoulder.

She glanced up at him, hoping to find enough condemnation in his expression to harden her backbone. But it was no use: his coldness had already evaporated, replaced by open concern. "Don't mind me, Adrian. I'm still in the throes of that awful dream, that's all," she lied.

"Would it help to tell me about it?" he asked. "Nightmares always seem less frightening in the light of day."

"It's the light of day itself that frightens me," she said, crumpling the handkerchief as if it had caused grave offense. "What am I to do, Adrian? I can't go back home. I just can't. I would rather die."

Adrian studied her for a long moment. She wished she looked better. There was nothing fetching about a tousled braid and an old chenille bathrobe to begin with, and she'd only enhanced their style with tearstained cheeks and red eyes.

At least he didn't seem to notice. "Come," he said. "Mrs. Vickery brought us breakfast this morning. I think the food will do you good."

He extended his hand. She allowed hers to rest inside it. His fingers were warm and strong, and an unexpected shiver raced through her. She glanced up, surprised.

"Cassie," Adrian said in a low voice, "you are worth so much more than you seem to think."

She wondered what he saw to make him think so. Damn him for going to Europe. Why couldn't he have stayed in Poughkeepsie where she might have confided the truth in him long before now?

She drifted into his open arms, resting her head against his shoulder.

"Perhaps we should play some backgammon." His voice was

soft in her ear as he stroked her hair. "For old time's sake. We can talk . . ."

Sleigh bells jingled outside, their gay chimes piercing the frigid air. Startled, Cassie stepped from the circle of Adrian's arms.

Peter Phillips's voice, unnaturally loud and hearty, penetrated the glass window pane. "Heigh-ho! Marjorie and I have come to rescue you from a day of boredom!"

Cassie hurried to the window, peering from behind the curtains so as not to be seen. "Dear God," she said, an excited flush coloring her face. "I'm not dressed. Adrian, can you talk to him until I'm ready?"

His only response was the slam of the bedroom door as he left the room.

FOR THE SECOND time in less than twenty-four hours, Catharine Walsh hauled her suitcase from beneath Liriodendron's guest-room bed. Kneeling on the floor, she flipped open the lid, propping it against the edge of the mattress. Although she'd returned most of her belongings to closets and drawers last night, she'd kept a few essentials packed away, just in case the need for an emergency flight should arise. None of that mattered now. Her hand slipped beneath a pile of lingerie, burrowing until her fingers brushed an object in the rear corner of the suitcase. She carefully withdrew a small bundle wrapped in a linen handkerchief. It was held together by a faded green ribbon, which came undone easily at her touch.

No matter how often she told herself that there was no need to look at these things anymore, there always came a time when the pull toward her past became more than she could ignore. Only two objects, but they were nearly all that was left from a time she could never fully reclaim.

She lifted a small sterling silver pendant first, willing her hands to stop trembling long enough to unlatch it. Nested inside was a curling lock of soft hair, so blond it was nearly white. The delicate curl had been clipped from Amy's head almost twenty years ago as the toddler tossed feverishly in her makeshift crib, leaving her anguished mother to wonder if she'd live until morning.

Catharine's stomach still clenched whenever she recalled that frightening winter. The sound of her child's piercing wails had been preferable to the possibility of only deathly silence coming from the crib.

She returned the pendant to the center of the unfolded handkerchief, then reached for the small tintype beside it. It had been taken in 1901, just after that horrible winter and shortly before she and Amy had left New York City for Chicago. Amy sat in an oversized chair, her little legs straight before her, hands clasped demurely in her lap. Her chubby cheeks reflected glowing health, as much a testament to her mother's sheer will as to the gradual sale of the few items of value Catharine had still possessed. Edith Delano's pearls, one of the final items to leave her possession, had paid for the heat, medicine, and food needed to restore Amy to health that winter, as well as for train tickets west and a fresh start. Even after all these years Catharine still blushed when she remembered the pearls. Desperation made people do despicable things. She still wondered what lie Adrian had spun to keep his family from pursuing her for theft.

Amy had survived, but she'd done so mainly because Catharine herself had always known how to endure in the face of adversity.

Catharine had always been able to see the bare essentials of any situation, and the truth had never burned more brightly than in that freezing New York garret during that dreadful winter: a marriage certificate might provide a thin veil of respectability, but one could neither eat nor buy medicine with it. In the end, it was merely a piece of paper, and a fairly useless one at that.

Catharine still didn't know what muse had inspired her to dress in her most refined attire that night Amy lay so ill, to scoop both child and blankets into her arms and carry her to the nearest doctor. "I need your help," she'd said, lower lip trembling. "My brother and sister-in-law have just died. I have little to offer you, but I promised them that I would do everything in my power to save their child. Please don't fail me."

The young doctor had straightened, eyes moist with emotion for the brave scene of dedication unfolding before him. For the first time, Catharine saw none of the pity or disbelief that followed her usual fable of widowhood. Suddenly she was a saving angel instead of a ruined girl, and Amy reaped the benefits.

It was a gift, this inherent knowledge of which part of her history could be jettisoned in order to stay afloat. Amy had not been the only one granted a new beginning through the fervent ministrations of the doctor. Catharine, too, had emerged reborn. Chicago had met the Walshes as aunt and niece, and if survival required the restrained distance of an aunt rather than the unbridled warmth of a mother, it seemed a small price to pay. Catharine had never looked back.

But, then, she seldom did. Even now, as she tenderly rewrapped her keepsakes, she did her best to avert her gaze from the initials embroidered in the corner of the handkerchief. Usually she paid them no mind. Today, however, it seemed that every steadfastly constructed wall around her heart had fallen. Her eyes focused on the initials as if there were nothing else in the room to see. AJD: Adrian James Delano.

Her head hurt. With a sigh, she leaned against the heavy night-stand and closed her eyes.

CHAPTER
30

Chloe Dinwoodie sat cross-legged on the flagstone terrace, eyes scrunched shut and palms upturned. Jim willed himself to turn straight around and head back toward the front of the house, but instead his pace slowed as he squinted in her direction. A votive candle burned next to her left knee, its flame flickering every time a breeze blew in from the ocean. Her lips moved in what he sincerely hoped was silent prayer, but as he drew closer, it became evident that Lady Dinwoodie would never be accused of doing anything silently.

"*Om mani padme hmmm* . . . Come to me, Spirit." Chloe's grating voice rose as the words rolled off her tongue. "Talk to me. I invite you! I *implore* you!" Her eyes flew open. "Damn it, Mother! Why do you show up for total strangers and not for your own flesh and blood?"

Jim tried to slip out of sight, but it was too late. Chloe nailed him with a gimlet stare. "Mr. Reid! No, no, don't slink away. I'm dying for some company. Let's face it, without Mother around to liven things up, this place is dull as nails."

There was no polite way to escape. Jim submerged a groan and made his way to the terrace.

"Please, Mr. Reid, tell me you've brought entertainment." Chloe blew out the candle.

"No. I'm sorry. Actually, I'm looking for Amy."

"Aren't we all? She tells us this morning that Mother has more to say, and then she vanishes from sight." She extended an arm. "Help me up, will you?"

"She's vanished?" Jim tugged Lady Dinwoodie to her feet, planting her firmly at arm's length before she could tumble forward into his arms.

Chloe glowered. "Oh, hold your horses, Romeo. I'm sure she's around somewhere. But, clearly, she's avoiding us all. Jesus, I'd forgotten how bloody boring it is here. You wouldn't happen to have a ciggie, would you?"

"Sorry."

She rolled her eyes. "No, of course you don't. I don't suppose the dashing Mr. de la Noye is anywhere nearby."

"Sorry again."

"Pity."

Chloe wore a bright saffron-colored frock with diaphanous scarves attached to the neckline. It didn't suit her, but Jim supposed she was trying for a free-flowing, spiritual effect. A thin line of gray detailed the roots of her bleached blond bob. One foot tapped an impatient rhythm against the flagstone terrace where, next to the pointy toe of her shoe, an empty flask lay on its side.

Chloe followed his gaze. "Yes, I'm out of hooch."

"I thought you—"

"Had given it up? I thought so, too. I had the best of intentions, but I'm bored to tears. If Mother doesn't plan to chat all that often, then what's the point of going clean?"

"Isn't it worth it for its own sake? Didn't you feel better?"

She stared at him, genuinely puzzled. "You really are a naïf, aren't you. Never mind, there's something quite fresh about it. How I'd love to be the one to corrupt you! Alas, there's no way to do it properly in this dull place. Now, if you ever find yourself in New York City . . ."

Jim took a giant pace backward as she stepped toward him. "I thought Newport was a party sort of town," he said, circling to the far side of the terrace table.

Either Chloe recognized defeat or she was just too bored to continue pursuit. She seated herself on the tabletop with an unladylike plop. "Not anymore, Mr. Reid. That ended years ago. Now this place just makes me feel old before my time, positively embalmed. Who'd want to live here, anyway?"

Voices carried from the garden. Bennett Chapman emerged from between the rosebushes, Catharine Walsh by his side. Jim peered more closely. Bennett's cheeks were ruddy, his posture straight. He looked fit enough to tackle a ten-mile hike.

"Perhaps *she'll* be willing to live here," Chloe said, tipping her head in Catharine's direction. "As far as I'm concerned, she's more than welcome to carry the keys to this colossal white elephant. I hate the place."

"You do? I should think Liriodendron would hold fond memories for you."

Her tone was positively withering. "Memories of what, Mr. Reid? Father didn't even begin building this place until 1897. I'd already been married off by then. And it's not as if Newport society was willing to embrace the Chapman family, anyway."

"Really?" Jim leaned slightly to his left in order to get a better view of Bennett and Catharine. They were too far away for him to hear their conversation, but even at this distance, he recognized indifference in the slump of Catharine's shoulders.

"New money," Chloe said flatly, following his gaze across the lawn. "Apparently it smells different from the old stuff, although I'm sure that distinction means nothing to our Miss Walsh there. Money is money, after all, and it all spends the same. Christ, Father looks wonderful, doesn't he? He's barely using his cane."

"Perhaps Miss Walsh is a tonic for him." Jim squinted. There wasn't a touch of the coquette in Catharine Walsh. Strange. A woman on the eve of her marriage ought to sparkle at least a little, whether or not her love for the bridegroom was lukewarm. Even the most jaded gold digger had the sense to keep her catch captivated through sheer flattery and appeal. Catharine looked about as lively as a human sacrifice.

"Perhaps she is," Chloe murmured. "And whatever I think of her, Mother must have her reasons for thinking Father should marry her. Who am I to go against my mother's wishes?"

Jim turned toward her, startled. "Does that mean you won't fight the new will?"

"It's hard to fight the dearly departed, isn't it? No, I'll leave the battling to my brother. He's got more at stake than I do, anyway."

Jim watched as Bennett planted an awkward kiss on Catharine's cheek. She accepted it with resignation. "Now that's something I have yet to understand, Lady Dinwoodie," he said. "I grew up in a family where making ends meet each week was a genuine challenge. Every day that ended with everyone gathered around a hearty supper was cause to celebrate. So, from my point of view, you and your brother have more resources than most folks could ever use in a lifetime. Why does it matter so much if your father changes his will and you have less? It seems a small exchange for his happiness. Unless, of course, you honestly believe that Miss Walsh will make him unhappy?"

"Oh, I'd worry more for Miss Walsh than for Father. She'll find out soon enough that he's an unprincipled old coot." Chloe's sigh blended with the soft swish of the surf. "No, you're right, Mr. Reid. My husband has enough personal income to keep me well. Nicky's another story. He's nearly flat broke. He's a gambler, you see, and he owes some dangerous people an obscene amount of money."

"How do you know this? It doesn't sound like the sort of conversation that comes up at the dinner table."

"Of course not. I found his cooked books in a drawer last year when I was looking for something to drink in the Boston house. He's been playing shady with his funds for years, trying to stay afloat until Pop dies and he can get his inheritance."

"Hmm. Unusually stupid to leave incriminating evidence lying about for your sister to find."

"Oh, he doesn't anymore. He keeps his paperwork in a safe here at Liriodendron now. The key never leaves his body. I think he even sleeps with it, which is just as well since he never sleeps with anything else."

Jim took a moment to digest the information. So Nicholas Chapman, with his superior airs and expertly tailored suits, was up to his ears in debt. "That certainly explains your brother's tenacity."

Chloe followed his gaze to Catharine Walsh. "He's going to need it. Catharine hates him, can you tell? She bristles every time he comes into a room."

"Yes, I'd noticed. Of course, he returns the favor. Lady Dinwoodie—"

She cut him off with a weary hand. "Just call me Chloe. It's clear I'm not your cup of tea, but there's no need to make me feel as if I'm moldering away in an English family crypt. I'm not that much older than you . . . am I?"

Jim calculated the decades between them and decided to sidestep the entire issue. "Chloe, why did you come to Newport if your father's will ultimately doesn't matter all that much to you?"

She flushed. "Mr. Reid, I take it your family is close?"

"Closer than I'd like, sometimes."

"Consider yourself fortunate. My father was a tyrant while we were growing up. Both Nicholas and I counted the hours until we could leave his home and strike out on our own. My brother may be difficult, but he is the only blood relation left who matters to me. I must make the most of it, despite the fact that I can no longer support his cause here."

"I understand."

Chloe stood, tugging her dress down across her hips as she did so. "As for me, I just want to leave. But I *would* like to speak to Mother again, learn how I can talk to my Margaret once I'm away from here for good."

"Your mother might be coming to the wedding."

"Oh!" Chloe stopped in mid-stoop, arm extended toward her flask. "Amy has agreed?"

"I haven't asked her yet. I suppose she could still say no."

"She could, but it's not likely if the request comes from you. She likes you, Mr. Reid."

His face grew hot. "Applesauce."

"No, really. A woman can tell." Her eyes strayed back to the couple down the lawn. "I'd say that Miss Amy Walsh carries a torch for you almost as high as the one Catharine Walsh carries for Adrian de la Noye."

Jim quickly wiped the surprised expression from his face. "Mr. de la Noye is happily married."

"As Catharine Walsh soon will be, we assume. What does that matter? Marriage has never been an impediment to true love, has it? You go find your Amy, Mr. Reid. I'll be in the dining room, refilling my flask from Father's stash."

He nodded an acknowledgment of her departure, but his eyes were fixed on Catharine Walsh.

So, now he could add Chloe Dinwoodie to the growing list of those who'd noted the connection between the bride-to-be and Adrian de la Noye. It didn't take a vivid imagination to recognize the unpleasantness that would arise should Nicholas catch on as well.

Deep in thought, Jim watched as Catharine Walsh planted a dutiful kiss on her fiancé's cheek and walked woodenly toward the house.

CHAPTER
31

Adrian brushed a speck of dust from Liriodendron's library desk blotter before setting his Corona 3 on top of it. Just unfolding the portable typewriter inspired hope. The Corona's presence meant that Bennett Chapman's Last Will and Testament would be typed in short order. Once typed, it was only a short step to the will's execution tomorrow evening, after which the town car could be called from the garage and pointed toward home. The Corona 3, inanimate though it was, held the golden promise that life might soon return to normal.

Fingers grasped his forearm. He swung to face his adversary, every muscle tensed.

"At ease," Catharine Walsh said. "It's only me."

He steadied his breathing. "I'm sorry. I didn't hear you come in."

Her hand brushed his sleeve before dropping to her side. "Good grief, Adrian. Are you always this jumpy these days?"

"No. But you must admit, these circumstances encourage one to remain on edge at all times."

She cracked a small smile. "I know what you mean. Chloe's blotto state of mind seems downright appealing."

He thought she looked pale. In general, she appeared more fragile than he remembered, but that might have been due to the library backdrop of massive wood furniture and rich colors. "Would you care to sit?" he asked, gesturing toward the chair behind the desk.

Catharine shook her head. "No. I'll be brief. Bennett is determined that you handle my legal affairs as well as his. I don't care what he tells you—I don't want our assets merged in any way. Do you understand?"

"Assets?" Adrian leaned against the edge of the desk.

"I have a few." Her finger traced the first bank of the Corona's keys. "I own my home in Sacramento, and there are some small bank accounts in my name."

"How have you managed all these years? How did you support both yourself and a child?"

A slight shrug made her gauzy dress shimmer in the sunlight that streamed through the window. "I've always been practical. You know that."

"What I know is that you've always mistaken scruples for jetsam and have never seen anything wrong in tossing them overboard whenever you deem it necessary."

Her hand froze above the typewriter keys. "I suppose you're entitled to that comment, Adrian. I may even deserve it. Say whatever you wish; just promise me that my current will can remain intact."

He tempered his tone. Surely the time for rancor had passed long ago. "I couldn't change anything without your consent anyway. You'd need to sign any final document I drafted."

"Give me your word all the same. I want everything I own to go to Amy. Nothing to Bennett."

The flush on her cheeks deepened as he studied her. "My word still matters to you?" he asked. "All right, then. I promise. But you shouldn't let it concern you so much. Bennett Chapman is nearly eighty years old. Chances are good you'll outlive him by decades."

"You never know. Life is full of unexpected surprises."

He didn't respond. He didn't have to. The fact that those words had fallen from her lips crossed so far into the realm of irony as to border on the ridiculous. Her gaze dropped to the carpet as the meaning of the sentiment sank in. He watched the motion of her throat as she swallowed, but it was hard to tell which emotions fueled her current silence.

When she finally looked up, her gaze was clear. "I've missed you, Adrian. How have you been?"

He caught the wistful note in her voice. She stood close enough that he could see the fine crow's feet at the corners of her eyes, the delicate lines framing her mouth. Occasional strands of silver threaded through her dark hair. As he'd noted before, they'd both grown older. But in the depth of her eyes, in that gentle curve of her jaw, she was still Cassie Walsh.

"I've been well, Cassie," he said, and this time, she did not flinch at his use of the diminutive. "But I won't lie to you: it took a very long time."

"I'm sorry." Her words trailed away. "I never meant to hurt you."

"Well then, what did you mean to do? What happened? Where did you go?"

She reached for his hand. "Does it even matter anymore? For what it's worth, I did come back to try and find you."

"You did?"

"Yes. I traveled to Poughkeepsie in early May after I . . . after we . . . parted. Rosie—the upstairs maid—was a friend of mine, and I tried to send you a message through her."

Adrian flinched as if struck. "I wasn't there."

"I know." Catharine squeezed his hand. "You'd gone to war. Rosie had to tell me at least three times before I understood the words. I couldn't believe it. Oh, Adrian, I wanted to see you so badly."

She might as well have kicked him in the stomach. If he'd only known that she needed him. So many of his decisions might have been different. "I . . . had no idea."

"No, of course you didn't. How could you? After the war, I couldn't find you. Now I know why. Rosie never said that you'd changed your name."

"Rosie didn't know. I first used de la Noye when I enlisted."

"Why?"

Her brittle shell had vanished. She stood before him so honestly vulnerable that there seemed no reason to keep his own defenses raised. The walls of the library slipped away as her hand nested in his.

He covered her fingers with his own. "I had to discover who I was without the patina of the Delano name. I needed to be taken at face value instead of sought after for my connections and wealth. And after our little escapade, you must admit that I owed my family a clean slate."

She stiffened. "Adrian, you do know that I never used you for your name."

"Now, how could I know that? I only knew that I'd apparently served your purpose and was no longer necessary."

"That isn't so!" she said fiercely. "It was never so. I knew very well what I was losing when I left you behind. Why do you think I tried to find you again? I never wanted to leave you!"

"Then why did you, Cassie?"

She stared at him, unable to speak. He recognized at once that any explanation would take much longer than the few minutes they'd allotted each other now. He thought of the thorny path she must have walked these past decades, all alone with a child to raise, and regret threatened to overwhelm him. If only he'd known. He could have made her way so much easier.

"Cassie, please. Tell me about Amy."

"There's so much I want to tell you," Catharine murmured.

A loud crash sounded from outside. Caught off guard, Adrian stood paralyzed for a moment before dropping Catharine's hand to rush toward the open window.

"What's happened?" Catharine appeared at his side.

"I'm not certain, but I have my suspicions." He leaned across the sill, scanning the landscape with a slow, practiced eye. A chair lay overturned on the grass below them. Farther down the lawn, a familiar figure darted in the direction of the garage.

Same jacket and knickers, same cap—spotting this character was becoming a habit that had to be broken.

"Please excuse me, Cassie," Adrian said as he hoisted himself through the window and dropped to the grass below. "We'll have to continue this conversation later."

CHAPTER
32

Jim emerged from the garage, stepping straight into the path of a rocket in tweed. His eyes widened as the tie pin he'd just fetched from the Pierce-Arrow slipped from his fingers. No doubt about it, this was the kid from the ferry—or, more precisely, the kid who'd been lurking around Liriodendron ever since their arrival, listening to conversations he wasn't meant to hear.

Hardly thinking, Jim took a step back from the boy's trajectory and stuck out his foot. The small figure tripped over it, stumbling into Jim's waiting arms with enough momentum to knock them both back against the garage wall.

"Caught!" Jim spun the boy around by the wrist, twisting his arm behind his back in a viselike grip. The kid struggled for a moment, then slumped in defeat. Triumphant, Jim yanked the concealing cap from his head.

Long blond curls tumbled down from beneath it.

"You're kidding," Jim groaned as Amy peered over her shoulder.

"Save me," she whispered, her face the color of paper.

He pushed her into the garage, then ducked in behind her. They pressed themselves flat against the inside wall as footsteps pounded past the door.

"Who's after you?" Jim whispered.

"I think it's Mr. de la Noye," she whispered back.

He stifled another groan. Just when he'd thought things couldn't get worse. "Ah, no, Amy, find another chump. I won't double-cross Adrian. He's not only my boss, he's my friend."

"It's not a double cross! Will you at least hear me out before you turn me in?"

He could barely make out her features in the dim light of the garage, but he sure could feel her shiver. Her slender fingers threaded through his.

He could see the face of his tombstone now—pudgy little cherubs hovering around one big fat word: *Sucker!*

Resigned, he dragged Amy toward the Pierce-Arrow, opened a rear door, and propelled her into the back seat. He closed the door behind them both with a quiet click. Together they slid down against the back of the seat.

"So, I was right before," he said beneath his breath. "This *is* how you do it. You listen in on private conversations and gather pertinent information to feed 'Mrs. Chapman.' Darn it, Amy, every time I accept the fact that she's real, you give me a reason to think otherwise."

"She *is* real." Amy's fists clenched into tight little balls. "I haven't lied to you, Jim Reid. Not once!"

"Oh, is that so? Then I suppose it's merely part of your daily routine to dress in disguise and tail people? You were on the ferry the night Adrian and I crossed from the mainland, weren't you."

"Yes, but—"

"And just yesterday Adrian caught you listening in on one of his telephone calls to his wife. Oh, yes. He noticed. I can only imagine how many other times we *haven't* caught you."

"It's not what you think!"

"What interests you so much, Amy Walsh? What information are you hoping to unearth by shadowing us?"

"I'm not interested in you at all!" Amy's voice rose.

Jim covered her mouth with his hand. "Shhh!"

She shoved his hand away. "You've got quite an ego, Mr. Reid. Did it ever occur to you that my reasons for sneaking around have nothing to do with you? I'm not tailing you and Mr. de la Noye. I'm tailing *them* . . . Nicholas Chapman and Lady Dinwoodie."

Jim blinked. "You are?"

"Yes! Catharine and I have been on the lookout for information ever since Bennett told us that his children were coming to Lirio-dendron to battle us over the will. I was on the ferry because I knew the chauffeur had orders to fetch Lady Dinwoodie when the boat docked. The reason Mr. de la Noye caught me outside the library is because that's my usual haunt. That's where the most private telephone in the house is located, so I can usually count on getting my best information there."

He felt as if a surprise witness had just undermined his case. "If you're not following us, then why did you listen in on Adrian's conversation with his wife?"

"Constance?" she asked brightly. "She seems quite nice."

Jim glowered at her.

"Oh, don't be a stick-in-the-mud. I listened because I was there. I listen to just about everything that goes on in that room. You wouldn't believe the things I know."

"Try me."

She twisted in her seat to face him. "All right. Nicholas Chapman is in debt up to his ears."

"No joke, Sherlock. I already knew that. It explains why he's so adamant about not changing the will, but it doesn't change much else, does it?"

"It does if you know the names and telephone numbers of his creditors, like I do. He's got some pretty shady characters on his back."

Jim dropped his head against the back of the seat. "Believe me, Amy—you don't want to get involved with that element."

"No, of course I don't. But Nicholas Chapman hates me and Catharine. He'd be thrilled out of his gourd to see us behind bars. You don't think I'm going to sit around and just let that happen, do you? If he pulls something on me, I'm going to pull something right back."

"Not above a little blackmail, then, are you?"

"You got that right. A girl's got to live defensively."

He was silent for a moment. In truth, Amy's tactics weren't all that different from the ones he'd used to thwart neighborhood beatings while growing up. What God hadn't granted him in brawn, He'd more than supplied in brain.

"Can't judge you when I've done it myself," he said. "What else do you know?"

"And why should I even bother to tell you?"

"So I don't turn you in, you bird."

Amy hesitated. "Do you want to know about the Chapmans, or about Cassie Walsh and Adrian de la Noye?"

His skin prickled in the dim light of the garage. "Come again?"

"You heard me, Jim. We've both wondered about that association, haven't we?"

Was it fair to gather information behind his mentor's back? After all, if Adrian wanted him to know something about his past, surely he would mention it himself.

On the other hand, everyone occasionally needed protection from himself.

He stared up at the automobile ceiling. "Okay, Amy," he said. "Spill."

CHAPTER
33

February 1898

Cassie shivered as Adrian knelt to lace her ice skates, but she had to admit that the bitter wind whipping across Almy Pond wasn't entirely to blame for the chill. She snuggled more deeply into her coat, searching for a spot of warmth. The boulder she sat upon felt as frigid and unyielding as the ice itself. Still, even that could not account for the cold lump of coal that had taken up residence in the pit of her stomach.

She jumped as a jolt of pain snaked through her toes. "You're lacing too tightly," she said, tapping the top of Adrian's glossy black head.

"Marjorie's skates are too small for you." He didn't look up. "Not unlike this entire situation."

She winced as he gave the lace another yank. "The skates aren't that small. I'll manage just fine. Besides, I don't plan to stay on the ice for long."

This time he did look up, cheeks nearly the same color as the scarlet earmuffs he wore. "What, pray tell, do you mean?"

"Ahoy there, you two!" Peter Phillips's voice, jolly in the extreme, floated across the ice as he skated toward them from the bluff where he and Marjorie had donned their own skates.

"Cassie, what do you mean?" Adrian hissed again as Peter weaved gracefully between other skaters on the pond.

"It's none of your concern, Adrian Delano. Ouch! Loosen the lace, will you?"

He untied the offending lace, easing her right foot into a more comfortable position within the skate shoe. "Everything about you seems to have become my concern," he said. "How did that happen, do you suppose?"

She opened her mouth to retort, but Peter had skimmed to a stop before them, hands clasped loosely behind his back. He seemed impervious to the cold, fueled perhaps by the fact that he was an excellent skater on a familiar pond, but probably more by the flask protruding from his pocket. "I know there's quite a crowd here today," he said, "but that's no reason to be unsociable. Marjorie and I would have gladly made room for you both on our roost over there."

"Appreciate it, Peter," Adrian said, frowning as his fingers nimbly looped Cassie's skate lace. "But why huddle together when there are so many other boulders and bluffs available?"

Peter bent toward Cassie, gloved hand framing one side of his mouth as he stage-whispered into her ear. "I'll tell you a secret, Miss Weld. Your cousin speaks of elbow room, but the truth is that he's given to fits of melancholy and far prefers to keep to himself. He's welcome to his solitude but, please, don't let him drag you into the cave with him."

Cassie ignored Adrian's scowl. "This isn't news to me, Mr. Phillips. And, please, do call me Kate."

"Peter, then. Adrian, I see you're already laced up and ready to skate. Why don't you go help Marjorie? She's painfully slow. I can help Kate finish here."

Adrian cleared his throat. "No, that's quite all right. I feel responsible for my cousin, you see, and—"

Peter's good-natured shove sent Adrian sprawling on the ice. "I promise to take excellent care of her," Peter said, crouching before Cassie. "Scat, my friend. Your cousin is safe with me."

Cassie rewarded Peter with a radiant smile as Adrian picked himself up and skated off, his clouded expression matching the ominous skies. Peter acknowledged Cassie's smile with a beam of his own, but it was hard to harness her attention to his gaze. He was handsome enough in a well-fed, florid sort of way, but a certain vacuity on his face made her wonder if his family had endowed Harvard in some fashion to ensure his graduation from its law school.

"Poor Kate," Peter said, enclosing her ankle in a firm grip. "I can't believe your family thought a visit to Mr. Misery would cheer you up. Might as well string up a noose for your use, or leave a cordial glass of strychnine lying about the house. Don't worry, I've come to rescue you. We'll remedy this sad situation at once."

"I count myself fortunate that you've arrived," Cassie said, allowing her gaze to stray above his head as he removed his gloves and bent over her skate. Adrian glided slowly across the pond, hands jammed deep into his coat pockets. Silhouetted against the silvery gray sky, his slouching figure conjured images of a prisoner meeting a firing squad at dawn. He straightened as he approached Marjorie, who offered him a sunny smile from her perch on a blanketed bluff.

Peter finished lacing and glanced up to follow her gaze. "My sister has been sweet on your cousin for years. Has she any hope at all, do you think?"

Cassie considered. Marjorie was nice enough, she supposed . . . getting a bit old to be a dewy society bride, but still attractive in a practical, capable sort of way. Still, Adrian could do better. "My cousin and I haven't spoken of it," she replied.

"Ah. That's not a good sign. If Adrian hasn't said a word, then he isn't smitten."

Adrian settled himself before Marjorie. His tug on her skate lace evinced more stoicism than ardor.

Cassie forced her attentions back to Peter. "And what about you?" she asked. "Do you babble incessantly when smitten?"

He glanced up, grin playing about his lips. "That all depends. Have I more reason to hope than my sister does?"

"Perhaps," she said, eyes downcast.

His hand rested lightly on her shin. "Then I might become very loquacious indeed."

Cassie cast a gaze from beneath lowered lashes. "I'm all ears," she said.

Peter's eyebrows disappeared beneath a shock of blond hair. "Are you, now. You're not as gloomy as your cousin, are you?"

She tossed a quick glance in Adrian's direction just as he rose to his feet. His eyes met hers. Her cheeks grew warm as she realized that Peter's hand still rested on her limb. "I'll let you be the judge of my disposition," she said, rising to her feet so that his hand slipped to the ice.

"I look forward to finding out." Peter stood as well, and the teasing note in his voice made it clear that the bait had been taken. Her heart skipped so erratically that she nearly lost her breath. She grasped the arm he presented, for without its support, she hadn't the strength to remain upright on the ice.

Peter squeezed her hand. "Have you never skated before? Don't worry. I'll keep you safe."

Her cheeks flamed. Of course she'd skated before. She'd spent childhood winters racing Adrian, who now narrowed his eyes in answer to the stare she sent across the ice. A slow, grim smile spread across his face. She watched as he turned to Marjorie and offered his arm with a graceful flourish. Marjorie blossomed under the unexpected attention, her face nearly glowing with delight.

"There. It's not so hard, is it. You're doing quite well." Peter's words made her realize that they'd begun to move. They glided between the other skaters on Almy Pond, Peter supporting her with a firm arm about her waist.

"I learn very quickly," she murmured.

Across the pond, Adrian squired Marjorie along the ice with exaggerated courtliness, beaming down at her as if she'd just said something terribly clever.

"Perhaps Cupid has heard my sister's pleas." Peter's lips were quite close to her ear. "Our Adrian seems to be paying a little more attention than before."

"Yes," Cassie said absently. Adrian didn't care for Marjorie in a romantic way. What was he doing?

Her train of thought came to a thudding halt as Peter pulled her even closer. His breath came in short little puffs. "Let's skate away from the crowd," he said. "It will be easier for you to learn if you're not tripping over other people."

Adrian's retreating figure flattened like a paper doll against a turbulent sky. Cassie allowed herself one last lingering gaze as Peter guided her toward a quiet cove.

"They skate quite well together," she said in a monotone. Then, swallowing back an unexpected swell of nausea, she drew in a bracing lungful of air and twisted artlessly toward the man beside her. Her lips brushed his. His brushy mustache tickled enough to inspire a nervous giggle but, fortunately, she didn't need to do much more to encourage Peter further. His arm tightened around her waist as he pulled her firmly against him, and his own lips pressed so hard against hers that she knew he'd been hoping for this opportunity all along.

The kiss was acceptable, urgent enough that she knew he'd welcome more, but not so passionate that she was in any danger of losing her head. She let it continue a few seconds longer than the rules of respectable coquetry allowed before pulling away.

"Oh!" she cried, hands flying to cover her mouth. At least the expression of raw longing on Peter's face made it unnecessary to feign her blush. "Oh, Mr. Phillips, you must forgive me!"

Peter tamed his own emotions quickly, arranging his face into a properly respectful mask as he reached for her hand. "No, please, I'm the one who must apologize. I quite overstepped."

"What you must think of me!"

"I have only the utmost admiration for you. You mustn't fret. Please. If you do, I'll live with the burden that I've behaved more monstrously than can ever be forgiven."

"That's never happened before," she said. "I can't imagine what came over me."

She checked for the expected hint of smugness in his pleased smile and found it. That did not surprise her; in her experience, most men thrived on flattery. But there was something else in Peter's smile, and she recoiled slightly as she realized what it was: Peter Phillips honestly believed that she'd been unable to resist the superior wonder of his masculinity.

"I can't speak to what came over you," he said. "I can only hope the impulse finds you again."

She rested her gloved fingertips atop his coat sleeve. "And . . . if it does, may I trust that you'll keep this matter confidential . . . a secret between us alone?"

A bright flush of anticipation colored his face up to the roots of his hair. "Oh, of course! Upon my honor. I would rather die than do you harm, Kate." He stroked her hand. "Perhaps, then, we have an agreement? I may come to call?"

"I'm afraid I won't be in Newport very much longer," she said.

He leaned toward her mouth again, but she turned her head. "I understand," he said, patting her hand in deference to her modesty. "But perhaps you will give me the opportunity to convince you that affection such as ours doesn't require much time to grow after all."

Cassie shot a glance across the ice as Peter led her from the cove. The spot where she'd last seen Adrian and Marjorie had filled with strangers. She craned her neck to find them in the crowd, but they were nowhere to be seen.

A fist tightened in her chest. "I would especially not want my cousin Adrian to know of this," she murmured.

Peter's arm stiffened as he drew her closer. "Believe me, Kate, neither would I. You may rest assured that the secret is safe with me. Shall we skate?"

Damn Adrian. Where had he gone?

"No," she said quietly, pulling herself back to the task at hand. "Could we perhaps sit in your sleigh for a bit? I've a chill."

Peter's voice turned to warm maple syrup. "Of course," he said. "Anything for you, Kate. Anything at all."

CHAPTER
34

Jim hoped that the dinner parties over which Mrs. Chapman had presided during her lifetime were more agreeable than the ones her spirit inspired now. He paused at the threshold of Liriodendron's dining room, reluctant to wade through the invisible waves of tension to take his place at the table. There was nothing new about the general disdain that emanated from Nicholas like a shriveled aura. Jim even understood Chloe's peripatetic dislike for the world at large. But there were new undercurrents at play here. It was hard to miss the poisonous glances Amy sent her mother. And here came a glare especially for him, as dripping with venom as the one Amy had just lobbed at Catharine. Of course, given the way their conversation in the Pierce-Arrow had ended, this wasn't a huge surprise. And if that was the way little Miss Walsh wanted it, he could take it.

But Adrian . . . Adrian, his friend and mentor . . . was it his imagination, or had Adrian become distant and overly polite toward him as well?

It was downright disconcerting, especially when any rancor between Adrian and Catharine Walsh seemed to have vanished. Was that an accidental brush of hands as Catharine reached for her water glass? It was hard to tell, especially when Adrian made no effort to move his own hand from her path.

"Mr. Reid." Adrian turned a level glance his way. "Do you plan to join us at the table?"

Jim lifted his chin and strode toward his chair. "Sorry to have kept you waiting," he said, staring Adrian directly in the eye. If the air between them had grown chilly, he had a sneaking suspicion he knew the reason why . . . and damned if he'd shoulder all the blame himself.

He'd half expected trouble when he'd knocked on Adrian's bedroom door earlier that afternoon. "Amy said she'd allow Mrs. C to attend the wedding," he'd announced as his colleague swung open the door.

An expression of surprised approval had crossed Adrian's face. "Good for you, Mr. Reid. You've outdone yourself with your powers of persuasion."

Truth was, persuasion had played a very small part in Amy's acquiescence. After listening to her account of Adrian's conversation with Catharine, Jim had simply turned the tables by offering to keep her spying expeditions a secret if she'd agree to let Mrs. Chapman through for the wedding ceremony. The use of blackmail in this situation had not sat well with him. Neither had the fact that after his chat with Amy, he now had secrets of his own to keep from the man he'd trusted all his life.

He'd shifted his weight from one foot to the other, eager to end the exchange. "Yes, well, at least that's taken care of. Let's go. We've got Mr. Chapman's will to finish, right?"

Adrian's searching gaze had practically seared a hole through his forehead. "Would you step inside here for a moment, Mr. Reid?"

"Sure."

The aroma in Adrian's bedroom was a soothing combination of vetiver oil and tobacco. Jim had breathed deeply and waited, a fraternity pledge bracing for a hazing.

"I caught sight of our little friend again today," Adrian had said.

"The boy? Where?" Jim's nonchalance had bordered on ennui.

"Listening at the library window. I took up chase this time, but he had a sizeable lead and I couldn't catch him."

Jim had nodded, marveling at how easily sins of omission seemed to come to him. "Do you think the kid heard anything he shouldn't have?"

Adrian's hesitation had not passed unnoticed. "No," he'd finally said.

Perhaps it had been unfair to push, but after hearing Amy's account of the conversation in the library, it had raised Jim's hackles that Adrian wasn't more forthcoming. "Another conversation with Constance, I suppose?" he'd asked casually.

"No. I was speaking with Catharine Walsh."

"Ah. I see." He'd paused for more, but it hadn't come. "Did the conversation turn up anything you'd care to share?"

Adrian had coolly met his gaze. "No."

"Nothing at all?"

"Nothing at all. And did you happen to catch a glimpse of the boy as he fled?"

For the first time he could remember, Jim had not blushed at an inopportune moment. He'd merely tilted his head in acknowledgment of the question. "No," he'd replied evenly, and his voice had echoed in the quiet room.

They'd spent the rest of the afternoon drafting Bennett Chapman's will, leaving little space for any discussion of a non-professional nature to pass between them. Now, noting the subtle glance Adrian sent Catharine, Jim wondered if that had been such a good strategy.

"Mr. Reid!" Bennett Chapman's booming voice reflected his newfound vigor. He alone seemed pleased to be seated at the table that night. "You've heard the good news? My Elizabeth will join us for the wedding ceremony tomorrow evening."

Jim ignored the murderous scowl Amy threw from his right; it only confirmed the fact that she was still steamed by the bargain they'd struck in the car. "You must be very pleased," he said. "It's not often a second marriage gets full endorsement from the first wife."

Bennett continued undeterred. "Very true, young man, and I can't tell you what a blessing it is."

"And my father's will, Mr. de la Noye?" Nicholas's words floated like toxic fumes from the foot of the table. "I suppose it's ready for immediate execution following the ceremony?"

"Yes," Adrian said. "Mr. Reid and I have done our parts to ensure that the events of tomorrow evening flow smoothly."

Nicholas shook his head. "You amaze me, sir."

"Thank you, but it's nothing astounding. I'm merely an attorney following the directions of my client. Bennett, I believe everything is in order, but since Mr. Reid and I are here, perhaps you'd care to review the document after dinner this evening?"

Bennett had lifted the silver dinner bell and sat poised to ring. "Oh, I'm sure the will is as meticulously drafted as is your usual custom, but I'll take a look later if you think it might speed matters along tomorrow."

"The will is incomplete," Amy said, so low that Jim was surprised anyone else heard.

"It's Mother who says that, isn't it?" Chloe clapped her hands. "She's come back!"

Bennett set the dinner bell down onto its clawed feet without ringing it. "I don't think she ever left," he said. "Elizabeth, my sweet! How lovely that you've joined the conversation. What's wrong with the will? I gave Mr. de la Noye very complete instructions based on your wishes."

"Mother dictated the will, too?" Nicholas asked. "Is there anything she can't do now that she's crossed over?"

Amy's knuckles whitened as she gripped the edge of the table.

"You don't have to do this," Jim murmured beneath Chloe's loud reprimand of her brother. "You only promised us tomorrow."

A fine sweat beaded her forehead. "I've been trying to ignore her, but she insists on being heard. Jim—I know things aren't right between us, but you'll look after me, won't you?"

"Of course. I gave you my word."

"Elizabeth," Bennett repeated, "what more does the will need?"

Jim followed the older man's gaze to a spot beside the fireplace. The teardrop crystal prisms dangling from a candlestick on the mantel swayed softly, as if teased by a summer breeze.

"Mrs. Chapman says that it will take very little to perfect the will," Amy said. "She says that Mr. de la Noye has done a thorough job with the facts you gave him, but that you did not have all the necessary information. Now you do. As written, the will directs that the bulk of your estate pass to your wife—Catharine Walsh Chapman—upon your death."

Jim checked: Amy had grown very pale but seemed collected.

"What more do you suggest we add?" Adrian asked.

"Issue," Amy said. "Catharine Walsh's issue."

"Ah." Adrian leaned back in his chair. "Children."

"Child," Amy corrected. "Mrs. Chapman wants to make it clear that all of Catharine Walsh's inheritance should pass to her child . . . to me. She wants no interference with that."

Nicholas's accusing stare landed on Catharine. "How surprising that this matter should arise," he said.

Catharine locked her own stare to his. "Kindly keep your vile insinuations to yourself."

"And how interesting that the point is brought up by the beneficiary herself." Nicholas's voice cut like a thin, sharp wire.

Adrian silenced him with an open palm. "Surely Mrs. Chapman knows that whatever Catharine inherits will become hers to do with as she pleases. The will can do very little about that. A trust, perhaps . . ."

The crystal prisms on the fireplace mantel swung back and forth as if trembling. "Write it as I say!" Amy commanded.

Jim snapped to attention, startled by her vehemence. Amy blinked hard, then relaxed in her chair. "I'm sorry," she said. "I'm not sure what just happened. But Mrs. Chapman is adamant that there be no misunderstanding."

"Of course." Bennett nodded, puzzled. "Whatever you think best, Elizabeth."

"I'll take care of the matter immediately after dinner," Adrian said. "Is that all Mrs. Chapman wants to tell us?"

Amy cocked her head for a moment, listening. Her shoulders relaxed as she breathed a relieved sigh. "That seems to close the matter of the will," she said.

"Then perhaps Mother could simply stay and chat," Chloe suggested hopefully.

"No." Amy lifted the napkin from her lap to blot her forehead. "I'm tired. I just want to eat my dinner and go up to my room."

"And that's it?" Nicholas asked. "You turn 'Elizabeth Chapman' on and off like a faucet, and we're to accept your edicts simply because you say they come from her? How foolish do you think we are, Miss Walsh? Or have you been so manipulated by your mother that you no longer recognize when your voice spouts her lies?"

Catharine shot from her chair, fists clenched. Adrian curled a warning hand around her wrist as she took a blind step in Nicholas's direction.

The candlestick on the mantel began to vibrate, knocking the crystal teardrops together in a cacophony of chimes. Amy rose majestically to her feet, head held high. She swiveled to face Nicholas, left hand slammed to her waist, right arm stretched straight before her, index finger extended toward his nose.

"You are indeed foolish beyond measure, my son," she said in a low-pitched voice. "You are to accept these words because I, Elizabeth Chapman, have indeed delivered them."

"Mother!" Chloe cried.

Jim stared into Amy's face. A pair of glittering, vacant eyes met his. He scrambled to his feet, sending his chair crashing to the floor.

Catharine Walsh rounded Amy's other side, landing a shaky hand on her shoulder. "Amy! Amy, stop this now!"

Amy's hand shoved Catharine away. "Please, Miss Walsh. I am very fond of you, despite your stubborn pride. 'O what a tangled web we weave when first we practice to deceive.' But I will not be manhandled. Step aside."

Jim grabbed Amy's wrists. Surprised, she turned toward him. "Give her back, Mrs. Chapman," he ordered. "She isn't yours. Give her back now."

A satisfied smile crossed Amy's face. "Good, Mr. Reid," Elizabeth Chapman said. "At least one person in this room has sense. Good night."

Amy's eyes rolled back as she collapsed into Jim's arms.

CHAPTER
35

S he's sleeping," Catharine said, pausing in the doorway of Adrian's bedroom like a street waif with no place to call home.

Adrian nodded slowly. "Did she say anything about what happened in the dining room?"

"No. She still won't talk to me. But Mr. Reid offered to stay with her a little longer. Perhaps she'll speak to him if she wakes up."

Adrian mulled over her words for a moment, surprised that Jim had elected to stay by Amy's side. After their conversation in town, he'd gotten the distinct impression that his associate preferred to relegate any further contact with the younger Miss Walsh to a purely professional level. Of course, Jim had been acting peculiarly all afternoon.

He slipped his arms from the sleeves of his dinner jacket, still deep in thought. "What did Mrs. Chapman mean tonight?"

Catharine entered the room, partially closing the door behind her. "Which part? I'm so very tired of everything Mrs. Chapman says."

"'O what a tangled web we weave . . .'"

"' . . . when first we practice to deceive.' *Marmion*. Sir Walter Scott."

"I'm aware of the source. I'd like to know why she said it to you."

Catharine sank into the armchair before the maple secretary. "Why does she say anything, Adrian? Why has she come at all? There are moments when I fear she'll stay with us forever. It's a nightmare."

She looked particularly wan, hardly a glowing bride on the eve of her wedding. A small shiver traveled through her, raising the gooseflesh on her slender arms. Without a word, Adrian crossed the room to drape his dinner jacket across her shoulders.

"Thank you," she said, raising her eyes to meet his. "Adrian . . . you do believe me when I tell you it's Mrs. Chapman who's decided I should marry Bennett? This isn't some plan I've devised. All of this is just as startling to me as it is to everyone else."

Adrian looked away. "Frankly, I don't know what to believe anymore."

"No, that won't do." She stood, clutching his jacket around her. "It would kill me to think you didn't believe me. I've never lied to you, Adrian . . . to others, perhaps, but never to you."

He could not help his rueful smile. "Yes, I remember. You never quite lie to me. You just leave out the details. What am I to do with you? All those wounds you inflicted so many years ago finally heal and then back you come, waltzing into my life as if we were merely parted by a few months abroad."

Her sigh pierced his heart. "I'm sorry. Is it so awful to see me again?"

"No," he said gently. "I wish it were. Cassie . . . tell me about Amy."

Catharine slipped past him, avoiding his gaze as she walked toward the nightstand by the bed. Adrian watched in silence as she reached for the framed picture there. He knew the photo well—he tucked it inside his suitcase whenever he traveled.

"Yours?" Catharine asked, raising it to take a closer look.

"Yes. My wife and children."

"You've a lovely family, Adrian." Her voice seemed pitched a little higher than usual. "How long have you and . . ."

"Constance."

" . . . been married?"

He crossed to her side, lifting the photo from her hand in one smooth motion. His wife's impish grin met his. "It's been over sixteen years now."

"And the children?"

"Grace is nearly fifteen, Ted is twelve."

"You're happy."

"Yes." The admission felt almost like a betrayal. "Jim Reid's father may have saved my life on the battlefield, but Constance saved my soul."

"I don't suppose you've ever told her anything about us?" She quirked an eyebrow, waiting.

He swallowed. "It's never seemed necessary."

Catharine drifted toward the window, parting the heavy curtains to stare down at the circular drive. "I see. So I'm not the only one who omits details that simply don't seem to matter."

Adrian rocked back on his heels. Bull's-eye. "You must understand that I needed to start again."

"Never mind. It's not important. You're content. You might even be at peace, provided you've learned over the years to let yourself be so. And with all that in mind, why should Amy's paternity even matter?"

"Don't you think it's something I should know?"

"It wouldn't change a thing that's passed between us, no matter how much I might wish otherwise."

He joined her at the window, staring out over her shoulder at absolutely nothing. The night sky glowed with a full moon and enough stars to lend a slight nimbus effect to Catharine's dark curls. Her perfume scented the air, as richly hypnotic as a field of poppies.

She was so different from Constance. His wife had been born with an innate honesty that left no room for emotional subterfuge. With Constance, one always knew precisely where one stood. She was as open and honest as a spring day on the prairie, delighting in the simple joys life offered. Cassie came with more mysteries than a man could ever hope to unravel in one lifetime. She surrounded herself with walls that required scaling, with layers that needed to be steadily stripped away. It took a lot of work to touch Cassie's heart.

Unfortunately, Adrian knew all too well how much that effort could yield.

He rested a gentle hand on Catharine's shoulder. She twisted around to face him, so close that he could see the tiny flecks of gold in her dark brown eyes. Responding to a distant memory, his arms wrapped around her, cradling her protectively as she rested her head against his shoulder.

She shuddered against him. "I want to tell you the whole story, Adrian, but I'm afraid."

"Afraid of what?"

"It's just harder than I thought. I had everything securely tucked away, hidden from view. I never expected to see you again."

"Perhaps telling me would bring you some peace," he whispered into her hair.

She raised her head to look at him. "I hope you've been able to find some," she murmured. "I've always wished it for you."

She eased herself from his embrace, allowing the dinner jacket to slip from her shoulders to the floor. When she curled back into his arms this time, the warmth of her body beneath her sheer frock made his heart pound. He drew her closer, half afraid she'd never leave, half afraid she would. Random details bubbled through his mind until it was hard to tell where memory ended and the present began. He remembered how she'd tremble if he kissed that spot behind her ear, how she'd loved when his fingers played through her curls. She'd liked to press her body so close to his that it seemed nothing could ever come between them. They stood that way now: hip to hip, breast to breast, so near it seemed they could block out the rest of the world.

He licked suddenly dry lips. "Cassie . . ."

Surprise lit her face as he eased her away.

"I'm not at liberty to do this." He hoped to eventually forgive himself for the undercurrent of regret in his voice. "And neither are you. You're engaged . . . nearly a married woman."

"Again," she said softly.

"Again," he allowed, although the word rekindled a sick roiling in the pit of his stomach.

"Just once? Could we be together just one more time? I would dearly love to feel something again. How wrong can it be if we've done it before?"

Years melted away as Cassie Walsh awaited his answer, each soft breath more hopeful than the last. All of her carefully crafted walls had finally fallen, leaving her more exposed to him than if she had slipped off her shimmery dress. Her yearning jarred his very core.

She studied his face. He could only stare back, unable to speak. For one brief moment, as she stood before him in the moonlight, 1921 collided with 1898, and he wanted her more than he'd ever wanted anything in his life.

"No," he finally said.

She hesitated, then brushed a kiss against his cheek. "You always were a gentleman at heart," she said wistfully. "And I loved that about you. Good night, Adrian."

He watched as she walked toward the door, unable to tear his eyes from her parting figure. A portion of his heart protested that he was making a terrible mistake, that he was once again allowing something dear and valuable to slip through his fingers. But Constance—his wife—was the one who'd defined dear and valuable for him in the first place.

His throat tightened. He could not leave Liriodendron fast enough. Until then, he would avoid Cassie Walsh, see to it that they were never alone. One more day; that's all that was required of him. He could manage anything for one more day.

Cassie turned as she reached the door. "Amy isn't yours, Adrian, but I wish with all my heart she were."

His stomach began to churn, sending bile to the back of his mouth. His vision blurred as he stared at her. "Whose then?" he demanded, and he barely recognized the hoarse voice as his own.

She said nothing, merely opened the door and slipped from the room.

A long-dormant image of Peter Phillips branded itself onto his brain. Time shifted as a jolt of red-hot jealousy raced through him. The injury was twenty-three years old, but felt fresh and new. "Cassie!" he started, but the only response was the sound of her heels clicking down the hallway.

Adrian bolted after her.

CHAPTER
36

February 1898

Somehow the seating arrangement in the sleigh got jumbled for the ride back from Almy Pond. Adrian crossed his arms against his chest and glared straight ahead. From the seat directly opposite, Cassie met his eyes and narrowed her own in response. With a regal lift of her chin, she turned to study the passing scenery.

He'd expected her to sit beside him, just as she had during the ride out to Almy Pond earlier that day. Of course, he'd also expected her to remain in clear view while ice skating. It had never occurred to him that she might disappear with Peter into hidden coves and inlets, oblivious to both her reputation and his own sensibilities. And as for leaving the ice to spend time alone with Peter in the sleigh . . . a muscle tensed in Adrian's jaw, sending an unpleasant clicking pulse through his brain. Exactly how much had Peter paid his coachman to look the other way?

He couldn't tell how long they'd been alone. It had felt like decades squiring Marjorie across the pond, smiling at her inane prattle until his face felt as frozen as the ice itself. He had no idea how much time had passed before he'd known—just known deep in his bones—that Cassie was no longer skating on Almy Pond.

Now Cassie and Peter sat side by side in the sleigh, but they did not touch. Cassie's hands remained hidden in her muff, her profile as immobile as Egypt's Sphinx. But Adrian recognized the expression on Peter's face: no matter how hard his friend feigned nonchalance, he could not hide the smug grin that tugged at the corners of his mouth. He looked like a child who'd consumed most of the holiday sugarplums before the family guests were even invited in to the feast.

Adrian had never hated anyone so much.

"My goodness!" Marjorie slid a little closer to his side, her voice bright in the frigid air. "This is the bumpiest sleigh ride I can remember." Predictably, her fingers tucked themselves beneath his arm.

"Do you think so?" he heard himself say. "Actually, I was just thinking that it was rather smooth. Peter, the trip to the pond was shorter than this. Is there a reason you've chosen a different route back?"

Peter caught the challenge in his voice. "Why, Adrian, you never miss a detail, do you? You're right, of course. I wanted to ride along the sea. I thought that Kate should make the most of the little time she has in Newport, and the ocean is such a majestic sight."

To Adrian's surprise, it was Cassie who protested. "A lovely thought, Peter, but I'm chilled straight through. Could we perhaps go home?"

Peter looked surprised. He moved as if to wrap an arm around her, but she'd managed to slide so far away from him that any attempt to touch her could only be perceived as gauche.

"Of course," he said, and there was a note of pleading in his voice that Adrian had never heard before. "Anything for you, Kate . . ." His words faded as Cassie turned her attention back to the landscape.

Adrian barely concealed his snort. Peter could very well join the ranks of men who'd been baffled and insulted by Cassie Walsh.

He straightened under the weight of his own thoughts. Baffled? Maybe—most women were baffling. But—insulted? It dawned on him that he knew very little about Cassie Walsh's romantic past. Why did it suddenly matter so much?

"I'm sorry I need to leave you," Peter said, as if this could be the cause of Cassie's coolness. "But I can't help it. There's much to do for the wedding tomorrow. You'll come to the ceremony and luncheon, won't you, Kate?"

Cassie turned toward him. "Do you truly want me to?"

"Yes," Peter said, and the low undertone in his voice made Adrian bristle. "More than anything. More than—"

"What's that?" Adrian interrupted, indicating the shell of a structure on a lot near the sea. Marjorie's hand slipped to the seat as he lifted his arm to point.

Peter stopped trying to gaze into Cassie's eyes and turned to follow the direction of Adrian's finger. "It's to be a summer cottage." He shook his head. "What this neighborhood is coming to."

"What do you mean?" Cassie asked as the massive "cottage" receded behind them.

Marjorie leapt in, clearly pleased to air her views. "Our new neighbors acquired their fortune fairly recently. They're hardly genteel. Textiles."

Adrian noticed the blood drain from Cassie's face. She was ever ready to expound upon the arrogant attitude of society's upper class, but to do so now would thoroughly destroy her masquerade.

"And who might they be?" she asked, and he caught the brittle edge to her words.

"Chapman. Bennett Chapman. The house is to be called Lirio-dendron." The sleigh turned left onto Bellevue, but the swish of its blades did not conceal Marjorie's unladylike huff. "Well, we shall see. They can build here if they like—there's nothing we can do to prevent that. But that doesn't make them one of us, does it?"

Adrian restrained himself from mentioning that although Marjorie and Peter had been born and bred in Newport, they weren't necessarily deemed part of the elite either. But now his attention was drawn toward Cassie. An unnaturally rosy blush broke the monochromatic pallor of her cheeks. Her breaths came short and fast, heralds of a bitter diatribe just longing to escape her lips. Adrian slipped his foot beneath the fur throw draped across her lap and pressed hard upon her toes. Her eyes met his, so blank that he longed for a blindfold to hide their emptiness. It lasted but a moment. A flash of comprehension crossed Cassie's face, followed by a brisk shrug.

"Imagine that," she said.

Adrian fumed as she inhaled deeply and settled deliberately against Peter's side. Why had he bothered to save her? Who cared if her duplicity was revealed, if Kate Weld was peeled away to reveal a stammering, scheming Cassie Walsh?

The answer to his own question raced unbidden through his mind. He cared. He'd given his word, and keeping it was about the only ounce of integrity he still had left, whether or not Cassie was worthy of it.

"Please take us home, Peter," Cassie said. "I'm sorry to be such a ninny this afternoon, but I'm cold and tired and won't be very good company tomorrow if I don't rest now."

"You're hardly a ninny." Peter's voice dripped with such intimacy that it was all Adrian could do not to lunge across the space between them to throttle him. "Of course I'll take you home if it means we'll see each other tomorrow."

"Yes, Peter," she said, and Adrian allowed himself to stoke his anger into a blazing orange flame.

Peter half rose as the sleigh slowed before the cottage walk, but Adrian bested him, jumping lightly to the ground before the last hoofbeat could fade away.

"Allow me," he said, extending one gloved hand to help Cassie alight.

"Thank you . . ." Cassie began, but he enclosed her hand so firmly in his that anything else she meant to say got trapped in her throat.

"You're not her warden, old man," Peter growled, but Adrian ignored him, turning toward the house with Cassie in tow. He vaguely registered the "Thanks ever so much" she flung over her shoulder, hardly noticed the wistful disappointment that echoed through Marjorie's forlorn "Goodbye, Adrian!" Instead he proceeded steadily down the newly shoveled walk, glancing at the gray sky with hopes that the thickening clouds might suddenly open to deposit a blizzard's worth of snow.

Cassie waited until they were inside the cottage before wrenching her hand from his. "Fine show that was, Adrian Delano," she said between clenched teeth. "Would you care to explain yourself?"

"I'm not the one who needs to explain." Adrian slammed the front door, turning its lock with a savage twist. "What did you think you were doing out there?"

"You know quite well what I was doing. And I'm so close to—"

"To what?" He yanked the scarf from around his neck. "To making Peter Phillips declare his eternal love for you? I hate to disappoint you, but do you know how many women Peter has promised to die for?"

She jerked the fur muff from her hand and flung it to the sofa, not even noticing when it rolled off the cushion and bounced to the floor. "This is different."

Her voice was a low-pitched warning, but Adrian didn't heed it. He unbuttoned his coat with such ferocity that it was a wonder the buttons stayed attached. "Different from what, Cassie? Do you honestly think you're different from every other woman Peter has seduced? How long were you alone with him in the sleigh? What happened?"

She turned away from him, pegging her cloak on the coat rack as she sailed down the hallway to her room. "I'm tired," she said. "I think I'll lie down for a bit. You needn't wake me for supper."

His hands balled into fists as he watched her retreat down the hall. Peter was nothing more than a libertine, which should have been obvious to Miss Cassie Walsh, with all her fine allusions to hours spent observing the upper class. Clearly, she'd neglected to pack pride and common sense when slipping her filmy white gown and his sister's pearls into his trunk back in Poughkeepsie.

Hardly aware of his own actions, he advanced toward her.

She stopped at the door to her room, surprised by his approach. "I believe we've ended this conversation."

"Please, Cassie. Tell me you didn't allow Peter to—"

"Of course not," she snapped. "I'm not stupid. I know that if Peter gets what he wants without consequence, then I've lost everything."

He stopped before her, at a momentary loss for words.

"Very well, Adrian." Although she aimed for authority, her voice sounded small. "Let's talk about tomorrow. I'm running out of time, you see, so we can't afford to bungle it. Peter says there is a luncheon at the bride's home following the wedding ceremony."

Adrian nodded dumbly.

"He'll drink, of course—he seems to do that so awfully well—and then, well, when we are quite alone"—at least she blushed—"I'll allow myself to be compromised."

He thought he might be sick. "Are you naïve enough to believe that once Peter has taken you, he'll propose?"

"No." A tremor ran down her left arm. "That won't happen until my enraged cousin Adrian demands that my honor be restored."

The angry flame he'd kindled in the sleigh glowed hot and white as he absorbed her words. He took in her dark eyes and quivering lower lip, the way she thrust her chin into the air while trying to stand her ground. Revulsion for her plan nearly robbed him of breath.

He turned his back on her, heading for the parlor where, hopefully, the room would stop spinning. "Pack your things," he said. "It's well past time you left."

Her footsteps skittered across the floor behind him. "Adrian!"

"You idiot. What made you think I'd help you sell yourself?"

Small fists pounded against his back. "Because you care about me!" she cried. "Because you're the only one who's ever seen me as anything more than a servant to the Delanos!"

He winced as her blows grew harder. "Then here's a pretty pickle for you: I also see you as more than a toy for Peter Phillips."

He turned to grab her wrists. Tears streamed down her face as she struggled to free herself from his grip. "Please, Adrian. You can turn over a new leaf and become the most righteous man on the face of the earth after you help me just a little longer!"

The tears startled him. He peered into her face, searching for an answer to the riddle that was Cassie Walsh. "Why are you doing this to yourself?" he demanded, genuinely puzzled.

She went limp in his grasp, suddenly drained. "Do you know what it's like to hate the hand you've been dealt?" she whispered.

He slowly lowered her arms until their hands were clasped between them. "Yes," he said fiercely. "You know I do."

A cloud crossed her face. "Oh, don't even pretend that your situation is anything like mine. You can change your destiny, Adrian. You're a man of means. Only cowardice keeps you from doing whatever you want in this world. Me . . . I've got to break every rule I know if I want to change a thing. But make no mistake about it: I *will* change it."

He wanted to protest that she knew nothing whatsoever about his life. With his parents at the helm of it, his destiny was etched in stone. He had no more choices on this earth than she did. But as he studied the desperation on her face, he suddenly understood that she was right. He'd been born a man of privilege. While his parents may have planned his future thoroughly, he was under no obligation to fulfill their ambitions.

Cassie loosened her hands from his grip to swipe away her tears. She was rapidly regaining control, pulling herself back behind the fortress walls she maintained so expertly. Her voice was cool. "The difference between us, Adrian, is that I know what I want and you do not."

But he did know. In fact, it felt as if he'd known for a very long time.

He pulled Cassie Walsh toward him, enclosing her tightly in his arms as his lips crushed hers.

CHAPTER
37

The light on Amy's nightstand cast a rosy glow across the bed, illuminating her sleeping form. Jim studied the delicate skin of her closed eyelids, the way her lashes shadowed her cheeks in fringed crescents. Golden curls fanned across the pillow as her clasped hands rose and fell with the rhythm of her gentle breathing. No doubt about it, she was lovely. If he ever planned to paint an angel, Miss Amy Walsh would be the perfect model.

Of course, he couldn't draw to save his life. And Amy had proved to be about as angelic as Mata Hari.

He slid deeper in his armchair, mired in thought. Amy was beautiful all right. Were he any less a gentleman, he'd be mooning over that bed this very moment with his lips poised above hers, ready to play Prince Charming for all he was worth. She brought out the best and worst instincts in him, all at the same time. He grimaced. Where Amy was concerned, he was well beyond what his parish priest called "impure thoughts." He'd moved on to impure hopes, impure dreams, and impure plans.

But the main reason she made his heart beat double-time was the very reason he had to watch his step: there was a brain inside that pretty blond head, one every bit as reasoned as his own.

Even if he believed that the spirit of Elizabeth Chapman was no ruse, he couldn't put it past Amy to use Mrs. C's bizarre arrival to her own advantage. He'd lost track: was he currently angrier with little Miss Walsh for the public betrayal about his eyesight, or was she angrier at him for manipulating her into speaking for Mrs. C at the wedding? Either way, there was plenty of reason to keep his distance, no matter how adorable Amy was.

Amy Walsh was a mystery, but she wasn't the only one. There were enough secrets around Liriodendron to keep even Harry Houdini scratching his head in an effort to sort them all out. Why had Elizabeth Chapman shown up in the first place? Why was she so insistent that her widower remarry? And, even if life were dull enough on the "other side" to induce Mrs. C to float around playing Cupid just for the heck of it, why choose Catharine Walsh? Not only was Catharine about half Bennett's age, she hailed from clear across the continent. Surely there was some nice eligible matron available here on the East Coast.

Jim templed his fingers above his vested middle and reviewed the facts of the matter at hand. He was no expert on the spirit world, but Granny Cullen had always said that folks never strayed outside the golden gates of heaven without a darned good reason for doing so. As dictated through his grandmother, his grandfather's "darned good reason" had usually involved lessons or advice for Jim and his siblings. Mrs. C, on the other hand, had a propensity to talk a great deal about people she'd never even known during her sojourn here on earth. In fact, much of what she had to say concerned the young woman named Cassie, whose story had unfolded decades after Elizabeth Chapman's death. Cassie—Catharine Walsh—held the missing key, and it didn't take Jim's Harvard sheepskin to figure out that her story somehow involved Adrian de la Noye.

Amy stirred, shifting to her side to rest with one hand tucked beneath her cheek. Jim braced his hands on the arms of his chair and raised himself to take a closer look. Her eyelids flickered as a fleeting smile crossed her lips; he mentally kicked himself for hoping she was dreaming about him. Her sleep seemed lighter now. Perhaps she'd wake up soon.

He settled back in his chair to wait.

There was apparently a great deal he didn't know about Adrian. Thanks to his father, he could picture the brave soldier who'd nearly sacrificed his life in battle. Courtesy of Constance, he knew all about the dedicated lawyer who'd spent long hours bent over his desk, working hard to build a successful practice. There were even stories from Grace and Ted, who were fond enough of their father to tease him, yet forever longed to make him proud. Adrian himself, however, seldom offered any autobiographical tidbits beyond the necessary professional and educational statistics. Why had that never seemed odd before?

Jim closed his eyes, suddenly tired. What could induce a man to distance himself from his history?

Noise from outside the open window jolted him from his reverie.

Rapid footsteps clattered across the flagstone terrace. Jim jumped to his feet, reaching the window just in time to see Catharine Walsh leave the terrace and hurry across the lawn. She cast a glance over her shoulder, and he quickly saw why. Adrian followed close behind. Jim squinted. He could just make out Adrian's balled fists and tensed arms beneath rolled shirtsleeves.

Catharine stopped to kick her high-heeled shoes from her feet, then broke into a full run toward the sea. Adrian was faster. He caught her at the edge of the grass, swinging her by the shoulders to face him so that she lost her balance and stumbled into his arms. She struggled for a moment, finally collapsing against him. Jim leaned as far as he could out the window, but it was impossible to hear whether or not they were even speaking, much less what was being said. Adrian pushed Catharine to arm's length for a moment, then pulled her back against his chest in a long, fierce hug. They stood that way for quite some time, as still as new topiary on Liriodendron's lawn.

What could a display such as this possibly mean? Adrian's actions were usually so measured, so . . . careful. What *was* this?

"Well." A low voice sounded from Jim's right. He looked down to see Amy beside him, blinking rapidly to clear the sleep from her eyes. "Are we going to let them get away?"

He took in her rumpled gossamer dinner gown and bare feet. She looked as unlikely a partner as any, and he still wasn't even sure he trusted her. But she was smart and as anxious to solve the riddle as he was. Most important, she was willing.

"Get your shoes." He turned back to the scene on the lawn, trying to maximize his fuzzy vision. "Hurry."

She dashed to the side of the bed to slide her feet into flat slippers, but it wasn't fast enough. Adrian and Catharine slipped through the low hedges that bordered the property and disappeared from sight.

JIM HELD ON tightly to Amy's hand as they flew noiselessly down the stairs and out Liriodendron's front door. By now he knew the way to the sea as well as she did, but there was no time to waste in adjusting his faulty night vision. It was best to let her lead as they quickly rounded the corner of the house.

They slowed to a trot, feet sinking into the plushy grass of the lawn. "I'm betting they've gone to the rocks," Jim said.

Amy nodded. "I wouldn't bet against you. Slow down. We don't want to get caught following them."

"Why not? I like the idea of a grand confrontation."

"Pity I forgot my boulders for the stoning," Amy said acidly. "A confrontation about what? No, we'll get more information if we stay out of sight and observe."

"Forgive me." Jim pushed his glasses up the bridge of his nose. "I forgot that you're the resident expert on stealth."

She gave him a withering glance but did not remove her hand from his as they silently approached the hedges at the edge of the yard.

Adrian and Catharine sat facing each other on a large rock overlooking the sea. Amy tugged Jim down until they were camouflaged by the bushes, but he doubted that it mattered: the two seemed lost in their conversation . . . a conversation that, try as he might, he couldn't quite hear.

"Blast," he muttered, peering through a bare spot in the bushes. "I can't make out a word they're saying."

"Shhh." Amy raised a finger to her lips.

The cadence of Catharine's voice rose and fell on the breeze from the ocean as she stared down at her hands in her lap. Adrian did not interrupt. He merely shifted position to face straight ahead, practically motionless as he looked across the waves.

"What do you make of it, Sherlock?" Jim whispered, gaze fixed on the tableau before them.

Amy moved closer to get a better view. "I've never seen my . . . Catharine . . . sit quite so still or talk so much to anyone. She trusts him, that's for sure."

Adrian's white shirt contrasted against the dark sky, making it easier for Jim to catch the sag of his shoulders as Catharine's voice trailed away. Silence descended between them, so dense and complete that they might have been sitting miles apart. Catharine reached out, her fingers floating on the air for a moment as if they couldn't decide whether or not to land. Finally she rested a hand on Adrian's shoulder.

Adrian slowly raised his hand to cover hers. Then he turned and drew her near, rocking her so closely against him that there was no longer any glimpse of ocean between them. He murmured into her hair, his words obscured, but even the poorest eyesight could make out the way his hand stroked Catharine's back.

Jim lurched forward, suddenly nauseated. Amy gripped his arm.

"You don't understand," he said, staring wildly at her. "I have to stop them. There's Constance to think of, and Grace and Ted . . ."

She held on tight. "No, *you* don't understand. You can't stop anything here."

She was right. He was powerless to alter whatever secret Adrian and Catharine shared, could do nothing to change the emotions that fueled their actions tonight.

He wanted to wail as Adrian planted a gentle kiss on Catharine's cheek.

"I have just as many questions as you do," Amy whispered. "But we won't get the answers now. We'll have to stow this away until its proper time."

Proper time? Could there ever be a proper time to watch a man destroy not only his life but the lives of those who loved him? A lump caught in Jim's throat as Adrian's arm encircled Catharine's waist. Her head dropped to his shoulder; together they faced the sea.

"Let's go," Jim said harshly, turning back toward Liriodendron. "I don't need to see what happens next."

Amy hesitated, obviously tempted to stay. Then she slid her hand against his cold palm and allowed him to lead her toward the house. "You can't leave Liriodendron yet," she said, and his head snapped toward her. How had she known that he wanted nothing more than to pack his bags and escape to a hotel in town?

"I'm not leaving," he said.

"Good. First of all, Mr. de la Noye is your friend, and you don't know the whole story."

"I don't want to know the whole story."

"Yes, you do. Secondly, I can't go through this wedding tomorrow without you. Thank you for saving me tonight."

He stopped, not even caring that they stood in clear view at the center of the lawn. "You're welcome," he said. "Amy, I won't hold you to your promise. You don't have to let Mrs. C speak through you at the wedding. You have every right to refuse after what happened in the dining room tonight."

"I know, and you're a peach to say it, but I've got to do it. I hate to admit it, but we've got to find out why she's come, what she wants. She might have the answers we need. Jim . . . has it crossed your mind that Mr. de la Noye could be my father?"

It seemed almost illegal to utter the words out loud. "Yes, damn it," he said, staring at the ground. "Of course it has."

"Then you see why I've got to finish this. I've got to find out, and I don't think we're going to get the whole story from those two down on the rocks, do you?"

He jammed his hands into his pockets. "You're sure you'll be okay?"

She hesitated. "No. What I'm sure of is that you'll do everything possible to protect me."

Jim cleared his throat. "I'll do the best I can."

"That's saying quite a lot," she said softly. "You're a good man, Jim Reid. Now, I need a drink. Join me?"

Surely Adrian would stride through that gap in the hedge, virtuously alone. But the leaves of the bushes fluttered in the breeze, almost teasing in their silence.

"Come," Amy said, extending her hand.

Casting one last futile glance toward the rocks, Jim followed her to the house.

CHAPTER
38

February 1898

Cassie shot up in bed, yanking the sheet up to her chin with one quick, defensive tug as the front door of the cottage banged shut.

"That will be Mrs. Vickery," Adrian murmured from beneath the quilt. "She told me this morning that she'd leave dinner for us."

"Adrian! Didn't you lock the door?"

"Of course I did. She carries a ring of keys, remember?"

"But what if she walks down the hall and—"

"What's this? Miss Walsh has a conscience?" A slow grin spread across his face; it had been years since she'd seen Adrian Delano in such good humor. "Both bedroom doors—yours as well as this one—are closed. If she decides to pry, then she deserves whatever offensive sights meet her eyes." His arm curled about her, hauling her back down beside him. "Although," he whispered, "I can vouch for the fact that there is nothing offensive whatsoever about any part of you."

A shiver danced up her spine as he kissed the nape of her neck. His left hand absently stroked her belly. A flush traveled from the top of her head to her toes as his lips moved to her earlobe. The truth of the situation splashed across her mind like a glass of icy water: she was lying naked in bed beside a man who wasn't her husband.

"Adrian." She twisted in his arms to face him. "What have I done?"

Adrian paused as Mrs. Vickery's efficient footsteps clicked through the front room toward the kitchen. Then he scooped Cassie close, easing her head to rest against his chest. "What have you done? You mean other than make me the happiest I've ever been in my life?"

"But at what cost?" To her utter embarrassment, her voice broke. His heartbeat skipped at that, but his arms remained wrapped securely around her.

"At no cost," he said quietly.

Mrs. Vickery had begun to sing, a dreary rendition of "Annie Laurie" that only served to make the situation seem even bleaker than it was.

"But . . . but my plans," Cassie started. "How can I marry Peter now that you and I . . . knowing that . . ."

Adrian continued to stroke her arm, but she felt his muscles tense. "Knowing what, Cassie?"

"I'm positively ruined, and—"

The stroking stopped. "That wasn't my doing," he said. "I won't ask you about it now, but I won't take the blame either."

She didn't refute his words. She might have found an artful way to feign virginity with Peter Phillips, but there was no point in even trying to fool Adrian. In truth, she didn't even want to.

"So, then," he continued, "what exactly has changed for you?"

She lifted her head to stare at him. Despite his rumpled hair and the evening stubble on his cheeks, his gaze was direct. He knew. He could read her heart as if there were words etched upon it, but he would make her say them out loud all the same.

Mrs. Vickery's singing stopped quite suddenly. Cassie froze. "She can't find me here," she said. "The talk—nobody will want me!"

"Cassie . . ." he prodded.

The lugubrious song began again, this time accompanied by the clatter of dishes and silver. Mrs. Vickery was apparently setting the tiny kitchen table, her attention captured by the minutiae of daily responsibility.

Cassie once again met Adrian's questioning look. "Oh, all right," she whispered, peeved. "How can I marry Peter when I'm in love with you?"

He lifted her chin with his finger. "You can be such a fool, Cassie Walsh. Do you honestly think I would ever let that idiot have you?" He kissed her, briefly silencing the words that bubbled to her lips.

"Adrian . . ." she said as they parted, but he kissed her again, so deeply that she couldn't help but lose herself in it. His body pressed the length of hers, as perfect a fit as if he'd been created for the sole purpose of making love to her. She wanted to tell him how wonderful he felt—that the only other time she'd been with a man had been the most horrible experience of her life. But it seemed a waste of words when his mouth felt so good, when the slightest brush of his fingers almost made her forget who she was. She hardly recognized her own sigh as she slipped beneath him, molding herself to each part of him as if she believed they could become one person.

What was done was done. She couldn't turn back the hours, undo what had passed between them. Nor could she lie and claim that he'd taken unfair advantage of her. She'd fallen willingly into bed with Adrian Delano. Even now, it was she who guided his hand to her breast as the room became nothing more than a rustle of soft sheets and quilts. Adrian's lips traveled down her neck as her nipple grew hard beneath his fingers.

They pulled away from each other as footsteps paced down the hallway toward the bedrooms.

"Dear God!" Cassie squeaked.

Adrian's head swiveled toward the door. "Ah. So Pinkerton's should employ our dear Mrs. Vickery after all."

"What cheek, prying like this!"

"Merely a benefit of her position, I suppose." Adrian leaned over the side of the bed to fish his trousers from the floor. Down the hall, the door to Cassie's bedroom creaked open. Mrs. Vickery's footsteps grew faint, muffled by the carpet as she entered the room. "Stay quiet, darling," Adrian said, landing a light kiss on Cassie's forehead. "I'll be right back."

She sank beneath the quilts as he pulled on his trousers and reached for his shirt. Benefit of her position? Had he forgotten that she came from that class as well? She dragged a pillow over her head, remembering the times she herself had "discovered" clandestine information while dusting a room or delivering a tray.

The door to the other bedroom tapped shut again. Adrian slipped his arms through his suspenders and ran a hand through his hair. Cassie dove beneath the bedclothes as their bedroom doorknob rattled from the outside. Mrs. Vickery was a more determined snoop than she herself had ever been. She heard Adrian unlock the door and open it a crack.

"Good evening," he said. His voice grew distant as he stepped into the hall, closing the door firmly behind him. Cassie could only imagine the discomfited expression on the housekeeper's face.

Occasional words floated through the closed door: "nap," "tired," "thank-you-for-dinner." Mrs. Vickery wouldn't dare ask questions, but Adrian included an offhand alibi all the same. Those words carried through the heavy door loud and clear: "I wish I possessed my cousin's vitality. She's spent the afternoon with Marjorie Phillips, but I expect her back at any moment."

Their footsteps retreated down the hall. Cassie emerged from her nest of quilts, topsy-turvy and out of sorts. Adrian would escort Mrs. Vickery to the door, see her safely down the walk before returning to the bedroom. They could only hope he'd done enough to quell the housekeeper's suspicions.

But Cassie herself wouldn't have believed their charade had she been in Mrs. Vickery's shoes. In addition to the thinness of their story, her coat hung on the coat rack in clear view, and her fur muff was probably still on the front-room floor, exactly where she'd left it.

Then there was Adrian. If his bare feet and general disarray hadn't given him away, then his general air of contentment would have. No nap on earth could confer such satisfaction. Cassie pushed a lock of tangled hair back over one shoulder. Mrs. Vickery knew very well how Adrian had spent the past few hours, and the identity of his bedmate was an easy deduction.

And, as Adrian entered the bedroom, she saw from his preoccupied expression that he had reached the same conclusion.

"How much time before word travels, do you think?" she asked, hugging her knees to her chest.

"There's no evidence of anything untoward."

"Gossip doesn't rely on evidence. Of course, you'll deny everything if Peter hears . . . won't you?"

His brow darkened. "Damn Peter."

"I wish I could. But now I need him more than ever."

"Marry me," Adrian said, slamming the door behind him.

Her stomach dropped. "I can't!"

He stepped toward the bed, eyes glittering. "Why not? Is Peter so much better?"

"No, of course not!" She scowled. "Peter's awful, a total dunce. But I don't care about him. You're different, Adrian. I care about you too much to force you into a situation that will surely ruin your life."

Adrian raised an eyebrow. "You couldn't force me if you tried, Cassie Walsh. I know exactly what I'm getting into. I proposed to you, not the other way around. Listen to me: you've taken every pleasure in informing me that I'm spineless, that I should decide what I want and then fight for it. Well, I've decided. I want you. Marry me, Cassie."

Her mouth tasted like ashes. "Your parents would never allow you to marry the cook's daughter."

"My choice of wife is my decision to make."

"Oh, brave words." She clutched the sheet about her as she pulled herself up to her knees on the bed. They were nearly eye to eye now, and that made her words flow more easily. "How cocky will you feel when your parents cut you off without a penny?"

He gripped her upper arms, drawing her into a long kiss. Her sheet floated down to the bed as her hands caressed his face. "Let them cut me off," he whispered, kissing her eyelids. "I can practice law somewhere besides my father's office. I can do anything with you beside me."

He would make a very fine lawyer. He would infuse his arguments with boldness born of conviction. But even the best attorney could not sway jurors whose opinions had been hardened before the trial even began. Cassie searched for the words to explain this but found they would not come. She shivered as his eyes swept across her naked body. How to express sentiments that she herself didn't even want to hear?

"Marry me, Cassie," he said again, holding her gaze as he unfastened his suspenders.

She said nothing, merely waited until he'd undressed completely before lifting the bedclothes so that they could disappear beneath them together.

CHAPTER
39

J im stayed in bed as late as he could the next morning, pulling the blankets over his head to avoid the sun's rays when they intruded through his window. He stubbornly ignored the rumbling of his stomach as the breakfast hour drew near, paying little attention to footsteps passing outside his bedroom door as others descended to the dining room in search of sustenance. But try as he might, he could not ignore the siren call of coffee, that rich, fragrant aroma that lingered on the air even after breakfast ended and everyone was set free to prepare for the afternoon's wedding as each saw fit. Resigned to his own addiction, he hastily dressed, grabbed his toiletries, and padded down the hall in slippered feet toward the bathroom.

He couldn't wait to get out of this place. Liriodendron made men do strange things. There was Bennett Chapman, acting more

and more as if he took daily showers in the Fountain of Youth . . .
Nicholas, muttering to himself as he passed through the hallways,
dry and nasty as an old turnip . . . and Adrian. Jim opened the hot
water spigot all the way and watched as water splashed against the
porcelain bowl of the sink. There were no words for Adrian. He'd
never in a million years suspected that his mentor could entertain a
dishonorable deed, much less commit one. Worse, the unspeakable
behavior would follow them straight off Aquidneck Island and back
to the de la Noyes' comfortable Brookline home.

He glumly twisted off the top of his Pepsodent tube, not even
noticing when a glob of paste fell from his toothbrush into the sink
below. He could always find a legal position elsewhere. He'd have
to, considering that he wouldn't be able to look Adrian in the eye
once the man deserted Constance and the children. Still, the friendship would be hard to replace. He already mourned the loss of
someone he'd looked up to for as long as he could remember.

What a treat it would be to shove everything into his suitcase and
leave Liriodendron right now. But that was not to be. He couldn't
justify anything getting in the way of his professional obligation . . .
not Adrian's fall from grace, not even Miss Amy Walsh.

With a sigh, Jim hung his shirt on the hook behind the door
and halfheartedly reached for the soap. Amy presented yet another set of worms to cram back into the can where they belonged.
Of course he'd noticed last night's flirtatious glances when they'd
slipped into the dining room for a swig of brandy from Bennett's
alcoholic contraband. He'd caught that wiggle of her little der-
riere as she bent to fetch the decanter kept stashed from sight in
the buffet cabinet. He had to admit he hadn't looked away. But
he'd done nothing more than look—had merely drained his glass

in one gulp and bid her a hasty good night. She was pretty damn alluring, but *somebody* had to hold on to his scruples in this cavernous den of iniquity.

He'd just lathered up when a knock sounded on the bathroom door. "Damn," he muttered beneath his breath. There went all expectations of sneaking unnoticed back to his room. He could only hope his visitor was a housemaid.

"Out in a jiffy," he said, slapping soap lather onto his face.

"I look forward to it," Adrian replied.

Jim stopped mid-scrub, staring at his image in the mirror as if it could tell him how to avoid a face-to-face meeting with the person he least wanted to see. But his reflection looked just as flummoxed as he himself felt.

Adrian was his employer, not his master. Said employer could jolly well wait until the completion of his employee's morning ablutions before demanding an appearance. Slowly, deliberately, Jim reached for his razor.

Adrian was studying a pad of notes when Jim finally stepped from the bathroom and into the hall. If he thought his wait unreasonable, he said nothing about it. He merely fell into step beside his associate, as unflappable as if they'd just met for a day's work at the office.

"Are you well, Mr. Reid?" he asked. "We missed your presence at breakfast."

"I'm just dandy," Jim said. "I wasn't hungry."

"That seems to be the trend of the day. Both Miss Walshes chose to remain in their rooms this morning as well."

Amy hadn't come downstairs? Jim made a note to check on her as soon as he could shake Adrian. "Perhaps Amy is still under the weather after yesterday's scare," he said, offering a noncommittal shrug.

"Perhaps. Did you have an opportunity to speak with her last night?"

The lies came far too easily by now. There'd probably be hell to pay somewhere along the line. "I sat in her room for a while, but she never woke up."

"I see." Adrian paused as they reached Jim's bedroom door. Jim waited there with him, hoping he'd been believable enough to be left alone until the afternoon. Instead Adrian reached out, turned the doorknob, and ushered him into what should have been a private sanctuary.

"This evening is pivotal," Adrian said, closing the door behind them. "We should discuss it."

Jim let his toiletry bag drop to the dresser with a loud thud. "I think I've got the schedule. Judge Bourne arrives around four o'clock and the wedding follows shortly after that. Then the happy couple executes the will. After that, it's a wedding feast, followed by our departure to the ferry and home. Thank God. It's about time."

Adrian remained planted by the door, his expression unreadable. "We may need to leave tomorrow instead."

"Oh, of course." Jim did not even try to disguise the sarcasm in his voice. "We wouldn't want to miss the wedding night, would we. Did you want to invite the late Mrs. C for that as well?"

"Interesting reaction, Mr. Reid. I was thinking more that we may miss the last ferry out tonight."

"Then perhaps we should leave before dinner." Jim folded his arms across his chest, chin raised in an unconscious challenge.

"Lord knows I've had more meals at Liriodendron than originally planned. I could stand to miss another one."

Adrian hesitated before replying. "This may be one we can't miss," he finally said.

Jim's eyes narrowed behind his gold-rimmed spectacles. Then he turned his back on the man before him, tugging open his top bureau drawer with enough force to nearly pull it loose from its tracks. "That's right," he said, yanking out a pair of socks. "I'd quite forgotten. Duty demands that we stay here as long as humanly possible, no matter what effect this place seems to have on us."

Adrian raised an eyebrow. "Suppose you end this tantrum and simply tell me what's on your mind."

Jim turned toward him, socks clenched tightly in his fist. "How is your wife, Adrian? Constance, remember her? Isn't she starting to wonder what's keeping you away for so long?"

Adrian crossed the room, lifted the socks from Jim's hand, and replaced them with a more appropriate color. "You may rest assured that I am in regular contact with Mrs. de la Noye. In fact, I plan to telephone her again when I leave your room."

His mild demeanor prickled. Jim slammed the drawer hard and paced toward the bed. "Oh, very good. Feed her the words you want her to hear before she figures out the truth."

"I beg your pardon?"

"What did you do last night while I sat with Amy?"

"I took a walk."

"Alone?"

"Obviously you know otherwise. I was with Catharine Walsh."

No attempt to lie? No remorse? The honesty landed like a kick to the gut. Suddenly deflated, Jim sank down to the mattress. "What are you doing, Adrian?" he asked bleakly.

"Jim." Adrian approached the bed. "I've never given you any cause to doubt me, have I?"

Jim could only shake his head. There was no way to deny that Adrian had always been a dependable rock.

"Then I ask you to trust me now. I can't say more just yet, but you must believe that I'll tell you everything when the time is right. In the meanwhile, try to be patient. I'm afraid the road might get a little rough tonight, and I need your help."

"Help or complicity?"

Adrian managed a faint smile. "Ever the wordsmith. Help. Nicholas Chapman means to ruin me if I don't play by his rules."

"Can he?"

"I don't know. What I *do* know is that I can't let him hurt my family while trying."

Jim looked away from his mentor's direct stare. "I don't know how helpful I can be," he mumbled. "I don't know what information he has to use against you. I suspect he has quite a bit, however, since I myself just learned that you changed your last name over twenty years ago."

Adrian didn't even flinch. "I'm surprised you didn't discover that fact earlier," he said. "It wouldn't have taken much to find out. You attended my alma maters; I graduated under the name Delano. I suppose it took an accomplished snoop like our young Miss Amy Walsh to awaken you to facts that have been right beneath your nose for years."

Despite his best intentions, Jim's stare returned to the other man. "Excuse me?"

"Of course I know that she's our little spy," Adrian continued calmly.

"How did you . . ."

"Oh, good Lord. I have eyes. I knew the first time I got a close look at her retreating form. You're smart, but still a bit green. Or perhaps Mrs. de la Noye is correct: it's time to find you a sweetheart."

The reference to Constance wrenched Jim back to the uncomfortable dishonesty of the situation. "Why did you change your name, anyway?"

Adrian's mouth twitched slightly, but he quickly regained his composure. "Personal reasons," he said. "We won't discuss them here."

It was oddly reassuring to see that the question could crack his mentor's stoic façade. At least Adrian's conscience still worked. "Perhaps the reasons aren't even mine to know," Jim conceded. "But surely you've shared them with Constance?"

"Yes." Adrian finally averted his gaze, studying his hands as if they were the most interesting objects in the room.

"Ah," Jim said. "You haven't told her the complete story, have you?"

"No."

Jim let those thoughts tumble through his brain. He'd seen with his own eyes the tenderness between Catharine and Adrian last night. Perhaps Adrian was correct about his naïveté, but he knew in his gut that there was more between those two than mere acquaintanceship, and that secrets kept from one's wife concerning another woman could only bode ill.

Adrian seemed to read his analysis. "Jim. You'll know more in time. I give you my word, and my word has always been good."

The images Jim had seen last night clashed with the words he heard now. "Give me something else to hang on to," he pleaded. "Please."

Adrian slowly rose from the edge of the bed. "I love my wife," he said, starting toward the door.

"But you have feelings for Catharine Walsh as well," Jim countered, strangely gratified when the other man stopped dead in his tracks. "I'm not as green as you think I am."

Adrian's shoulders slumped. "Just follow my lead tonight. And, if by the end of the evening you still question my character, I will provide the references necessary for you to obtain an excellent legal position elsewhere."

He exited the room with a quiet click of the door, leaving Jim to realize yet again that the rational analysis so useful in resolving legal issues left much to be desired when applied to matters of friendship and the heart.

CHAPTER
40

Constance answered the telephone immediately, although Adrian couldn't determine if the breathlessness he sensed emanated from his wife or from a rogue crackle on the wire.

"I could set our clocks by your promptness," she said, and static or not, the teasing lilt in her voice sounded loud and clear through the line.

"You're on time, too," he replied. "I'm impressed."

"As well you should be. Promptness is not the religion to me that it is to you."

He'd already closed the library window and surveyed the room for intruders, but he glanced beneath the desk again for good measure. "How are you, my dear? Has anything changed since we spoke last night?"

"Not really. A man's been by."

She delivered the words casually, but his muscles tensed all the same. "When?"

"This morning. I thought it best to walk with the children to school—it's a most delightful day here, so it was easy enough to convince them that I wanted nothing more than to take the air. I noticed him when I returned."

"Where?"

"Across the street, hovering near the Nelsons' mailbox. As if Eleanor Nelson would entertain anyone before noon, let alone a strange man. I watched him from behind the parlor curtains for a bit."

His fingers tightened around the telephone. "Constance, listen to me. Meet the children after school. I want all three of you to stay with your parents until I get home."

He could almost hear the roll of her eyes. "Don't be silly, Adrian. How can I be of any service to you from my mother's stuffy parlor?"

"It's more important to me that you remain safe. I can manage this matter on my own from this point."

"You most certainly cannot."

He recognized the tone from her days in the law office. It was her "Let *me* handle this, Mr. de la Noye" voice, the one that surfaced whenever she believed he hadn't seen the whole picture. It had been perfectly acceptable in the relatively secure setting of a day's work, but this was an entirely different situation. "I need to know that you're protected," he said. "If that man was sent by Nicholas Chapman—"

"Oh, he was."

"How do you know?"

"I asked."

Adrian's heart sank. He'd forgotten how independent his wife could be. "Constance . . ."

"Well, it was just silly. There he was, pacing back and forth across the sidewalk, obviously surveying our house. I felt like a bug beneath a microscope. I dashed next door to tell Nellie Patterson I was inviting a salesman onto the front porch for a cup of coffee, but that I might need her to interrupt should he become tiresome. She was outside gardening, after all, in perfect earshot. She agreed to listen for a signal to come over and help me get rid of him."

Adrian leaned against the desk, not sure that he wanted to hear more, but knowing that he had no choice.

Constance barely took a breath. "I walked across the street and told Mr. Parker—that's the name the man gave me, although I don't believe for one minute it's real—that since he'd obviously been stood up by someone, he should come over for a cup of coffee and a piece of cake before moving along."

"Constance . . ."

"Don't sound so weary, Adrian. You know perfectly well that I'm able to take care of myself. You also know that nobody can resist my raspberry coffee cake. Would you like to hear about our conversation?"

"Actually, I'd like to shake you for putting yourself in danger. But of course I want to know what was said."

He heard the clink of silver against china and remembered that Constance herself could not resist her raspberry coffee cake. "First of all," she said, "he's definitely in Nicholas Chapman's employ, but he doesn't think much of the man. I suspect he'd throw his loyalty behind anyone who paid him even a nickel more."

Adrian could not deny that Nicholas Chapman lacked the usual qualities that encouraged devotion from employees.

"He was mostly interested in your personal life," Constance continued. "That came as no surprise: although Nicholas Chapman takes issue with your legal decisions regarding his father, you are professionally beyond reproach. One would have to dig a little deeper in order to ruin you."

"What sorts of questions did he ask?"

"Totally improper ones. How long we'd known each other, how we met, how a delightful woman such as myself had been captured by a dull, dreary lawyer . . . oh, he thought himself so clever, trying to insinuate himself into my good graces through idle flattery." She paused to chew. "Mind you, he was quite good at it, and were I so inclined, it might have worked."

He couldn't help it; he had to smile. "He just asked whatever he wished with no thought that you'd find the questions suspicious?"

"Sometimes, Adrian, there are benefits to being a woman. Most men consider us quite stupid, utterly incapable of seeing through clumsy attempts at intrigue."

"I see." Poor man; he'd had no way of knowing that Constance was not a woman to underestimate. "Go on."

"He wanted to know if I knew your family—the Delanos. He watched my reaction as he enunciated the name, trying to gauge if I knew you'd been born anything other than de la Noye. I ignored the question and prattled on about the difficulty of dealing with in-laws until his eyes glazed over with boredom. Then, when I finally stopped to breathe, he asked about Catharine Walsh."

The smile slipped from his face. "What did he want to know?"

"If I knew anything about her."

"And what did you say?" His mouth felt dry. The library verged on stifling without a cooling breeze wafting through the usually open window.

"I told him that I knew she was Bennett Chapman's fiancée, but that you would never do anything as unprofessional as discuss a client's business with me at length. I fluttered my eyelashes a great deal and said that I knew nothing more."

He shook his head at the image of his canny wife pretending vacuity. "And?"

"And he said I was a charming woman whom he didn't wish to bother further and could he please have another piece of cake? I gave him one, of course, then sent him on his way. I told him I'd pass you his regards."

Adrian pulled his collar away from his neck with a crook of his finger. The gesture provided only slight relief. "I'd rest more easily knowing that you and the children were safely out of the house. Just once, my dear, could we pretend you are the subservient sort of wife who follows her husband's requests?"

"No, Adrian, we could not. But don't worry. Mr. Parker won't be back."

"How can you be so sure?"

"He's accomplished his task. His only point in coming was to make his presence known to you. His questions to me involved matters of public record or information he would already have, and he did nothing to hide himself when observing the house. I told you, he looked a perfect fool loitering amidst Eleanor Nelson's azaleas. No, he wanted me to notice and report his appearance to you. Since

I told him I'd do that, he has no reason to return. Wouldn't you agree?"

Adrian eased his handkerchief from his pocket and dabbed his brow. Her analysis, as always, seemed sound. Of course, whether he agreed or not was irrelevant; his wife would do as she pleased. "I would. But, Constance, don't take any chances. If you begin to feel nervous for any reason, you must promise me you'll go to your parents'."

"Of course, Adrian," she said sweetly. "I'd be so much safer there. My father can fend off intruders with his cane while my mother lobs dumplings at them."

"About the other matter we discussed last night . . ."

"I took care of it. The envelope was in your desk drawer, exactly where you said it would be. You should receive it as planned."

Despite himself, he exhaled a long, relieved sigh. "Thank you, Constance. You are a jewel."

"And you thought you could handle everything yourself. Adrian . . ."

He couldn't remember the last time he'd heard that hesitant note in his wife's voice. He closed his eyes, anticipating her words before they could leave her mouth.

"I respected your request not to open the envelope," she said. "I must admit, though, that I'm curious to know what's inside."

"I know you are, sweetheart. But this is neither the time nor the place."

She was well aware of the need for discretion on a telephone line. "I understand. But perhaps we might discuss it when you come home."

"I will answer whatever questions you have, Constance," he said gently. "We have been partners for a long time, and I owe you the world."

"Yes, Adrian." He was pleased to hear her usual resilience re-emerge. "I know that. Whatever would you do without me?"

It was a thought he didn't care to ponder.

CHAPTER
41

The cloying fragrance of too many flowers wafted through the open bedroom door as Jim set his closed suitcase firmly on the floor beside his bed. He wrinkled his nose in response, trying to ward off a sneeze.

"Packed and ready, I see." Adrian stepped into the room, dressed for the impending wedding in a crisp ivory suit.

"Yeah, well, I thought I'd be hopeful." Jim fumbled for his hand-kerchief as the expected sneeze overtook him.

"Bless you. And if it makes you feel any better, I've packed my bags as well. I'll do my best to get us off Aquidneck tonight, but I can't make any promises."

"Thank you." Jim allowed himself a halfhearted smile. The jury was out as to whether or not he could trust Adrian de la Noye one hundred percent just yet, but it felt right to give a friend a chance.

"I'll observe closely tonight and try to follow your lead."

Adrian acknowledged the words with a brisk nod. "I'd appreciate that. I'd tell you more, Jim, but I think it would be best if your reactions were unrehearsed."

"I understand."

There was no hesitation about Adrian now. He wore his professionalism as easily as he wore his linen suit and finely pressed shirt. He shot a glance toward the bureau clock. "Are you ready?" he asked.

"Sure." Jim shrugged. "Why not?"

"Then let's go down to face the lions, my friend." Adrian clapped a hand on his associate's shoulder and propelled them both toward the door.

The flower arrangements began in the foyer, where roses of yellow and red spilled from vases of all shapes and sizes.

"Jeez," Jim murmured as his foot left the last step. "There are enough flowers here for a funeral."

"The analogy is not entirely inappropriate," Adrian replied, snapping a small rosebud from an overstuffed vase. "The late Mrs. Chapman should feel quite at home."

Mention of Elizabeth Chapman brought other thoughts to mind. Jim cleared his throat. "I'd like to check on Amy if you don't mind."

"I was hoping you'd offer." Adrian slipped the stem of the rosebud through his lapel buttonhole. "I've matters of my own to manage this evening."

"Manage fast. Here comes Lady Dinwoodie and, as usual, she has eyes only for you."

Indeed, Chloe came bearing down on them from the back of the house like a miniature tank, her feathered headdress mirroring the reds and yellows of the roses so perfectly that they could only have been dyed to match. "Mr. de la Noye!" she cooed, and the sway in her step left little doubt that she'd spent much of the afternoon tippling. "D'you like the flowers? Catharine wasn't planning to have any, but if we're going to endure a wedding ceremony, we might as well do the damn thing right, don't you think? I ordered them. At least we'll have a bit of festivity here before either Nicky sends everyone to jail or Little Miss Gold Digger takes Pop for everything he's got."

Jim slipped into the parlor before he could hear Adrian's response, but he knew it didn't matter. They couldn't afford for him to ride shotgun anymore. It was time to move from behind Adrian's shadow and operate according to his own instincts.

Someone—probably Chloe—had arranged the parlor sofa and chairs into a long row with an aisle in between. That made little sense since only five guests would witness the ceremony, but if it kept Lady Dinwoodie happy and quiet, then Jim was all for it.

Amy sat on the sofa to the left of the aisle, facing a podium set near the far right-hand wall. Her head was bowed, but hardly in supplication. Based on her flushed profile and the stiffness of her neck, Jim would have bet the farm that nothing even close to prayer raced through that blond head at the moment.

His nose itched. This room had not escaped the invasion of the roses. They flanked the podium in two determined clumps, daring anyone to object to their presence. Another bouquet sat in a vase on the floor behind the sofa. Jim figured he'd have to move that batch lest the entire marriage ceremony be punctuated by sneezes and honks.

He grabbed for his handkerchief just in time to catch his sneeze.

Amy turned around. "Oh," she said, "you've come back."

It was as good a reaction as any. He walked around to the front of the sofa to face her. "You look down in the dumps," he said. "Are you all right?"

She slumped further in her seat. "How can I be all right, Jim? I'm attending the wedding of a woman I always assumed was my aunt, but recently discovered is my mother. I still don't know who my father is. And I'm about to speak for the dead first wife of the groom, a man old enough to be the bride's grandfather."

Jim nodded. "The situation is hardly copacetic."

"There's more."

"How can there be?"

Her brows lowered, but she didn't turn away. "I think I'm falling in love. Who the heck needs a complication like that?"

His handkerchief stopped halfway back to his pocket. So much for the yo-yoing question of what to do with Miss Amy Walsh. When on earth had she found time to fit anyone else into her schedule?

"Oh," he said, aiming for indifference. "I'm sorry. I didn't know."

"Men never do," she said darkly.

Not that he gave a fig about the cherub on the sofa . . . but would it always be his lot in life to serve as the pal, the trustworthy guy a girl could count on for sound advice and a strong shoulder? And could Amy's timing be any worse? There were already enough tangles in the current situation to trip up a tightrope walker. Still, she looked so small and miserable nestled in the corner curve of the sofa that there was no way he could walk away.

"Oh, all right," he said with a sigh. "We have a few minutes before chaos descends. Did you want to tell me about it?"

Those big eyes would be his undoing. Fortunately, the flowers made him sneeze again as he settled beside her, and the action tore his gaze from hers.

"You may not be the right person to tell," she said.

"I'm always the right person to tell."

"This happens to you frequently?"

"Constantly. I'm everybody's choice." Another sneeze ripped through him.

She looked puzzled.

There wasn't much time for this, and Amy would need to be as focused as possible if Mrs. C was going to come through clearly. "So, what's the problem?" Jim prodded. "Doesn't the fellow like you back?"

"You tell me," she said. "Since you're the fellow in question."

He stared at her as if she'd spouted quantum theory. "I am?"

"Who did you think it was, you idiot?" She scowled. "Falling in love with you is the last thing I need right now, but there doesn't seem to be a thing I can do to stop it."

His nose began to itch again. "Excuse me," he said, leaping to his feet. With renewed vigor, he transported the hateful vase of roses from behind the sofa to the opposite end of the room. Then he returned to Amy's side. "Would you say it again for me, please? Slowly enough that I can understand?"

"Why? I thought you were everybody's choice."

He draped his left arm around her shoulders and drew her toward him. Then he kissed her, not even pausing to wonder whether or not it was a good idea. The kiss she gave in return made it clear that there'd never been any reason to worry in the first place.

"Fine time for this to happen," Amy whispered as they parted.

"It could be a very fine time indeed." Jim kept her close. "I'm willing to give it a whirl if you are." He leaned toward her mouth, but she stopped him with an insistent hand flat against his chest.

"I've a favor to ask," she said.

"I knew there was a catch."

"Don't think ill of me, Jim. It's all right if you say no. But, God willing, this will be the last time I speak for Mrs. Chapman—and believe me, I'm going to do everything I can to keep her from taking over. But if I can't do it, I need you to ask her something on my behalf. I want to know who my father is."

"Perhaps it's your mother who needs asking."

"I . . . I haven't really spoken to Catharine since learning the truth. I'm not sure I trust her anymore."

He covered her hand with his own. "You've got to repair that, Amy. Like it or not, Catharine Walsh took care of you, raised you, loved you. And you loved her back. You can't just discard people like that, especially when you don't know the reasons behind their actions. Aren't you the lady who said that very same thing to me where Adrian was concerned?"

She sank against him. "Skewered by my own words. I'll think about it. But, please, Jim—for my sake, if I can't do it, ask Mrs. Chapman about my father."

"I'll do that."

"Promise? Even if there's a chance her answer might place Mr. de la Noye in a delicate position?"

Jim briefly considered everything he knew about Adrian. "I think he would want to know."

This kiss was even nicer than the ones before, and Jim would have forgotten his surroundings entirely were it not for the quiet "ahem" he thought he heard from somewhere far away. With difficulty, he disengaged himself from Amy's arms and glanced over his shoulder. Adrian stood behind the sofa, accompanied by a short, round gentleman of perhaps seventy.

"Judge Thomas Bourne"—Adrian spoke as if he'd just interrupted a friendly game of cards—"allow me to introduce my associate, Mr. James Reid. And this young lady is Miss Amy Walsh, daughter of the bride."

Jim scrambled to his feet, dragging Amy up along with him. "Pleasure to meet you, Your Honor," he said, pumping the judge's proffered hand a little harder than necessary. "And I do apologize for our . . . uh . . ."

" . . . youthful indiscretion?" the judge supplied, but anything else he might have said disappeared as Bennett Chapman entered the room, flanked by his son and daughter.

CHAPTER
42

T om Bourne!" Bennett boomed, striding into the room. The walking stick in his hand served as little more than an accessory now. "So good to see you again! I believe you've met my son, Nicholas . . . my daughter, Chloe . . . we'll talk more during supper, but for now, Tom, let me take you to meet my bride." He leveled first his daughter, then his son with a stare that dared them to protest. "We'll begin the wedding ceremony as soon as possible," he said, drawing out each word long beyond its natural length. "I find I'm more eager by the minute to once again embrace the blessed state of matrimony."

"Yes," Nicholas said beneath his breath as his father and the judge left the room. "Go right ahead and speed things along, you old goat. The sooner we begin, the sooner we can end." He grimaced at the ceremonial arrangement of sofa and chairs. "Oh, dear God. Whose harebrained idea was it to set up the room like a bloody church?"

"Mine," Chloe said brightly. "I thought it might make Mother happy."

Her brother's gaze followed her as she reached beneath the hem of her dress for her flask. "You need to stop drinking, Chloe," he said. "It's getting too hard to tell if your actions are the result of alcohol or stupidity."

"Oh, Nicky, can't you simply get along for a change?" She tilted her head back to take a quick swig. "Don't worry. I'll ask Mother about it when she comes through today."

Nicholas turned away abruptly, seating himself in the first chair to the right of the aisle. "Mr. de la Noye, I suppose it's useless to ask if you've changed your mind. Will you let the current will stand due to my father's lunacy or must we drag through this ludicrous charade before reaching the same conclusion anyway?"

Adrian approached the sofa, reaching for his pocket watch along the way. "I will continue to stand by my client's sanity."

Nicholas's hand landed on his forearm, stopping him flat. Surprised, Adrian looked down to meet his gaze.

"The groom may be your client," Nicholas said, "but I won't be surprised if you choose to sit on the bride's side of the aisle." The coldness of his fingers underlined the chill in his voice.

Adrian took a long moment to check the time on his watch before pushing the offending hand away. "Thank you for the suggestion," he said.

"What is it with you, Mr. de la Noye?" Nicholas asked softly. "Are you really so impervious as to think you'll escape this fiasco unharmed?"

Adrian considered. "No, Mr. Chapman. Not impervious at all. Just willing to take my chances."

Bennett's voice carried into the parlor from the foyer. "Catharine! You look ravishing, my dear. Judge Bourne, my intended, Miss Catharine Walsh."

"Uh-oh." Chloe steadied herself with a shaky hand on the back of her brother's chair. "We should have stopped him. It's bad luck for the groom to see the bride before the ceremony."

"Oh, for heaven's sake." Nicholas reached up and pulled her into the seat to his right.

"I'm just repeating what people say." Chloe landed with a plop. "It's supposed to be a bad omen . . . although I think *every* wedding is a bad omen, whether or not the bride and groom have seen each other beforehand. Good grief, though. Even a blind person would have to admit that Pop looks better than ever. And I'm sure that Catharine—perhaps I should begin calling her 'Mother'—is ridiculously radiant."

"You're babbling, Chloe," Nicholas said. "Of course it's a bad omen. This whole marriage is doomed. Has anyone bothered to explain the guest list to Judge Bourne? Does he know yet that this wedding will be attended by its deceased matchmaker?"

"We'll leave that little detail to you, Mr. Chapman," Adrian said as he sat down on the sofa.

"Oh, don't make it quite this easy, Mr. de la Noye. You'll take away the sport of it."

Adrian smiled politely. "Please accept my apologies," he said, glancing toward the parlor door.

He shouldn't have. Catharine Walsh stood in the doorway, an ethereal vision in an ivory drop-waist dress that fell in a jagged hemline below her knees. Her hair framed her face in wild tendrils, setting off the intricate seed-pearl headdress she wore and making her eyes look even darker than usual. She held a bouquet of red and yellow roses with both hands. Bennett Chapman appeared by her side, finely dressed in a well-cut dinner jacket, one hand resting against his fiancée's hip in a proprietary fashion that made Adrian's jaw clench.

Nobody else in the room could possibly sense the conflict behind the regal lift of her chin. No one would guess that she felt as anxious and vulnerable as a lioness outnumbered by her hunters. But Adrian knew. Her desperation raced through his own veins, calling to him so loudly that he wondered why no one else could hear it.

He'd saved her from such rashness before. Would it really be so difficult to save her again? He started to rise, desperate to assure Cassie Walsh that there was no need to sacrifice herself in a marriage she didn't want.

Jim stopped him with an iron grip around his wrist. "Sit down," he whispered, eyes straight ahead. "It's her wedding, and you're not the groom . . . at least, not this time."

Adrian froze.

Jim readjusted his spectacles with a small, smug smile. "Again, Mr. de la Noye: I'm not as green as you think."

CHAPTER
43

February 1898

I suspect we've cooked our own goose." Cassie frowned out the window of the brougham as it slowed before the bride's home. "Really, Adrian, nobody will want anything to do with us now that we've managed to miss the wedding ceremony. Perhaps it would be best to turn around right now and miss the luncheon as well."

Adrian attempted to look remorseful, but it was an impossible task. Even though she sat demurely clothed beside him, every inch of Cassie revived memories of pleasure. Her gloved hands rested neatly in her lap as the carriage rolled to a stop, but that did not block the recollection of her fingertips sliding down his body as he gathered her close beneath the sheets. Her wild curls had been tamed into a modest chignon, but he didn't even need to close his eyes to see her thick hair cascading across the pillow as he poised himself above her. And how could he forget that her lips, although pursed at the moment, offered so much more than words alone?

He moved close enough to inhale the bewitching fragrance of her skin. "That's a tempting thought," he whispered into her perfect ear. "It would please me beyond measure to miss the luncheon. More than anything, Cassie, I want to go back to the cottage and take you to bed. But my friends would swarm the place in concern, and no good could come of that."

She planted a kiss on his cheek, not even pulling away when the coachman opened the carriage door. "We'll have to attend to your druthers later, then, Adrian Delano," she murmured, and he wasn't sure whether it was her words or her touch that caused the delicious waves that rippled through him.

"Look," she said, nodding toward the house as the coachman handed her down from the carriage. "Peter Phillips is perched on the windowsill, just waiting for us to arrive." Sure enough, Peter burst through the front door of the comfortable home, a glass of champagne punch in one hand, forehead creased in a vexed frown.

Adrian alighted beside her. "It isn't 'us' he cares about, my dear. He couldn't care less about me. It's Kate Weld he wants."

"Oh. Of course."

He caught the slight quaver in her voice. "Whatever were you thinking when you started this, Cassie?" he asked gently. "No, don't answer. It doesn't matter anymore."

She had no time to reply, but the trusting squeeze of her fingers as she slipped her hand through the crook of his arm spoke loudly enough to straighten his spine.

Peter met them halfway up the walk, his florid face more flushed than usual above his stiff white collar.

"Kate! Where have you been?" Fumes of champagne punch mingled with the bay rum of his cologne as he pried Cassie's hand from Adrian's arm and eased it into his own. She steadied him midsway. Undeterred, he led her toward the house, maneuvering the path as if it were the rolling deck of a ship.

"I'm so sorry we're late." Cassie planted herself in the walkway. "Was the wedding quite lovely?"

"I don't know," Peter said, and the words were rimmed with fretful accusation. "I spent most of it wondering where you were. You said I'd see you today, Kate, so I could only imagine the worst." He stroked her fingers in a slow, even rhythm. Adrian gritted his teeth.

Peter moved closer to Cassie, his tone so intimate that a soft blush tinged her cheeks. "I couldn't stand the thought that something might have happened to you," he said, bending toward her to brush his lips against hers. She dipped her head.

Adrian quirked an eyebrow in Cassie's direction. She telegraphed her permission from beneath fringed eyelashes.

He cleared his throat. "No worries about me, Peter?"

"None whatsoever." Peter frowned at the interruption. "I'm sorry, old man, but you're nowhere near as enchanting as your cousin."

"You mean my wife," Adrian said.

Cassie withdrew her hand from Peter's and drifted back to Adrian's side, her face the color of chalk. Peter stared from her to Adrian, his mouth agape. It took a long moment for comprehension to dawn.

"You married her?" The words rolled through his mouth as if foreign to his tongue.

"Yes." Adrian slipped an arm around Cassie's waist. "Last night.

There's a most obliging justice of the peace just on the outskirts of town."

"Married?" Peter repeated, and Adrian felt Cassie cringe in anticipation of the expected torrent of anger.

Instead, Peter threw back his head and laughed, each peal closer than the last to a donkey's bray. "You *married* her?"

Adrian said nothing, merely pulled Cassie closer.

"I'm sorry, old man," Peter said, wiping tears from his eyes. "It's just that . . . forgive me—I know she's your cousin, however distant. And she's beautiful, no doubt. But, Adrian, did Europe teach you nothing? She made it perfectly clear to me that she was willing. Did she even bother to tell you about our little . . . rendezvous . . . at the pond yesterday? It's quite natural to succumb to women like that, but one needn't ever marry them."

Adrian's fingers clenched into a hard ball. Suddenly Peter lay on the ground at his feet, hand pressed to his eye as blood spurted from his nose. Adrian stared at his own fist, momentarily surprised.

"Come." Cassie yanked on his arm as Peter struggled to rise.

Adrian faced him squarely, both fists raised to strike again.

"Leave him be!" Cassie cried, hustling him down the walk before the other man could regain his balance.

"I'd just as soon knock his teeth down his throat," Adrian said, but Cassie broke into a run, dragging him along with her. Her fingers gripped his arm like a vise; he had no choice but to keep up.

"It isn't worth it," he heard her say. "He's drunk."

He had no idea where she thought she was going. She didn't know Newport at all, but it didn't seem to matter. She hauled him down unfamiliar streets, darting past houses as if trying to escape something far more dangerous than Peter Phillips could ever be.

Their breath hung frosty on the air as they raced toward the ocean. Only their footsteps in the snow marked that they had ever come this way at all.

The snow accumulation lessened as they neared the water. The rocks by the sea were merely wet, their colors muted by the heavy gray clouds billowing low in the sky. A sharp dampness in the air pricked Adrian's nose, promising snow again by nightfall.

His heart rammed hard against his chest. "Cassie!" he called over the wind from the sea. "Stop!"

She did as he commanded, her breathing punctuated by ragged jolts and jags. "I'm sorry, Adrian," she gasped. "I'm so, so sorry."

He caught her in his arms, rocking her close. "Sorry for what?"

"Peter . . ."

"He's an oaf. I don't care what he says. You had a lapse of judgment where he's concerned, but it's over."

But her tears flowed fast, almost more quickly than he could wipe them away.

"He saw through me the whole time." Her words spiraled upward. "Peter, of all people! That stupid, conceited . . . even he could tell that I'm nothing better than a common—"

"Stop." Adrian shook her. "Cassie, you punctured his pride. He lashed back in the only way he knew how."

Her shoulders shook even harder as she sobbed against the front of his coat. "Oh, Adrian, what I've done to you. And you don't deserve it. You've always been so good to me. You—"

"And what have you done to me?" He cut her off, more concerned with her growing despair than with the words themselves.

She collapsed against him, finally spent. He rested his cheek against her hair and waited. Finally, she drew in a long, shaky breath. "Peter will talk," she said. "He'll make you a total laugh-ingstock."

"Peter's a clod. Anyone who listens to him deserves to be misled."

"But he doesn't even know my station yet. He doesn't know I'm nothing more than a cook's daughter. If that was his reaction even without knowing, can you imagine what your parents will say?"

Adrian didn't need to imagine what his parents would say. He already felt the quiver of his father's rage, cringed at the expected wrench of his mother's heartbroken sobs. It just didn't matter any-more. All that mattered was the woman in his arms, the beautiful, intriguing puzzle he now called wife. The rest would take care of itself.

He raised her chin until her eyes met his. "Listen to me, Cassie Delano, because I only intend to say this one last time. I don't care about your family lineage. I don't care what my parents think about it either. And I certainly don't care about anything Peter Phillips has to say. I have willingly pledged my life to you. I love you . . . madly, ridiculously. There's a part of me that can't exist without you. With you by my side, I can take on the world. Do you under-stand?"

She didn't answer. He thought he saw a flicker of sadness cross her face, but it might have been a trick of the clouded sun.

"Cassie," he said softly, "let's go back to the cottage. We'll leave for Poughkeepsie in the morning. Either my parents will under-stand or they won't, but it won't make a difference. We'll be just fine no matter what."

She didn't say a word, only clung tightly to his hand as he led them both away from the rocks toward home.

CHAPTER
44

Adrian's stunned expression was proof that Jim had been dead right: the bride trembling on Bennett Chapman's arm by the door of the parlor had once been married to Adrian de la Noye. Jim would have enjoyed basking in the glow of success just a little longer, but there wasn't time. Judge Thomas Bourne approached the podium, Catharine Walsh and Bennett Chapman following closely behind. Chloe reached out to take the bride's bouquet, but Catharine gripped it as if it were a lifeline, her stare never leaving the riotous colors she held before her.

"I applaud you, Mr. Reid," Adrian murmured, his emotions once again concealed behind a neutral mask. "You must tell me later how you managed that particular parlor trick. In the meantime, look sharp: the roller coaster ride is about to begin."

Amy had grown so pale that Jim could have traced the delicate blue veins beneath her skin. "Are you ready?" he whispered, squeezing her hand.

"I have no choice," she whispered back. "Mrs. Chapman is just itching to talk. I can't hold her off much longer. You'll keep me safe, Jim, won't you?"

"Are you kidding? You're my girl now; there's not a chance you're getting away from me that easily."

Judge Bourne smiled out at the small group before him. "Good evening," he said, setting the book he carried down onto the podium. "We're gathered here today to celebrate a most happy occasion: the marriage of my old friend Bennett Chapman to Miss Catharine Walsh."

Nicholas's head swiveled toward Adrian, his silent question hanging on the air: *Will you bring matters to a head or should I?*

"I know we're family and friends here," Judge Bourne continued. "And we're all eager to get reacquainted over the fine wedding supper I smell even as we assemble in this room. With that in mind—and at the request of both bride and groom—I will keep this ceremony short." He lifted his book, flipping the pages in search of the proper spot. "I assume no one objects to this marriage," he said with a chuckle.

Catharine tensed. Nicholas opened his mouth, but Bennett cut off his words. "Of course not," he said, glaring at his son and daughter. "But, Tom, before we continue, I must ask your indulgence to invite another guest. Would you mind if Elizabeth attended the wedding?"

The pages stopped flipping. "I'm not sure I understand the question," Judge Bourne said. "You are, of course, at liberty to invite anyone you please."

"I'm glad you don't mind." Bennett absently patted Catharine's hand. "It shouldn't take long to call her up. She'll be delighted to see you after so many years." He turned toward Amy. "Are you ready, my dear?"

Amy's hand shook in Jim's grasp. "Mrs. Chapman, are you ready?" The name had barely left her lips before her body grew rigid. "She's here," she said faintly. "She's been waiting. She bids you all good evening and says that the bride looks beautiful. She's delighted to see everyone . . . especially you, Judge Bourne."

The judge wrinkled his brow. "I don't understand."

"Of course you don't," Nicholas said. "No reasonable person would. My father has just invited my late mother to witness his wedding ceremony. In fact, it's his belief that she handpicked Catharine Walsh to be his bride. You asked if there were any objections to this marriage taking place. Well, I object. I believe my father's state of mind speaks for itself. He's insane, Judge Bourne, fit for neither marriage nor executing a new will. This should be obvious, yet I cannot convince Mr. de la Noye of the fact."

A fine sweat broke across Judge Bourne's forehead. "Mr. de la Noye?" He slowly lowered his book back to the podium. "Can you explain?"

Adrian's voice was calm. "Bennett Chapman is my client," he said, and at the sound of his voice, Catharine finally looked up from her bouquet. "He summoned me to Liriodendron to draft a new will, one that would reflect his marriage to Catharine Walsh. If I thought him insane, I could not in good conscience follow his directive. But I believe him to be of sound mind, and it's therefore my fiduciary duty to do as he requests."

Bennett Chapman smiled into the air. "Elizabeth, my dear, we are happy to have you join us," he said.

"Where is she standing, Father?" Nicholas enunciated his words as if speaking to a child.

"Oh, Nicky," Bennett sighed. "Perhaps you'd see her, too, if you didn't fight her visits so hard. She's standing to the left of Amy." His eyes filled with tears. "And she's wearing her own wedding dress. Elizabeth—how gracious of you to allow me a second chance. I never did deserve you."

Judge Bourne followed Bennett Chapman's gaze. It rested to Amy's left, where a doily draped across the sofa arm nearly brushed the wall. The judge studied the empty space for a moment before facing Amy. She met his unspoken query with a blank stare.

Catharine was next in line for his scrutiny. "There's nothing amiss here," she said, cheeks scarlet.

The judge reached for a handkerchief to mop his brow before meeting the adoration on his old friend's face.

"There you have it, Judge Bourne," Nicholas said. "You've heard it yourself. And I would suggest that if Mr. de la Noye finds even a shred of sanity in the belief that a dead woman arranged this wedding and now attends it as an honored guest, he himself is a few shades south of sound."

Adrian stood. "Oh, no need to concern yourself over my state of mind, Your Honor. I'm perfectly sound. We don't need to consider the existence of life after death. We need only determine whether it's reasonable for Bennett Chapman to believe that he's communicating with his late wife."

"How could that ever be reasonable?" Nicholas exploded. "It's clear what's happened here. In his weakened mental state, my father has been duped by Catharine Walsh, who obviously wants to get her dirty little hands on his fortune."

"That's a lie!" Catharine's bouquet slipped from her hand to the floor, forgotten.

"I am more sane than you'll ever be, you little wart!" Bennett snarled.

"Bennett," Adrian began, shooting Catharine a warning glance, "I beg your indulgence to let me speak on both your behalf and that of Miss Walsh. Judge Bourne, I've appeared before you in court on numerous occasions, haven't I?"

The judge pulled his bewildered gaze from the flowers strewn across the floor. "Yes, Mr. de la Noye, of course you have."

"Have I ever given you cause to doubt either my word or my sanity?"

"Indeed you have not. You remain one of the most competent attorneys to appear before me. That's strictly off the record, sir. Don't let it go to your head."

"Thank you, Your Honor. And I don't mind telling you that I've always found you to be open-minded and fair, even when ruling against me. I rest on my reputation when I ask you this: please, suspend judgment until Elizabeth Chapman has had an opportunity to speak for herself."

"Speak for herself?" The judge blanched. "You mean . . . through this young lady here?" He pointed toward Amy, who shrank a little farther into Jim's side.

"I'll agree to that," Nicholas said. "The more you see Amy Walsh weave her fiction, the more obvious my father's insanity will become."

Catharine steadied herself with a hand on the podium. "Or perhaps, Mr. Chapman, the more your mother speaks, the more obvious your own hateful truths will become."

"Careful, Miss Walsh," Nicholas said in a low voice. "I hold all the cards here, and I am not a gracious winner."

A gust of cold air whipped through the room; Chloe's feathers dipped and danced. She whirled to discover the source of the draft, hand clapped firmly to her head.

"Your mother is growing most displeased with you, Nicholas," Amy said, rising from the sofa on wobbly legs. Jim dropped her hand but positioned himself on the edge of his seat.

"Yes, let's have more theatrics," Nicholas said. "They can only prove my point."

Judge Bourne glanced sadly at his old friend. "I'm sorry, Bennett, but on the face of it, I must confess that your son's arguments are compelling. I . . . I had no idea you might be in a state of decline."

Bennett pointed a finger, ready to protest. Adrian held up a quelling hand as the judge continued.

"I am gravely concerned, both as an officer of the court and as a friend. But out of respect for you—and for your attorney as well—I am willing to listen to what the young lady has to say. Mr. de la Noye, you have five minutes to convince me of your argument."

"It should take less time than that for you to see right through it," Nicholas said.

Adrian turned toward Amy, who stood quaking in the middle of the floor like a lost child. "The floor is yours, Miss Walsh. What would Mrs. Chapman like to tell us?"

Amy's eyelids flickered as she closed her eyes to listen. "As I said before, Mrs. Chapman is particularly pleased to see you, Judge Bourne. She has fond memories of your visits and feels it most appropriate that you be here for Bennett tonight."

Jim's skin prickled. Although a frigid wind had blown through the room moments ago, only the left side of his body felt chilled. The cold seemed to spring from the empty space between sofa and wall, the very spot where Bennett Chapman had placed his wife.

"What is that?" Judge Bourne's voice cracked as he pointed a shaky finger toward the wall.

A concentrated ball of light glowed against a small portion of the wall, perhaps five feet up from the floor.

"Mother of God," Jim breathed. Catharine gasped.

Chloe's face lit up like a Chinese lantern. "That's you, Mother, isn't it. You're truly here!" She extended an entreating hand, but Nicholas lowered it with a press on her wrist.

Amy opened her mouth to speak, but only a little gulp came out. Jim half rose as a minor spasm jerked her body, but when her blue eyes opened wide, it was clearly Amy still behind them. "Your Honor, Mrs. Chapman sends her condolences on the loss of your wife," she said.

This time the gasp came from Judge Bourne.

Amy continued as if she'd heard nothing. "She says not to fret. Lavinia is happy, and she sends her love."

The glow on the wall brightened; Judge Bourne gripped the podium as an overpowering fragrance of bergamot laced the room. "That's my Lavinia's scent! Or was . . ."

"Wonderful, isn't it?" This time, Chloe's excitement fueled the quivering of her feathers. "Mother has been most kind in delivering messages from my departed daughter, too. I tell you, Judge Bourne, I don't like Catharine Walsh one single bit, but I can't agree with my brother that she and Amy are perpetrating a fraud."

"Shut up, Chloe," Nicholas said. "With all due respect, Judge Bourne, your wife's death certificate is a matter of public record. Once the Walshes knew you would be joining us this evening, they obviously dredged up all the information they could find about your personal life. Surely you're aware that there are ways to do that."

As quickly as it had arrived, the scent of bergamot faded away. Judge Bourne inhaled a last whiff of it, looking like a man whose dearest possession had just been laid to a bonfire.

"Mrs. Chapman wants Judge Bourne to know that she especially enjoyed the conversations you two shared about books," Amy said. "Her husband was always too busy to read. She found your conversations quite a welcome exercise of the mind."

"She often told me that!" Tears sprang to Judge Bourne's eyes. "Bennett! This is really quite extraordinary!"

Nicholas slowly stood, pivoting to face Amy. She ignored him, head cocked as if eavesdropping on a faint conversation in a crowd. "Mrs. Chapman especially requests that I tell you how grateful she remains for your recommendation that she read dear Mr. Thoreau. And as for *Les Misérables*, well, she quite forgives your opinion of Fantine and only hopes you've come to understand the miseries women are so often forced to endure."

"You may tell Mrs. Chapman that I've grown softer in my old age . . . perhaps even wiser," Judge Bourne said, his face shining.

"Oh, she can hear you," Amy said. "She says she's very glad to know that."

The spot of light on the wall faded for a moment, then glowed with even more intensity than before. The temperature emanating from it remained constant now, until Jim felt as if he'd settled beside an open icebox.

"Extraordinary!" Judge Bourne repeated.

Nicholas took a measured step toward Amy. "How do you do this?" he demanded, incredulous. "How do you know the things you know?"

Jim shot to his feet, reaching Amy's side at the same time Nicholas stopped before her.

"It's not that I want to," Amy answered quietly.

"It isn't real," Nicholas said. "It can't be real, no matter how many convincing words you utter, no matter how many strange effects you and your mother manage to conjure." His fingers landed on her shoulders like the talons of a great bird. "How do you do it?" he shouted, shaking her so hard that she slumped like a rag doll in his grip.

Both Catharine and Jim started toward him, but Amy regained her strength first and shoved the man away. The slap she delivered echoed through the room. Nicholas stumbled backward, hand covering the burning outline of her fingers on his cheek.

The light on the wall churned in a waterfall of color, then grew still.

"Your mother says," Amy said through torn breaths, "that you grew into a monster of a man, Nicky, and that you haven't yet received half of what you deserve."

"Does she, now," Nicholas said, chest heaving. "And let me guess: you share this opinion so strongly that you might have created it yourself."

"I will be quite honest with you." Amy's voice grew stronger. "I don't speak for your mother because I want to. I do it because I have no choice. She won't go away until she's had her say. And, since I want her to leave me alone for good, I plan to do everything in my power to see that she gets her way. She wants a wedding, Nicholas, and she wants it now."

"As do I," Bennett Chapman said loudly, reaching out a firm hand to tug a shocked Catharine to his side. "Damn it, Tom, can we just get this thing done?"

"Your Honor," Adrian spoke gently. "Can you understand now why I believe my client is perfectly sane?"

Thomas Bourne cleared his throat. "I've seen enough," he said, reaching for his book. "Nicholas, do you still contest this marriage on the basis of your father's sanity? Because if you do . . ."

"No," Nicholas said suddenly. "I withdraw the protest."

Even Adrian appeared surprised. "You do?"

"I do." A jagged smile broke across his face. "Why continue? It appears I'm in the minority here, doesn't it? Everyone—including those who no longer walk among us—seems to want a wedding. Very well. Let's have one." He approached the podium, arms opened wide. "Father," he said, enveloping Bennett in a huge hug. "Miss Walsh . . ." He turned toward Catharine, who recoiled so sharply that it appeared she might be ill. "Ah, Catharine, is this any way to treat family? Of course not." He lifted her limp hand to his lips and kissed it; she yanked it away as if burned. "Let's begin the ceremony, shall we?"

"Is Elizabeth ready?" Bennett asked.

Amy nodded. "She's quite eager to witness both the wedding and the execution of the will afterward."

Nicholas backed toward his seat. "Of course. We mustn't forget the execution of the will."

"What do you make of it?" Jim whispered as Adrian sank down to the sofa beside him.

Adrian shook his head, lost in thought.

CHAPTER
45

Never underestimate an adversary. That lesson had not been taught at Harvard Law School, but Adrian had learned it early in his career. Nicholas most certainly hadn't capitulated out of a kind change of heart. There had to be a damn good reason he'd switched tactics and now welcomed a wedding. Unfortunately, a "good reason" for Nicholas could only mean trouble for everyone else.

"Let's begin." Judge Bourne cast one last awed glance toward the glow on the wall, then squared his shoulders to signal a return to the reason they'd assembled in the first place.

Amy wedged herself between Adrian and Jim on the sofa. Adrian unconsciously shifted to accommodate her, attention riveted on the scene unfolding before him. To his right across the aisle, Nicholas leaned back in his chair, arms crossed.

Judge Bourne looked down at his book on the podium. "As I said earlier, we are gathered here to witness the union of Bennett Chapman and Catharine Walsh as man and wife. And I will cut to the quick, since we've already had enough excitement for one evening."

Catharine and Bennett flanked the podium, stiff and ill at ease. There were no shy, excited glances exchanged; no trembling fingers intertwined in anticipation. Bennett rocked his weight from one foot to the other, one hand jiggling nervously in his pocket. Catharine stared at the floor.

Adrian's thoughts drifted decades back to the overheated parlor of a sleepy justice of the peace on the edge of town. Cassie's cheeks, rosy from the cold . . . her hand so confidently tucked in his . . . they'd looked so improperly mussed that surely any fool could tell they'd celebrated the honeymoon before the wedding.

Judge Bourne's voice forced his mind back to the matters at hand. "Bennett William, do you take Catharine Mary to be your lawful wife, to love, honor, and protect her, forsaking all others?"

Set free after years of suppression, Adrian's memories would not be denied. Cassie's anxious half-smile as the justice of the peace paused for his response . . . the tug of his heart at her obvious concern that he might change his mind. "I do," he'd said, so emphatically that the worried lines on her face had disappeared into a wide, happy beam.

"I do," Bennett said now, shooting his cuffs like a man late to a board meeting.

"Catharine Mary, do you take Bennett William to be your lawful husband, to love, honor, and protect him, forsaking all others?"

Catharine kept her eyes averted from the man by her side. That hadn't been the case twenty-three years ago. Then, the eager warmth of her gaze had almost melted her young groom on the spot.

"I do." She whispered the expected words to the floorboards.

Adrian's fingers drummed an even tattoo on the arm of the sofa. Cassie didn't want to marry Bennett Chapman any more than she'd wanted to marry Peter Phillips.

"No best man?" Judge Bourne asked, apparently noticing for the first time that Bennett and Catharine stood alone.

"No." Bennett withdrew a small box from his pocket. "I didn't think it necessary. Mr. de la Noye and Mr. Reid will serve as witnesses, and I've got the ring right here." He flipped open the box; diamonds glittered as he lifted the ring from its satin nest. It was clearly worth quite a bit, no matter how hastily it had been procured.

Adrian and Cassie had made do with rings they'd already owned, grinning at the cleverness of imbuing treasured possessions with entirely new meaning. "I, Adrian, take thee, Catharine . . . ," he'd intoned, watching the amethyst crest of his signet ring turn toward the floor as it dangled, too big, from her ring finger. She, for her part, had slid her own imitation ruby halfway down his pinkie before squeezing his hand and giving up.

But despite the haste with which that ceremony had been arranged, it had mattered to him, mattered deeply enough that it seemed almost a mockery to hear Bennett Chapman repeat the words he himself had once said to this same bride: "I take thee, Catharine, to be my wife, and pledge my love to you forever."

How was it that the woman who'd first inspired him to stand up for himself had been the very one to cut him to the quick?

Judge Bourne waited until Bennett had slid the ring onto Catharine's finger before continuing the ceremony. "Catharine and Bennett, insomuch as the two of you have agreed to live together in matrimony . . ."

Adrian had meant every word of the vows he'd uttered before the justice of the peace that night twenty-three years ago. He'd have loved Cassie forever had she let him. And, had Cassie been able to trust that, perhaps it might have been enough. How could she have doubted that he would stand by her, no matter what?

" . . . and have promised your love for each other by these vows . . ." Judge Bourne went on.

Catharine slowly exhaled, her color high. Adrian straightened. He couldn't save her now any more than he'd been able to save her then. But, as if of their own accord, his thoughts caressed another bride, a small blond stenographer of lively intelligence who fearlessly countered his legal arguments at the office, yet quaked with visible nerves as she stood beside him at the altar.

"I thought every woman longed for marriage," he'd teased when he and Constance had finally walked down the church aisle as husband and wife. "I'm supposed to be your savior, Constance, not the greatest terror of your life."

Constance had managed a crooked smile. "Oh, I love you, Adrian . . . although not as a savior, you poor fool. But, marriage! What I've just promised you . . . my God. How can anyone on earth entertain such vulnerability without experiencing waves of nausea?"

" . . . I now declare you to be man and wife."

Catharine's long exhalation echoed his own. He sensed invisible walls rise quickly around her, caught the determined set of her jaw as she reached for Bennett's hand.

Catharine Walsh could never let down her guard enough to fully trust anyone other than herself. Constance had been right: loving another person left one entirely unprotected, and Catharine was fundamentally fashioned to survive.

With a jolt, Adrian realized that she had never needed saving at all.

A movement from across the aisle caught his attention. Nicholas leaned forward, poised at the edge of his seat. He was too eager, and that expectant look on his face could only bode ill.

"Congratulations," Judge Bourne said. "You may kiss the bride."

And, as Bennett bent forward to plant an awkward smack on Catharine's lips, Adrian knew the answer in a flash. Of course! It was so obvious—only the distraction of past memories had prevented him from anticipating Nicholas's most effective moment to attack.

Judge Bourne closed his book with an authoritative slap. "My friends, allow me to present Mr. and Mrs. Bennett William Chapman."

"My congratulations," Nicholas said, rising to his feet before anyone could even think to applaud. "And my sympathies as well. Judge Bourne, I assume bigamy is still an offense in the state of Rhode Island?"

Catharine stepped forward, fists clenched. "Enough," she said. "Keep him out of it. He doesn't deserve it."

"Why, Catharine. Are you begging me?"

Cold fury drained Catharine's face of the little color it had left. "I would *never* beg you," she spat. A collective gasp arose as she lunged toward him, fingernails raking across his vested torso as if she thought she could draw blood through the silk.

Adrian shot from his seat, pulling her against him in a straitjacket hold. "Don't, Catharine," he murmured. She stared at him for a moment, her clenched fist resting against the soft skin above her lace neckline. Adrian waited until her fingers relaxed before releasing her from the safety of his arms.

Nicholas adjusted his vest and lapels, cold eyes glittering like glass. "Don't be such a killjoy. I'm finally starting to enjoy this dismal visit." With an exaggerated clearing of his throat, he turned to face Bennett.

"Father, I'm sorry to cause you grief, but I'm afraid your bride will be spending the honeymoon in jail. It seems the new Mrs. Chapman and your lawyer are already married . . . to each other."

CHAPTER
46

J im leapt to his feet as Bennett Chapman swayed backward, but Adrian was already there, supporting the older man with a strong hand beneath his elbow.

"I don't understand," Bennett said, slumping against his attorney.

"It's not difficult." Nicholas advanced until he and Catharine stood nearly toe-to-toe. She pulled herself up to her full height, the hatred in her eyes as sharp as any weapon. "Catharine Walsh and Adrian de la Noye were married here in Newport in February 1898," Nicholas said, plowing through Chloe's gasp. "Do either of you deny this?"

Catharine's questioning gaze flickered across Adrian's face; he nodded.

"No," she said. "I don't deny it."

"And neither do I." Adrian's steadiness seemed to bolster Catharine's nerve. Her expression remained serene, her figure a study in regal fortitude.

Nicholas paused, obviously expecting more, but it was Bennett who filled the gaping silence.

"I don't understand," he repeated, and this time, his words came out in little more than a croak. Jim leaned across the aisle to grab Nicholas's chair, dragging it across the rug just in time. Bennett gratefully sank into it as if every year of his age had finally caught up with a vengeance.

"I don't blame you for feeling poorly, Father," Nicholas said. "You've been hoodwinked twice, haven't you? First by the charming Miss Walsh and then by Mr. de la Noye . . . or is it Mr. Delano? Did he ever tell you that was his family name? But, of course, knowing what we all know now, it makes perfect sense that he would want to change it. It's so much easier to keep the past a mystery if you leave your old identity behind."

Judge Bourne opened his mouth to interject, but Adrian stayed his words with a polite wave of his hand.

Amy cleared her throat. "I'm sorry, but Mrs. Chapman . . . the first Mrs. Chapman . . . would like to speak."

"Oh, I'm sure she would," Nicholas said, "because you're as deep into this scheme as your mother and . . . dare I say it . . . your father."

"That's not true!" Catharine and Adrian both said at the same time, but Amy's voice floated above their protests. "Mrs. Chapman says you are mistaken," she said. "Adrian de la Noye is not my father." She froze, momentarily stunned by her own words. "Jim . . ." she began, confusion clear on her face, "he's not my father!"

Jim swiftly returned to her side, steadying her with an arm around her waist.

Adrian placed a firm hand on his client's shoulder. "Bennett . . . I owe you an apology as well as an explanation. Perhaps I should have been more forthcoming about my past relationship with Miss Walsh. But the fact is, I've never even shared this information with Constance, and I was caught entirely off guard when I saw Miss Walsh again after all these years. Twenty-three years, Bennett. It's been that long since I had any contact with—"

"—your wife." Nicholas's words landed like a boulder in the midst of them all.

Adrian shook his head. "She's not my wife, Mr. Chapman. My wife is at home in Brookline with our children." He reached inside his coat pocket. "Judge Bourne, now would be a good time to give this back to you, I think. This seems the right moment to open it."

The judge cleared his throat as he accepted the proffered envelope. "Bennett, let me be clear: I carried this envelope with me from Boston today. Constance de la Noye had it delivered to my home before I left for Newport. I don't know what it is, but she requested that I give it to her husband, so I did."

"Why would you do that?" Nicholas demanded. "Are you in the habit of providing courier services?"

The judge's face softened. "Sir, have you ever met Constance de la Noye?"

"No."

"Obviously, or you wouldn't be questioning me. It's hard to refuse Constance anything. An utterly charming woman . . . and my goddaughter to boot."

For the first time, Nicholas looked a bit nonplussed. "Adrian de la Noye's wife is your goddaughter?"

Judge Bourne nodded as he unsealed the envelope in his hand. "I think the world of her. Which means, Adrian, that you'd best have a very good explanation for all of this."

"Your Honor, I believe you'll find that all is in order," Adrian said quietly.

The room grew still as the judge withdrew a thin piece of paper from the envelope. He unfolded it and read silently, taking a moment to absorb the words before looking up. "It would appear that the marriage between Catharine Walsh and Adrian Delano was annulled in September 1901," he said.

"Let me see that." Nicholas lifted the paper from the judge's hand. "Annulled on what grounds?"

Adrian hesitated as Catharine bowed her head. "Does it matter?" he asked. "The fact is that an annulment is a judicial declaration that no marriage ever existed between the parties. In the eyes of the law, Mr. Chapman, Catharine Walsh and I were never married. Not only is there no bigamy involved, but one could even argue that there was no need to address this youthful folly at all."

"Where was this filed?" Nicholas's voice trailed. "I did considerable research on you, Mr. de la Noye . . . you know that. Rhode Island, Massachusetts . . ."

"New York," Adrian said. "The information is in your hand. Read the document. I suppose you assumed that when I changed my name, I cut off all contact with my family. You were mistaken. My father was delighted to use his influence to help me bury an embarrassing mistake. I was forgiven that particular indiscretion." He managed a small smile. "What he hasn't quite accepted these days is the fact that I married my stenographer."

Nicholas slowly lowered the paper in his hand. "So this decree . . ."

"Let's just say that it isn't easy to find."

"Then Catharine Walsh couldn't have known about it either." Nicholas stared into his father's stony face. "She'd have married you, Father, whether her first marriage had been annulled or not."

Catharine's composure finally cracked. "I knew Adrian would take care of it somehow," she whispered, staring at the floor. "It's his nature to put things to right. What happened twenty-three years ago was my fault, not his. He's a good man and deserves no censure from anyone here." She rounded the chair to kneel before her husband. "Bennett, I have not knowingly duped you. I will stand by this marriage no matter what, even if you choose not to execute your new will."

Bennett Chapman pierced her with a searching look. "You will?"

"Yes. I will."

The clock on the mantel exploded in frantic ringing, its chimes slicing the air like a series of small, sharp slaps. Brightness splashed across the wall as the ball of light pulsed and sparked with indignation.

"Oh, my God," Chloe moaned, eyes wide. "What does Mother want? Amy, tell us."

"I'd rather not," Amy said. "You and your brother already think badly enough of me . . . oh!" She doubled over, arms wrapped around her stomach. Jim reached for her hand, but she waved him away, struggling to pull in a deep breath. "All right! All right, I'll say it. Mrs. Chapman wants the new will executed. Immediately."

Bennett stared from his bride to the vivid glow. His brows lowered as his face contorted into a scowl: apparently his romance with his first wife had reached the same bump in death that it had experienced during their time together on earth. Catharine quickly rose to her feet to retreat to the relative safety of Adrian's side.

"Why does this matter, Elizabeth?" Bennett demanded, every inch the intimidating magnate he'd been in the prime of his life.

Amy spoke, but all eyes remained glued to the light, which now seemed to protrude as if someone had attached a shimmering bas-relief to the wall. "Mrs. Chapman says that she will answer all your questions once you've done as she requests."

"That's insane!" Nicholas shouted. "He's supposed to officially change his will before knowing why it even matters? This situation has gotten entirely out of hand—Judge Bourne, surely you can see that my father has lost his mind if he even considers . . ."

"You've already lost that battle, Nicky," Bennett said flatly. "No more. I am of sound mind and body, entirely capable of making this decision without your intervention."

But whether or not Nicholas heard a word his father said was irrelevant. The glow had left the wall to become a floating ball of light. It hovered in the space between sofa and wall, close to Amy's blond head. Jim felt her shudder against him as an involuntary grimace crossed her face.

"Mr. Chapman," he said, "with all due respect, you'll need to make your decision quickly. I'm not sure Amy can hold this communication for much longer."

"Elizabeth says to sign the will now, Bennett," Amy said faintly. "She says to do it for redemption, as a way to gain her forgiveness for all the pain you caused during your life together."

"Pain? What is Mother talking about?" Chloe turned to her father for an explanation.

"Who cares, Chloe?" Nicholas said, a fine mist of sweat beading his brow.

A tremor raced through Bennett Chapman's frame. "No, Elizabeth, don't . . ."

"She says she would be happy to enlighten those gathered here unless you comply." Amy's eyes were closed now, the motion of her eyelids reflecting the jumble of thoughts behind them.

Jim's eyebrows rose at the thought of a blackmailing ghost. It didn't quite jibe with expectations of a rosy afterlife. But there was no time to ponder eternal truths: he was nearly carrying Amy now, and the weaker she became, the stronger the angry ball of light blazed.

"Mr. Chapman," he said, trying hard to keep his voice steady, "suppose you execute the will so that we can hear Mrs. Chapman's rationale. If the answer is unsatisfactory to you, Mr. de la Noye and I can immediately draft whatever new will you'd like. Ultimately, sir, you are still our client, and we won't leave Liriodendron until you're content."

"Yes," Adrian echoed as Catharine nodded her agreement. "Excellent plan, Mr. Reid. Bennett, will that do?"

"I can't deny that some unexplainable force is at work here," Bennett murmured. "Bring me the will. I'll see this through for Elizabeth's sake . . . and, apparently, for my own."

Adrian crossed to an end table, where the document lay waiting atop a lap desk. Only Nicholas's harsh breathing broke the silence in the room as he carried both will and lap desk to Bennett, who sat up tall in his chair.

"Judge Bourne, Mr. Reid, would you serve as witnesses, please?" Adrian asked, pressing his Waterman into Bennett's waiting hand.

The flap of paper broke the stillness. Bennett skimmed each page, initialing it before turning to the next. Finally he came to the end. The nib of the pen paused above his signature line for a moment, then landed in a series of loops and dashes as Bennett William Chapman signed his name. Catharine let out a long breath; Nicholas swore and retreated to the window to stare out at the front yard.

"There," Bennett said, handing the will to Judge Bourne. "Sign it and be done. And now, Elizabeth . . . are you satisfied? Will you tell me why this was so important to you?"

The light roiled in and about itself, bright and clear. Eyes closed, Amy stepped toward it, right hand still enfolded in Jim's. She frowned, listening hard to something nobody else could hear.

Suddenly her eyes flew open. Her left hand flew to her mouth. "Oh!" she cried, mouth curled in disgust. "Oh, no!"

CHAPTER
47

February 1898

Cassie propped her head on one hand to study Adrian asleep beside her. "We'll go back to Poughkeepsie," he'd said, as if the two of them would be greeted at the Delano home by a wedding banquet instead of by enraged parents. Back to Pough-keepsie, where his father had probably worn a rut in the floor after pacing for days, all the while sharpening well-crafted lectures enti-tled "Family Embarrassment in Europe" and "The Need to Accept the Responsibilities of Manhood." Adrian's latest escapade—the one called "Abominably Unsuitable Marriage"—would probably end in disownment. Yet her new husband slept untroubled beneath the eiderdown, so much at peace with himself and his bride that one might imagine he'd unexpectedly married into royalty.

If he didn't fear returning home, then why should she?

She let her head fall back against the cool pillow, eyes unblinking as she stared up at the ceiling. Adrian Delano was the best friend she'd ever had, well worth loving—how on earth could she have let this happen to him? Hot tears started in the corners of her eyes. Irritated by her own weakness, she reached up to angrily brush them away. The time for crying was long past.

Adrian shifted to his side, instinctively pulling her close. She clutched his arm as if it were a life preserver.

"Cassie?" He struggled to open his eyes. "Go to sleep, sweetheart. The train home leaves early."

She couldn't help flinching at the word "home."

He tucked her more securely against his chest, already lost to the tides of sleep. "Stop worrying," he mumbled. "I'm not afraid. I'm ready to deal with this."

She bit her lip. He could deal with what he knew. It was the part she hadn't told him that plagued her.

Adrian had been away from his family for a very long time. He hadn't spent the winter holidays with them in the New York town house, enduring all the pomp and pageantry surrounding his sister's debutante ball. There'd been the business of dress, of escorts, of guests, followed by a stupefying procession of bachelors who'd graced family social events in order to see if Edith Delano suited their fancy. Parties at home, dinners and dances about town . . . Cassie had watched them all from her vantage point as Edith's lady's maid, had learned about each eligible bachelor well before he crossed the marble threshold.

Her fingers slid down Adrian's arm to entwine with his. He murmured his approval, although she could tell from his breathing that his sleep had grown deeper.

Maybe he was right after all, and everything would be fine. He seemed so certain of it. Besides, what good did it do to doubt? They were married now. Perhaps the ceremony had been less than dignified, but it was legal all the same, performed by a reputable officer of the court. And as for Adrian—she'd loved him since girlhood. She would do her best to make him happier than he'd ever been.

She fell into a restless sleep as new snow swirled in the night air.

The dream, of course, was waiting, just as it had waited nearly every night for almost two months now. There she was again, sorting hair ornaments in Edith's New York City bedroom, half listening to the rise and fall of voices from the dining room downstairs as the current crop of gentlemen tested their wit over dinner. Time became jumbled in dreams: it seemed only seconds before *he* was at her elbow, the suitor who should have been tucked away in the dining room with the rest but had somehow managed to climb the stairs to find her alone.

The smell of tobacco pierced her nostrils as a hand clamped across her mouth. Strong fingers closed around her throat, loosening just in time for her to drag in a ragged gasp before passing out. A man's body pinned her against the mattress; his rough hand explored beneath her petticoats. She pushed against him as best she could, but over and over and over again pain ripped her apart as he grunted like an animal above her.

Cassie bolted upright in the cottage bed, hot tears mixing with the perspiration that dripped from her brow. Adrian stirred, but she calmed herself enough to murmur that all was well. He smiled in his sleep, turning his back to her to burrow more deeply into the quilts.

It would never, ever end. She would live with the results of that horrible night forever.

The dream was kind in one respect: it never forced her to revisit her assailant's face. But she knew it well enough . . . she knew everything about the man. He was heir to a fortune, considered quite an eligible catch. His people hobnobbed with the wealthiest of families . . . that fact had been brought back to her with an alarming thud when she'd seen the newly constructed Liriodendron rising proudly above the crashing surf. If his tentacles could reach her even here, in Newport, then was any place safe?

Taking care not to disturb Adrian, Cassie left the bed and reached for her robe on the bedpost. Her hand hovered above it as she glanced down. Illuminated by the brightness outside, her naked body seemed nearly otherworldly. She ran a tentative hand down one full breast, finally letting it caress the slight fullness of her abdomen. There was nothing otherworldly about the baby she carried.

She should have continued to play her game with Peter, no matter what the outcome. Perhaps she never would have fooled him, and maybe he never would have proposed marriage. But once he appeared to be the father of her child, he might at least have done the honorable thing and supported the baby. Lying about the baby's paternity to Peter would have been easy, for she didn't care a fig about him. But Adrian . . . Adrian, who had always been so kind to her, who was willing to risk his own inheritance to stay by her side . . . how could she put him in this position? How long would it be before social paths crossed and he found himself face-to-face with her past? She knew how it would go: her assailant would find a way to reveal everything, to destroy her husband's reputation along with his love for her. And Adrian would have risked all to end up a pathetic fool.

She shivered as she pulled on her robe, drifting toward the

window as if the answer to her dilemma lay outside in the soft snow.

She deserved disdain. She knew this deep in her soul, for the dream, however persistent, always omitted one important fact: she had met that heinous man before, back in Poughkeepsie. And she had flirted as coyly with him as she flirted with all of the suitors who found her such a delightful change from plain and awkward Edith Delano. She'd allowed pride to cloud judgment, taking secret pleasure in the knowledge that all of Edith's wealth could not make the young woman more desirable than Cassie herself already was.

She had brought this on herself, no doubt—but Adrian did not deserve to share her downfall.

Willing each foot forward, Cassie slowly crossed the room. Her open carpetbags were already packed for the trip tomorrow. The robe dropped to the floor as she stepped into her drawers. Her fingers fumbled with the buttonhole, their clumsiness a silent protest; she pushed the button through with a savage shove. At least Adrian's sleep seemed sound enough. Even so, she quickly donned chemise and corset but did not waste time tightening the laces. Gaining speed, she yanked on her corset cover and all four petticoats from her carpetbag . . . she'd need the space they occupied.

Transformed into a silent whirlwind, she rummaged briefly through Adrian's packed trunk to draw out his gold cufflinks and studs, along with Edith's pearls. Her heart burned with her own deceit as she counted the money in his billfold. It was for his own good. The loss of money and objects now was nothing compared to what he'd lose if she stayed. Someday she'd find a way to return it all: the cufflinks, the pearls . . . everything. She left him a little more than the cost of his train fare home.

Her breath caught as she remembered the amethyst-crested signet ring. Now, that was rightfully hers. Hadn't Adrian implied as much when he'd slid it onto her finger during their vows? Grateful for the slightest shred of honesty, Cassie skimmed across the floor to retrieve it from the nightstand by her side of the bed.

She turned toward Adrian one last time. His tousled hair reminded her of the boy she'd known, but the angular cheekbones and stubble of his beard made it clear that the time for their childhood games was over forever. The corners of his lips turned up in a slight smile, as if he visited a marvelous dream. She gripped the bedpost to keep from diving back into the snowy sheets beside him, where she could entwine herself around his warm body and never let go. A deep, empty chasm gaped open within her. Carefully, she bent toward her husband.

Adrian shifted in his sleep with a sigh. Cassie pulled back, stung.

Quietly, she lifted both carpetbags and slipped into the hall. She stopped just long enough to reach for Adrian's heavy coat as well as her own, sliding both over her shoulders as she disappeared into the night.

CHAPTER
48

Enough." Jim grasped Amy's arm in concern. "She's had enough."

Amy did indeed look slightly green, but she shrugged away from his hold, advancing toward Nicholas Chapman with a slow, even gait. She stopped a foot away from him, as if closer contact might contaminate.

"You're my father," she said in disbelief.

Nicholas stared at her. "Don't be ridiculous."

"Mrs. Chapman says . . . you're my father."

Jim caught her as her legs gave way, scooping her up into his arms as if she weighed nothing at all. One quick glance toward Adrian and he nearly dropped her back to the ground. Her words should have induced an emotional earthquake, yet his friend stood silent and calm. A quick image of Adrian and Catharine on the rocks the night before flashed through his mind: Adrian already knew.

Nicholas swiveled toward Catharine. "Does she understand

what she's implying? That you . . . that I . . . it's insane! I never met you before this past week. Tell them!"

Catharine bit her lower lip. The ball of light glowed near the sofa, steady as a sentinel.

"Put me down," Amy said, and Jim obliged. She placed a light fingertip on each temple, closing her eyes in concentration. "Mrs. Chapman says that a wrong must be righted, and that since the living were too spineless to do it, she had no choice but to do it herself."

"Mother . . . what are you talking about?" Chloe's quizzical haze transcended alcohol.

Ashen, Bennett turned to his bride. "What is the meaning of this?"

Catharine stepped past him to face Nicholas, a barely suppressed tide of anger causing the pearls on her headdress to tremble. "You don't remember me at all, do you."

"No, of course not. Why would I?" He stood his ground as she drew closer.

"Then your hatred for me has been born of nothing more than fear that I would gain your father's fortune?" She was genuinely surprised.

"What else could it possibly be, Miss Walsh?"

She allowed her scorn free rein. "You may call me Mrs. Chapman. I rather like the sound of that name dripping from your lips. And you are mistaken. We met many, many years ago, although you certainly never bothered to ask my name."

Amy's eyes remained closed, her voice as plaintive and clear as a child's. "Nicholas, your mother suggests that you remember a certain dark-eyed lady's maid in Poughkeepsie . . . and later in New York."

The words seemed to unfurl through Nicholas's mind like a ribbon. Slowly, his face changed to putty, the eyebrows dropping from their haughty arch, the cheeks slack. A vein throbbed in his forehead as he flexed his fingers. "My God," he said. "You're . . . that girl. Edith Delano's maid."

"Catharine." A quaver in Bennett's voice betrayed his authority. "I must insist on an explanation."

"And you've every right to one, Bennett," Catharine said. "Perhaps Nicholas might provide it since I've wanted one myself all these years."

"I owe you nothing," Nicholas said, but his gaze strayed from Catharine to Amy as if the young woman's existence was even more unbelievable to him than that of his late mother. "You were there for the taking."

"You're right, you owe me nothing," Catharine countered coldly. "Your mother has taken care of your debt in full, hasn't she?"

The ball of light grew more diaphanous. Jim looped a defensive arm through Amy's as it passed by, but it no longer seemed interested in her. Instead it bobbed before Bennett, almost as if inviting him to dance.

"Can you hear her?" Amy asked. "She wants to be the one to tell you what happened. She thinks it's important that you know."

"It's all lies!" Nicholas shouted. "It's clever effects with lights and mirrors, concocted by the most brilliant grifter I've ever met. Watch!" He punched through the light, only to pull back with a cry of pain.

Chloe sprang to his aid, gasping as she covered his fist with both her hands. "Your skin! It's like ice!"

Bennett stared into the light. "Elizabeth?" Pale splashes of gold and pink illuminated his countenance as he leaned toward the essence of his first wife. "What did you want to tell me? I'm listening."

The light brightened and dimmed in response.

Bennett recoiled. "Amy, perhaps it would be best if you just told me what she's saying."

Amy listened for a moment. "She won't say. She prefers to tell you herself."

A shadow of fear crossed the old man's face as he stumbled backward. "Elizabeth . . . my sweet . . . you know I never meant you any harm, don't you? I've tried my best to repent for my boorish behavior. I've done all you've asked me to do. I've married Miss Walsh . . . I've changed the will . . ."

The light intensified.

Color flooded back into Amy's cheeks as she tugged Jim's arm. "She's finished with me . . . for good," she whispered, and Jim wondered if relief might have temporarily blunted the shock of discovering her father's identity. "She only wants Bennett now."

Bennett glared at his son, then turned to plant an awkward kiss on Catharine's cheek. With a resigned nod, he bent toward the ball of light. "Very well, Elizabeth," he said. "It appears I must do your bidding for the rest of my days in order to keep peace between us. Tell me."

Suddenly his eyes opened wide in shock. His body grew rigid as he began to wheeze. One arm flailed through the air.

Judge Bourne started forward as Bennett Chapman collapsed to the ground. "Bennett!"

Adrian dropped to one knee beside the old man, grasping his wrist in search of a pulse. "Jim. Telephone for help."

"Look!" Chloe jerked a shaking finger toward the light. The

iridescence had elongated into the shimmering shape of a woman. Resolute even in shifting form, she hovered above Bennett's prone body.

"M-Mother!" Nicholas nearly choked on the word.

The figure turned its head. Nicholas shrank from the disdain etched in the milky features. Elizabeth Chapman returned her attention to her husband, extending her hand in a shadowy invitation before vanishing.

"She's gone!" Chloe cried.

Adrian gently lowered Bennett Chapman's arm to his chest. "So is he, I'm afraid," he said. "I'm so sorry."

CHAPTER
49

J im drained his fourth cup of coffee, staring out at the sea from Liriodendron's terrace as the morning sun arched its way across the sky toward noon. There'd been little for him to do since Bennett's sudden death last night. Adrian and Judge Bourne had accepted the sad tasks involved in making the necessary arrangements, and while Jim had politely offered his assistance to Chloe and even to Nicholas, he hadn't been surprised when both declined. Neither seemed particularly distressed by their father's passing. In fact, after the initial shock had dissipated, Chloe had taken herself to bed, transparently relieved that she might soon leave both Liriodendron and Newport behind. She'd left her flask behind as well, propping it beside Bennett's walking stick in the parlor and exiting the room without a single parting glance.

Nicholas, too, had secluded himself, but not before a hurried conference with Catharine Walsh Chapman and her attorney, Adrian de la Noye. Catharine had kept that conversation brief, for Amy had been waiting her turn, finally ready to talk. Jim had sent her to her mother's room later that evening with a kiss for luck.

"Jim."

Jim's thoughts returned to the present as Adrian crossed the terrace. Adrian had spent most of last night on the telephone, but only the faintest shadowing beneath his eyes hinted at his lack of sleep. He was clean-shaven, every dark hair on his head expertly in place. His suit looked freshly pressed. Best of all, he carried the folded Corona 3, an indication that perhaps the car had been called around, and they might actually leave Aquidneck some time soon.

"How is everyone?" Jim asked.

"No hearts are breaking." Adrian set down the typewriter and reached into his coat pocket for his cigarette case. "Lady Dinwoodie and her brother have agreed to accompany their father's body to Boston. The funeral will be there. After that . . . well, they are aware of the contents of his will, and that's all they really care about. Our firm will handle that, of course."

"Does Nicholas plan any further challenge?"

Adrian opened the cigarette case. "No. Certain bygones— however egregious—will remain bygones as long as he agrees to leave Catharine alone."

"That's all?"

"It's not my decision to make."

Jim watched as Adrian slid a cigarette from the case, closed the lid, and returned the case to his pocket. He wondered what thoughts raced behind that smooth exterior. Surely the emotions of the past few days had pounded his friend hard, yet there he stood, calmly cupping his cigarette with one hand as if lighting it efficiently were the most important thing on his mind.

"By the way," Adrian said after a long, slow exhale, "Bennett Chapman's official cause of death was heart failure."

"Ah. I see. Understandable."

"More understandable than the truth, which I suggest we keep to ourselves. How much time do you need before you're ready to leave?"

"Hope has been springing eternal for days. I can leave any time you say."

"Good. I still have business to finish here, but one of us should drive back to the office. Could you manage our affairs there?"

Jim eyed the typewriter. "Sure. If you think I'm up to the task."

"Oh, you are more than up to the task," Adrian said dryly. "I trust you to keep the home fires burning until I return. I'll only be a day or two behind you. I plan to take the train no later than—"

Pounding footsteps cut him short.

"Jim!" Amy flew through the French doors, so out of breath that he knew she must have run from upstairs. He opened his arms just in time for her to catapult into them, but the impact knocked the wind from him. "She's gone!"

Adrian's cigarette stopped halfway to his mouth. "Catharine?" he asked.

Amy nodded. "We were up so late talking last night that I thought she'd decided to sleep in this morning. But I've just been by her room and . . . she's gone, suitcases and all! She left a note for me on the bed."

For the first time, Jim noticed the envelope in her hand. The way she carefully smoothed it against her body told him that she would keep it someplace special for quite some time.

"She promises she'll be back," Amy said. "She's decided to travel a bit, that's all, and will call me as soon as she has more definite plans. She said your law office was authorized to handle the matter of the will in her absence, and that you'll administer her assets until she returns. She said you could help me should I need any money from the estate."

Adrian absorbed the information with no apparent emotion. "Some things never change, do they?" he said.

Amy turned toward him. "She's left you a note as well, Mr. de la Noye. Here." She teased a sealed envelope from behind her own.

Adrian stubbed his cigarette against the side of the retaining wall before taking the letter from her trembling hand. He turned toward the sea to unseal it, slowly withdrawing a single sheet of stationery from within. Something else came with it: Jim caught a glint of gold in the bright sun, thought he glimpsed a purple flash of amethyst as a ring fell into Adrian's waiting palm. Adrian paused for a moment, as lost in his own world as a man could be, while the gulls screeched overhead and the waves smashed against the rocks. Then he read.

Amy waited until he looked up before clearing her throat. "Mr. de la Noye, my mother would do anything for you."

Except stay, Jim thought, and despite the placid expression on Adrian's face, he suspected that the same words splashed through his mind as well.

"Thank you, Amy," Adrian said. "And we, of course, are at your service."

Amy rested her head against Jim's chest. "That's good to know because I've a favor to ask. Might I travel with you back to Boston?

I've nearly finished packing. I've no desire to stay here at Liriodendron with Chloe and Nicholas, that's for sure."

"And after Boston?" Adrian asked.

"I'm not sure yet. I could always return to Sacramento, of course, but it seems so terribly far away now." Jim caught the glance she sent him from beneath lowered lashes.

Adrian absently traced the outline of the envelope in his hand. "I'm afraid Nicholas Chapman took possession of the family house in Boston years ago, but you've other houses at your disposal. The town homes in New York and London belong to your mother now, along with Liriodendron itself."

"It will take a while to get used to that. In the meantime, I thought I'd perhaps find a hotel in Boston until I can think clearly."

Jim's cheeks burned as Adrian studied him. He tightened his arms around Amy and met the scrutiny with a nonchalant shrug. "That makes perfect sense," he said.

"Amy, my dear," Adrian began, "Mrs. de la Noye would turn me out on the streets if I let you stay anywhere but with us. And Jim will be pleased to have your company this afternoon, since he was making the drive back to Boston alone. Finish packing; Jim will be up shortly for your bags."

"Thanks awfully, Mr. de la Noye." She stood on tiptoe to kiss Jim's still-warm cheek, then dashed into the house.

"I echo that notion," Jim said, shoving his hands into his pockets. "Thanks."

Adrian nodded. "I take it that young Miss Walsh's detective skills were instrumental in revealing my past to you?"

"You might say that. We started working on it together yesterday morning."

"She works fast."

"She has her ways, and it looks like I'll get the chance to discover what, exactly, they are. I suspect I should be afraid."

Adrian shook his head, turning his gaze back to the ocean. "No, don't be afraid. Take the chance. A little bravery in matters of the heart is exactly what you need."

"Oh, is that so?" Jim folded his arms against his chest. "Maybe I'm not the only one."

Adrian's stare whipped toward him, then dropped to the envelope in his hand. "You are definitely not the only one," he murmured. He fumbled for his watch. "Jim. You'll excuse me . . . I've one more errand to run, and I'm already years late. I'll have the car back within the hour." He jammed Catharine's letter into his jacket pocket and turned away.

"But . . ." Jim lifted a finger to punctuate his question, but his words died on the air as Adrian broke into a full run across the lawn.

CHAPTER
50

The outside of the train depot looked shabbier than it had when he'd last seen it through snowfall twenty-three years ago, but Adrian paid little attention to that now. He reached the tracks just as a train slowed to a stop. A stream of passengers jostled him in eager pursuit of the beach. He stood his ground against their tide, craning his neck in an attempt to see through the crowd. It was impossible. But as quickly as it had come, the swarm was gone, leaving him alone to search the passenger platform as the train chugged away toward its next destination.

She sat alone on a bench at the end of the platform. The wide brim of her hat obscured her face, but he would know her anywhere. The graceful arc of her neck as she dipped her head over the book in her hand, the pleasing curves of her body, the way she tucked one slender ankle behind the other . . . his pulse raced as he walked slowly toward her. He'd tried for years to protect his heart from the emotions she stirred in him. What a waste of time that had been!

He paused above her. "May I?" he asked, gesturing toward the empty space beside her.

She calmly turned a page, not bothering to look up. "If you'd like," she said.

"I'd like nothing better." He sat beside her. Her perfume teased his nostrils; he drank it in as he reached for her hand. Raising it to his lips, he planted a gentle kiss against the inside of her wrist. "Put down the book, my dear, and greet your husband properly."

Constance turned toward him, lips curved into an impish smile. Her familiar prettiness made his throat catch, yet it seemed he saw her fully for the first time. "Really, Adrian," she said, placing the book facedown on the bench. "What took you so long to send for me? I'd been expecting last night's midnight call hours earlier. With all due respect to Jim, you know I've always been your best partner when there's work to be done."

The hat toppled from her curls as Adrian gathered her into his arms and kissed her long and hard. Her inadvertent gasp as they parted told him that he'd managed to surprise the one person on earth who knew him better than anyone else did.

"I'm an idiot," he murmured into her delicate ear. "That's the only explanation I have for my actions. But believe me, Constance, I will never be so stupid again."

"Goodness!" Constance pulled in a startled breath, then nestled against him. "First you replace the chauffeur and come to fetch me from the station yourself, then you indulge in a public display of affection . . . whatever have you done with my oh-so-proper husband? I should alert the authorities, let them know he's missing."

Adrian stroked her hair, then cupped her chin in his hand. "You do that," he said, gently kissing her eyelids. "Tell them that he seems to have vanished, and that he's not likely to return." He kissed the tip of her nose. "Although, my darling, perhaps you'd like to wait a bit, just to see if you really want him back at all." His lips found hers, searching as if they had all the time in the world.

"Perhaps I should," Constance gulped when he finally let her up for air.

Cradling her hand in his, Adrian raised his wife to her feet, lifted her suitcase, and guided them both out into the bright Newport sun.

THE BUSTLE OF Fifth Avenue fell away as Catharine stepped into Cartier. A middle-aged jeweler closed the front of a showcase and discreetly turned the key. His practiced gaze took her in from the top of her demi-veiled hat, past her jade silk day dress, to the tips of her French-heeled shoes.

"May I offer madame assistance?" he asked, and she could tell from the tone of his voice that the assistance he thought she might need was a polite suggestion that she'd perhaps wandered into the wrong store.

"Yes," she replied, studying the jewelry displayed before her. Diamonds and precious gems winked at her, their sparkling facets changing with each tilt of her head.

The jeweler remained in his spot, smile pasted to his face. Catharine casually tucked the envelope she held alongside the purse beneath her right elbow and, very deliberately, worked her glove over the fingers of her left hand. Set free, the diamonds of her wedding band glittered along with the rest of the jewelry in the room, serving as a calling card few could ignore. She noted the quick appraisal the jeweler gave her ring and knew that he'd immediately recognized its unique design as one of Cartier's own.

"Mrs. Chapman," he said. "Please accept my condolences on the loss of your husband. Naturally, we were shocked to read of Mr. Chapman's passing so soon after his happy purchase of your ring. He was very specific about its design. On behalf of all of us here at Cartier—"

"Yes," Catharine said absently, turning away. "These past few weeks have been difficult."

The showcase she wanted was mounted on the opposite wall. Reaching up to curl the net veil of her hat around its brim, she crossed the room. The jeweler followed close behind.

"You're interested in pearls today, madame?" he asked.

She peered at the elegant strands displayed. "I have a very specific necklace in mind . . . a triple-strand choker, cream-colored natural pearls. It came from your Paris store about twenty-five years ago, but I don't see it here."

"That style was very popular a generation ago. But wouldn't madame prefer something a bit more chic?"

"This isn't for me."

The jeweler nodded. "Come with me," he said, leading her from one hushed room into another. "I have two possibilities in this floor case here."

She saw what she wanted at once. The necklace blurred before her eyes as a familiar pang knotted her stomach.

She blinked, and the pearls snapped back into focus. "This one," she said, pointing. "I'd like it delivered to Edith Delano White in Buffalo." She laid her envelope down on the showcase just long enough to open her purse and withdraw a business card. "The address is on the back of this card."

"Do you wish to include a message of some sort?"

"I wish to remain anonymous, thank you." She flipped the business card over and laid it on the case, running a well-manicured finger across the embossed LAW OFFICES OF ADRIAN DE LA NOYE. "You may bill my attorney's office. I sail for England tomorrow."

The jeweler glanced at the card before tucking it into his breast pocket. "Very good, madame," he said, raising the glass lid. He reached beneath the showcase for a narrow box, popping open its top with a smooth flick of his thumb.

Catharine watched as he lifted the necklace from the case and lowered it carefully into the padded box. His expert fingers quickly pinned the pearls into place so that they would not jostle during their journey.

"Mrs. White will have her pearls by the end of the week," he said, hiding the necklace from sight with the close of the lid. "And should I say *au revoir* or *adieu* to you?"

"Pardon?"

"Your trip. *Au revoir* means you'll return. *Adieu* means farewell forever."

"I see." Catharine traced the edge of her envelope, lost in thought.

"I'd be happy to post that letter for you," the jeweler said, following the motion of her fingers.

Snapped from her reverie, Catharine lifted the envelope, truly seeing the address for the first time since she'd carefully written it earlier that morning: Mr. Frank J. Wilson, U.S. Treasury Department Intelligence Unit. A slow smile crossed her face as she pressed the padded outline of the key she'd plucked from Nicholas Chapman's vest pocket during their last altercation. Mr. Wilson would know just what to do with the doctored books and documents he'd find in that safe at Liriodendron.

"Thank you," she said, "but I'll mail this one myself." Nicholas would look absolutely smashing in prison garb.

"As you wish, madame. At your service."

Layers of the past peeled away like cumbersome winter clothes at the start of a warm, fresh spring. Catharine let out a long-held breath. "It's *au revoir*," she said, tapping the envelope one final time against the case. "I'll be back."

The jeweler looked up in time to see the last glint of Catharine's wedding ring as she passed through the doorway on her way to rejoin the flurry of the outside world.

About the author

About the book

Insights,
Interviews
& More . . .

Read on

Meet Jill Morrow

JILL MORROW has enjoyed a wide spectrum of careers, from practicing law to singing with local bands. She holds a bachelor's degree in history from Towson University and a JD from the University of Baltimore School of Law. The author of *Angel Cafe* and *The Open Channel*, she lives in Baltimore. ᔕ

2

An Essay:
The Lure of the Séance

ONCE, MANY YEARS AGO, I attended a séance. The medium, Mrs. B, had since childhood been talking to people nobody else could see. In her eighties when I met her, she'd been a minister in the Spiritualist church for years. Turns out she was part of a long tradition.

The modern American Spiritualist movement dates back to 1848, when the Fox sisters of upstate New York convinced the world that the mysterious raps heard in answer to their many questions were responses from unseen spirits. Of course, people throughout the ages had longed to cross the borders to the afterlife, if only to know more about what awaited them beyond death. But with the evangelical Second Great Awakening challenging traditional Calvinist beliefs, the mid-nineteenth century offered particularly fertile ground for an emotional religious revival that spawned trance lecturers and camp meetings. More than ever there were séances, meetings where people gathered to receive messages from the spirit world delivered through a medium who claimed to be in touch with the dead.

Anyone could make money as a medium, and anyone did. Séances and readings proliferated as newly minted mediums—usually women—contacted the spirit world via spirit guides (discarnate entities relied upon for ▶

spiritual guidance) or the deceased themselves. But alongside those willing to believe sat the skeptics. It was easy enough to expose fraud. Close observation revealed levitating objects suspended by string and tables tilted by nothing more "spirited" than the medium's knee. Supernatural "manifestations" by spirit guides turned out to be dolls, while plaster casts served as "materialized" ghostly hands. Yet after even the Fox sisters admitted in 1888 that their spirit rapping had been the result of cracking toe joints, people continued to believe. By the turn of the twentieth century, Spiritualism had more than eight million followers in the United States and Europe. And despite the movement's glaring lack of credibility, there was more to come.

As the 1920s dawned, the world struggled to recover from the one-two punch of the Great War and the 1918 influenza pandemic. Nearly 120,000 Americans died in World War I. The flu surpassed that figure, sweeping across the landscape in 1918–1919 and taking approximately 500,000 to 675,000 American souls with it. Almost everyone lost someone dear to them, taken suddenly and with little warning. Not surprisingly, Spiritualism experienced a new surge of popularity as, fueled by sorrow and desperation, people flocked to séance tables in search of closure.

As before, fraudulent practices flourished. Mediums continued to glean their information about the deceased from the words and descriptions of those trying to contact them. There was ectoplasm made of butter, muslin, gauze, chewed paper, or sheep's lung. Materialized spirits (including Woodrow Wilson and King Ferdinand of Bulgaria) turned out to be cut-out faces clipped from magazines. Spirit photography—photographs of living sitters with images of their beloved deceased floating around them—was revealed to be nothing more than double exposures. The deceptions seemed so clumsy and obvious, yet still people flocked to séance tables, longing for answers and comfort that traditional religion and modern science could not provide.

Mrs. B's "circles of enlightenment" were held at her home, in a room set aside as a chapel. A little altar with a cross atop it sat on one side of the room; Mrs. B identified herself as a devout Christian. Instead of the expected round table, there was a circle of chairs. Spirit pictures—pastel portraits of Mrs. B's spirit guides—lined the walls. Quartz crystals and religious artifacts were set on side tables, while bookshelves held Bibles, metaphysical books, and Spiritualist pamphlets. The air was dense, as if walking to one's seat involved passing through several sets of velvet curtains.

Six of us settled into our chairs. Mrs. B reached for the light switch. As total darkness settled around us, she ▸

asked if anybody in the room saw "anyone." Nobody did. She herself saw points of light, which she identified as spirits. She received information from several spirit guides who had been with her for decades. Frequently she spoke in one-size-fits-all generalities that invited personalized interpretation. Some of her pronouncements seemed like obvious follow-up statements to information gleaned from a participant's question. Nothing "appeared," thank heavens: no ectoplasm, thumps, or unusual noises announced otherworldly guests.

I started wondering if anyone else in the room had noticed that, except for changes in hairstyle and clothing, all the spirit pictures on the wall looked exactly the same. And did anyone really believe that the beautiful rose quartz necklace Mrs. B wore had been materialized long ago as a gift from a spirit guide?

Mrs. B thoroughly believed in her own ability to communicate with spirits and didn't care whether other people thought her legitimate or not. Neither did the couple she comforted with words from their deceased teenage son. Nor did the woman who had come that evening to ask her late husband for a little guidance about where he'd left his will. Mrs. B listened to a voice none of us could hear and repeated what she heard. I later learned that, based on that information, the woman did indeed locate the will.

Perhaps this is the fundamental reason why belief in Spiritualism continues. For each uncovered act of fraud, there are stories that cannot be explained in logical terms.

Our world moves forward in a steady flow of scientific and medical advances. Technology allows us to be in nearly constant contact with each other, no matter where on (or off) the planet we may be. But despite these changes, people today experience the same curiosity and emptiness as did those so willing to believe the Fox sisters back in 1848 or to once again touch the loved ones lost in the Great War.

For those who yearn for something "more," Spiritualism will always offer hope. ❧

The Four Hundred: An Aspirant Inquires

The Four Hundred? What exactly is that?

Oh, my dear. You don't know? It's only the annual list of New York City's social elite. The crème de la crème of society. It's . . . well, who's in and who's out. It's everyone who's anyone.

How did it start?

If you have to ask, then you probably aren't on the list.

The list was started by *the* Mrs. Astor. (I shall require my smelling salts if you ask which one. It's Mrs. William Backhouse Astor Jr., of course.) Mrs. Astor— the former Caroline Webster Schermerhorn—is the perfect gatekeeper of old money and tradition. She's not only an Astor through marriage, she's descended from New York City's original Dutch settlers. But the Four Hundred isn't her work alone. It's actually the notion of her protégé, Samuel Ward McAllister.

Please, dear, close your mouth. No need to advertise your ignorance.

Ward McAllister arrived in New York City from Savannah, Georgia, in 1872. Using his wife's wealth (he married an heiress) and his own family connections (he is a distant cousin by marriage of Mrs. Astor), he crowned himself the expert in all things related to high society.

How is the list compiled?

You must understand that Mrs. Astor acts only for the good of society (and perhaps her own social standing). Since the end of the War of the Rebellion, there are entirely too many new millionaires crawling around New York. (You didn't hear it from me, dear, but some of them are worth more than, well, Mrs. Astor.) Still, the nouveau riche can be so vulgar. Just because one has a fortune does not ensure acceptance by the fashionable elite.

Mr. McAllister once declared that amongst the wealthy families of New York City, there are only about four hundred who matter in society. He devised a plan to appoint twenty-five "patriarchs" chosen from the New York Knickerbocracy. Each of those patriarchs would then select four ladies and five gentlemen (of pure bloodlines, of course) to receive invitations to Mrs. Astor's famed Patriarchs' Ball. The list of invitees, compiled in the winter season and kept absolutely secret, forms the society guest list for the New York social season.

(Well, it wouldn't do to let *everybody* in, dear. Besides, we've left a bit of room for important people, visiting dignitaries, and a handful of debutantes.)

Mrs. Astor wants only the cream. Are you perhaps descended from an old merchant family that can trace its lineage back to colonial New Amsterdam? No? Hmm. Pity. ▶

The Four Hundred: An Aspirant Inquires
(continued)

What good is this list of Four Hundred? Why should I want to be on it?

I'll pretend I didn't hear that, dear.

Do you ever want to attend another society party or ball in New York City again? Mrs. Astor's Patriarchs' Ball launches the social season! Once invited, you are assured a year's worth of invitations to other balls and events given by the patriarchs. (Even then you'll be vetted to make sure you remain worthy of the next round of invitations.)

But not so fast . . . You can't attend *any* Astor event unless you receive a calling card from *the* Mrs. Astor herself, and I wouldn't count on that unless she deems you worthy of the Four Hundred.

Who's already on the list?

As the *New York Times* noted in 1880, "The [Patriarchs'] society . . . was originally founded for the purpose of giving social entertainments of undoubted tone and exclusiveness . . ." It should be abundantly clear that those selected as patriarchs must be leaders, both socially and financially.

The names may vary somewhat from year to year, but one is always safe expecting to see Messrs. Belmont, Schuyler, Howland, Kane, Schermerhorn, Livingston, Forbes, Bliss, Rutherford, Winthrop, Irving, Stuyvesant. You may also expect Mr. Royal Phelps, William

Butler Duncan, William R. Travers, Archibald Gracie King, and William Langdon Jr.

By the way, dear, pay no attention to the fact that the list actually falls short of four hundred names. Nobody cares.

What if I'm not in?

You probably aren't. The push to be included is simply crushing. You wouldn't believe the gambits people employ to join our ranks!

Or perhaps you would. Lean in closer, dear. I'll tell you of a manipulation that worked.

I'm sure you know that the Vanderbilts were exactly what Mrs. Astor *didn't* have in mind for the Four Hundred. They are out and about in New York, of course, but, my dear, they have *earned* their money rather than inherited it. And Cornelius Vanderbilt . . . so uncouth. Mrs. Astor refused to call on anyone in the family, which meant they simply hadn't arrived. Cornelius's granddaughter-in-law, Alva, refused to accept the snub. She built a magnificent mansion at Fifth and Fifty-Second, then planned an opulent costume ball as a housewarming for it. She invited the press in to admire the extravagant party preparations, thus ensuring enough publicity that everyone wanted an invitation. Then . . . she did not invite Mrs. Astor's daughter! Inquiries, of course, were made. Alva said (regretfully!) that proper etiquette did ▶

The Four Hundred: An Aspirant Inquires
(continued)

not allow her to invite strangers who had never called upon her socially. Mrs. Astor had no choice; she dropped off her visiting card at the Vanderbilts' new home, thus formally acknowledging them as socially acceptable. Young Caroline Astor got her invitation, and Alva Vanderbilt broke into the Four Hundred.

So, dear, there you have it. Good luck. I'm sure you'll find something to do should you fall short this year . . . some dreary little party or other, perhaps, or a dismal dinner filled with others who are not quite up to snuff. Chin up. There will be . . . something.

And do let me know how you fare so that I'll know if I'm ever to call upon you again. ❧

Reading Group Guide

1. At the beginning of the novel, Adrian keeps tight control over his passions and emotions. Why does he do this, and what allows him to finally let those defenses fall?

2. Catharine leaves Adrian as an act of love. Had she stayed, do you think their marriage would have been successful? Would they have been happy with each other?

3. What might Jim's life have been like had Adrian not stepped in to help fund and mold his future?

4. Bennett Chapman has been belligerent, self-centered, and ill-behaved throughout most of his life. Why, then, is he so willing to believe that his wife, Elizabeth, has come back from the dead to contact him via séance? Why is he determined to follow her directives?

5. As you read, did you believe that Mrs. Chapman was indeed appearing in spirit, or were you skeptical? At what point did you feel that perhaps this was real? Or did you still have doubts at the end?

6. Catharine's plan to quickly snag a wealthy husband in Newport seems rather a long shot. What compels her to try it? What other choices were open to a woman of her social status in her situation? What were the potential outcomes to those choices? ▶

7. Catharine obtains the key to Nicholas's incriminating documents through uncharacteristic physical contact with him after her wedding ceremony. Do you think Adrian knew of her plan?

8. Have you ever attended a séance or received a psychic reading? If yes, what made you go and what was the experience like? If no, is this something you would ever want to do? Why or why not? ∽

Further Reading

Currently on my nightstand . . .

I read without rhyme or reason and love having a stack of books waiting for me. Already read or about to be read, this is what's currently stacked within easy reach:

A Hundred Summers by Beatriz Williams

97 Orchard: An Edible History of Five Immigrant Families in One New York Tenement by Jane Ziegelman

Orphan Train by Christina Baker Kline

Miss Manners' Guide to Excruciatingly Correct Behavior by Judith Martin

Garment of Shadows by Laurie R. King ∽